For Ramon.

From our first kiss

to our inevitable last,

you are the one.

PART ONE

The Video

1

Jessica

"Morning, beautiful."

I flip over and there's his face, inches from mine—Jake, my boyfriend and my next-door neighbor. "You scared me," I whisper.

His shadowy lips curve into a grin. "I was shooting for romantic."

"Well, you missed."

He rolls off the bed and turns on my light, posing in the most un-Jake-like outfit I can imagine: a cute dolphin-print shirt with matching dolphin-print shorts and a pair of white-rimmed sunglasses. "At least I'm well-dressed."

"Oh my god, why?" I sputter.

"Because I'm taking you to the beach to see the sunrise. I even packed food."

I stretch and roll onto my side, prop my head up in my hand. "You look like a tourist."

He adjusts the brightly colored shorts and slides off his glasses. "A sexy tourist?"

"No such thing."

Jake sweeps me up, tucks my legs around his waist, and nuzzles my neck. "So, are you up for a sunrise surprise? We have to hurry."

I gaze into his eyes, sweet caramel-brown framed by long black lashes. I already know this picnic will be missing napkins or drinks or something essential, and Jake will insist on bringing his obnoxious dog, Otis, and there's no way we'll get to the coast in time for the sunrise, which happens in the east, not the west (and I think deep down Jake knows this), but none of it matters. The date will be perfect because we'll be together, so I agree. "Yeah, I'm up for it."

Jake inhales in that slow way of his, as if he's breathing me into his lungs. Then he sets me down and enjoys the peep show while I change into jeans and a sweatshirt, beachwear in Northern California. "Ready, Mrs. Healy?" he asks, giving me his last name.

"Ready, Mr. Sanchez," I reply, giving him mine.

Jake collects his backpack and drops his sunglasses back over his eyes. "Otis is going to be very happy you said yes. He's already in the truck."

I lead Jake out of my bedroom with happiness blooming in my stomach at being correct, because *of course Otis is in the truck.*

◆ ◆ ◆

As we crest the last bluff, the view of Blind Beach fills Jake's windshield. Doesn't matter that we were born here, doesn't matter that I jog here every day after school, doesn't matter that the ocean never changes—the sight of the endless sea sucks our breath from our lungs as if we're drowning in it. This is the most dangerous stretch of coastline in California. The continental shelf drops quickly

FRIENDS LIKE THESE

JENNIFER LYNN ALVAREZ

PENGUIN BOOKS

PENGUIN BOOKS

UK | USA | Canada | Ireland | Australia
India | New Zealand | South Africa

Penguin Books is part of the Penguin Random House group of companies
whose addresses can be found at global.penguinrandomhouse.com.

www.penguin.co.uk
www.puffin.co.uk
www.ladybird.co.uk

First published in the USA by Delacorte Press, an imprint of Random House Children's
and in Great Britain by Penguin Books 2022

001

Text copyright © Jennifer Lynn Alvarez, 2022
cover image © Shutterstock, 2022

The moral right of the author and illustrator has been asserted

Typeset in 12-point Adobe Jenson
Printed and bound in Great Britain by Clays Ltd, Elcograf S.p.A.

The authorized representative in the EEA is Penguin Random House Ireland,
Morrison Chambers, 32 Nassau Street, Dublin D02 YH68

A CIP catalogue record for this book is available from the British Library

ISBN: 978–0–241–47613–0

All correspondence to:
Penguin Books, Penguin Random House Children's
One Embassy Gardens, 8 Viaduct Gardens, London SW11 7BW

from a few dozen feet below the sea's surface to several hundred feet, creating riptides that will kill you if you aren't careful.

Sleeper waves are another risk. They hide in deep water, but when they meet the shallow portion of the shelf, they rush past previous waves and swallow whoever is standing on the shore. The water is cold enough to silence human screams, and if none of that kills you, the great white sharks that prowl offshore might. Visitors die here each year. Last summer, two local boys drowned when a sleeper wave dragged them into the ocean.

Today the waves are white-capped and violent, assailing the huge boulders that rise as ancient monoliths from the deep. The tide swallows the shoreline in greedy gulps, and the brightening sky reveals a layer of gauzelike mist, veiling the horizon. Seagulls dive and screech as they scavenge on creatures washed ashore—crabs, abalone, and starfish. In the dark depths, humpback whales, dolphins, seals, and sharks flick their tails, invisible to us until they decide to be seen.

Jake glances at me, smiling. "We're here."

But I'm surprised to see we're not alone. Our friends Chloe and Manny, and Manny's girlfriend, Alyssa, are nestled in the sand. "What's going on?"

Jake parks and turns off his engine, rubs his hands together for warmth. "I want to hang out, just our group, one last time before school starts on Monday."

Oh, I think, *not this again*. Jake is terrified of senior year. I can't talk to him about my college applications or my AP tests without him getting moody and quiet. I won't get into an Ivy League school, but my dream of attending the University of Colorado is pretty attainable, and that has Jake worried. *It's so far*, he says. He believes I'll forget about him at college—*as if I ever could*—but

I think he's more afraid to lose a person he loves, like he and his little brother Cole lost their dad two years ago. Maybe it's why he clings so hard.

But today he invited our friends. He did that for *me*, and I smile back at him. "This is perfect."

He opens his door, and Otis streaks out and down the trail, bounding toward the beach like a puppy. I sigh. "He's going to get wet."

But Jake ignores Otis and grabs our gear—two beach chairs, a blanket, and a cooler full of food. His thick eyebrows crinkle as he tries to wrangle it all. He looks so cute, I almost don't want to help him, but I reach for a chair.

"Nope, I got it," he says.

We hike down the trail to the beach, and Manny spots us first. "Hey, hey, the cabana boy is here!"

Jake drops everything and slaps Manny on the back. Alyssa and Chloe huddle by a small driftwood bonfire, with the massive stone cliffs at their backs, blocking the worst of the wind. The sky is ash gray and getting lighter.

I drop in next to my friends, and they scoot over so I can share the blanket draped over their laps. Alyssa glares at Jake on the other side of the flames. "Your boyfriend texted at five this morning and told me to hurry, and then he has the balls to show up late—wearing that." She laughs.

I peek at Jake's tan muscular legs, clad in dolphin-print shorts. "He pulls it off."

Alyssa snaps a picture of him.

"Don't post that!" I grab for her cell.

She grins. "Too late."

The boys join us, and Jake pulls out the food he brought: a collection of sodas, a clump of grapes, and frozen breakfast burritos he must have heated in the microwave this morning. "Shit," he says, rummaging in his backpack. "I forgot the salsa."

The rest of us exchange a look, not surprised he forgot something. Jake and I started dating ten months ago, and I've learned I can rely on him to be exactly who he is—my easily baffled and mostly disorganized boyfriend who tries harder than anyone else I know to do the normal shit, but then crushes me with gestures so tiny and sweet that I wonder if I deserve him at all.

Finally he passes out the burritos, which are now dusted in brown sand from the gusting wind. "No charge for the seasonings," he says.

We brush the tortilla wrappings clean and dig in, sometimes hearing the slight crunch of sand between our teeth. The beans are ice-cold in the center of my burrito.

"Delicious," says Manny, tossing his into the fire with a shake of his head.

Jake passes out the sodas, and we watch the crackling flames as Manny adds another driftwood log. "Who's going to Tegan's party tonight?" Manny asks.

"We are," says Jake, wrapping his arm around me.

"We are?" I ask.

His brows draw together. "Yeah, weren't you on the group chat?"

"What group chat?"

"Uh-oh," says Alyssa.

"The invite chat," he says. "Tegan invited us."

Anger slithers through my belly. "Us or just you?" Tegan is Jake's ex, and she doesn't bother to hide the fact she still has a crush on him.

"Us, all of us," he says. "She told me to bring you."

Manny pokes at the hot embers, causing sparks to dance in the wind.

"Everyone is going, Jess," says Alyssa. "It's Tegan's end-of-summer bash."

I nod but feel my heat rising. I don't subscribe to the "everyone is going" peer pressure bullshit. I don't like parties; they're too chaotic. Everyone drinks and acts stupid and they're not fun. They're loud. Tegan's Fourth of July bonfire earlier this summer was a disaster. Parties are one area where Jake and I don't see eye to eye. He loves them, and I've made him skip quite a few.

Chloe snorts. "I can't believe she invited you through your boyfriend. Oh wait, yes I can." Her sarcasm masks the hurts from our past. Tegan and I were best friends until I befriended Chloe in the third grade. The three of us tried to be friends for two years, but Tegan treated Chloe like crap and eventually forced me to choose between them—I chose Chloe.

"Are you going?" I ask her.

"Yeah, Grady invited me. It's his house too." Grady is Tegan's younger brother and Chloe's best friend, next to me. They met when Chloe and I used to sleep over at Tegan's, and then reconnected when they bought goldendoodles from the same litter three years ago. When the Sheffields are out of town, Chloe is their dogsitter. Grady's had a crush on Chloe since he was a kid, and I think she likes him too, but Chloe won't do anything that takes her focus off gymnastics, and that includes dating.

Jake gently tilts my face, so our eyes meet. "It's the last party of the summer, Jess."

I shift my eyes to the bonfire, to our friends, and to our ruined burritos. *This* is my idea of a party, time with the few people I truly care about. But I know Jake wants to savor the beginning and end of senior year—the final leg of our high school journey—so I let out my breath. "Okay."

He grins and kisses the back of my hand, and Alyssa snaps a photo. "So cute," she says.

The others finish eating while I pet Otis to hide my sulk. If it was anyone else's party, I'd feel better about it, but Tegan Sheffield? Our friendship exploded in the fifth grade during lunch period when Chloe and I declined to join Tegan at the popular table. We didn't like Tegan's new friends, not because they were popular but because we had nothing in common. She was furious when I stood up to her that day.

"Sit down," Tegan insisted.

"No," I whispered, feeling my face grow hot.

"You're being a baby." She eyed my horse-graphic T-shirt. "You look like a baby."

We were eleven years old, and an epic shouting match followed that resulted in Tegan slapping me and making me cry. Chloe shoved her, and Tegan stumbled and tripped over a bench. Her skirt flew up, showing her underwear, and her new friends laughed at her.

After the fight, Tegan and I stopped speaking and Chloe became my best friend, and Tegan never forgave either of us. And now that the boy who dumped her is in love with *me*, our feud has reignited.

Tegan wages her war by posting candid pictures of Jake on her social media account. She draws little hearts around his ass or around his face, using the hashtag #TheOneThatGotAway. Once she posted a shot of both of us, Jake looking gorgeous and me looking frazzled, and tagged it #BeautyandtheBeast. It probably counts as online bullying, something we could turn her in to the principal for, but Jake and I decided to ignore the pictures. No response is a response, right?

Alyssa doesn't agree. "Hell no, I got you," she said after the #BeautyandtheBeast pic. Now she posts cute pictures of Jake and me on her popular photography account, with the hashtag #CrystalCovesCutestCouple. The photos are adorable—Alyssa has a good eye—but this is a battle I didn't start and don't want to fight. It's just bullshit anyway, sticks and stones and all that, but it hurts. No one, not even Jake, knows how much.

Jake leans over and whispers, "Where are you, Jess?"

"Sorry, just thinking." I lean against his warm body and focus on the beach. As the sun rises higher, it illuminates the mist in a pink glow that's ethereal.

Chloe tugs on Alyssa's arm. "Ooooh, will you get a shot of me doing a handstand in the fog?"

Alyssa rolls her eyes toward me, because we know it won't be *one* handstand. Chloe won't quit until her tiny gymnast body nails the perfect angle.

In a flash she's upside down with her toes pointed toward the sky. Arching deeply, she bends her legs in a leaping stag pose.

"Damn, that's hot," hoots Manny, and Alyssa jabs him in the ribs. Then she starts shooting photos with the Nikon she brought.

Chloe had a shot at the National Junior Olympic team once, but then an awful balance beam accident stole her confidence. She's better now and has her eyes set on a new prize—an elite gymnastics scholarship to UCLA. The Region One college showcase is three weeks away, and I'm impressed she's here and not already at her gym.

"Do you like your surprise?" Jake asks, wrapping his arms around my waist and resting his chin on my shoulder.

The fog envelops us like a wet blanket, cold but insulating, and I must admit, this was a good idea. We're going to be busy this year, and everything will be for the last time—my last year going to high school football games, my last homecoming dance, my last season running track, and my last prom. In November, I'll turn eighteen. I'll be old enough to vote. "I do," I tell him.

"I hoped you would." Jake kisses the side of my neck, his lips hot and light on my skin. His heart thumps against my back, and he pulls me tighter against him. "I wish today would never end." His hands slide below my waist and into my jeans. I twirl away, laughing. "Not here."

"In my truck?" He pulls me into a hug.

"Maybe." His heart beats faster and harder against my chest, and his warm breath brushes my ear. Jake is zero to sixty when it comes to sex.

Right then Chloe comes down from her handstand and Otis thinks she wants to play. He circles her, shaking his wet fur and soaking her in cold droplets of Pacific Ocean.

"Damn it, Otis, why'd you go into the water?" Jake asks.

"You know he can't resist," gripes Chloe.

"I got an awesome shot of him splashing you." Alyssa shows Chloe her camera.

Chloe shrugs. "If you like fails."

"Who doesn't like fails? I'll send these to you on the way home."

We don't stay much longer, because Otis and Chloe start shivering and we're all getting hungry since the burritos were also a fail—but the morning was not. It was perfect.

As we drive back to town, Blind Beach vanishes behind us. The biggest thing on my mind is whether Jake will be ready on time for school Monday. If I'd had any idea then how our lives were about to change, I would have whispered into Jake's ear, *Whatever happens at the party tonight, stay away from Tegan Sheffield.*

Or maybe I would have shouted it.

2

———

Jake

Jess is miserable. I feel it in the tightness of her fingers around mine. Maybe I'm a shitty boyfriend for bringing her to this party, but I hope she'll loosen up and enjoy it with me. It's the last one before senior year, and I don't want to miss a thing.

We walk up Tegan's slate driveway toward her family's house, a gigantic prismlike structure made of glass and concrete and metal that overlooks the Pacific Ocean. Its sharp angles gleam with designer lights and sparkling floor-to-ceiling picture windows, like a lighthouse except it beckons teenagers instead of ships.

Her parents travel a lot, and the house has been party central since Tegan started high school. She moved here from Alabama eleven years ago. Her mother was a one-term US senator, and her father is a "businessman," but no one knows what he actually does. Bottom line—the Sheffields are loaded.

The party is in full swing when we arrive, music thumping, laughter drifting, and the poolside waterfalls splashing. My heart kicks and I walk faster, dragging my reluctant girlfriend toward the fun. Rare August rain clouds pile overhead, thundering and flashing, and the ocean whispers below, as if the sea and sky are alive. Colored strobe lights illuminate the lawns, trees, and the swimming pool. "Tegan went all out," I say.

Jess nods, looking sick.

I turn her beautiful face to mine. "It's a party, not an execution."

Her amber eyes reflect the lights as she blinks at me. "I don't want to stay long."

"Are you going to turn into a pumpkin?"

"Jake," she warns.

"Okay, okay, we won't stay long." I squeeze her hand, and she squeezes mine back.

Up the steps we go. Tegan's front door is unlocked, and the noise and heat hit Jess and me like a concussion as we enter. I kiss my girlfriend's lips, laughing against her mouth. Finally she smiles.

The living room is packed. Tegan's friends dance in small groups with their drinks sloshing. Their sweating bodies reflect in the panoramic windows that overlook the ocean. The beat rocks my chest, fills my ears, and I lean into Jess. "Want to dance?"

"Maybe later?"

"Sure." I catch sight of my buddy and his girlfriend in the kitchen by the keg. "Hey, there's Manny and Alyssa."

After Jess and I navigate the gauntlet of bodies between us and the kitchen, Manny drags me into a hug. "Dude, you made it!"

"Wouldn't fucking miss it. When'd you get here?"

"Two beers ago, man. You've got to catch up. Jess, you look fucking hot!" He hugs her and lifts her off her feet, making her laugh and squirm until he puts her down. Alyssa and Jess start whispering, a new song starts, and Manny bobs his head. "You should see the spread downstairs. More food, Jell-O shots, pool, Ping-Pong, empty bedrooms." He wiggles his eyebrows at Alyssa.

She makes a face. "Gross."

I fill a plastic cup with beer for me and hand Jess a hard seltzer from the ice bucket. She accepts it with a whispered plea. "Don't drink too much, okay?"

The comment stings, so I ignore it. I drank a lot after my dad got sick, and even worse after he died, but I've turned myself around. A few beers to mourn the end of summer won't hurt me. I peer into my cup. The beer is the color of morning piss, but it's ice-cold as it glides down my throat.

We spot Chloe, chowing on snacks laid out in the family room. That girl packs away more food than most guys, usually healthy stuff, but right now, she's oblivious to everything but the nachos. Jess smiles and scoots away from me. "Alyssa and I are gonna catch up with Chloe."

"Yeah, okay. I'll find you later."

She kisses me and veers toward her best friend. Hypnotized, I watch her hips flick side to side in her skin-tight jeans as she walks away. Jess has no idea how sexy she is.

"That girl will do anything for you," Manny says. "Fucking anything. You know she doesn't want to be here."

I blow out a breath. "Yeah, I know. She'll loosen up." We talk about surfing and watch people come and go. A tray of pot stickers catches my eye, and I down six of them in one breath. Tegan's best friend, Shawna, joins us—with her boyfriend, Marcus, shadowing her like a bodyguard. He looks about as happy to be here as my girlfriend does. He's older, a college guy.

Shawna catches me eyeballing her boyfriend. "Jealous much?"

she teases. The scent of her designer perfume mixes unpleasantly with the taste of pot stickers in my mouth.

I ignore her question and reach for a napkin. Marcus's eyes skip around the room like security cameras, observant yet detached. I hear he's rough with Shawna. "How old is he?" I ask under my breath.

"Older than you." She slides her eyes up and down my body, smirking. Shawna is beautiful in an off-center kind of way, like a Picasso—hard-set eyes, pouting lips, razor-sharp cheekbones—all askew, and framed by the brightest, reddest hair. "Have you seen Tegan yet?" she asks.

"Nope." My gaze drops to the floor, and my shoulders tense. Everyone knows that Tegan and I dated for six totally insane and intense weeks, and that I ended it. The news shocked the school, probably because I'm nothing special—not a jock, or a prep, or a rich dude—just a guy trying to graduate. Or maybe it was because we made out all over campus—no shame—our hands everywhere. Several teachers complained.

When I broke up with Tegan, I couldn't believe the fallout—the posts, the comments, the criticism from the guys, the instant obsession from the girls. Breaking up with the hottest girl in school put me on the map in ways I never expected.

I tried to please Tegan when we were together. I posed for her pictures, raved about her on my account, returned her sexual ambushes at school, took her to parties, and gave her my favorite sweatshirt to wear—but it wasn't enough. She criticized everything about me as soon as we were alone. It was fucking confusing. One day Manny said, "Is she worth it, Jake? You're miserable."

And that was it; I was done. I moved on, and now she's crushing harder. Her friends still believe we're destined to end up together. Such bullshit.

"Dude, I'm gonna check things out," I say to Manny. He grabs a handful of chocolate-covered pretzels and follows me away from the keg. We discover Tegan's pool table in the basement and play for an hour or so with her brother, Grady, and his friends from the baseball team. The music is loud, vibrating my chest, and I love it. I want to find Jess. I want to dance.

I wander out of the basement to the swimming pool area. There's another keg down here and more people. A couple that I don't know swims in Tegan's infinity pool, and I watch them for a few seconds before I realize they're *not* swimming.

Suddenly my girlfriend appears beside me and nods toward the submerged couple. "Enjoying the show?"

"You know it." I slide my arm around her waist, relieved. We're together, as we should be.

"Want to know what I've been doing?" She lifts her chin. "I've been playing spin the bottle with the football team."

I laugh. Jess won't share her drinks with me, let alone kiss random dudes. I grab a loop in her jeans and tug her closer. "Yeah, well, I played two minutes in the closet with the girls' basketball team."

She shakes her head. "You're not tall enough."

"Maybe not for kissing."

She laughs and I nod toward the pool. "Want to get in the water?"

Jess glances at the couple already in there and pulls a face. "Um, no thank you." Then her eyes meet mine. "I want to go home."

My arms droop because I'm not ready to leave, and she reads me like she always does.

"You want to stay, don't you?" she asks.

"Yeah, Jess, it's the last party of the summer."

"You keep saying that." She crosses her arms, and I know she's pissed, but we always do what she wants. "Are you drunk?" she asks.

"Getting there," I say, grinning.

It's meant as a joke, but it hits Jess like a challenge. "Fine, Jake, drink, get wasted, whatever. It's not the last party for me. I have college."

I glare at her, helpless. She has no idea what goes through my mind when she talks about going away. Mostly it's *Other guys, other guys, other guys*, with a plentiful helping of *We're going to drift apart* on the side, and if I think about it one more time, I'm going to lose my fucking mind. She needs to let me deal with my shit my way. I throw back my third beer and slam down the cup. "You know what, Jess, sometimes you're no fun."

She stares up at the moon and exhales a long, gauzy breath. "I'm leaving in an hour, with or without you." She stomps up the steps toward the balcony.

My eyes and heart follow her, and I feel instant regret. I don't want to fight; I want to dance with her. I turn around, wondering where everyone went. The couple in the pool has vanished, and dark clouds have rolled over the moon. The air is charged with static and the scent of rain.

I walk to the edge of the lawn and peer over the steel-landscaping guardrail. Far below, the ocean waves chomp at the high cliffs, clawing at them like hungry dogs at the end of their chains.

A chilly breeze wafts over me, carrying with it a voice. "Jakey! There you are."

17

Every muscle in my body cringes because I'd know that sweet-but-sour Southern accent anywhere; it's Tegan Sheffield. I turn to face her.

"Don't tell me there's trouble in paradise," she drawls, glancing at the balcony where Jess vanished.

"No trouble."

She smiles so wide, I can see her back teeth, and as usual, her hotness strikes me like a punch—big sultry eyes, curvy lips, a body to match. When she moved to Crystal Cove, she brought the South with her—charm, sweet tea, and a Bible she doesn't read. Tegan's carrying two shot glasses, and she clinks them together. "You look thirsty."

I stare at the alcohol, then into her glittering blue eyes. Our past throbs between us—the sex, the kisses, the fights—six weeks I'll never forget.

She hands me one of the shot glasses, and I read the writing etched on the side. It says *Drink Me*. Thanks to countless hours of Jess's tutoring, I recognize this as the *command* form of the sentence. Okay, I'll play; one shot won't hurt. "Thanks." I down the liquid. It sears my throat and opens like a flower in my stomach.

Tegan follows suit, making a face as the alcohol flows across her tongue. "Wow!" she cries, swaying.

I reach to steady her, and her loose top gapes open. My eyes steal a glance, and Tegan notices. She drags her gaze across my face and down my body. "You look good enough to eat, Jake."

Like an idiot, I nod, realizing how alone we are. Her friends are sprawled all over her house and throughout the basement, but no one is within thirty feet of us, as if there's a force field keeping them back. The force is Tegan herself. She's giving off her stalker

vibe. *Stay away; he's mine.* I know it well. "What do you want?"
I ask.

She gazes at the roiling clouds, then straight at me. "Can a girl
get a dance?"

It's what I want too, but not with her.

Tegan shouts toward the open sliding glass door: "Turn up
the music!" Someone does, and the bass pounds my rib cage. The
rhythm strums my ears. She beckons, and her friends rush out
to join us. I glimpse Shawna and Marcus by the downstairs bar,
watching. Marcus looks pissed. Tegan's personal paparazzo, Brendon "the Cameraman" Reed, is in the background taking videos,
like always.

Tegan's friends seem surprised to see us standing so close together, but we're not *together.* I'm being polite, that's all. It's her
party. I close my eyelids and let the music flow through me. Overhead, the sky thunders. Everyone cheers when the scudding summer clouds finally drop their rain, drenching us. The falling crystal
droplets reflect the colored lights from the infinity pool.

"Yes!" Tegan shouts, throwing up her arms.

Shawna leaves Marcus and switches on a wireless strobe light,
and the teens of Crystal Cove dance in wet clothing. More shots
are distributed, and Marcus offers blotters of acid and ecstasy. No
one pays any attention to me. I shake off my gloom and lift my
hands toward the sky. I feel good, warm and happy. This is why I'm
here—to let go. I glance around for Jess because I want to dance
with her, but she's nowhere.

I dance alone. Surrounded, but alone.

3

Jake

Time passes—I have no idea how much—and Jess's beautiful face grows in my mind like an inflating balloon. I decide to look for her, stumble into the house, and bump into a chair. Fuck, I'm wasted. Voices and faces blur together. How many shots did I have after that first one? I can't remember. Jess is going to kill me.

Everywhere I look, people are dancing, laughing, making out, or staring at their phones. I exit the kitchen and veer into the wall where the stairs begin. As I grab the railing to steady myself, a hand squeezes my wrist. My gaze follows tan fingers up to a shapely arm to glassy blue eyes. Tegan again. "Jake," she says, and her smile separates from her face and floats in the dark, like that grinning cat from *Alice in Wonderland*. "Whatcha doing?"

"Lookin' for Jess."

"Jake and Jessica, sitting in a tree," she purrs. "You know the rest."

"Yep, I do." Her head brushes my chin, and I smell strawberry shampoo. Without thinking, I touch the silky strands. Then I flinch, and my heart beats suddenly faster. What am I doing?

Tegan's lips twist into a lazy smile. She's drunk too and she wraps her arms around my waist.

"Have you seen Jessica?" I ask, trying to pry her off me, which is like playing with an octopus. It becomes a game, and we both start laughing, me pushing her away, her reattaching in new places, and the result is that our hands are all over each other. The stairwell is dark and private, and the walls throb, my head buzzes, and her skin feels insanely smooth.

"Did you check upstairs?" she asks.

"Nah." I blink, but all I can see is Tegan. The music and conversation blend into a steady hum that washes through the house like a pulse.

"Come on, silly. I'll help you." She takes my hand and leads me up the stairs. A thought flashes in my mind, *Don't follow her,* but my feet don't listen. I'm eye to eye with Tegan's ass as we climb. Tripping on a stair, I fall against her, and we tumble. My hands grip her legs, feeling a pleasing combination of fat and muscle. My head lands in her lap.

Her laughter is like breaking glass in my ears, pretty but sharp. "Lord, we should not be walking right now," she drawls.

We help each other up and reach the second floor. "Jess?" I call out. "Are you up here?" We search a bathroom and a guest room, and then arrive in front of a white door. Tegan is so close behind me, I feel her warm breath on my neck. "Isn't this your room?" I ask.

She reaches around me and opens the door, revealing a queen-size bed. It's covered in white satin, with pink accent pillows and furred throw blankets. A striped cat hisses at me before leaping off the bed and running out of the room. Tegan pushes me inside and shuts the door.

"I don't think Jess is here," I say, turning.

She backs me against her huge picture window. One pane is propped open, and I smell brine-soaked ocean air as she presses her body against mine. I sway, listening to the surf. My heart thuds faster. "Do you hear the ocean?" I ask as the room swirls around us.

"Let's lie down," Tegan suggests. "Get sober."

Her gaze delves into mine, and her eyes are like her family's infinity pool, deep and endless and tempting. I fall into them, but I can't swim inside eyeballs. I will drown. I lurch for the door.

"No, no, rest a minute." Tegan takes my hand and tugs me closer. I inhale her strawberry hair and cherry-gloss lips. Every nerve is on fire, and then the feel of satin meets my skin when she guides me to sit on her bed.

She brushes her fingers down my chest to my stomach, and my lust stirs, waking like a dragon. I'm curious and obedient and drunk on tequila. Jess's scowling face flashes in my mind, and then disappears when Tegan slips off her top.

"We shouldn't," I whisper. Her lace bra is pale blue and overflowing. Her waist is so narrow, I lose my breath.

"Kiss me," she murmurs.

My blood is hot now, coursing south, and I pull her lips to mine, my tongue reaching, my eyes rolling back. Finding her mouth is like finding another bed of satin.

Tegan pulls off my T-shirt and lowers herself to my lap. Our kisses deepen. My hands squeeze her hips. "Take off my bra," she says.

I fumble for the clasp and undo it, and she spills free. My drunken brain sizzles and switches to autopilot. The rest of our clothes slide off, our limbs entwine, and then I'm between her legs, and then I'm flying.

I'm no longer in Tegan's bedroom. I'm not in her house at all—I'm soaring over the ocean. My mind is blank, my thoughts nonexistent. I'm a ball of tingling heat, building and budding, rhythmic.

I fly higher and higher, too far from the earth to survive. I strain toward space, toward the stars, to worlds unexplored, and when I can soar no higher, my body explodes into a thousand points of ecstasy. My wings, full of holes now, stall, and I crash into the sea, but I don't care. There's no fight inside me, no thoughts, no commitments, no *nothing*.

The water flows over me, pushing me into its depths. There, it is cold and dark. There, I rest alone. There, I drown. But it's not the sea where I have sunk; it's Tegan's soft satin bed. Time passes, I don't know how much, and a lone thought wisps across my brain, like the gasp of a dying man, *I cheated on Jess.*

Glancing at the gorgeous, naked girl beside me, my first reaction is not my best: *I have to hide this.*

4

Tegan, June

"You're wearing that?"

I halted midstep. My mother sat at the breakfast table, reading the *New York Times* and drinking iced lemonade. A view of the Pacific Ocean filled the glass wall behind her, and the surf churned in aquamarine bursts. The brightness of the sun paired with my mother's stark tone made me squint down at my outfit—tight jean shorts, crop top, bikini—nothing unusual for the rare days when it's hot here, but my mom could find fault with Jesus. "What's wrong with what I'm wearing?"

She flicked her paper closed. "You're not the twig you used to be, sweetheart. It's time to cover up." She looked pointedly at my dimpled thighs, straining against my shorts.

"Mom!"

"Don't kill the messenger." She studied me. "Go on, Pea, get upstairs and put yourself together more decently."

Pea was my childhood nickname and I was obviously not

pea-sized anymore. Tears of humiliation collected in the corners of my eyes. "I'm just going to the beach." School was out for the summer and Mom usually let me wear what I wanted.

Her lips tightened at the corners. "Wherever you go, you represent this family. We might live in California, but we're not *from* California. What's next? Ripped jeans? Wearing sweats to school? Tattoos?"

Mom was a US senator in Alabama for six years before losing her seat to a relocated Yankee, something she couldn't quite live down. It's what precipitated her "retirement" out of state so she could live closer to her brother, but losing her seat did not quench her obsession with our perfect and unassailable public image. My mother had no idea that I changed my outfit in the school parking lot each morning, exchanging ugly khakis for skin-tight ripped jeans, Gucci footwear for Converse, and my slicked-back hair for a messy bun. If she was going to start harassing me about my beachwear too, then this was going to be a long, unbearable summer.

My mother didn't understand the relationship between trendiness and relevance, between fashion and friendship. This *was* California, and if she didn't like it, then she shouldn't have moved us here. But I didn't say any of this to her. I tromped upstairs, changed my shorts, and flat-ironed my hair.

+ + +

As I descended the steep trail from my cliffside house to the beach below, my heart lifted. The coast was everything my geometric home was not—loud, wild, unpredictable. It had its way with you, no apologies, like the older boys with their slippery hands. The ocean breeze whipped my freshly glossed hair and blew up my top, exposing my bikini-clad chest and narrow, flat stomach, body parts that still held my mother's approval. I felt free.

Shawna spotted me first, and then the others did—Brendon, Marcus, Hailey, and Chiara. They'd staked out an area of dry sand protected from the wind. I waved. "Hey, y'all, great spot!"

The girls rushed to greet me, cooing over my new white bikini. "Is that from New York?" Hailey asked.

My mother had been in the city the week before, but her famous travel gifts had become more difficult to earn lately. My grades dropped last year, and there was talk that I might not be a varsity starter this year in volleyball. My serve was off, and I couldn't jump like I used to. The coach insinuated that I should lose weight, and with that dire pronouncement, my mom's desire to give me expensive presents had dried up like a peach in the sun. "It's from Vilebrequin," I lied.

Hailey's eyes filled with envy. "You're so lucky. Is that new makeup too?" She admired my glittering eye shadow and the thick black lashes I'd applied this morning, cheap crap from CVS.

"Chanel," I said, another lie. I moved past them and plunked my bag in the center of the beach blanket, scattering my girlfriends to the edges. The boys lounged on a large driftwood log, Marcus whittling with a four-inch carving knife and Brendon with his camera, always with his camera.

"Drink, please." I threw out my hand, and seconds later, a White Claw materialized within it, compliments of Hailey. I took a sip and licked my lips.

Marcus smirked at me in a disapproving way that made my stomach burn. He was a loser with a capital *L*, and he was judging *me*? Did he even have a job?—I had no idea. He supposedly went to community college, but I never heard him talk about his schedule or classes or saw him do homework. Shawna had met him five months before at a gas station, of all places, and now he was part of our group.

I flipped back my hair and addressed him coolly. "Did you get the fireworks for my Fourth of July bonfire?"

His nod was so slight, I almost missed it. Well, good, that was taken care of.

"Can anybody come to the party?" Chiara asked. "Or is it just for us?"

"The Sheffields don't own the beach," Brendon said, cracking open a beer.

I lifted one shoulder, not bothering to correct him, because we did, in fact, own a small section of the beach that fell outside the state park. "A party for just us would be boring," I said instead, watching the sea. A few tourists strolled near the water's edge, letting the waves lap their feet, and that was how I knew they were tourists. Locals knew better than to get close to the water at this beach.

Then two teens appeared at the north end of the shore, walking their goldendoodles on the sand, and by their height difference alone, I knew it was Grady and Chloe. Besides the fact that my brother towered over her—he was six foot four and the youngest pitcher on the varsity baseball team—there was that thousand-watt smile he wore whenever she was around that was probably visible from space.

I've hated Chloe from the first moment I met her in third grade—maybe because she didn't like me either, or maybe because Jessica, my best friend at the time, liked her so much. I put up with her for two years before she and Jessica dumped me. Everyone was starstruck over Chloe back then, Crystal Cove's Olympic hopeful. Even my mom went to a meet once, just to see what all the fuss was about. So Chloe could do tricks like a monkey. Who cared? She wasn't any *fun*. I blew out a breath and turned away from her and Grady.

"What's left to do?" Shawna asked, referring to my Fourth of July bonfire. We put our heads together and decided who would collect the driftwood, who would bring extra chairs, coolers, music, and who had the alcohol covered. Marcus was twenty-two, so he agreed to buy it, with my money of course. I'd brought cash for this purpose.

"Three hundred enough?" I asked, pulling the bills out of my pocket.

He stared hard at the money. "Why, you got more?"

Behind my big sunglasses, I rolled my eyes, and then I added a fifty, my lunch money for the week. "It's all I have on me."

When he took it, his fingers grazed mine. "That'll do, darlin'."

His touch made my guts shrivel, and I snatched my fingers away. He stared harder, that snide smirk still on his face, and I glanced at Shawna, who was clueless and slathering sunscreen onto her pale skin. Annoyance rippled through me that Shawna couldn't control her boyfriend. "No amount of sunscreen's going to lighten those freckles," I blurted before I could stop myself.

Shawna's head snapped up, and her mouth fell open. She hated her freckles, and I knew that, but I doubled down, using a phrase I hated. "Just sayin'." Then I peeled off my crop top and mother-approved shorts, adjusted my bikini, and stretched my long legs across the blanket, letting the warm sun tan my skin. I might have been getting thicker, but it didn't stop my friends from peeking at my curves, especially Marcus. His eyes swept over me so openly and thoroughly that Shawna turned a new shade of white. There. Now maybe she'd see what a loser boyfriend she had and dump him.

To break the tension, I called out to Brendon, "Cameraman, get a picture of us."

He jolted out of whatever reverie he'd been lost in and lifted his camera. "Get closer," he said, motioning us together.

My friends gathered around me, choosing their smiles and poses. I lifted my sunglasses to hold back my hair and stared deeply into the lens, to the one person who wouldn't "like" this photo, to the one person who wouldn't leave a comment full of fire emojis, to the one person who didn't want me at all—Jake Healy. I pulled back my shoulders, tightened my waist, and angled my head until I felt the sun catch the color in my eyes. Maybe I'd tag Jake in this shot to be sure he saw it.

"Don't get my legs," I said to Brendon, thinking of my mother's comment.

He snapped away, and when he was satisfied, we girls broke apart and Hailey passed out the sandwiches she'd made at home. Grady and Chloe walked past us without stopping, and my friends and I spent the rest of the afternoon playing volleyball, sunbathing, and drinking. Brendon told a story about his dad trying to put together an Ikea cabinet that had us bent over, laughing. Hailey braided everyone's hair, except Marcus's because his was too short. Chiara gushed about Chase Waters, a varsity baseball player on my brother's team, and I smirked because Chase had a crush on me. "You should pick someone you have a chance with, Chiara," I said, gulping my drink.

Marcus shook his head at me. "You are *such* a bitch."

I threw up my hands. "Don't kill the messenger." Then I peered at my lap, hating that my mother lived in my mouth.

The silence that followed was a bit too heavy, so I wrapped my arms around my girlfriends and dug into what was left of my Southern accent. "Y'all know I love you to the moon and back. I would do *anything* for you." I kissed their cheeks and gave each one a smile that reached my eyes, letting them know they were special. Even Shawna melted toward me. I didn't know what I'd do without these people. Make new friends, I supposed, but there weren't many to choose from in Crystal Cove.

"Let's check out the new sunglasses at the surf shop," I said impulsively. "Who's coming?"

"Liar. You want to check out Jake," Shawna slurred, well into her fourth or fifth White Claw.

I glared at her. "This isn't about him."

"What hasn't been about him since he dumped you for Jessica?"

I lurched to my feet, tightened my jaw. "Jake didn't—it wasn't because of *her*."

"Then why can't you leave them alone?"

Marcus stood too and kicked sand all over our blanket. "This is so high school. I'm out." He pulled on his T-shirt and baseball hat and took off.

"Thanks a lot," Shawna growled at me, and then chased him.

"We *are* in high school, asshole," Brendon muttered, making the others laugh. I crossed my arms and watched Marcus stalk away, hoping he'd get bored with Shawna and move on. She caught up to him and tugged on his arm, pleading with him to come back to the blanket. *Marcus might tire of her*, I thought, *but will Shawna tire of him?*

He shook her off and kept walking. Shawna caught up and grabbed him again. This time he shoved her so hard, she fell down, and her head smashed into her knee and whiplashed back. He ignored her and kept going.

"Hey!" I threw on my shorts and ran as fast as I could across the sand. The others followed. I reached Shawna first and dropped next to her. "Lord, you're bleeding." I cupped my hand over her split lip. "You can't let him treat you like that."

The others arrived, and Chiara gaped at me. "This isn't Shawna's fault."

I rose up and towered over her. "Did I say it was her fault?"

"I—yeah, you implied it."

Fury roared through me. I pointed at Shawna, whose red hair had come undone from one braid. "That's *my* best friend. I think I know what she needs to hear."

Chiara backed off, but the set of her chin told me she didn't agree.

My phone beeped with an alert. I swiped the screen and groaned. "Shit, my massage therapist is coming at two; I have to go. Y'all take care of her, okay?" I focused on Hailey and Brendon and ignored Chiara.

"We will," Brendon said, helping Shawna up.

"Shawna, call me later." With that, I left my friends, still fuming, and snatched my top off the beach blanket on my way home, leaving the rest of the mess for them to clean up.

If Chiara knew so much, then *she* could listen to Shawna moan and cry about Marcus on the phone every night, because I already knew what was going to happen next. Shawna would apologize to *him* for what he'd done to her, and it would start all over again.

Some people never learned, and babying Shawna wasn't going to change anything. She needed to leave Marcus or stand up to him, not lick his boots. No one bullied me, because I didn't allow it.

I stomped up the sandy trail, frustrated that I'd missed seeing Jake at work, but I hadn't been lying about the massage therapist. My parents had hired the woman, and a personal trainer, to keep my body in top form for volleyball season.

As I approached my house, I caught sight of my mother in the panoramic family room window, her body stiff, her mouth frowning, her critical mind churning, always churning. Bracing myself, I smoothed my hair, adjusted my shorts, and walked inside.

5

Jessica

From Tegan's gigantic family room window, I gaze at the ocean, the backyard pool, and the immaculately landscaped grounds, but really, I'm looking for Jake. I spot Manny, chatting with a guy from the gym, but Jake's not with him.

Earlier, maybe an hour ago, I checked the kitchen and ran into Tegan. She whirled around, grinning, ready to tease whoever bumped into her, but when our eyes met, the smile slid off her face. Her eyes raked over my outfit. "Having fun at my party, Jessica?"

Be nice, I told myself. "Yeah, it's good."

"Where's your beau?"

"Around."

Tegan's gaze hardened and chilled. "Jake loves parties, doesn't he?" She reached out and touched my arm, as if we were still friends. "We went to so many when we were dating. I can't believe you're not with him right now. He's such a good dancer, I might need to round him up." Her eyes challenged me, bringing up the awful words we spoke at her Fourth of July bonfire this summer. The memory ricocheted between us.

My muscles tightened, and heedless fury spilled from my mouth. "Why don't you leave us alone?"

"Leave you alone?" she sputtered. "This is *my* party, sweetheart. You didn't need to come."

"You know what I mean."

She crossed her arms, sucked in her cheeks. "Enlighten me."

God, was she going to make me spell it out—the online posts, her stupid hashtags, her obsession with Jake? She knew *exactly* what I was talking about. I glanced around, noticed the other people in the kitchen, pretending not to eavesdrop, and felt like I was back in fifth grade, at the lunch table where our friendship ended.

Truth is, I was sad when I lost Tegan. I'd spent years sleeping over at her house, watching movies, teasing Grady, playing dress-up in her mom's gigantic closet, and sharing secrets with Tegan in the dark. I'd loved her sparkling eyes; her Southern accent; her pink canopy bed; her Irish Setter, Maggie; her laugh—I'd loved everything about Tegan and her beautiful life. We'd been *best friends*.

Until I started hanging out with Chloe, who was more like me—basic, normal, not rich. When we tried to hang out as a threesome, Tegan would shut Chloe out, forget to invite her to things, and belittle her gymnastics competitions. *You're so good, Chloe, you could join a circus!* The tension built and eventually led to the shouting match that resulted in everyone seeing Tegan's underwear.

I peered at her, standing aggressively in her kitchen, and visualized the little girl she used to be—the girl who got jealous whenever I met someone new—and I wondered if her anger was about losing Jake, or losing me. "Never mind," I muttered.

Tegan smirked. "If Jake's so sweet on you, where is he now?" Without waiting for an answer, she brushed past me, leaving me feeling stupid and abandoned and sad in the middle of the party I hadn't wanted to attend in the first place.

Now, with my stomach gurgling, her words eat at me because I can't find my boyfriend anywhere. I told him I was leaving in an hour. Doesn't he care?

My friends find me sulking beside an antique spinning floor globe, and Chloe is flushed from the contortionist show she performed on the dining room table a few minutes ago. It drew a crowd. Everyone cheered and took videos to post to their stories.

She guzzles from a plastic water bottle and wipes her lips. "Where's Jake?"

My smile falters, and Alyssa joins in, shaking her head. "Did Crystal Cove's cutest couple have a fight?"

I shrug one shoulder.

Chloe pokes at me. "You two shouldn't go to parties—not together."

Alyssa snorts. "How many times have I said that? No one listens to me."

"Where've *you* been?" I ask Alyssa.

"Beating everyone's ass at darts downstairs, until they came up to watch Chloe's little performance, that is."

Chloe lifts her eyebrows. "No shit, you're that good?"

Alyssa shows us the wad of cash she won. "They're that drunk."

We laugh and I glance toward the bedrooms upstairs. "I haven't seen Jake in a long time. We're supposed to be leaving."

"You know he's not up there," Alyssa says. "Jake would never."

Chloe glances out the picture window, her breath fogging up the glass. "Don't worry about him. We can have our own fun!" She grabs our hands and tries to get Alyssa and me to dance in the family room.

Across the sea of heads, I notice Brendon Reed watching us. No, not us, he's watching *me*. He's Tegan's closest neighbor and personal paparazzo. I straighten up and inhale. "What's up with Brendon? He's staring."

Alyssa rolls her eyes. "He probably likes you, duh."

"God, I hope not." No one likes Brendon, not really. His nickname is "the Cameraman" because he's a try-hard YouTuber who's obsessed with getting popular and moving to LA. He thinks mean videos and pranks are funny, and he's got a few thousand followers. Tegan only puts up with him because he takes sexy photographs of her for free that she posts on her account. If her account were public, she could be an influencer, her pictures are that good, but her mom squashed any hope of Insta fame. In politics, even ex-politics, a wholesome image is currency.

My thoughts return to my dilemma, that I want to go home. "When are you and Manny leaving?" I ask Alyssa. "I might need a ride."

She shrugs. "I don't know. Depends on—"

"What the fuck!" a guy shouts, distracting Alyssa.

We turn and notice that everyone is watching the ninety-inch television mounted over the fireplace. I blink rapidly at what has appeared on the TV screen—it's Jake, and he's standing in a girl's bedroom. My eyes dart around the living room and then back to the flat screen. "Is that real?" I blurt.

Jake isn't alone. Tegan Sheffield is in the bedroom with him.

She wraps her arms around his neck while Jake smells her hair. My body starts to tremble.

Alyssa glances toward the staircase. "What the hell! Is this live? Are they upstairs?"

"That's Tegan's bedroom," Chloe says, and we exchange a tangled glance. The décor has changed, but not the huge canopy bed that we remember from childhood sleepovers.

My stomach lurches. Is this a joke? Why are Jake and Tegan on TV? I half expect Jake to face the camera and shout, "Got you, Jess!" But it's not funny, not at all.

"Are they—?" Alyssa doesn't finish her sentence.

The family room goes silent as Tegan guides Jake onto her bed. Bile rises in the back of my throat, and my heart whirrs, like a helicopter about to take off.

Then Tegan slides off her top, revealing a pale-blue lace bra. The boys in the room lose it:

"Fuck yeah!"

"Get it, Jake!"

Someone points at me. "Shut up. His girlfriend's right there."

"We shouldn't," Jake says, his voice amplified by the state-of-the-art sound bar beneath the TV.

"Kiss me," Tegan insists. And then he does. He kisses her, his eyelashes fluttering, his tongue curling. I inhale sharply, and half the people in the room spin around to stare at me.

"That's your boyfriend," a guy calls out, because everyone here knows I'm dating Tegan's ex, *the one that got away*.

Chase Waters from the baseball team mutters a stream of curses and tries to turn the TV off, but the remote is nowhere to be found and the screen is hardwired into the wall above the massive fireplace. He's not tall enough to reach the TV, and he storms downstairs, calling for Grady.

An indiscernible noise emits from my throat as Tegan pulls off Jake's T-shirt and his smooth muscled chest fills the screen. She peers over her shoulder, and I feel as if she's looking straight at me.

My hands rise to my face. I blink, and tears rain down my cheeks. My mouth goes slack.

"Can you turn it off?" Alyssa shouts to Tegan's best friend. Shawna has dropped her drink and is staring at the screen, a stunned look on her face.

"I don't know how," she mouths, also too short to reach the TV's off button.

Meanwhile Jake and Tegan kiss in full-color HD. She straddles his lap, facing him, and we watch them in profile. "Take off my bra," she says.

There's a collective burst of shrieks and babbling in the living room.

"Shut up!" shouts one of the guys as he strains to hear.

"No," I gasp. "No."

Jake reaches around Tegan's back and unhooks her pale lace bra. It slides off her chest, and catcalls erupt as Jake lowers his lips to her skin. I collapse onto a recliner and only then do I notice all the cameras. Everyone has their phones out, filming Jake and Tegan, except for one lone holdout—Brendon Reed, who is filming *me*.

Then the rest of Tegan's and Jake's clothing comes off.

Chloe's hand covers her mouth. "Oh my god, stop."

Grady sprints up from the basement. Silence drops on the house as his eyes dart from the crowd to the screen. "Tegan?" His jaw loosens. He looks sick as he darts toward the main staircase.

Brendon intercepts him. "Don't go up there, man. Your sister's busy."

Grady's bronzed skin reddens.

I'm no longer watching the screen, but the lustful, rhythmic sounds emitting from the speakers send my mind into dark and twisted loops of despair. The noises are unmistakable. Jake and Tegan are screwing, on-screen, in front of everyone.

"Can you turn it off?" Shawna asks Grady, and her request sets him in motion. He's just tall enough to reach the off button, and suddenly the noises stop.

"Let's go, Jess." Chloe hauls me to my feet and drags me away as voices follow us.

"You okay, Jessica?"

A girl from English pats my arm. "He's not worth it."

A different guy from the baseball team shouts, "If you want revenge, Jessica, I'll make a video with you!"

"Coming through," Chloe pipes, but at four feet eleven inches, she's no bouncer. She elbows me through the crowd and into a darkened bedroom, with Alyssa trailing.

A couple argues inside, but they scatter when they see my face. "She's gonna puke," the guy comments as they exit.

He's not wrong. As soon as I glimpse the en suite toilet bowl, my stomach heaves up everything I ate tonight—Flamin' Hot Cheetos, a Red Bull, and two Bud Light seltzers. Chloe strokes my back as I splatter the porcelain with orange liquid.

Alyssa hands me tissues, her high ponytail swinging angrily. She texts and chews gum and taps her thigh. "Tegan Sheffield deserves to die for this."

I flush the toilet, wipe my eyes, and blow my nose. "Maybe not *die.*" Warm tears slide down my cheeks. "She didn't force him."

"But she filmed it. Gross," Alyssa adds.

"And Brendon filmed *me*. Why?"

"'Cause he's a dick," says Alyssa, and Chloe nods.

I cry quietly, miserably. "Guys, I can't go back out there."

"To get to my car, we have to go through the living room," Alyssa points out.

I'm not ready to pass through the gauntlet of Tegan's friends, including Shawna and Brendon, so I lean against the bed with my best friends beside me.

Alyssa scrolls on her phone, cursing about the posts populating on everyone's stories. "Is it legal to post real sex online?" she asks, popping her gum.

"Not when one of the people is under eighteen," Chloe says, turning pale. "A girl on my team did it and got arrested. Well, she used to be on the team." She holds my hands, her large eyes rolling over me like marbles.

I groan. "Do you know what Jake said to me by the pool?" I tug at the silver heart necklace he gave me for my seventeenth birthday. "I told him I wanted to leave, and he said, 'You know what, Jess, sometimes you're no fun.'"

"That's not fair. He knew you didn't want to come," says Chloe.

Alyssa sighs. "You're not fun at these kinds of parties, Jess, but that's no excuse for what he did." She blows a bubble and lets it pop. I gape at her, and Chloe throws her a withering scowl. Alyssa softens. "I told Manny to catch a ride with a friend. I'll drive you home, Jess."

"You should go up there and confront them," Chloe says. "I can't believe Jake did this to you."

"No," I cry. "No way."

"Jake is drunk. He'll regret it tomorrow," says Alyssa.

I shrug. Jake is drunk, obviously, but what do experts say about alcohol? It's liquid courage? It helps you say and do the things that you're normally too afraid to say or do? Jake dated Tegan for six weeks and swears he's not into her anymore. I believed him, until now.

But even worse was the expression on Tegan's face when she looked at me in the kitchen earlier. In hindsight, it wasn't challenging. . . . It was triumphant. She planned this, and I know why. The battle we've been in since fifth grade isn't over.

The video is proof of that.

6

Jessica

While we wait for the party to die down, my friends and I kill time, scrolling on our phones. Chloe sneaks out and returns with Red Bulls and Takis. "All they had left was this crap," she explains. "Hey, I saw Grady on his way out to spend the night at Chase's. He asked if you're okay, Jess."

"Is *he* okay?" Alyssa asks. "That was his sister on the screen."

"I don't think so," Chloe murmurs.

Alyssa takes my hand. "You know I love Jake, but if he's going back to his old ways, it's better you find out now, before senior year and prom and all that."

This starts me crying again. Could Jake be slipping? After his dad died of pancreatic cancer, and before we were dating, he partied a lot and hooked up with random girls. Everyone believed I changed him, but I don't think that's true. Jake felt bad about how his behavior was affecting his mom.

Still, when people at school saw us holding hands for the first time junior year, no one could believe it. He'd broken up with Tegan, and then he'd fallen for *me*—the plain girl who wears flannels and sits in the front row and does her homework—and we became #Goals overnight.

I close my eyes and inhale a shallow, hiccuping breath. Jake with his unruly hair, velvety lower lip, and eternally perplexed eyebrows. Jake who tries so hard to make me happy—it seems like all the girls want him now that I have him, but none more than Tegan Sheffield.

Outside the guest bedroom, the party has wound down, so I borrow Chloe's sweatshirt and pull up the hood. "Let's go," I say.

My friends usher me out, and I keep my head down, like an MMA fighter departing the Octagon after a brutal loss.

How do you feel about that last round, Jessica?

No comment.

It's not the worst analogy because I *feel* like a defeated fighter. My eyes and lips are swollen from crying, my nose is packed with snot, and my head pulses. My heart is smashed.

Every day Jake wakes me with a text: *Good morning, beautiful*, with hearts. Jake and Jessica, Jessica and Jake. Everyone thinks he has eyes only for me. It's why we're Crystal Cove's cutest couple, until now. God.

Chloe, Alyssa, and I pass through Tegan's family room, where her exhausted friends drape over the furniture like dirty laundry. Some are asleep; some are stoned, and some are still making out. My drama has faded, for now, and my friends and I make it outside unnoticed.

"Shit, it's still raining," says Chloe. We huddle together on the front stoop and prepare to run into the chilling rain.

I spot Jake's truck in Tegan's driveway, and my stomach flops. "He's still here, with *her*."

Chloe scans the grounds, as if Jake might be near, then shakes her head. "Don't think about it."

I turn on my phone, see no texts from Jake. It's 3:07 a.m. Then I glance at Alyssa, who is unsteady on her feet. "I'll drive us home, okay?" I say.

"No, Jess," she whines.

"You'll thank me later."

With a grunt, she hands me the keys to her dad's BMW. "Don't wreck it. My dad's out of town and doesn't know I took it."

We hunch our backs, sprint to the BMW, and pile inside, Chloe taking the back seat. The car is a classic from the seventies, worth a small fortune, and my heart kicks at the responsibility of driving it. But the engine turns over and then purrs with a confidence that settles me, as if it's saying, *I might be old, but I know what I'm doing.*

I press the pedal, and we roll quietly down Tegan's long driveway with the windshield wipers sliding away the raindrops. The moonlight reflects off the hood between drifts of heavy clouds. The rain strikes the car in splattering bursts.

I pull onto the country road that leads out of the exclusive Cherish Heights neighborhood and toward Crystal Cove a few miles away. There are no streetlights, and the dark asphalt snakes ahead, wet and gleaming in the moonlight, with no real shoulder, just a deep ditch on either side. We locals nicknamed it Blood Alley because people crash and die on this road every couple of years. I grip the steering wheel with both hands, and Alyssa cranks up the stereo.

The song playing happens to be *our song*, the one Jake and I first danced to at homecoming last year, and fresh tears skid down my cheeks. "Turn it off," I say, but Alyssa doesn't hear me. "I said turn it off." I reach for the car's unfamiliar buttons and start changing stations, until I end up on an AM frequency. Hissing static fills my ears.

"What are you doing?" Alyssa shoves my hand away.

"Trying to change the song." I glance at the road, feel the pull of the tires as the BMW veers toward the ditch, and I overcorrect the wheel. The car fishtails.

"Jesus, pay attention," Chloe shouts from the back.

I squint into the blackness ahead. It's so dark, it's difficult for me to distinguish between the wet asphalt, the dark ditch, and the velvet sky.

My phone pings with a text, and my heart zooms. Is it Jake? Risking a glance at my cell, I read the message, but it's from my mom: *Where are you? It's after 3.*

No, I'm so late. "Alyssa, text my mom that I'm okay."

"Bossy," Alyssa grumbles. She texts my mom and then turns the radio to the original station, which is still playing our song.

I think about Jake's lips on my neck while we danced last year—his featherlight kisses, his eyes pouring into mine—and grief like fire rolls up from my toes, blasts through my veins, and comes to a cold, stuttering halt in my heart. The words Jake whispered to Tegan fill my ears. *We shouldn't.*

But then he did, and I know how intense it must have been for Tegan. Kissing Jake is like riding a rocket—body floating, heart thudding, breath gone.

Losing Jake is like crashing back to earth.

A sob breaks from my chest, and salty tears overflow from my eyes, blurring everything as I wonder, *Is this my fault?* My foot tenses, pressing harder on the accelerator.

Chloe screams in my ear, "Watch out!"

I wipe my eyes, see the ditch coming at us, and slam on the breaks, swerve toward black space. The car skids. The rubber tires scream and slide. I spot a flash of movement, some creature running across the road. Horrified, I accidentally steer toward it, and before I can correct the wheel, the car smacks it with a light thump. The skidding tires grind to a halt.

We're thrown forward and then back in our seats. My hands tremble. Chloe gasps.

Alyssa's thin voice brings me around. "We hit something," she whispers.

I stare into the darkness. "Or someone."

7

Tegan, June

"You're going too fast," Brendon snapped at me.

"Just keep filming." I stepped harder on the pedal and tightened my grip on the steering wheel, my tires screaming down Blood Alley. In the lane next to us, Marcus's Mustang nosed ahead of my Audi. Grady sat beside me. Chiara, Hailey, and Brendon rode in the back seat, with Brendon recording the race. When I beat Marcus, I'd have a video to prove it.

It had been Marcus's idea to race, and the fact that he'd *had* an idea had been surprising enough, but I had to win, and I would. "Hold on!" I steered the car around a tight curve. Marcus's tires squealed beside us.

"What are you doing, Pea?" Grady asked between clenched teeth.

"Chill," I scolded, using a term my mother hated.

Marcus and I snaked up the two-lane road, each of us heading north. It was as dangerous as hell, but at least he was the one driving in the wrong lane. Blind curves and towering redwood trees blurred past us. I blocked out all sounds except his rumbling engine and the deep whir of my own.

✦ ✦ ✦

The day hadn't begun with a high-speed illegal car race. It'd started this afternoon when Shawna had dragged us to Bodega Bay for clam chowder bowls. It had been sunny and unusually humid, a whiff of brine on the breeze, and we girls had thrown on our cutest, tightest tops, our shortest shorts, and our biggest sunglasses, and stuffed our pockets with cash. We were determined to enjoy our normally foggy coast as we imagined people in LA enjoyed their sunny one. I'd flat-ironed my hair, and it tickled my lower back as I walked. I was excited, ready to flirt and enjoy my first summer without a boyfriend in years.

Then Shawna invited the guys. "No testosterone," I said.

"Too late," she answered, her green eyes swimming. She was already high.

I gave in, to make her happy, and we ate our clam chowder at wooden picnic benches that overlooked the Pacific. Seagulls soared overhead like winged rats, waiting for scraps. Brendon and Marcus argued about some new rap song while my brother hunched over his bowl, sulking because he'd wanted to invite Chloe and I'd flat-out refused.

Whenever Chloe came over to see my brother, we passed each other in the halls of my house like war submarines, no acknowledgment of the other but always, always the *awareness*. Grady has a crush on her, but, Lord. She's four feet eleven and he's six feet four—they might as well be from different planets.

We finished our clam chowder bowls and walked to the beach for pictures. On the way home, Marcus and Shawna pulled up beside my Audi, and he gunned his engine.

Brendon snorted from my back seat. "Does he want to race?"

I met Marcus's hooded gaze through our car windows, and it was his ugly smirk that did it—that wry grin that said he was better than me. The hair on my neck lifted, and I gunned my V-6 in return, knowing he'd sucked me in, and not giving a damn. I toggled to manual transmission and placed my fingers over the paddle shifters. My dad had enrolled me in an offensive driving school last year, held at a racetrack, and Marcus was about to find out that I knew how to drive. He yanked up his emergency brake and spun his tires, a wicked grin on his face.

"Please don't race," Hailey said, gripping the door handle.

"What is she supposed to do, back down?" Chiara huffed.

I swept back my hair. "Buckle up, y'all."

Marcus nodded at me, and our tires squealed, leaving trails of smoke as we rocketed onto the street, side by side.

It was not a good day to race. The fog had dropped while we'd been taking pictures, and now it floated above the road and shrouded the trees. My headlights beamed on as a little Toyota appeared around the bend, driving toward us. My heart juddered.

"Watch out!" Grady braced as my steering wheel pulled hard against my hands, fighting the curves, but I kept my pace, ignored the slam of my pulse. Marcus didn't budge either.

The oncoming driver waffled between lanes. It was going to be a head-on collision or a deadly trip into the ditch if Marcus didn't drop back and move over. Instead he shot forward, thinking to pull ahead of me, but I downshifted and thrust the Audi faster to block him.

With bare seconds to spare, he tucked behind me, and the Toyota passed us with a long, whining honk. I whooped. "Did you see that!"

"Oh my god, oh my god," Hailey cried.

"Okay, you're good," Brendon said to me. "You won."

Marcus veered back into the wrong lane and tried to speed past me again. He also owned a V-6, but mine was newer and faster, and I had turbo. I shifted, nosed ahead of him, and made the sliding turn onto Blood Alley, my tires screeching. This stretch of road was six miles long, and we raced it, trading the lead as the curves favored either him or me.

"You're going too fast," Brendon snapped from the back seat.

"Just keep filming."

We hit a sharp curve and I leaned into the turn. "Hold on!"

My brother took deliberate slow breaths beside me, sometimes closing his eyes and moving his lips. Praying, I imagined. "What are you doing, Pea?" he asked.

"Chill," I said, but I knew Dad would tar and feather me if he found out I'd driven like this on a public road. My heart knocked inside my chest.

Another car appeared in my windshield, barreling toward us. Marcus edged the hood of his Mustang ahead of mine and veered toward me, pushing me toward the ditch. "Screw that," I muttered, veering closer to him. Our mirrors collided, metal against metal.

But then a quick glance at Marcus showed me something I'll never forget—his eyelids peeled back, his jaw muscles tight, his smile loose—as if he had a death wish or he was high on drugs— and it was the first time during the race when I felt scared. Marcus didn't care if he died, or if *we* died.

Grady also noticed Marcus's unhinged expression, and his hands flew to the dashboard. "He's not gonna back off, Pea."

"I know; I see it." I let off the gas. Marcus blasted ahead, cut away from the oncoming car just in time, and dived into my lane, ahead of me. He gave a long victorious honk of his horn.

I offered a half-hearted wave, ceding victory. Now that it was over, I noticed my hands shaking. What was more dangerous? I wondered. Racing on Blood Alley, or hanging out with Marcus? Shawna didn't even know his last name. I twisted around to face Brendon. "Erase that video."

"Why? I got some good shit."

"Because I lost, Brendon. Delete it." He mumbled a few choice curse words that I ignored.

Hailey's hands trembled in her lap. "You could have killed us," she said when I pulled safely into my driveway, as if the race were *my* fault.

I put the car into park and flashed her my biggest, brightest smile. "But I didn't, did I?"

At the end of the day, that was all that mattered. That no one had gotten hurt—at least not permanently.

8

Jessica

"I'm gonna throw up." Alyssa grasps the door handle of the BMW, shoves the door open, and retches into the middle of the rain-soaked road.

Chloe unbuckles and stares out the windshield as the wiper blades squeak, swishing back and forth, clearing the thick droplets. "Why did you say we hit *someone?*" she asks, her voice tremulous. "It was a deer, Jess."

"It was?" I curl my hands into fists to stop them from trembling. I remember the glint of an eyeball staring back at me. The impression of the creature in the dark was so quick, so fleeting, plus I was crying. "I—I don't know why I said that. Did you see it?" I ask Alyssa.

She wipes her mouth clean and glares at me "My dad's car— I told you not to wreck it." I start to apologize, but she waves at the hood of the BMW. "Check the front, see if it's dented!" Her mascara has smudged, and one set of eyelashes dangles.

"Okay." I pop open my door, emerge into the wet night, and turn on my phone's flashlight. First I crouch and peer under the chassis, and breathe a sigh of relief—no creature's body there. I inch forward, dreading what's next, because I know I hit something *living*. Inhaling, I swipe the rain off my eyelids, round the corner of the BMW, and shine my light on the front of the car. Dark liquid dribbles down the grille.

"What is it?" Alyssa asks, coming around to the front. Seconds later, she's growling at me. "Jesus, no wonder the road looked so dark. You never turned on the headlights!"

I blink at her, dazed. "Aren't they automatic?"

"It's a classic, dumbass, of course they're not."

We each exhale angrily, standing on opposite sides of the front hood. There's no body—no animal—but there's that dark substance on the grille.

Alyssa sees it too. "Is that . . . blood?" she whispers.

I bring the light closer, touch the sticky residue, and then raise my finger to my nose. The acrid scent of blood is unmistakable, and without thinking, I wipe it on my jeans. "Yeah, it's blood, but where's the animal?"

Chloe's voice startles me because I didn't hear her get out of the car. She gapes at the blood, glances around. "It's gone. After you hit it, it leaped over that ditch." She points to the depression on the side of the road, right next to a DEER CROSSING sign.

It doesn't escape me that she said *you* and not *we*. I turn in a circle, gazing into the woods on either side of the road. "Let's look around, okay? Whatever I hit might need help."

"Pull the car over first," Alyssa insists.

I park her dad's car as close to the ditch as possible without sliding into it. Once I'm standing beside Alyssa and Chloe again, I point to the ground. "There's a few droplets of blood leading that way."

My friends turn on their phone flashlights and we climb across the ditch to the other side. This is the first rain of the season, so the soil is still packed and hard from the long, dry California summer. Deer cross this road and get hit rather frequently, which is why the county installed the DEER CROSSING sign in the first place. Chloe's right, I probably hit one. I keep searching anyway, bent low, inspecting the undergrowth for blood or animal tracks.

"It's probably hiding in a thicket," Chloe says.

Alyssa snaps her gum. "A thicket? Like in *Bambi*?"

Chloe snorts. "Deer do that in real life."

"I've just never heard anyone say *thicket*." There's a drunken slur to Alyssa's words. "Thicket, thicket, thicket." Suddenly she groans and smacks at her phone. "Damn it. It died."

Chloe halts. "What died?"

"My phone, it died." She reels unsteadily. "There better not be a dent on the car, Jess. if there's even a scratch, my dad's going to kill me. He forbade me to drive it after my last accident. Like, I'm not even allowed to sit in it. He said that before he left, 'Don't even sit in it, Alyssa.'" She laughs grimly.

"Just keep looking," I say.

"Why, for what?" She gestures around us. "Chloe saw a deer, Jess. If it was a person, they would still be here, right, calling their lawyer." She blows a bubble, sucks it back in. "What time is it, Chloe?"

Chloe glances at her phone. "Three-seventeen."

My heart rate slams into overdrive. "God, I'm late. My parents are going to murder me."

"I don't see anything. Let's go," Chloe says, shivering without her sweatshirt. She and Alyssa hike back to the car.

A ribbon of lightning flashes in the sky, followed by a clap of thunder, and the drizzle turns into a roaring downpour, soaking my clothes in seconds. A whoosh of wind sends the rain flying sideways. There's nothing here.

Shivering, I trudge back to the car and settle into the front seat. "I guess it ran away."

Alyssa cranks the heat as our breath steams up the windows. Then she reaches over me to turn on the headlights. "Good. Let's go home. Please."

I grip the wheel for a moment, feeling overwhelmed.

"This isn't the end of the world, Jess," Alyssa says softly. "You and Jake can work this out."

A laugh gurgles from my throat. "Work it out? Did you see him on that TV? No, it's over."

I start the car and press the gas pedal, and we roll smoothly toward town. I keep my speed to twenty-five miles per hour even though the speed limit is forty-five.

Alyssa borrows my phone and starts reading posts. "Epic hookup at Tegan's," she says, snorting. "Everyone's posting pics and clips of that video. Jesus, it got kind of X-rated."

"Are you trying to make her crash again?" Chloe says, rubbing her forehead.

My grief returns. The image of Jake is burned into my brain, his wet tongue, his closed eyes, his voice. *We shouldn't.* He was undeniably *into* her, and everyone from school saw it, not just me. My foot twitches, making the car lurch faster.

"Why is she still driving?" Chloe rails from the back seat.

"'Cause we're wasted," Alyssa replies.

"Jess, the turn!"

I glimpse the turn that leads to Chloe's house and whip the wheel to the left. The BMW glides around the corner, and I'm grateful we're not in my little Honda with bald tires.

"So, how are we going to handle this on Monday? Do we kick Tegan's ass or what?" Alyssa asks.

I shake my head. "No, she didn't force Jake to kiss her."

Alyssa twirls her long shiny hair around her finger and then shrugs. "Just say the word if you change your mind."

I steer us onto Chloe's street and drop her off first. "Thanks, Chloe. You saved me in that family room. I—I didn't know what to do."

She smiles sadly. "What are friends for? I'm sorry about Jake and Tegan, but maybe those two deserve each other, you know." She squeezes my arm. "It's senior year. It might not be so bad to be free."

Instant tears pool in my eyes. Do I want to be free? I'm not sure. I wait until she lets herself in, and then drive to Alyssa's house and pull the BMW into her garage.

"Let's check the car again," Alyssa says. We squat to inspect the front end.

To my relief, the heavy downpour washed away most of the blood. "Do you have any spray cleaner? I'll get the rest of this off."

Alyssa finds bleach and a clean rag, and I scrub the last remaining blood droplets off the car and run my hands long the metal grille. It might be slightly bent, but I don't think anyone will notice unless they're looking for it. I toss the bloody rag into her garbage can. "All done." I wipe my forehead and turn to leave.

Alyssa stops me. "Are you going to *walk* home? This late? You can spend the night if you want."

"No, I'm in enough trouble. It's just two blocks. I'll jog."

She pulls me into a warm hug. "I'm sorry too, Jess. What a shitty night."

"It's okay. I'm okay." Five minutes later, I'm home. Inhaling a huge breath, I walk inside, hoping my parents are asleep.

One is not.

Mom sits at the kitchen table, a half-empty cup of what appears to be tea in front of her. Emotions dance across her face as she surveys my wet hair, borrowed sweatshirt, and damp clothing.

"I'm sorry—" I blurt out.

She rises, using both hands to push herself up. "You have no idea," she rasps.

"Mom, I'm sorry!"

"Your father and I will speak to you tomorrow."

"Mom . . ."

She looks straight at me, her lips tight, her robe inside out. "Tell Jake I want to speak to him too. This is unacceptable. I'm so disappointed. Did you two . . ." She can't finish the question that I know she's dying to ask. *Did you two have sex?* We've been having sex for months, but she doesn't know that, and it remains her biggest concern when it comes to Jake.

I shake my head, crying. "No, we—"

She throws up her hand, cutting me off. "You know what, Jess? The sun is coming up soon and I'm exhausted. You're safe. That's all that matters. Tell me tomorrow." And she heads upstairs.

As my mother disappears into the shadows, my answer trails her in a whisper, "We broke up."

9

Jake

A wet nose and bad breath wake me in the morning—Otis. When I try to scoot him over, he dives at me harder, licking and wagging. *Get up*, he says with his entire furry body.

"Go away," I mutter.

Every fiber in my body aches, and I feel wrung dry, shriveled and empty. My brain pulses as if it no longer fits inside my skull. My eyeballs are so dry that blinking is like rubbing sandpaper over them, and all movement is agony. How did I get home? What happened last night?

Glancing around my bedroom, I spot my shirt and jeans piled on the floor. The underside of my foot throbs, and when I pull it out from under the covers, I find a deep gash in my skin that's covered in dried blood. The last thing I clearly remember is standing beside Tegan's swimming pool with Jess.

I reach for my phone and slide it beneath the blankets with me. A streak of unread text messages fills my screen.

dude, tegan sheffield? Props!

your dick looks huge on a ninety-inch, man

you better get that shit deleted porn star

jess is going to kill you

Porn star? My dick? I start to text Jess; she'll know what I did. But then I pause, vaguely remembering a Southern drawl, a blue bra, and some hot kissing. Did I imagine that? Shit, if I did something with Tegan, Jess will be pissed. I text Manny instead: *what did I do last nite*

Gray dots, and then Manny, answering, *you don't remember*

Me: *dude im asking arent i*

Manny: *call me*

Me: *im sick. Just tell me*

Manny pauses, then, *you and Tegan screwed in her bedroom. she had a camera. It played live in the family room.*

My stomach lurches. *no fucking way*

Manny: *dude, i saw it. So did Jessica. Brendon filmed her watching the live feed. He posted an edited version on youtube.* He adds a link.

My chest tightens and my eyes start to burn. *jess watched us?*

Manny: *yeah, everyone did. you should prob stay away from jessica rn. tegans hot dude but you went too far*

A low moan pours from my mouth and reactivates Otis into nuzzling me. I sit up and roar at him, "Get out!"

My dog flees, and I cover my face as chills rush through my body. I had sex with Tegan Sheffield and people *watched*?

I need to see the video, and not the edited version.

As soon as I log into my account, people's stories from last night populate my screen. First it's just the usual posts, beer bongs, dancing, spilled snacks . . . but then there's a video of a ruckus in the family room—catcalling and people shouting my name and Tegan's name. Guys cheering us on, and yelling "Take it off" and "Hit that."

Then there are close-ups of the flat screen as people zoom in on us. It's such a shock, I almost drop my phone.

There I am, making out with Tegan. I'm watching Brendon's story now, where he posted the unedited version of what he put on YouTube. Brendon briefly turns his camera toward the crowd to film Jessica's reaction, and I watch as my girlfriend self-implodes. I watch as her faith in me drains from her eyes.

Holy shit! I tug on my hair. My girl! Jess! Another moan rises, and my throat tightens around it. I might as well have taken a baseball bat to her. In the video, she hyperventilates and then drops slowly into a chair, like a building crashing down, one floor at a time. Jessica looks away from the video, and Brendon swivels his camera back to Tegan and me on the screen.

I don't remember any of this—well, hardly any of it. The Jake on camera has taken off Tegan's bra, and now he's pulling down his jeans, his underwear. Everyone at the party watches me strip.

And then—oh, shit, I'm going for it, every naked inch of me.

My stomach lurches, and I stumble into the hallway bathroom and dry heave into the toilet.

When I'm done retching, I flop onto the cold tile floor and stare at the wall. I'm the world's biggest asshole! I didn't use a condom; I didn't think about my girlfriend. So what if I was drunk? That's no excuse. The drugs—did I take any? Or did I drink so much after that first shot of tequila that I blacked out? Shit, it's been almost a year since I woke up like this—sick and confused and wondering if I picked up an STD. Fuck me. I start to cry.

Right then the bathroom door bangs open, and my mom

materializes in the doorway. Her horrified expression flays me. "Jacob Healy!"

"Please, don't yell at me."

"Why?" she shouts. "Are you hungover?"

"Mom, please." I feel as if gravity has increased and it's pinning me to the floor. My tongue is as dry as desert sand. I want to die.

"You drove home like this? You know better, Jake. How many times have I told you to call for a ride? How many?"

Her voice blasts through my brain like buckshot. My stomach heaves harder, and I grip the toilet.

But she won't stop. "I had to move your car when I got up this morning. Do you know why? You parked in the *grass*, Jake. You completely missed the driveway."

My body shakes, but there are no tears left, and it hurts too much to cry anyway. "I'm sorry," I rasp, curling into myself and shuddering.

"What else did you do last night? Do you even remember? Damn it, Jake, we've been through this. I—I thought you stopped drinking like that."

Mom doesn't know about the sex posts, thank god. I hide my face, can't speak.

After a minute, she squats, touches my forehead, and softens. "You feel hot. If you're done throwing up, get back into bed." I nod, and she leads me to my room. "Are you limping?"

"I'm fine," I say.

She pushes back her curls and stares me down. Looking at Mom is always like looking at myself, same dark hair and puffed lips, except I'm rough where she's smooth. "You're not fine. Let me see." She makes me sit, pulls my foot toward her, and inspects the bottom of it. Her eyes widen. "It's glass, Jake. Looks like part of a mirror." She grabs tweezers, pulls sharp fragments out of my foot, wipes the wound clean, and then wraps it in gauze.

Afterward Mom tucks me into bed, a bit rougher than necessary, but her rage has melted into something worse. Disappointment. Since Dad died, she's extra terrified of something bad happening to my little brother or me.

"At least you're home safe," she says, wiping the hair out of my eyes. "I checked the car, and there's no sign you hit anything, but I'm taking your keys. Jessica can drive you to school until you earn them back."

I doubt Jessica will be driving me anywhere for a while. Why the fuck did Tegan film us? Does she need attention that badly? I release a breath. It doesn't matter; the damage is done. Jess will hate me forever for cheating.

My mom tiptoes from my room and returns later with a bowl of steaming tomato soup, a large glass of ice water, and a handful of vitamins. The sound of the lawn mower kicks on, and I groan. "Does Cole have to do that now?" My brother just turned seven, and he insists on mowing the lawn, which was Dad's job when he was alive. It makes Cole feel good to help Mom, but it takes him forever to mow the lawn.

She sighs. "There are tire tracks in the front yard, Jake, so yes, I'd like those erased. Can Otis come in? He's upset."

Otis whines outside my door, the world's most insecure dog, and I feel terrible that I yelled at him. "Yeah, go ahead."

Mom lets him in, and Otis curls next to me, content to breathe the same air as me. I scratch behind his ears, my apology for snapping at him. Mom tilts the blinds to keep the sun out of my eyes and shuts my door on her way out.

The blood-colored soup she left burns my tongue, so I suck down the water in one greedy gulp and then text back a few friends. They offer heartfelt congratulations on my conquest, which I ignore. Then I text Tegan: *why did you film us?*

She doesn't answer.

I glance out my slatted blinds to Jess's house next door, and my fingers hover over the screen. I'm dying to text her, but what do I say? *Sorry I cheated, please forgive me?* How do I explain that I drank too much and ruined the best thing in my life? Forget losing her to college. I lost Jess before the first day of senior year. I'm such an idiot.

I settle on a simple text—*please call me*—and then drop my phone and try to sleep as images scroll through my head: Tegan's lace bra, her smooth skin, a shot glass of tequila with the words *Drink Me* etched across the side, and Jess by the pool. We fought because she wanted to leave the party early. I said something about her being *no fun*. Why did I have to fight with her? Jess is right; parties are overrated. I should have listened.

All day long, I ignore my phone, which is blowing up. People from school rapid-share the sex video. Brendon Reed's YouTube post is also blowing up. Manny texts me updates of how many views it's getting, and it's almost to one hundred thousand.

Brendon titled the video **sshole Breaks Girlfriend's Heart— Live!* It's an edited, PG-13-rated version of what Tegan and I did, but Jess is the real star. Sex is everywhere online, but a girl's live reaction to her boyfriend cheating is raw, unscripted . . . *genuine*. It's real life, and it's going viral. When the viewer count passes a hundred thousand, I turn off my phone.

The next time I see Brendon Reed, I'm going to beat the living shit out of him.

I lie back and stare at the ceiling, arms behind my head. The sex—that was both our faults—but the video is Tegan's fault. She must have set it up before we got to her bedroom. She planned the whole thing—she got me back for dumping her and she humiliated Jess, in one fell swoop. I'm no longer *the one that got away*. And the worst thing is, I went along with it.

Around two p.m., I finish the tomato soup, which is cold now, and drink the ice cubes in my cup that have turned to water. Feeling only slightly better, I haul myself out of bed and into the shower. When I emerge with a towel around my waist, I bump into my little brother. He stares up at me, looking suspicious. "Are you sick? You look sick."

I force a smile. "Nope, just tired, little man."

"So, you don't have germs?" When our dad died of cancer, Cole was five years old and he misunderstood all the extra hand washing we did. He thought Dad died of a virus, not cancer—and even though we've explained it to him, Cole can't let go of his war on germs.

"If I had any germs, they're gone now," I say, holding up my hands like a surgeon.

He sidles past me to avoid touching my skin. "If you're not sick, why'd you drive on the grass? Couldn't you see the driveway?"

I shrug. "It was too dark."

After a beat, Cole decides to believe me and shuts the door.

In my room, I peer out the window, squinting through the fog that has rolled in and muted the sun. I notice a figure emerging from Jess's house next door, and my heart wallops. It's her!

With my injured foot aching and my head throbbing, I tie on my shoes and stumble out my front door. Jess is already out of sight, but I know the trail she's taking because she runs it every afternoon. It leads to Blind Beach.

I break into a jog and chase her.

10

—

Jessica

Sunday afternoon, after hiding from my parents all day, I decide to go for a run to clear my head. I've avoided looking out my window to Jake's window, which is directly across from mine, because—of course—we're still neighbors. Breaking up doesn't change that, and I assume he knows it's over between us. I shouldn't have to say it, right?

My stomach clenches, and tears sting my eyes. The video of him and Tegan has gone viral, and the whole school knows my boyfriend cheated on me. How am I going to survive Monday? I change into shorts, tie on my Asics, and trot downstairs. But first I must face my parents.

Stomach twirling, I approach the kitchen. I'm not afraid of the punishment for blowing my curfew; I just don't want to tell my parents about Jake. Dad already doesn't trust him for all the partying he did after his dad's death. We had a front-row seat to that disaster. Jake pissing in the bushes, Jake singing—badly—at the top of his lungs at two a.m., waking everyone up, and Jake bringing different girls home each weekend. The last thing I need to hear right now is *I told you so.*

My parents are sipping coffee at the table, as if they've been waiting for me all day.

"Sit down, Jessica," says Mom.

"Can I have a cup?" She nods, and I pour myself a mug of hot coffee from the half-empty pot. After adding cream and four spoonfuls of organic sugar, I stir and then drink, enjoying the sweet warmth in my throat, and then slide into an empty seat. On another day, I might have argued or pleaded my case. Today I simply confess. "I know I was late. I'm sorry. I have no excuse."

Dad's head flips up, and he glances at Mom, then back at me. He looks baffled, probably because I'm not begging for mercy or denying what happened. He prods me. "We were worried sick."

"I know."

"Don't tell us you lost track of time. You're glued to that phone of yours."

I say nothing to defend myself, just nod and swallow another sip of coffee.

Mom takes a swipe at me. "We've supported your relationship with Jake, and you know how much we—I—like him, but if you stay out that late again, you two need to take a break."

Tears fill my eyes, and I push my cup aside, trying to hold them in. *Do not lose it, do not lose it!* I nod furiously and rise halfway up. "Can I go?"

"Jess, what's wrong? Why are you crying?" Mom's anger switches to fear.

A sob ripples through my body.

Her hand flies to her mouth. "What happened?" Mom believes

that teenagers lose their minds when they hit high school—we get into drugs, screw every other teen we see, get pregnant, fall for online stalkers, run away, or get murdered—and this is the moment she has dreaded. Surely I've been raped or drugged or bullied. And I guess it is *a* moment, if not *that* moment.

"J-Jake and I broke up," I whisper.

Her sigh of relief fills the kitchen. Even Dad takes a steadying breath. It's as if I can hear their thoughts. *It's just a broken heart, no big deal.*

Mom pets my hair. "Oh, honey, I'm sorry, but this happens when you're young."

"When you're *young*? You don't get it!" I run outside and slam the front door.

Since there are no police to call and no funerals to plan—since it's just a broken heart, something that happens *when you're young*— my parents let me go.

Outside, the August air is warm and humid from the recent rain from Mexico. As I start walking, I switch on my phone. Text messages fill the screen, the most recent at the top.

Chloe: *ARE YOU OKAY*

Alyssa: *call me*

Jake: *please call me*

His voice whispers through my brain. *We shouldn't.* "But you did," I whisper. Rage and shame and horror swim through me, and my feelings flip-flop so fast that I get dizzy. This was going to be *our* year—classes together, road trips, spring break with friends, prom. Jake was scared about graduation and what might come next—and yes, we had a few fights about how he'd started to cling to me—but we would have gotten through it, and graduation feels so far away.

Now, as I pass his house, my heart squeezes. Did he sabotage us on purpose, or did I? I'm the one who threw down an ultimatum: *I'm leaving in an hour, with or without you.* I'm the one who abandoned him in enemy territory. I'm the one who . . . No, this isn't my fault.

There's a trail behind our houses that leads through the redwood groves to Blind Beach, and today of all days, I need to run. It's four miles round-trip, a nice, flat, easy workout to clear my head.

I set my fitness watch and think about the deer I hit last night. God, I practically aimed for it. I didn't mean to, of course. My shoulders rotated with my head, and the BMW followed the line of my eyes—like a skier who stares at a tree and then rams into it—but the accident adds to the sourness in my gut. I'll go back to the spot after my run and check the road in daylight, make sure the creature is truly gone.

When I reach the trailhead that leads to Blind Beach, I ease into a jog, thinking about Jake.

Our friendship started a few weeks after his dad died, when I spotted him sitting on his porch, alone. His family had moved next door from another part of Crystal Cove just a few months before, but I knew who he was—Tegan's ex-boyfriend. "Hey, are you okay?" I asked.

He sat scrunched over his lap—his dark hair in his eyes, his hands clasped in front of him—fifteen years old. He'd broken up with Tegan a month earlier, and his social status was still out of whack. When a *nobody* dumps a *somebody*, well, it's strange, like a dog that can talk. No one in our little town knew how to rate Jake anymore. Was he crazy, stupid, or just way cooler than the rest of us?

"Do you want to see a secret place?" I asked, since he seemed upset.

Jake leaped from his seat. "Yes."

Later I learned that he'd been taking a break from his mom, who'd been inside crying, which she did a lot back then. I think Jake would have agreed to anything. *Want to pull our fingernails out one by one? Sure. Want to jump off a bridge with me? Why not? Want to poke out our eyes with sticks? I thought you'd never ask.*

Jake followed me down this very trail to Blind Beach, and I showed him the cave I discovered when I was eleven. During high tide, the front half becomes submerged in seawater. During low tide, it's home to stranded crabs and starfish and sometimes abalone. Once a seal was inside, and it hissed when it saw me coming.

Turns out it's not a secret cave, other locals know about it, but it felt like it was ours alone. Jake and I hung out, exploring, until the water began to rise. That's when a real friendship developed between us, but also when Jake backslid into drinking and short-term relationships. I had no idea then that I'd one day fall in love with him, but two months after he turned himself around, we had our first kiss in that very cave.

I always wondered if he regretted leaving Tegan and if he thinks of her the way she thinks of him—as *the one that got away.* Well, now I have my answer.

As I enter the forest, I pick up my pace. Mist floats between the redwoods like wet cotton candy, and as I get closer to Blind Beach, the path becomes loamy and riddled with shells. Another mile, and the redwoods blend into a cove of shorter cypress trees with crooked trunks. The soil edges into sand dunes, like rounded ski moguls, and the wind whips harder. The humid fog frizzes my hair, and my clothes grow damp.

I hear the seagulls before I see them, screeching as they dive and glide. When I pass the last dune, the ocean appears, ancient, endless. Its foam-topped waves smash the coastline and drag thick tendrils of dead seaweed off the beach. A sharp ache pinches my side, and I bend over just as a familiar voice rips through the wind.

"Jessica!"

11

——

Jessica

It's Jake, my brand-new ex-boyfriend. His familiar voice thrills then disgusts me.

"God!" I stagger away from him. "Did you follow me?"

"I did." His skin is drained of color, and his eyes are hollow and dark. He's out of breath, not a runner. He edges closer, his fists clenched, and I take another step back. "Don't run away," he says. "Please."

I bite back a sob. "What do you want?"

"To talk."

"No!" I stomp away as forcefully as one can in deep sand.

He follows, his words strangled. "Jess, I'm sorry. I wasn't trying to hurt you. I was—I was stupid. I drank too much. I—"

"That's not an excuse!"

"I didn't know she was filming it."

I whirl on him, feel the blood rush to my face. My thoughts

scream and my muscles vibrate. "You're upset that you got *caught*? Is that it? How many times have you done this, Jake? *Who are you?*"

Tears streak his cheeks. His lower lip quivers. "It's the first time."

"The first time," I repeat, incredulous. "Am I supposed to believe that? I can't believe *anything* you say. Ever." I turn and start to run.

Jake cuts me off. He's taller and stronger, and he grabs my arm and spins me around. Grief explodes across his face. His grip tightens like a vise. "Please don't run away, Jess. I love you."

"Let go!"

He does, but he steps closer, blocking my escape. His eyes probe mine. "Jess, I'm serious, I didn't mean it. I can barely remember it."

"Well, I can't forget it!" My voice cracks, and my heart squeezes inside my chest. "I thought you'd changed."

He flinches and his expression crumbles. He rubs his hands through his hair. "I'm sorry. I—I don't like her that way."

I laugh. "Right, Jake! There's a very graphic video that says otherwise. A video every single person at school has seen by now." Bile rushes to my mouth as I remember his giraffe-like tongue plunging into her mouth. I clutch my stomach, sick and thirsty. "Leave me alone. Please!"

"I love you!" Tears wash down his face. "Don't do this. Talk to me."

I straighten and find my core, my strength. I'm not the prettiest girl, or the most popular. I'm not the smartest or most athletic— but I'm strong. My voice rises from my chest, cold and flat. "It doesn't matter what you say; we're over. I don't date cheaters. Life policy."

He gapes at me and his jaw works silently. His tears dry in the wind. The waves gobble the shoreline behind him, seeking land and then retreating, an endless cycle they will never win.

I turn and jog back home, leaving Jake standing in the sand. Alone, wounded.

What he deserves.

♦ ♦ ♦

When Mom sees me through our window, she motions me inside, looking strained. She's a real estate agent and dressed for a showing—heels, pencil skirt, blouse—but the blouse is untucked and her hair is only half-curled.

"What, Mom? I need a shower."

"Dad saw Jake heading to the beach. Did he follow you?"

My heart rattles at Jake's name. "Yeah. He wants to talk. I don't."

"Boys don't always handle breakups well, Jessica. Be careful with him."

"I can handle Jake." I notice a sheen of sweat across Mom's forehead, and her fingers are tapping her thighs. She's not done. "What's wrong?" I ask.

"It's probably nothing." She exhales loudly. "Shawna Moore's mother contacted me. She and Senator Sheffield are calling Tegan's friends, trying to find her."

"Tegan's mom isn't a senator anymore, you don't have to call her that, and I'm not Tegan's friend."

"Well, she's gone, Jess. She vanished from that party you went to."

"Vanished?" I lift an eyebrow. Mom is so dramatic.

"Went missing," she amends, which is no less dramatic, in my opinion.

"So?" I ask, growing more annoyed because I don't know or care where Tegan is.

Dad's large shape darkens our doorway. He pulls off his glasses and rubs his eyes. "Tegan missed a senior photo session that was scheduled for today. Her mom's worried. She's not with Jake, is she?"

"What! That's ridiculous."

"Well, you went to that party with your boyfriend and came home single," he says, as if that proves anything.

Mom intercedes. "Did Jake and Tegan get back together? Is that why you broke up?"

"This is stupid." I whirl around and stomp up the stairs, battling tears.

Dad mutters some version of *I told you so* that I ignore. He never could see past the drunken neighbor boy who kept us up with his partying and once puked on our driveway. He believes Jake is bad news, and worse, Dad might be right.

"We're not finished here, Jessica." His tone halts me in my tracks.

Mom drops her purse in the foyer. "Shawna's mom said Tegan left behind her car, purse, and debit card. Her phone is missing, but turned off. They're very concerned." She pushes her fists onto her hips. "Did anything unusual happen at the party? This might be nothing, Jess, but it could be very serious."

Anything unusual? Underage drinking, drug use, cheating on girlfriends, running over animals in the rain—in Crystal Cove, we call that *the weekend*. The live broadcast wasn't normal, but Jake's cheating is none of my parents' business, so I shrug and shake my head. "Nothing unusual."

Mom sighs and peers at Dad. "The Tegan I remember wouldn't miss a photo shoot," she says.

My pulse speeds as images ricochet inside my head—the lace bra, the kissing, Jake's hands on her body—the worst night of my life. The truth is that I don't give a flying fuck why Tegan missed her photo shoot. I tug on a loose strand of hair. "I don't know anything, Mom."

She sighs deeply, and I absorb her expression—the set of her chin, the worry unlocked in her eyes—and realize she's right. It is strange that Tegan missed her senior photo shoot. Her parents hired a renowned photographer from San Francisco six months ago—Tegan bragged about it at school—and I wonder if Mom's worst fear has been validated.

Maybe there *are* worse things than a broken heart.

12

Tegan, June

Shawna pulled into the parking lot at Salmon Creek Beach and grinned at me. "Lookie who's here—Jake."

I grabbed my surfboard from her truck and followed her eyes, ignoring the stupid smile on her face. Jake and Manny stood side by side with their boards jammed into the sand, watching the waves. As the rose-gold afternoon sun dropped toward the horizon, backlighting their bodies, the familiarity of Jake's silhouette sent shivers through me. The tilt of his head, the flex of his shoulders, those big hands that knew right where to go—the only boyfriend who'd ever broken my heart.

Jake had been my first time, and I'd been his. No one knew that but us, and I'd loved him so much, I'd often felt sick. Our relationship had been too much, too intense. He'd wanted *everything*, all the time, all of *me*. When I'd get annoyed, we'd fight, and then I'd miss him. I couldn't eat, couldn't sleep. He swallowed me whole and then, when I pushed him too hard, he spit me out so fast that I wanted to die.

As if he felt me watching him, Jake twisted his body, and our eyes met across the windswept sand. His lips parted and my legs turned to water. I could taste his kisses as if they'd happened yesterday, but he didn't look happy to see me.

"Jake and Jessica will never be Crystal Cove's cutest couple," Shawna said, slamming her door shut and locking it. "You and Jake were."

"We still could be," I said, wondering if that were true.

We staked out our own spot on the beach, away from Jake and Manny. Shawna covered herself in sunblock, and the wind gave a ferocious howl, stirring the waves, making them bigger, messier. My nerves quivered at the sight of the larger rollers, curling like claws, their crests reflecting the sunset in tones of pink and turquoise. Waves like this scared me.

As Shawna stepped into her wet suit, a new bruise caught my attention, the outline of four purple fingerprints on her upper arm. I swore under my breath, and then asked her point-blank, "Did Marcus do that?"

Shawna quickly zipped up her suit and glared at me, her red hair framing her face like a lion's mane. "Don't—"

"Your skin shows everything, Shawna."

She leaped on that as an excuse. "I bruise easily, that's all. He doesn't . . ." Her voice trailed into the wind. Shawna won't lie to me, and that's why she's my best friend. It was true that she bruised easily, but not *that* easily. We both knew why she defended Marcus. For some reason only the Lord knows, she was obsessed with him.

"If you ever need help . . ."

A smile danced across her lips. "Text *beetlejuice*."

I smiled back, happy she remembered. *Beetlejuice* was our absolute favorite movie, a classic her mother made us watch that we fell in love with. We decided that if we ever needed the other, we'd text the word *beetlejuice* and our location. It meant "Come now, guns blazing," and it was only to be used in a matter of life or death. Back then, we couldn't imagine ever needing it.

"Day-O!" Shawna crooned, singing the Harry Belafonte song from the movie. I joined in, and she danced and snapped her fingers, imitating the Winona Ryder character, while we finished getting ready.

A few surfers checked us out, and we hammed it up for them, then danced to the water's edge to study the incoming set of waves. Jake and Manny were already out, paddling toward the breakers.

"Jake's boring since he hooked up with Jessica," Shawna said.

"Because *she's* boring."

Shawna laughed. "Remember when Jake sent Austin to the hospital at last year's bonfire? That's the real Jake, the one who beat the shit out of a senior for spitting on his truck."

"Not Jake's best moment," I added. The fight with Austin began the way everything begins with Jake—as play. Jake was drunk and hanging all over Austin, trying to force him to wrestle. Austin got annoyed and spit on Jake's truck, and Jake lost it, beat him so badly that he cracked Austin's rib and fractured his eye socket.

That was the thing about Jake—he couldn't keep his hands off *anybody*, for any reason. He got lucky that Austin's family didn't press charges, because honestly, Jake should have gone to jail for what he did.

"It'll be dark soon. Let's hit those barrels," Shawna said,

drawing me back to the beach. She sprinted into the ocean, her red hair streaming behind her. I followed more slowly. I'd learned to surf because I refused to be one of those hodads who cheered everyone on from shore, but I didn't trust this ocean. I preferred the Gulf Coast, where the water was calm and clear, where I could see danger coming.

As I paddled out on my board, the waves slapped my face.

"Dive under them!" Shawna yelled.

My heart dipped. These waves were too big for me. I duck-dived beneath the next set, and the next. Each time I popped up, freezing-cold salt water sprayed my face and chilled my body through my wet suit. I glanced down, saw maybe ten feet into the depths, and wondered for the millionth time why Mom had bought a beach house in the north! Sure her brother lived nearby, but we didn't visit him that often. I think she just wanted to punish us for her loss in the senate.

But I'd learned quickly that if I wanted to hang out with the right crowd, I had to get into the water, and here I was—shark bait on a plate—paddling through the Red Triangle. It galled me that no one here seemed to care about the great whites. As hard as I tried, I didn't possess their level of West Coast blasé about losing body parts.

A glance around showed me six other surfers, including Jake and Manny. At least I was a strong swimmer. If I saw a fin, all I had to do was out-stroke these fools to the beach, and I could do that.

Shawna headed to the lineup where surfers waited for the best waves, but I stayed closer to shore. When a small, clean wave with a nice curling lip appeared, I dropped in and stood, and it swept me toward the beach. I'll admit, I'd come to enjoy this moment—surfing was like riding a magic carpet. My heart thudded against my bikini straps, my toes gripped my deck, and a smile spread across my face.

I felt Jake's eyes on me and tried to carve, but I wasn't warmed up and I took a header over the front of the board. The wave broke over me, and my surfboard shot away. Shit! I'd forgotten to tether the leash to my ankle. I struck out after the board, my face flushed with humiliation. Only kooks lost their boards.

A fresh wave picked me up and then shoved me back into the soup. I was locked in, tumbling, thrashing toward daylight. My mouth filled with salt water. My pulse thrummed. *Keep your head; stay cool.* I forced my body to go still, tried to feel my buoyancy in the deep water, but just as I started to rise toward the surface, a third wave pounded my back and sent me rolling again.

Right as I ran out of breath, a pair of hands yanked me to the surface and tossed me across a surfboard. Without speaking, my rescuer paddled us outside the lineup, and we floated a moment, silent, me catching my breath. I could only see his body from the waist down, but at this angle, I knew he was a man. My humiliation shifted and darkened. I pushed myself off my belly. "I was fine. You didn't need to—"

Our eyes met—it was Jake.

He crinkled his brow and crossed his arms, amused and irritated. The sea and sky spanned behind Jake, sparkling in the pink hue of sunset. "I didn't need to do what?" he asked.

"Save me," I whispered, my heart dipping in a whole new way.

He lowered his eyelashes, and I absorbed the view of his face—the rough stubble; his sharp cheeks, always flushed; his curved lips, dark red and full of blood. Droplets of ocean water glittered on his bronzed skin. He lifted his eyes and thrust my tether at me. "Leash your board next time, Tegan."

I grunted, frustrated and annoyed at myself. But the way he said *Tegan*—my name husky and familiar and gentle in his mouth—took root inside my chest.

I slid off his board and onto mine. Straddling it, I attached my leash and adjusted my bikini top beneath my wet suit. Jake watched, his eyes flickering, and I could tell he was remembering *us*. He could dote on Jessica and pretend to ignore me all he wanted, but he still had feelings for me. Maybe all he needed was an opportunity?

"Thanks for nothing." I splashed him and paddled away, my pulse kicking the way it did when I was about to serve the volleyball.

This game wasn't over.

13

Jake

Monday morning, twenty-four hours after Tegan's party ended in disaster, is the first day of senior year, and she is still MIA. The news hit my phone Sunday, after my awful talk with Jessica. I don't know why anyone's surprised. Tegan might have liked making that video when she was drunk, but in the light of day, it's pretty fucking bad. Her family thrives on image, and that video will wreck them. I'd hide too if my mom had been a senator.

Shawna Moore texts me: *Where's Tegan? Is she with you?*

I delete her message. Fuck her and Tegan too. I don't need any more of their drama.

Since my mom took my car keys, I ride the bus to school. Sitting in the back row, watching the streets flash by, I feel my heart like a cold rock in my chest. I should be with my girlfriend on the first day of school, watching the morning sun brighten her hair as she hands me a homemade coffee and asks her usual litany of questions: *Do you have everything? Calculator, laptop, highlighters?*

Did you see Mr. Lopez's note about the comp books? Did you get one? Here, drink your coffee and try not to look like an idiot when Ms. Lui does her pop quiz thing. You know she will.

I'm the only senior riding the bus, and the freshmen girls stare hard. I'm not sure if it's because they've seen the video or if it's because I've upset every social hierarchy known to mankind by riding a school bus when I'm old enough to drive. The truth is that a walk of shame through downtown Crystal Cove is not what I need right now, because everyone knows who I am and what I did.

Which is why I believe Tegan is hiding and why everyone needs to calm the fuck down. She's eighteen, not twelve. They just need to give her a minute.

But in the back of mind, I have doubts. I have flashes of memory. Something happened in her bedroom after the sex . . . something bad.

As the bus pulls up to the school, the first thing I notice is a police car and a shiny black sedan parked at the curb, not a normal sight for a Monday, or any day. There's already a rumor that *I* did something to Tegan, so I hope she turns up fast. I deboard, flip up my hoodie, and head straight to my first class.

"Dude, you're famous!" someone shouts.

Students turn and stare at me. "It's Jake, from the party."

I hunch deeper into my sweatshirt. The air is damp and cold, but embarrassed heat sweeps through my body. I can hide, but I can't *hide*.

Ducking into an alcove to take a breath, I notice it's already occupied. "Sorry."

A girl whirls around, sniffling. It's Tegan's best friend, Shawna. Her eyes are swollen, her face is red, and she's trembling. "Jake," she whispers. "Where's Tegan?"

"Fuck you." I turn to go.

She grabs my arm. "Jake, I'm worried. Grady skipped school today, and he's not talking to anyone. Police are still at his house. Something's wrong."

I yank free of her. "I don't know where she is. She's your friend."

Shawna backs away, her eyes round, her lashes soaked in tears. "You're the last one who saw her."

"So?"

Her mouth slides open and closed. "So—she's missing."

"She's *hiding*," I say, breathing faster. "Did you see the video Brendon posted of Jessica? Some friends you have, Shawna."

Her lips tighten. "It—none of that was supposed to happen."

"None of *what*?"

She cries harder, shakes her head. "The video—it all went too far. You were only supposed to kiss. I'm—I'm sorry."

I lunge toward her. "What do you mean, we were only supposed to kiss? What are you talking about?"

She glances behind me and lowers her voice. Her light red curls blow across her pale skin. "I'm scared, Jake."

"Why? Tell me."

Shawna's black-smudged tears smear her cheeks as she stares up at me, her breath coming in sour puffs. "The FBI is here, and everyone is lying. No one wants to get arrested."

"*The FBI?* Holy shit." I grab her arms and squeeze. "Who's lying and why is the FBI in Crystal Cove? Stop fucking around and talk straight."

"I can't," she rasps, her eyes bouncing across the campus. "I need to talk to Tegan first. Just, stay away from me, okay? Please."

"Stay away from you?" I gape at her and then lean closer, backing her thin body against the brick wall. "When you find Tegan, you tell *her* to stay the fuck away from *me*. You got that?" My chest squeezes painfully.

Suddenly Manny is at my side, pulling me away. "Dude, you're scaring her." The bell rings, and Shawna ducks out of the alcove and scurries away. "What's going on?" Manny asks.

I rub my head. "I have no idea. She said something about the FBI and getting arrested."

"Arrested for what?"

"She wouldn't say, but there are cops in the principal's office."

Manny swipes at the air. "They're overreacting because of who Tegan is, man. Don't worry." He swings his arm around my neck. Manny's bigger than I am, and his body shields me as we walk across campus. "How's Jessica?" he asks. "Alyssa says she's pretty upset."

"She won't talk to me. Do you know how many people watched her on YouTube?"

Manny nods. "Almost half a million views now. And there's a new hashtag: 'JakeIsMyHero.' You're trending, man."

I cross my arms over my chest. "Everyone's laughing at us."

"Not at you." Right as he says this, a passing student punches me on the shoulder and shouts his congratulations. Manny waves him off as I shrink into myself. No one understands how embarrassed I am.

The first bell rings. "See you at lunch," says Manny.

I drop my head and walk through a wind-buffeted doorway. By pure luck, Jess and I have two classes together this year, and art happens to be the first one. Considering what I did, though, it may not be so lucky after all.

Jess is already here, sitting at one of the large work desks. When I enter, she glances up, and her cheeks flush bright red.

Guys enter from the quad and knock me playfully, throwing me fist bumps and slaps on the shoulder. Without thinking, I knock a few fists in return. It's automatic. It means nothing—I'm depressed as hell—but Jess sees, and her breath hisses from her lips. Then a junior from the football team tosses a condom at me. "For next time, man." Half the class starts laughing.

My brain whirs and I can't speak. Every single person in this classroom has seen my dick. Sick shame rises and shakes me so hard, my guts turn to jelly.

The art teacher, Ms. Lui, saves me. "Everyone, sit please."

I slide into a seat in the back of the room. Feel the heat radiating off my cheeks.

Ms. Lui pulls out a sheet of paper, and the class groans, expecting her infamous first-day pop quiz on the famous artists of the world. It's harder than it sounds because she makes you guess the artist based on a partial image of one of their lesser works. It's tough to prepare for that, which I didn't. "I have a statement to read to you," the teacher says, clearing her throat. "You may have noticed the police car outside?"

Whisperings erupt in the classroom. Ms. Lui waits for us to settle and then begins. "Something very serious occurred at a party this weekend that some of you may have attended. This statement is from our principal, and it's being read to every class this morning."

I sink lower into my seat.

"It has come to the attention of school administrators that a questionable recording is circulating among our student population that features two Crystal Cove High School seniors engaged in sexual activity, one of whom is a minor."

I sit up so fast, my knee strikes the bottom of my desk. I'm seventeen—I'm the minor! Snickers erupt around the classroom.

The teacher continues. "Crystal Cove's police department contacted the local branch of the Federal Bureau of Investigation for help in eradicating this recording. Please be advised that sharing it is a felony offense and that the school has a zero-tolerance policy for cyberbullying and sexting. Any student caught storing or sharing this media will be held accountable and could face prosecution under California Penal Code section 311 that deals with child pornography."

There are hoots and jeers as my classmates pull out their phones to delete their posts. My body goes hot then cold. Child pornography? Prosecuted? No wonder Tegan is MIA. She's worried about getting *arrested*. Not even her friends know where she's hiding. Is this why Shawna said we're in trouble? Could I be arrested too?

Ms. Lui shushes the class and continues reading the statement. "Police have been unable to locate the adult student involved with the recording. If you have any information about her whereabouts, or about the video's production or distribution, please contact the front office. The Crystal Cove Police Department and the Redwood Unified School District are taking quick and decisive action to protect and maintain the welfare and safety of this campus and its students and families." Ms. Lui finishes and gathers a fresh stack of papers.

Jess shrinks into her seat and starts sniffling. I've never seen her lose it in public before, and it makes me sick that I'm the one who hurt her.

The infamous pop quiz comes next, and I blink at the pictures that seem to float and shift before my eyes. I try to guess the first few artists, but then give up and turn my quiz in blank except for my name at the top—*Jake Healy*.

Halfway through first period, the classroom telephone rings. Ms. Lui answers, murmurs quietly, and then calls my name. "Jake, you're wanted in the front office." Every eyeball in the classroom rolls in my direction.

The teacher writes a pass and hands it to me. Our eyes meet, and hers are sympathetic but also *knowing*, and my heart stutters. Holy fuck, she's seen the video too. Is there *anyone* in Crystal Cove who hasn't watched me have sex? Tears fill my eyes, and when I blink, they splat onto her desk.

"Jake, are you okay?"

I rush out of the class and skid into the men's restroom on my way to the office. It's empty. I'm alone. I bend in half and scream into my hands. "This can't be happening!"

It hits me—all of it—not just what I did to my girlfriend, but what I did to myself, and my family. The FBI can take that video down, but it will never, *ever* go away. It will live on the internet somewhere—forever. People will watch it, might even get off on it—people who know me and people who don't.

Shit. I can't breathe. My chest rises and falls too fast. I stumble toward the sink. Wet my face. *Get it together, Jake!* I gulp for air; my breathing grows forced and shallow. The edges of the bathroom walls blacken. I careen and slam into a stall door and then crack my head against the toilet. As my body crumples, my thoughts gloriously dissolve. My cheek hits the grimy tile, and the world goes dark.

14

Jake

When I open my eyes, I'm in the school nurse's office. The principal, the nurse, a student advisor, and two police officers surround me. I sit up, and the nurse urges me to take it slow. "A student found you in the men's washroom," she says. "An ambulance is on the way."

"Ambulance, no," I mutter. My shirt is filthy and reeks of human urine.

"Can you tell us what happened?" the principal, Ms. Clark, asks. "Did someone attack you?"

I shake my head, rub my neck. "I—I couldn't breathe."

The nurse nods. "It sounds like you had a panic attack, Jake." She asks me to follow her finger with my eyes and then shines a light in them. "I don't believe you suffered a concussion, but it's school policy to have you checked out if you lose consciousness on campus."

"Yeah, okay." My gaze drifts toward the cops.

The male studies me, his expression unfriendly. "Jake, we need to speak to you about events that occurred at a party Saturday night."

Events that occurred—that's one way to phrase it. My stomach drops and sloshes like I've fallen off the crest of a killer wave.

The second cop is Officer Lee, a recent Crystal Cove graduate herself. "We're also interested in the whereabouts of Tegan Sheffield," she starts. "Have you seen her or had any contact with her since Saturday night or early Sunday morning?" She clears her throat. "After the . . . incident in her bedroom, that is."

The cops have seen the video too, which is no surprise, considering they called in the FBI to help them eradicate it. I shake my head as Tegan's huge blue eyes fill my brain. Why did I follow her? Why did I drink with her? "I don't know where she is and I don't care," I answer.

The principal nudges me. "Jake, this is serious."

"I haven't seen her!" I sit up fast and bump the nurse, making her stumble into a cabinet.

It was an accident, but the cops pounce on me, lock up my arms, and bend me over the recovery cot, facedown. The principal scoots out of the way.

"Calm down, Jacob," orders the male officer.

"I'm calm," I shout, struggling as he squishes my face deeper into the mattress.

"It's okay. I don't think he meant to push me," the nurse says, trying to help.

"If I let you go, will you behave?" the male cop asks.

Kiss me. Take off my bra. Apparently, I'm good at obeying, so I nod, and the cop lets me go. Officer Lee pulls out a pad of paper. "Your mother will be here as soon as she can leave work."

I twist uncomfortably. "You talked to my mom?"

"Just got off the phone with her."

I gaze at Lee's dimpled chin and memories from past school rallies and football games flood me. "You were a cheerleader, right? A flyer?"

She smiles warily. "Yes, when you were a freshman."

I sit back and take a breath, feeling calmer. Officer Lee doesn't look like a cheerleader anymore, not with her hair in a low tight bun, but she's one of us, and I hope that means she's on my side.

Her smile falters as she continues. "Jake, you should know, the video of you and Tegan that circulated at the party falls under federal child pornography laws, due to your age."

My scalp slithers. "I didn't—"

She raises a hand. "You're not in trouble for the video. You're the victim, and we'll do our best to protect you."

"Victim?" I laugh and glance around the room, but no one else seems amused.

She nods. "Whose idea was it to broadcast the encounter to the television downstairs, yours or Tegan's?"

"Not fucking mine," I mutter.

Lee tilts her chin. "Do you know what happened to the camera? We've searched, but it's missing." I shake my head, and she nods. "All right, we'll get an official statement from you later. Also, and there's no graceful way to put this, Jake, but as a minor, you don't have the legal authority to consent to sex. What Tegan did to you is statutory rape."

Another laugh sputters out of me "You're kidding, right? I've been consenting since I was fifteen years old."

The principal shoots me a look that says, *Not helpful, Jake.*

Lee knocks her pen against her pad. "The FBI would like you to undergo a sexual assault exam, for several reasons." When I balk, she raises her hand, and suddenly the fact that she's almost my age is *not* comforting. It's fucking embarrassing. "Hear me out, Jake. An exam will preserve physical evidence in the event there's a trial over this video, and it will include STD and other infectious disease testing, and open up services to you, including trauma counseling. It might seem too late now, but it's best to cover your bases."

I mouth the words and then spit them out. "Trauma counseling? No. No way." Are they for real? I would never describe sex with Tegan as traumatic.

Officer Lee leans closer. "Is it normal for you to have panic attacks at school?"

I close my lips. "Can I go? Please."

Her eyes rapidly scan mine. "We're very concerned about Tegan's whereabouts, Jake. The circumstances around her disappearance are suspicious, perhaps criminal." She clicks her pen. "What time did you last see her?"

I think back to the party—Tegan's satin bed, her mouth on mine, my fingers digging into her hips, and then falling asleep after. "I don't know."

"Did you drink at the party or take drugs?"

"Shouldn't his mother be here for this?" asks the principal.

Officer Lee sighs. "Her presence isn't required, unless Jake wants her here. We're just trying to find Tegan. We have reason to believe she's injured." A line forms between Lee's brows as the mood in the office shifts. Lee pauses to see what I'll do and when I say nothing, she continues. "Did anything happen in Tegan's bedroom besides the sex? Did you two have a fight?"

The principal moves between us. "Hold on a minute. I thought Jake was the victim here. Are you saying he's a *suspect*?" When Lee doesn't immediately answer, Ms. Clark rests her hands on her hips.

"I think that's enough with the questions. Jake told you he doesn't know where Tegan is, and I really believe his mother should be present for this."

"Sure." Lee releases a breath and hands me her business card. "I've got a few other interviews to conduct, but, Jake, please call if Tegan tries to get in touch with you, or if you remember anything helpful, okay?"

"Yeah, I will," I agree.

"And, Jake, don't leave town." Lee winks at me, but the hard set of her chin tells me she's not joking. I swallow, starting to get the picture—I *am* a suspect.

Two EMTs arrive then with their medical kit, and Officer Lee closes her pad. "Your mom also has my number. She can call anytime if she has questions about the video. The FBI is doing their best to scrub it."

I nod, but none of this feels real except for losing Jess, which is like a bomb exploding in my heart. It's the same fucking terror I felt when Dad died. Except this time, it's my fault.

I have to hide this. That was my first thought when I woke up in Tegan's bed—but hide what, the sex, or something else? I squeeze my eyes shut, remember the sound of breaking glass, a cry of pain, and a sharp pain in my foot. Plus, there's the *thing* I hid in my bedroom closet this morning. I don't understand why I have it or how I got it, but it's starting to make sense, and not in a good way. I may be more involved than I think.

The truth is, I'm afraid of finding out what happened at Tegan's party. I thought I was a loyal boyfriend, but if I drank so much that I slept with Tegan, what else did I do to her?

Maybe I'm just a few beers shy of being a total fucking animal.

15

Jessica

The first day of school is over, and it was worse than I imagined. Everyone heard the announcement about two seniors "engaged in sexual activity" and about the FBI's arrival in Crystal Cove. They're spreading rumors that Tegan fled the state and went back to Alabama. And maybe she did. Tegan had her fun but didn't factor in Jake's age, and now she's in trouble with the Feds. She's hiding because she's scared, obviously.

As I cross the school parking lot, I remember the blood on the BMW's front grille and the flash of a terrified eyeball. I didn't make it back to Blood Alley yesterday to look for signs of the animal, but I have time now. Chloe said it was a deer, but what if it wasn't?

I find my little car parked between two huge trucks, unlock it, and scurry into its quiet safety. As I inhale, the smell reminds me of Jake, warm and a little bit dirty. There are no people here to laugh at me, no questions, no pitying glances, and no syrupy murmurs of "Are you okay?"

I grab my phone and turn it on, and texts from people pretending to care bombard me. They send screenshots of Jake and Tegan kissing, with messages like—*Jess, did you see this?*

I rev my engine to warm it up and then peel out of the lot, on my way to Chloe's to see if she'll come with me. She left school early today and she doesn't have gym until seven.

She answers her door and drags me into her bedroom, eyes wide. "I heard the police talked to Jake at school? Do they think he did something to Tegan?"

I fall onto her unmade bed and stare at the horse posters that still decorate her room from when we were kids. Her gymnastics medals and photos overshadow them now, but somehow they comfort me. "They probably talked to Jake about the video," I answer. "They're calling it *child pornography*. Can you believe that? Jake's and Tegan's birthdays are, like, six months apart."

"I told you, this exact thing happened to one of my teammates last year," Chloe says. "She filmed sex with her sixteen-year-old boyfriend and texted the video to us, thought she was so cool. One of the mom's saw it, and Charlotte got charged with distributing child pornography, and the coach let her go. It was a big deal."

I rub my eyes, not wanting to think any more about the video. "I wonder if Tegan went back home. Remember her grandparents have that huge horse farm in Alabama?"

Chloe plays with my hair, her look wistful. "Yeah, she promised to take us there one day, before . . . you know, the fight."

I sit up. "She can really hold a grudge, can't she?" I shake my head, change the subject. "Jake tried to apologize."

"For what?" Chloe asks.

"For cheating on me! What else?"

"I don't know, for doing something bad to Tegan. He was the last one with her."

"No, Jake wouldn't hurt anyone." My heart flutters, because that's not entirely true. I stand up and try to pull Chloe to her tiny feet. "Come with me. I'm going back to Blood Alley to check on that deer."

She blinks at me, confused. "The deer you ran over?"

"Bumped into."

"Why?"

"What if it's still there, injured or something? I feel ... responsible, I guess."

"That's weird, Jess, but I can't go anyway. Gymnastics is early tonight."

"Skip it."

She glances at her medals and the trophies on her bookshelf. "No way. The college showcase is in three weeks. If I nail my beam routine, Coach says I have a great shot at the UCLA scholarship. My parents hired a beam specialist in Rohnert Park. They took out a loan on our house, Jess. I can't skip."

It was her balance beam routine that ruined her chances at the Junior Olympics when she was eleven, and it's plagued her ever since. "Geez, Clo, that's a lot of pressure."

"It takes what it takes."

She lifts one muscular shoulder, and my throat tightens with pride. She deserves every ounce of bronze, silver, and gold she's won, and I can't let my roadkill stand in her way. "All right, I'm out."

We hug, and I wave goodbye to her parents as I leave.

◆ ◆ ◆

On the way to Blood Alley, I click the radio off and listen to my tires roll across the road, retracing in reverse my drive from Sunday morning as angry tears slide down my cheeks. Why did Jake make me go to Tegan's party, of all parties, when he knows how I feel about her and how she feels about him? I flip the radio back on and squeeze the wheel harder. Maybe it's good that we went and I left him by himself. Now I know who he really is.

As the road snakes through the coastal redwoods, narrow but gorgeous, sunrays burst through the gauzy fog and stab the ground, creating vibrant spotlights. A moody love song emits from the speakers, and my feelings flip-flop. No, I should have danced with Jake when he asked. I should have paid him more attention. I might as well have escorted him to Tegan's bedroom myself. Then my thoughts recoil because he could have said no.

I stomp on my brakes, realizing I've reached my destination— the DEER CROSSING sign on Blood Alley, not far from Tegan's home. My car skids to a halt because the stupid tires are bald, and my heart rate jumps as I remember the big eyeball and the soft thump of metal against flesh.

Shuddering, I pull the Honda as far onto the side of the road as possible, flip on the hazard lights, and exit the car. It's late afternoon, and a soft breeze whispers through the ancient redwoods, energizing the birds and squirrels. They forage overhead, singing and chirping. I hike into the woods, searching on Tegan's side of the road for an injured animal.

The ground is still soggy from Saturday night's downpour, and covered in fallen tree needles that mute my footsteps. As I walk, Jake's betrayal burns hotter within me. He was the first to say *I love you* in our relationship. He said it without hesitation, without shyness or fear. He just leaned back, threw his arms behind his head (he was shirtless, very distracting!), and said, "I love you, Mrs. Healy."

It was the first time he gave me his last name and called me Mrs., and the title spun dreamily in my head as I wondered what it meant to him. Jake jumped into *us* with both feet and then swept me off mine. But just as quickly, he slid out and landed in Tegan Sheffield's bed.

As I tromp through the woods, my hurt shifts back into anger. Sleeping with him wasn't enough—she had to film him too? I hope Tegan is hiding under a rock like the snake she is. I hope she goes to prison.

Pausing against a tree, I study the ground for hoofprints, blood droplets, or tufts of fur, but any tracks or blood traces that existed washed away in that horrible rainstorm. The only signs of life here are the footprints I'm leaving now. I should go.

A voice rings through the woods. "What are you doing here?"

I stumble backward and then spot a clean-cut man in a business suit walking toward me. He's tall and trim against the wild untamed woods. "Don't move," he says, holding out his hand.

I spot a flash of metal and duck, my heart in my throat. Is he a hunter, a hiker, a well-dressed serial killer? I cover my head. "Don't shoot me!"

"I'm Detective Green. I'm not going to shoot you. This is my badge."

I peer between my fingers, see he's telling the truth. He walks closer and faces me, his feet wide apart. "I didn't mean to scare you. I'm a detective with the Sonoma County Sheriff's Office, helping out Chief Waylon. What are you doing here?" he asks again.

My hands tremble as I answer, as if he's caught me doing something illegal. "Just walking," I say.

"Do you live nearby?"

I shake my head.

"This is a possible crime scene."

"Wh-what?"

"A girl went missing from her home, over there, early Sunday morning." He points toward Tegan's glass prism of a house, which is partially visible through the veil of needle-laden branches. Her property covers over sixty acres of bluff and forestland and a ribbon of beach, and I've never understood the boundaries. He squints at me. "Her name is Tegan Sheffield. Perhaps you know her?"

I nod, chewing on the inside of my lip. "I thought she ran away?"

"Doesn't appear so." He pulls out his smartphone and poises his fingers to type. "Can I get your name?"

I gape at him, still trying to process this tidy man standing in the woods.

"Your name, please."

"Jessica Sanchez."

His eyes widen as he types my answer. "I recognize that name from the witness list. You're Jacob Healy's girlfriend."

"Yeah, no. . . . We broke up."

"How convenient," he says, smiling curiously. "Not the breakup, but that you're here. You're on our list of people to talk to. Do you have time for a few questions?"

"Now?"

"Sure, why not?" His smile broadens, as if chatting in the woods about a missing girl is natural. Heck, maybe it is for a detective.

"Oh, okay. I guess so." My palms feel instantly wet.

He begins. "Just a few clarifiers. We know you were at Tegan's party. What time did you leave?"

I blink at him, remembering. "Around three."

"Three a.m. Sunday morning?" I nod. "How do you know that? Did you check the time?"

"I checked to see if I was late for my curfew. I was . . . late," I add weakly.

He writes this down. "Were you with anyone?" I nod and give him Chloe's and Alyssa's names. "Who drove?" he asks.

"I did." He writes that down.

Detective Green tilts his head. "When did you become aware of the situation in Tegan's bedroom that involved your boyfriend?"

The breath leaves my body. *Situation.* I don't want to talk about that.

He lowers his hands. "I guess I'm asking—were you aware of their interaction before the live broadcast or after?"

"During," I whisper.

"How did you feel about it?"

My mouth goes dry. "Not good."

"I imagine it was a surprise," he says kindly. "But can you elaborate? Were you angry, sad, jealous? Can you clarify the feeling for me?"

I feel my cheeks start to blaze. "I don't know. I felt a lot of things at once."

"Makes sense. Did you see Tegan again after the video ended?"

My stomach thrashes. "No."

"You're sure? Can anyone vouch for that?"

I explain that my friends never left my side once the video started and that I arrived home around four a.m.

"The Crystal Cove Police Department will talk to your friends to verify that. We're interviewing everyone who attended the party." He types a note, continues. "Has Jake indicated to you where Tegan might be or what happened to her?"

"He and I aren't speaking right now."

Green considers me a moment and then lowers his smartphone. "I'm sorry. I'm not trying to upset you, Jessica. When a student goes missing, especially when it's uncharacteristic for them, time is urgent. We have reason to believe Tegan was harmed and could be in danger."

He studies my face as I bite back my reaction. Harmed? Oh no.

"Here, take this in case your parents have questions." He hands me his business card. "You've been very helpful. Detective Underwood from the Crystal Cove Police Department will follow up with you if she has any more questions. I'm just helping out."

"Thanks."

"One last thing." He flashes a broader smile, one that quickly fades. "What made you decide to walk in these woods today? You indicated you don't live nearby."

The breeze ruffles the hair around my face as I briefly close my eyes and then open them. "I—I hit an animal on the road, and it ran this way. I was looking for it."

He gives a perplexed frown. "I see. You didn't mention that before. What kind of animal was it?"

"A deer."

"And you hit it just now?"

"Yes," I whisper, and my bladder loosens like it always does when I lie.

"Is your car damaged? Are you hurt?"

I shake my head, but I can barely process what he's saying, still stuck on the fact that I lied to him and I don't know why. Does it matter *when* I hit the animal? But the truth suddenly seems too suspicious—that I struck something on this road, not far from Tegan's house, around the same time the detective said she went missing. But Chloe said it was a deer. There's no reason to feel guilty.

"If there's a carcass or an injured animal out here, we'll find it, Jessica." The detective prods me. "You should get back to your car. That road is pretty narrow, not safe for parking."

"Yeah, okay, but . . . why are you looking for Tegan out here?"

He cocks his head, smiles gently. "That's all I can tell you, Ms. Sanchez. Now scram. You're contaminating the field."

He's not angry, he might even be joking, but he's serious about me leaving. "I'm sorry. I didn't know."

"In either case, this is private property." He winks. "I won't arrest you for trespassing, not this time. Good day."

I return to my car and inhale deeply. I can't believe this has gotten so serious so fast. Tegan really is missing, is possibly injured, and Jake was the last one with her. Does that make him a suspect?

I notice smoke coming from a chimney on the other side of the street, about a half mile away. It's Brendon Reed's house, the jerk who put me on YouTube. He's Tegan's closest neighbor and part of her crew. His channel is full of stupid video pranks, but the truth is, no teen in Crystal Cove can work a camera better than the Cameraman. My foot tenses, gunning my little engine. He's got to be involved with what happened at the party.

I clunk the Honda into first gear, ease back onto Blood Alley, and drive straight to Brendon's. If anyone knows what is going on with Tegan and that awful video, he does.

16

—

Jessica

Brendon's driveway is long and unpaved and full of potholes. His house is custom-built, like Tegan's, but instead of glass and concrete and metal, the Reed house is built of solid cedar. It's three stories tall with enormous windows facing the coast.

But the cedar planks have turned black, weeds have grown up in the rosebushes, and the windows are dull with filth. The house has gone to ruin since Brendon's dad lost the multimillion-dollar garbage collection contract he had with the city three years ago. The news made the *Crystal Cove Gazette,* and Brendon missed an entire week of school. It's why he's trying so hard to get famous; Brendon wants to be rich again.

His dad answers the door, wearing Bermuda shorts and a stained polo. "Who are you?" he rasps.

That's his greeting. No hello. No smile. And he smells like a distillery. "I go to school with Brendon. Is he home?"

He glances over my shoulder, toward the woods. "Did anyone follow you?"

"What?"

Then I hear Brendon's voice. "I got it, Dad."

As Mr. Reed melts back into the house, Brendon shuffles across the slate foyer to the front door. He looks like shit, tired and hollow-eyed, but unlike his frumpy father, Brendon is wearing designer jeans, a Champion sweatshirt, new Jordans, and a B. B. Simon Swarovski-studded belt—branded to the hilt as usual. It appears that any money the family has left gets funneled straight into his closet. Brendon doesn't seem surprised to see me. "Let's talk outside. Dad doesn't like anyone in the house."

Brendon shuts the door, and we pass through his side yard to the back deck. Fallen pine needles and dust cover the furniture, as if no one has sat out here in years. He tries to brush a chair clean for me, but his hand just smears the grime into dark swirls. I sit anyway and cut to the chase. "Why did you put me on YouTube?"

He shrugs. "For the likes."

My breath rushes from my lungs. "That's so messed up, Brendon."

"I know. I took it down."

"Because the FBI made you?"

"No, I got copyrighted because of the song playing in the background. Rookie mistake."

"You're an asshole."

He smiles at me. "Being an asshole is kind of my thing, Jess."

"Don't call me 'Jess.'"

"Whatever. I picked up over thirty thousand new subscribers and my first sponsor." His eyes brighten. "I owe you one."

God, why did I think he would explain anything, or care that his video hurt me?

Brendon laughs. "Calm down. I'm an asshole, right? I have to stay in character."

Something inside me loosens. "At least you own it."

"Damn right. We all need to own our shit and stop pretending. Like you—you need to own that ass of yours and stop hiding it with those ugly flannels you tie around your waist. You're, like, every dude's secret crush."

I throw up my hands. "Okay, we're not doing this. I came here for answers."

He smiles, and the faded freckles sprinkled across his nose remind me of Brendon in second grade, when we traded lunches every day. That was before his parents fell into financial ruin, sold off their fancy cars and their second home in Lake Tahoe, and canceled their yearly trips to Europe. They kept this huge beach house, though.

Ugh, I'm off track again. I hate Brendon Reed. He's not the same boy I knew in second grade. I swallow and start over. "Do you know where Tegan is?"

His smile dissolves. "No, but I hear your boyfriend does."

I ignore that. "Do you know why she made the video? Did you help her?"

His eyes dart toward Tegan's house, barely visible between the trees. "Look, I can't talk about the video. The police already questioned me, and I have an interview with the FBI later." He chews on his thumb, like he used to when he was little. Maybe he's not that much different from how he was in second grade. Brendon spits out a chunk of skin. "I can't believe Tegan didn't think about Jake's age. When's his birthday?"

"In December." I peer at him. "You helped her, didn't you? You set up the camera."

His expression darkens. His amiable mood vanishes. "I didn't fucking say that."

It occurs to me that if Brendon set up the video, he probably also broadcast it to the family room, which would make him in the most trouble with the FBI, so of course he won't cop to setting it up. Tegan might be the only person who knows the truth—and that's a good motive to get rid of her. Chills sweep my spine. "So you haven't heard from her? There are cops at her house right now. They're calling it a crime scene."

Brendon sucks in his cheeks, and his eyes narrow. "Look, I left the party right after I filmed you, okay. I was home when Tegan took off or . . . whatever happened to her. The police checked my alibi, so don't try to pin this shit on me." He rises so fast from his dirty deck chair that he trips over it and lets out a stream of curses when the wrought iron slams onto his thigh. Blood darkens his jeans.

"Are you okay?"

Hatred flickers across Brendon's face. "Since you came all the way out here, Jessica, I'm going to tell you something I shouldn't."

I cross my arms, waiting.

"You lost your boyfriend to a bet." He grins, enjoying the look on my face. "At her Fourth of July bonfire, someone bet Tegan fifty bucks she couldn't get Jake to kiss her." He studies me, his head tilting. "Looks like Tegan won that fifty bucks."

My stomach loosens. "Do you know who did it?" I whisper.

"Someone who doesn't know Jake as well as they thought they did."

I feel as if I'm drowning, as if waves are rolling over me, beating me toward the bottom of the sea. My cheeks suck together as I pull for air.

He spreads his arms, still smiling. "I think Tegan filmed it to prove she won the bet. What a surprise when they went all the way, huh? Jake's no longer *the one that got away*. See, I'm not the only asshole in Crystal Cove."

"But you knew it was about to happen. You were watching me."

His cheeks redden. "I was just looking at you, Jessica. I wasn't 'watching.'"

You're, like, every dude's secret crush, he said. Maybe he does like me. I shed the idea and move on. "Okay, fine, but when the video started, you filmed me."

He peers coldly at me. "Yeah, I did. I've got fans to please, Jessica, and the look on your face was fucking priceless."

My head reels. My thoughts clump together and form into red-hot rage. "You know what, Brendon? You deserve this."

"Deserve what?"

I kick the bleeding wound on his thigh, and Brendon goes down hard, screaming in pain.

"That!" Then I run, darting around the side of his house, dodging low branches, racing toward my car, and leaving him and his conscience to think about what he did. Brendon's curses follow me, a slew of profanity that ricochets between the trees.

The front door bangs open, and his dad rushes outside, wielding a shotgun. "Get off my property," he screeches. "Leave my son alone!"

Jesus! I leap into my car and back toward the road. When I get to Blood Alley, I gun the engine and drive away as fast as one can in a 2002 Honda Civic. I pass the DEER CROSSING sign on my way home, thinking about Tegan and the *bet*. She must be laughing at me.

Wiping my eyes, I slow down. The last thing I need today is another wreck, another ruined life. My own is in tatters. Since no one counted on Jake's age (or realized that kissing him is more addictive than crack), Tegan—or whoever set up that camera—is in huge trouble, and that's my consolation prize—that they'll probably end up in jail.

As far as pranks go, this was a doozy. But somehow it backfired. Tegan is missing and Detective Green called her house a possible *crime scene*. Things did not go as planned.

Or did they?

My scalp tightens, and I wonder, What if the video isn't about Jake and me? What if the real target of the prank was Tegan herself? It appeared she looked right into the camera, but maybe she just looked in its direction and didn't know it was there. If that's true, then someone at the party planned to embarrass her, but who?

I think there's more to this video than any of us realize.

17

Tegan, July

Two days before my Fourth of July bonfire, Grady, Brendon, Shawna, Marcus, and I drove east to the Cow Mountain shooting range, Marcus's idea. The range is located in the Mayacamas Mountains on twenty-six thousand acres of forested government land. We brought lunch and hiked in from the parking lot.

"This is where serial killers bury their victims," Marcus said, swatting at a spiderweb strung between two oak trees.

"Not cool to bring that up while carrying a gun," Brendon said, adding a laugh that sounded deranged. He was dressed head to toe in a color-coordinated Nike tracksuit, and he'd applied so much bug spray in the car, I couldn't get the scent out of my nostrils.

Marcus turned to Brendon, his gray eyes as cold as the metal rifle he carried. "Why not? It gives you time to *run*." He pointed his gun at Brendon and made a popping sound, and then bent over laughing. "Your face, man," he said, laughing harder.

Brendon grimaced. "That's not funny."

Grady stepped between them, a giant boy among men, and poked Marcus in the chest. "You point that gun at someone again, I'll take it from you."

Marcus stopped in his tracks. "Holy shit, the kid speaks." He dropped the rifle to his side and stared up at Grady.

"I'm serious," Grady continued. "Don't aim unless you intend to shoot." The words coming from my brother's lips sounded exactly like our grandpa Jeb.

"Well, give me an A and call me schooled," Marcus said. "Fine. Next time I aim at someone, I'll fucking shoot them." He grinned and resumed hiking.

Grady turned to me, his breath hissing. "I don't like this, Pea. Let's go home."

"We're fine," I grumbled. Marcus was showboating, and my friends let him intimidate them too easily. I plunged past Brendon and Shawna. If Marcus was full of shit, I wanted to know it. "What serial killers?" I asked.

He grinned back at me. "The Speed Freak Killers. You heard of them?"

"If I had, would I be asking?"

He shrugged. "They're a couple of dudes who killed over seventy people, claim they buried a bunch of them here at Cow Mountain. The bodies have never been found. See? It's a good place to get rid of someone."

"I'll keep that in mind," I warned him. My friends and I agreed to go to this remote outdoor range with Marcus because he'd promised to let us shoot his gun, but he didn't have to be such a jerk about it.

As we hiked toward the range, Shawna and I dropped back. "He's just messing around," she whispered.

"He'd better be," I snapped.

"Maybe we'll find one of those bodies and solve a crime," Brendon said, back to his optimistic self-centered self.

A low cloud drifted across the sun, and my mood shifted with it. The fact that I went along with this adventure said more about how desperate I was to get out of my house than about how fun I thought it'd be.

Dad came home from a business trip last night with a pile of gifts for Grady and me. I got a platinum pinkie ring, a silk beach wrap, two signed novels, champagne truffles, and a miniature wooden puzzle.

"You spoil them," Mom said, her disapproval ringing from the polished hardwood floors to the metal beams that crisscrossed our ceiling.

Dad slipped off his suit jacket, looking short and old in the oversize room. "That's how you say hello to me?"

Their eyes locked across the designer furniture, and Grady set his new autographed baseball on the counter, as if rejecting the gift might stall the fight, as if *anything* he did could have an effect on them. From an open window, the rumble and spray of the Pacific filled the space between us, drowning the silence.

Mom forced a smile and peeked toward Dad's suitcase. "We're happy you're home, Charles. Did you bring a gift for me?"

Dad's face shuffled through several perplexed contortions, all of which meant that he had *not* brought her a gift, and the longer he stood there, looking helpless, the more loudly the ocean seemed to laugh at us, the tide hissing in and out in monstrous breaths.

But Mom softened. Sometimes she took pity on weaker things, and this was one of those times. She saved Dad with a suggestive smile. "Perhaps you'll give it to me later?"

"Yes," he said, grasping her lifeline and setting the room back into motion.

Grady and I cleaned up our gifts as Mom poured Dad a glass of bourbon. They sat on the sofa together, and Grady and I vanished quicker than we did when they were fighting, hoping that if we weren't around, they'd talk, really talk, and get over whatever it was that made them distrust each other. Grady guessed that Dad had cheated on Mom on one of his business trips, but I thought it was worse than that. I worried that Mom didn't care about Dad at all.

Their truce lasted until this morning. Right before I left the house, Dad stormed out, shouting at Mom about why they bothered to live together anymore. She stood in the kitchen, arranging flowers in a two-thousand-dollar vase, not bothering to look up as the garage door slammed shut and he drove away.

When Mom became aware of me, waiting for Shawna to pick me up, she flashed the vacant smile she'd worn since losing her re-election. "Don't get too much sun at the beach, sweetheart. You'll get wrinkles."

But I was dressed in hiking boots and jeans, not beachwear, which meant that Mom hadn't really looked at me at all. Sometimes that was a blessing.

◆ ◆ ◆

"There's the range," Marcus said when we emerged from the woods into a clearing of dried grass dotted with dirty picnic tables. A series of targets was set up across a hundred yards of open space.

"You're sure this is legal?" Brendon asked.

"As legal as marrying your sister," Marcus said. "Or am I confusing our laws with Alabama's? Maybe I should ask the senator's kids. Y'all married?"

Grady snatched the rifle from Marcus. "I'll shoot first."

To my surprise, Marcus stepped back and threw one arm around Shawna, amused. "Damn boy, all right. The safety's—"

Grady pushed back his blond hair. "I got it. I could shoot before I could drive."

Marcus smiled. "They do shit right in the South."

Watching my little brother stand up to this guy, I felt proud. We Sheffields didn't allow people to ride roughshod over us. Grady couldn't legally drive, though. His permit test was in two weeks, but Marcus didn't know that.

Brendon glanced at each of us, looking like he'd swallowed a frog. "I'm serious. We're really allowed to shoot shit out here?"

"The targets, yeah," Marcus answered, and Brendon started pacing. I forgot sometimes that not everyone was raised hunting and target shooting with their grandparents.

Grady flicked off the safety, chambered a round, and shot the middle target, fifty yards away. He missed. He tried twice more.

Shawna laughed. "What are you aiming at, New York City?"

"The sight is crooked."

"Like your dick," Marcus huffed.

I picked up the binoculars Marcus had brought and checked where Grady's shots had landed. "Aim a hair right of center, Grady."

Shawna sidled up to me. "We should have ditched these guys and gone to the mall," she said, but her eyes remained glued on her boyfriend, though "boyfriend" seemed a loose term for their relationship. Marcus had a fresh hickey on his neck that Shawna hadn't given him, but she ignored it the same way she ignored everything else bad. At least no one was drinking alcohol, which would have flushed this day even farther down the toilet.

Grady shot twice more and nailed his final targets. Then he handed the rifle to me.

I brought the gun smoothly to my shoulder and peered down the sight. The wooden target stared back.

While Shawna and Grady spread a tablecloth for lunch and Brendon played with his phone, looking for a signal, Marcus sauntered up close behind me. The back of his hand grazed my ass and his deep voice purred in my ear. "When I shoot, I imagine the target as whatever I want most. If I hit it, it means I'll get what I want."

I snorted and edged away from him. "How's that working for you?"

"Real good. You know what I'm gonna think about today?"

"A million dollars?"

"I'm gonna think about you."

He pressed himself harder against me, and fury rose like bile in my throat. My voice dropped to a rattling hiss. "Get the fuck off me, or I'll knock you to next Sunday."

Grady's head popped up, and he started walking toward us, but my expression stopped him cold. I didn't want any help.

Marcus laughed the way guys do when they think a girl's anger is cute. I compressed my feelings into one churning ball and faced him. "You're dating my best friend."

He tossed his head back. "So?"

The teasing, the banter, the acceptance of him because he was with Shawna—I released it. I dropped the veil and revealed my disgust for him. That heat in his eyes wasn't sexy; it was mean. That smirk on his face wasn't smart; it was dumbass laziness.

He recoiled at my expression. "You're one cold bitch, you know that?"

Now you see me, I thought.

"Girls like you should watch their backs," he said. "I gotta piss." He tromped into the woods, and Grady shot me a worried look. I lifted a shoulder and forced a smile. It seemed I'd have to work harder to get Shawna away from Marcus, because he obviously didn't care a lick about her.

I turned back to the target and thought about what Marcus had said. Imagine what you want most, and if you hit the target, you'll get it. He wanted me, but what did I want? My lips curved into a smile as I stared at that dumb wood stump—I knew exactly what I wanted.

I chambered the gun, released a breath, and fired—thinking of Jake. The wood shattered in an explosion of splinters.

Bull's-eye.

18

Jake

After the paramedics determined I didn't have a concussion from hitting my head in the restroom, I texted Mom to stay at work and pick me up after school. Now I'm waiting for her in the office, smelling faintly like the men's urinal. When she arrives, she's overloaded as usual with an oversize purse and a coffee, her keys dangling, a high heel sliding off, and her curls falling over her dark eyes. Mom's a tornado—a pretty, whirling tornado—murmuring apologies and littering debris as she spins through the doorway. She halts abruptly when she sees me. "Jake!"

I slip my backpack over my shoulder and decline a hug. "Let's go outside."

We emerge into wisps of fog and Mom flings her arms around me, her purse smacking against my back. "Are you okay? The police officer who called told me about the video. You should have let me come earlier. And your head, does it hurt?"

"I'm fine, Mom. I know how your boss is about taking time

off." Mom works full-time as an administrative assistant at a car dealership, a soul-sucking job, for sure. Before Dad died, she was always home, cracking jokes, turning the music on high, and she DIY'd our aging, drafty bungalow into a home rivaling those on the Design Network.

Dad's death transformed her into a quieter, less colorful version of herself, but she's getting better. Just last week she turned on the radio and danced while cooking dinner, but today, standing on campus with her purse hanging off her arm, the shock and grief in her eyes is all too familiar.

I lean into her. "Don't worry, Mom."

"I am worried, Jake. You and Tegan?" she asks, frowning. "What were you thinking? What about Jessica?"

I have no good answer for that.

Mom pats my hair smooth and gently squeezes the back of my neck. "We'll talk at home. Let's go. I'm late to get your brother." She fishes for her keys, and I follow her to her car, a maroon minivan she got a deal on at work. When we arrive at Cole's school, the pickup area is empty. All the kids are gone.

"Shit," Mom says, ready to cry. "I told aftercare I was picking him up today. Where is he?"

"I'll check the office." I pop into the school and find out Cole walked home with his best friend, Sawyer Salisbury. When we pull up to Sawyer's immaculately landscaped home and honk, the Salisburys practically shove my brother out the front door.

"What was that about?" Mom mutters as Cole jumps into the back seat. He and Sawyer have been friends for years, but the Salisburys are one of those "perfect" families, and Mom can't compete. She doesn't attend the monthly PTA meetings, and she shocked a lot of parents when she admitted she doesn't help Cole with school projects. ("They're *his* projects" was her defense, but the truth is, she's too tired after work.) Also, she doesn't pack organic lunches (too expensive), which is practically a sin in Crystal Cove.

"Were they nice to you today?" Mom asks Cole.

"Yeah, they're always nice."

"Did they say anything weird? Anything about your brother?"

"Mom, let it go," I mutter. Like me, she's probably worried someone will tell Cole about the video. People think kids are on their phones a lot, but parents are just as bad. By now, the whole town knows what I did.

We're halfway home and my little brother is still fussing with his seat belt, so I lean into the back seat and buckle it for him. His eyes are huge in the new glasses he got last month. He thanks me and then says to Mom, "Sawyer's mom asked if you ever leave us alone with Jake."

"What? How did you answer that?"

His eyes grow wider. "I told her yes. You said to always tell the truth, remember? Why are you mad?"

"I'm not mad." Mom blows out a defiant breath. "Jake is a good big brother and fully capable of keeping an eye on you and your friends. It shouldn't be a problem."

When Mom turns onto our street, I tense at the sight of our green 1950s, wind-battered bungalow, thinking about what's hidden in the back of my bedroom closet, and the officer's comment *Don't leave town.* I think she suspects me, even though she hasn't accused me yet.

As we exit the minivan, I rub my eyes, exhausted. Today is surreal, from the humiliating bus ride this morning, to the announcement that I starred in an illegal video, to passing out in a smear of urine, to being informed I was raped—by my ex-girlfriend, of all people.

Cole tugs on my hand. "You look like you need a hot chocolate."

I squeeze him into a hug, inhaling his scent. "Yeah, okay." My little brother smells like fog and hand sanitizer, and my muscles unclench.

Cole squirms away. "You stink, Jake."

"I'll go shower. You make the hot chocolate."

Upstairs, I balk when I see my bedroom. It's a mess. The clothes I wore to the party—the clothes I stripped off in front of *everyone*—are strewn across the floor. I ball them up and toss them into my trash can on top of the bloody glass shards Mom pulled out of my foot. Then I dart downstairs and empty my trash into the outside garbage, to be whisked away on Wednesday.

When I return to my bedroom, my eyes shift to the closet where "the thing" is hidden. I can't throw it away, and I can't keep it. I can't even think about it! With a groan, I bang my head against my wall. My bedroom seems to shrink around me. What happened in Tegan's bedroom? What did I do to her?

Cole's high-pitched voice wafts from the kitchen. "Jake, do you want mint leaves in your hot chocolate? JAKE!"

"Yeah, give me mint leaves," I call back.

In the upstairs bathroom, I turn the shower to its almost hottest setting and step into the stream. I soap up three times and shampoo my hair. When I'm done, I wipe the fog off the mirror and stare at myself, wondering what people see when they look at me. Do they see a minor? A child? I lift weights four days a week with Manny, and I've built a layer of muscle over my once skinny body, and even though I shaved this morning, a shadow of fresh hair darkens my jaw. I glare at my image, flex my arms, show my teeth.

I might be a minor, but I'm not a fucking child.

No one took advantage of me. I wasn't *raped*.

My anger at Tegan resurfaces. If this was her brilliant plan to get me back for dumping her, it's working.

I glance at my face in the mirror again—my long lashes that Jess calls "pretty," my lips that look like my mom's, and my floppy waves of hair that Jess likes to braid. Suddenly I hate the way I look—like a pretty little boy. I rip open the cupboard, grab my dad's old electric clippers, wrap a towel around my neck, and buzz off all my hair.

Standing back, I turn my head from side to side. The skin around my hairline is lighter, but it'll tan up quick. I rub my hands across my skull, smiling. It's good; I look older, tougher. I flex my traps and exit the bathroom, feeling in control.

Dressed in clean sweats and a T-shirt, I trod downstairs.

When Mom sees me, she drops the plastic cup in her hand, spilling water across the floor. "Jake! I didn't recognize you."

"Sorry." I grab paper towels and clean up the spill.

Mom watches me, worried. "Why did you cut off your hair? Is this because of what happened at the party, or . . . something else?" Her voice thins. "Do you remember when I cut off my hair?"

I shoot her a warning glance because I do not want to talk about the shit that happened after Dad died. "It's just a new cut, Mom."

"Your hot chocolate's ready, Jake!" Cole blasts into the kitchen with Otis, and startles. "Whoa, you look scary."

"Thanks a lot, bud."

Mom gives me a look that says we're not done and heads

upstairs. Then my little brother serves me a too-sweet hot chocolate and a lot of chatter about a stray dog that ran across the school playground today, exciting stuff when you're seven. I hear Mom in her room, probably crying about Dad. My heart shifts, trying to fit her grief beside my own, and it doesn't work; it never has. Suddenly all I want is to load this hot chocolate with shots of Kahlúa.

"Why is everyone acting weird?" Cole asks.

I squat down, figuring he's going to hear about what I did eventually, and tell him a G-rated version of what happened. "I kissed a girl I wasn't supposed to kiss."

His eyes widen. "Ohhh."

"It was an accident, but someone put it on YouTube." Cole nods, as if that makes perfect sense. "Your friends might see the video and try to show it to you, or you might want to see it yourself. Just—don't watch it, okay. Promise?"

"I promise," he says, crossing his heart. "Is Jess mad?"

"Yeah, pretty much. We broke up."

Cole throws his arms around my waist. "I like her."

"I know. Me too."

◆ ◆ ◆

After a quiet dinner of warmed-up spaghetti, I stand by my window and stare at Jessica's, next door. Her blinds are shut, and her light is off. Maybe she's at work. I want to go over there and talk to her. Apologize again.

My mom knocks, startling me. "Yeah?"

She opens my door, her eyes red and strained from crying, and I'm so sorry I did this to her. "The officer just called, Jake."

My newly shaved scalp tingles. "Why?"

"She wanted me to know you declined the . . . the assault exam."

"I wasn't assaulted. Jesus, let it go."

Tears trickle from Mom's dark eyes, and I swallow thickly. "She recommended you see a private doctor for STD testing. She said you didn't use a—"

I turn sharply away. "Fine. I will."

"Jake?"

"I said *fine*. I don't want to talk about this."

Mom looks confused. "Maybe you should see a counselor too? You had a panic attack at school, you cut off your hair, your privacy's been violated by that video—it's a lot, Jake."

I grimace because there's no way that's going to happen. "I'm tired, Mom."

She sighs and gently shuts my door, but not before Otis slinks in. As she retreats down the stairs, my dog flops beside me, panting and licking my arm, his tail thumping against the blankets. He doesn't care what I did at that party, and I love him extra for it.

After powering up my laptop, I find a news story about Tegan that was recorded about an hour ago, and turn up the volume.

"Tonight authorities are searching for former Alabama senator Aubrey Sheffield's daughter, Tegan Sheffield. The Crystal Cove twelfth grader went missing under suspicious circumstances during a party at her home early Sunday morning. If you have any information about her whereabouts, please call the Crystal Cove Police Department."

It's a short piece and doesn't mention the illegal video or any suspects. Tegan's mom must be pulling every string she has to try to squash that story.

I spend a few hours playing video games and ignoring my phone, too amped up to sleep. I visualize the vodka bottle my mom keeps on the top shelf downstairs. A couple of shots would help me sleep. Help me forget . . .

No. Fuck no—drinking is how I got into this mess.

I return to my window. Across our side yards, Jessica's room is still dark. I could sneak into her house later and surprise her. I used to do it all the time. Maybe she'd let me talk, apologize.

Movement across the street catches my eye. There's a strange car parked down the road with someone sitting in the driver's seat, drinking from a bottle or a cup. It's not normal for strange cars to park on our cul-de-sac.

Shit. I duck down. *Don't leave town*, Officer Lee said. Is that her outside, or another officer? Are they *watching* me?

Sliding my hands over my head, I feel the hard planes of my skull as panic slithers through me. This thing with Tegan is turning into a news event and a police investigation. If she doesn't come home soon—assuming she's *able* to come home—they're going to look harder at me, and I'm not sure I'll survive that.

A memory surfaced after Officer Lee questioned me this morning. It was Tegan's voice saying, "Let me go. That hurts." I glance at my closet where I've hidden "the thing." I'm fucked if the cops get a search warrant.

Jess is the only person I trust, besides my mom, and the last person who might say yes, but the truth is, I need her help. I don't know if she's home, though, and I've already decided I'm going to skip school in the morning.

Tomorrow night. I'll talk to her then.

19

Jessica

Today is the second day of senior year and Jake's not here. It rubs me the wrong way. I'm the one who got cheated on. I'm the one who should be too upset to go to school. Maybe Alyssa was right; maybe I'm better off without him, but as soon as I think it, tears burn my eyes. I miss him. I'm so confused!

When my last class is over, I duck out, race to my car, and drive home to change for my daily jog to Blind Beach.

It's a terrible workout. My rhythm is off and I can't catch my breath. Afterward, I blast through my front door and slam straight into my dad.

He's home early, and his face is bright red, his hair messy, his glasses askew. "Did you know Jake and Tegan made a *sex video?*"

I grunt and push past him. "I think you're the *last* one to know, Dad."

He follows with a mumbled comment to Mom: "I'll deal with

this." Upstairs, he lectures me from my doorway. "If Tegan isn't found soon, they could *arrest* him, Jessica. He was with her when she disappeared."

"No, they won't, and she didn't *disappear*." My head starts to pound as I lean against my headboard. "Tegan will come back when she's ready."

"A cop was parked on our street all night, watching his house. Why do you think that is? I don't want you near that boy again."

"He's our *neighbor*. I have to be near him."

Dad's left eye twitches. "Don't be facetious and don't defend him, not after what he did to *you*."

"Jake didn't mean to hurt me, Dad. He was drunk. He said he's sorry." As soon as the words leave my mouth, I hear how pathetic they sound. It's a habit, defending Jake, because Dad never liked him. That's all this is.

Dad is not mollified. "Have you noticed that your boyfriend's always sorry about something? There's a pattern here, Jessica. He's manipulative, a liar, an alcoholic—he's going to crawl back here, crying and apologizing, until *you* feel guilty and take him back. Watch! You may not understand this, but Jake's not worthy of you."

"I'm not a princess, Dad."

He stares at me, his only child, and emotions spasm across his face. Then his eyes grow softer and his shoulders droop as he changes the subject. "Is your homework done?"

"Yep," I lie.

"Okay, then." He turns to leave.

"Shut the door!" Dad closes the door and retreats, his knee joints creaking as he plods down the stairs.

This has gotten out of control. I pull on a pair of pajamas and flip through my apps. People at school are starting to truly worry about Tegan.

Maybe she ran off to Mexico?

No way can she survive this long on one outfit

If Tegan's dead, who killed her?

It's always the boyfriend

She doesn't have one

She has Jake

I pull up Alyssa's photography account and scroll through the pictures she took at the party. I'm looking for clues. There's Manny, riding a cue stick like it's a stick horse, with Jake slapping his ass. There's Chloe, doing a back bend on the dining room table with a Cheeto clenched between her teeth, and there's me, watching everyone else party. *You know what, Jess, sometimes you're no fun.*

I zoom in on other friends' posts from the party, studying the people in the background—Grady, Shawna, Brendon, Chiara and Hailey, and Shawna's boyfriend, Marcus. In one wide-frame picture, Marcus's jaw is clenched and his expression is murderous. I follow his gaze and recoil in shock. He's watching Tegan dance with Jake beside the pool. I zoom in until Marcus is pixelated. He looks angry, but why? Was he jealous?

Next I study Jake and observe the casual, familiar way his hand rests on Tegan's hip. My stomach wrenches, and I toss my phone aside and draw my knees to my chest. Unlike Marcus, Jake doesn't look like he wants to hurt Tegan—quite the opposite, in fact.

I believed he'd never cheat on me, but then he did. Alcoholic? He used to drink too much and then do wild stuff and forget it. Like when he beat up Austin Smith for spitting on his truck. The next day at school, Jake wondered why Austin was in the hospital. Jake had no clue he was the one who'd put him there.

And once, he came home drunk and bloody from a fight with an exchange student, singing at the top of his lungs. My dad complained the next day, but Jake had no memory of that either. He got his act together over a year ago, though, so what changed? Why did he get so wasted at Tegan's? Is he stressing that hard about senior year and me going to college? And where is Marcus? Have the police questioned him about Tegan?

I try to do my homework but can't concentrate, so I turn off my light and lie in bed, staring up at my ceiling fan. As time marches slowly toward morning, I must fall asleep, because suddenly I hear squealing tires and the patter of rain. A terrified eyeball flashes in front of me.

There's a dull thud, and then a deer appears beside my bed. Blood drips from its nostrils to its soft fur. I reach out to touch it, and the deer morphs into a human shape and leaps out my window, shattering the glass. Sharp pieces rain down on me and strike the floor.

I wake up, rush to my wall, and flip the switch. Light floods the room. There's nothing, no creature by my bed. The window is closed and unbroken; my floor is clean. Why is that deer haunting me? Or was it ever a deer? God, did I hit Tegan with the BMW?

No. No, no. Her body would still be there if I hit her. Or she'd be suing me.

I glance at my phone. It's almost eleven and I'm covered in sweat.

A noise from outside makes my heart kick. It sounds like someone or something bumping into our trash cans. The rattling is probably what woke me up, and I hope it's not Jake. He sometimes uses the cans to climb into my bedroom, but Dad will kill him if he tries that now, and if Dad doesn't, I will.

I hear the noise again, hurry downstairs in my slippers, and open the back door.

It's cold enough I can see my breath. I slip through the door and listen for the noises I heard. My backyard merges seamlessly with the woods, just a few feet beyond our garden. Rubbing my arms for warmth, I keep walking until I enter the forest, my exhales creating cloudy puffs. The giant redwood trees filter the moonlight, and the smell of wet mulch rises from fallen, rotting trunks. "Jake?" I call out.

A voice drifts toward me. "Yeah, it's me. I thought you were your dad and ran."

"Smart move. Where are you?" Surrounded by tall shadows, I can't see him.

"Here," he says.

Gliding through the redwoods, I angle toward his voice. The plants rustle and an owl hoots, but otherwise it's quiet.

As I creep deeper into the woods, my skin begins to crawl. Why is Jake drawing me out here? I glance back at my house, which is now a dark shape in the distance. "Screw this." I start to walk back. Then a man steps into a patch of moonlight, blocking me.

It's not Jake!

20

Jessica

I break into a run just as the stranger careens out of the fern grove, crashes into me, and slams his hand over my mouth. We fall, and my face smashes into a tree root. His heavy body pins me down.

I try to flip over, to bite. My teeth scrape against his palm.

"Don't scream." He has Jake's voice, Jake's scent. "Promise not to scream, and I'll let you go."

When I nod, he releases me, and I sit up, blinking back tears. The man's head is shaved, giving his eyes a hollowed appearance and his cheekbones a vicious slant, and it takes me a second to realize that it *is* Jake. "You hurt me," I gasp, cupping my face.

"Shit, I'm sorry, Jess. Let me see."

"No." We're each covered in pine needles, and hot fluid splats into my hands. "I think I'm bleeding."

Jake leans forward to inspect me. "It's your nose."

I shove him away and plug my nose as it begins to throb. Anger and sadness mix with my pain, leaving me confused. "Were you trying to sneak into my house, or what?"

"Yes," he breathes, and there are a thousand unsaid words locked inside that *yes*. His brows wrinkle together, and his pupils grow large and pleading. "I can't stand not being with you," he says. "I'm—"

"Shh." With one hand pinching my bloody nose, I press a finger to his lips. "Just because we're neighbors doesn't give you the right to sneak into my room, not anymore." Dad's words echo in my brain: *He's going to crawl back here, crying and apologizing, until you feel guilty and take him back. Watch!*

Jake inches closer. "I just want to talk. Please, I'm so sorry, Jess."

I hate that my dad predicted this, but Jake really *is* sorry; it radiates from every bone in his body. He made a mistake that has crushed us both. We're kneeling in the fairy ring—a near-perfect circle of redwood trees that sprang up after loggers murdered the mother tree hundreds of years ago. Layers of cool mist float around us, masking the tops of the ancient trees. The forest feels small—encapsulated and quiet—like a stage waiting for its players. I lower myself onto the stump and watch him.

He crawls closer, his eyes glistening. I touch his shaved head, and the short dark hair feels like velvet.

"I love you," he whispers. "Give me another chance? Please. I'll do anything."

His voice conflicts with the words in my head: *You know what, Jess, sometimes you're no fun.* Does he think that after x number of days, I'll forget what he did, that there's an expiration date on this? He can't screw Tegan and then run back to boring old me. "I-I'm not ready for this."

He starts to cry.

"Hey, aren't I the one who should be crying?"

That makes him cry harder, and I feel a stab of resentment as Jake unloads his guilt onto me. "I ruined everything good in my life," he says. "I'm so fucking sorry. I'm such an asshole."

I release my injured nose and we stare at each other, bound tight, and maybe forever, by that awful video. His regret pulses like a wound, and I can't help but take pity on him. "You drank too much." It's not an absolution, just an acknowledgment.

Jake doesn't respond. He crumples into himself, his tears spiking his eyelashes.

My stomach unknots as I exhale a breath of steam. Every inch of me wants to hold him because I still love him—my feelings didn't cut off on Sunday morning. I want to kiss his cheek, wipe his tears, assure him he has nothing to worry about. And I want to feel his strong arms around me because I'm sad too. Is this what manipulation feels like? Maybe Jake's beautiful face is a trap and I need to stop walking into it.

I force myself to recalibrate to what is, not what was. "I heard that the police questioned you at school, and my dad saw a cop watching your house. What do they want?"

Jake gets quiet. "I came over to talk to you about that."

"Okay?"

"They think I know where Tegan is or what happened to her." His jaw muscles twitch; shadows slice his face. "But I can't remember anything after . . ."

Warning signals blare inside me.

"I didn't do anything bad to her, Jess."

"But?" I prod, sensing there's more.

He wipes his eyes. "I found this in my truck yesterday morning."

He reaches into his sweatshirt pocket and pulls out a cell phone with a cracked screen.

My breath leaves my body because I recognize the phone's glittering plastic case. I've seen it in her hands a million times. "That's Tegan's phone."

"I know," he says. "Why do you think I'm freaking out?"

I rise to my feet and back away from him. "Do you know how guilty that makes you look?"

"Guilty of what?" he asks. "I don't know where she is. No one does."

"You have to give that phone to the police."

He shoves it toward me, his hands trembling. "I know, but I can't. If I do, they'll arrest me for sure. And I'm afraid to leave it anywhere. What if someone threw it away? I think the police should have it. It might hold clues. Will you turn it in?" He reaches for my hand. "Tell them you found it at the party or something? Just don't tell them I gave it to you. Please."

My eyes bulge against their sockets. "*This* is why you came over? To ask me to hide evidence from the police?"

He chews his lip and shakes his head vehemently. "No, no, Jess. Not hide it. Turn it in for me."

We stare at the crystal-studded phone between us, and I observe how scratched-up it is. Tegan keeps everything she owns in pristine condition. Something bad happened to this phone. "Oh god," I cry. "Is it on? They can track the signal, you know."

"It's off." Jake blinks slowly. "I don't even know if it works anymore. I was too afraid to power it on to check. I found it in my glove box Monday morning when I was looking for my sunglasses. I swear, I don't know who put it there."

"But it could have been you?"

He gazes up at the moon, and fresh tears skid down his cheeks. "I hope not."

I see that he's wrecked, and I believe he doesn't remember. I wonder if he even remembers the sex with Tegan. "Is the *whole* night a blur?" I ask, my throat tightening.

"Not really," he answers. Even in the dark, I notice his face redden. At school yesterday, he was accepting congratulations, but maybe deep down he's embarrassed about what he did. "I can't believe she filmed it to win a bet."

"You heard about that?"

"Yeah, the whole thing was a big joke." His mood shifts. "Fuck me. My family will never, ever live this down."

My guilt for ditching him at the party bubbles to the surface. I pace through stripes of moonlight as my feelings twist between grief and fury and regret. "You didn't have to go along with it," I point out.

His shoulders curl toward his chest. "You're right. I'm a piece of shit boyfriend."

He makes it *so hard* to stay angry with him! I drop my head into my hands and say the one thing I know is true. "I miss you."

Jake rears up, crosses the space between us in one violent stride, and sweeps me into his arms. "I miss you too!" He hugs me tight, breathing me in.

I try to resist, but when his scent envelops me, it feels like coming home. I have been so lonely since Sunday morning—I need to be held, I need support, but he's the one who hurt me. My confusion intensifies.

Jake's blazing eyes meet mine. "I love you," he murmurs, his muscles quivering beneath my fingertips. "You make me crazy, Jessica."

His love is like a shield around us. He presses his lips to mine, and then I remember that he kissed Tegan just as hard, just as deeply, and the shield suddenly feels like a prison.

I break away. "Stop."

Jake leans back, breathing fast, eyes half closed. Zero to sixty, my Jake. It's not always a good thing.

I pull out of his arms and realize why this has been so hard for me. It's because the boy I love, the one I trust the most, is also the one who broke my heart. The fog descends, making me shiver. "I'm cold. Let's go."

As we start walking again, he switches back to blaming others. "Shawna said that everyone at the party is lying and that things went too far. She was probably talking about the bet. They planned this. Tegan and her friends are protecting each other. Maybe one of them put her phone in my truck, to make me look guilty."

I twist a lock of my hair as we walk toward our houses. I shouldn't feel relieved that Jake has her phone, but it makes me feel more certain that I didn't hit Tegan on the road.

I offer Jake my other theory about the party, the one that came to me at Brendon's. "What if Tegan was the victim of the prank?" He peers at me, and I continue. "I don't think she knew about the live broadcast downstairs. If she had known, she wouldn't have let things . . . go so far with you, right? She would have stopped at the kiss. I think someone hacked the camera to mess with her and it got out of hand, and that person could go to jail. Do you know where the camera is?"

"How would I?" he growls.

I release a tight breath, thinking back to fifth grade, when everyone saw Tegan's underwear after she slapped me and Chloe pushed her. If that shame caused a seven-year-long vendetta against me, I can't imagine her wanting everyone to see the *rest* of her body. Even her *brother* saw the video.

The evening wind buffets my hair around my face as I follow my thoughts. "It had to be one of her friends who hacked the camera, someone who knows where her room is and that she planned to kiss you that night."

"Like Shawna?"

"Or Brendon, since he knows all about cameras. I asked him about it, though, and he wouldn't admit to anything."

Jake swipes at an ant crawling up his leg. "You talked to Brendon?"

"Yes, Jake. I'm not hiding phones and skipping school. I'm trying to figure this out."

He flinches and I see I've hurt him. "I have been trying, Jess. I've been texting Shawna since Monday to talk to me."

Several quick bats swoop overhead, making my heart rate skitter. Jake reaches for my hand, but I stuff it into my pajama bottom pockets. We walk through the woods, together but apart. "I'm sorry about your nose," he says.

Between his shaved head and Tegan's missing phone in his hand, I wonder if I know him at all. "I'm fine," I say.

His cell beeps, and he slides it out of his pocket. A smile spreads across his face. "It's Shawna. She says she'll talk to me."

"Now? It's almost midnight."

"Yeah, at Falcon's Peak. Can I borrow your bike? My mom took my keys."

"Sure, I guess."

We arrive back at our houses, and he holds out Tegan's phone like an offering. "Will you take this, Jess, please? I know I don't deserve your help, but I need it."

I stare at the battered phone. Taking it feels wrong, but Jake wants me to turn it in to the police, not get rid of it. He's trying to figure this out too, so I relent and agree.

His tears have dried, and a fresh smile transforms his face. "Thank you. I owe you." He passes the phone to me, and as soon as I touch it, an oily feeling slicks through me.

"I know things look bad with Tegan being gone and stuff," he says, narrowing his eyes, "but that camera didn't connect to the TV by itself. Tegan and her friends did this to me, to *us*, Jessica, on purpose and they're going to pay for what they did."

Far away, a dog starts to bark, and I can't believe this angry guy is my fun-loving boyfriend of just last week. "Be careful," I tell him because I don't know what else to say.

Jake grabs my bicycle from our side yard and takes off—searching for redemption or revenge. I'm not sure which. As soon as I get to my room, I call Chloe. I need her calm, rational voice to ground me, because my head is spinning.

21

—

Jake

Wednesday morning, Mom sticks her head into my room at seven. "Rise and shine, sleepyhead. The train leaves at eight." Mom's minivan is the *train*.

I groan. "But—"

"Get up. You can't miss another day of school." She vanishes back downstairs.

The sun glints through the open window, and I roll over to avoid it. Shawna didn't show up at Falcon's Peak last night, and she hasn't answered any of my texts since. I'm back where I started, totally fucking clueless about how Tegan's phone ended up in my truck and why everyone is lying.

Footsteps and loud panting breaths precede Cole and Otis before they burst into my room and leap onto my bed. My brother yanks off my blankets. "Will you drive me to school? Please!" He's already dressed. Otis circles us, his black fur shedding into the air.

"I can't drive you. Mom took my keys."

Cole jumps onto my back, wraps his arms around my neck. "Please, Jake!"

There's nothing cooler than your big brother driving you to second grade, I get it, but I can't do it, and I hate disappointing him. Then I have an idea. "Tell Mom to give me my keys back, and I will."

"Really?"

I rub my eyes and yawn. "Really. Go ask. Hurry up!"

Cole sprints from my room and skitters down the stairs into the kitchen. Otis chases him, diving off my bed so fast that he skids across the hardwoods and slams into the wall. After shaking it off, he plunges down the stairs and lands with a thud at the bottom. Not an athlete, that boy.

I hear Cole begging Mom to give me my keys back, and if this works, I'm a genius. Seconds later, she yells from the kitchen. "Nice try, Jake!"

I get up, shower, throw on jeans, a T-shirt, old Vans, and a flannel in case the fog rolls in later. I grab five slices of cold bacon and a can of yerba maté tea and then race Cole to Mom's van. After school, I'm scheduled to work a shift at Wipeout, the surf shop off Highway One, but first I need to get through my classes. A glance down our road shows me that the strange car is gone.

In the driveway, Mom drops her keys, and when she tries to pick them up, her heavy purse slides down her arm, making her spill her coffee. "Damnit!" She wipes at the stain on her dress with a clean tissue.

Cole squeals with laughter. "Mom said a bad word, Mom said a bad word."

"Get in the van," Mom huffs. Then she scurries to the curb to throw her tissue into our garbage. When she opens the lid, she pauses and calls over her shoulder, "That's weird. Our trash is gone, but I didn't hear the truck. Did you boys hear it?"

I shake my head and climb into the van. Why is our trash gone? Down the street, I notice a few overflowing cans, which means the garbage truck *hasn't* come yet. Mom gets into the van while I feel suddenly sick. I didn't see the strange car last night, but maybe it came back while I was sleeping. Maybe the driver went through our garbage on the curb. No one but a detective would steal trash, right? Shit. My party clothes and the glass from my foot were in there. I'm stupid. I've always been stupid.

Mom drops me off on her way to Cole's school. "Hey," she says as I exit the car, "keep your chin up."

I nod, but as I turn to face the high school, dread oozes through me. On the way to my first class, a group of ninth-grade girls goes silent when I appear. They push off the wall where they're hanging out and advance toward me.

I'm the guy who screwed Tegan Sheffield and then possibly murdered her. I'm famous, infamous. Their phones materialize in their fourteen-year-old hands, recording me. One girl—a skinny redhead with freckles on her cheeks—blocks me. "Kiss me, Jake," she says, exaggerating Tegan's Southern drawl. The others giggle and grab each other.

Nope. I can't do it. Not today.

I veer off campus as the girls shout lewd suggestions at me, and walk into downtown Crystal Cove. I feel exposed outside, like a lone coyote out of its den. I slink around, looking for somewhere to hang out. First I try the coffee shop and ice cream parlor called Cool Beans, but what I see inside stops me cold. It's Tegan's mom and Chief Waylon, at a table together. The ex-senator's eyes are swollen, and her expression is desperate.

When she tilts her head, her eyes catch mine, and hatred swirls across her face. I watch in horror as she lurches to her feet, pointing at me and mouthing horrible words. The police chief pushes back his chair.

Fuck! I turn and blast down the street as a car suddenly speeds up behind me—the same one that was outside my house the other night. I'm definitely being followed. No, chased!

I sprint as fast as I can, darting in and out of alleyways, climbing over fences, taking shortcuts. The car careens around turns, tires squealing. It circles the block and catches up to me, but then it gets blocked in a one-way street by a car driving the correct direction. I charge down two more side streets, slowing as my injured foot begins to throb. I think the gash has reopened, because my sock feels wet.

I duck behind the movie theater and lean against the brick siding, wanting to throw up. I can't believe I slept with the senator's missing daughter and then hid evidence that might help find her, and I have no fucking idea why I did either. I hope Jess turns the phone in today. *Let me go. That hurts.* Tegan's voice resounds inside my head. Did she and I fight? Did I lose control?

A scream climbs up my throat, and I bite it back down. I don't know where to go, where to hide, and I'm breathing too fast. I feel dizzy. There's the local library, a nail salon, some clothing shops, the post office—nowhere I want to hang out, though.

I text Manny, my fingers shaking: *dude come get me*
im in class shithead

I stare at my cell, my panic rising and turning darker. Nowhere in Crystal Cove feels safe, and I don't want to be alone. The morning air is crisp, but the sun pulses overhead, promising to bake the coast later. My muscles tighten. I want to run, fight, shout, hide.

No.

I want to lie on Jess's miles of soft skin and feel her lush body in my hands. I want to taste her mouth on mine. I'm in trouble and I need her now more than ever. If her arms were tight around me, squeezing me, I'd feel calm. I'd be okay. Jess is safe. She's the only place I want to be.

Turning toward the wall, I place my cheek on the cool brick building and close my eyes. Then Manny texts back: *schools overrated. where are you*

My impending sob evaporates in my chest. "Yes, I fucking love you, man!" I shout at my phone and my mood skyrockets. *Behind the theater*, I text back.

Ten minutes later, Manny pulls up in his Dodge Charger, revving the engine like a fucking hero. "Get in, shithead," he says.

Before I can buckle my seat belt, he takes off and I feel rescued. "Thanks, man."

He knuckles my shaved head. "You joining the army, or what?" When I glance away, he changes the subject. "We should hit the gym."

"Not open yet. Let's go to the beach."

"You want to surf? We don't have our boards."

I throw back my arms and stare out the windshield. "No, I just want to drive. Get out of Crystal Cove."

"Can do, buddy." He downshifts and squeals around the next turn, and minutes later we're on Highway 116, driving west. He shifts again and the engine hums; the tires swallow the road. DragonForce plays through his speakers, and he turns it up. The manic beat fills the car, and I holler out the window as we fly around the curves. The sky unfolds overhead, the town shrinks behind, and Manny lets go of the wheel to play air guitar. I steer for him, hollering louder. The car skids between the lanes and we laugh. We're free!

At the beach, Manny parks crossways, taking up three spots because he can, because there's no one here except for a couple of dog walkers.

We hike down to the shore, and the wind gusts, whipping up sand and stinging our faces with it. "Dude, we didn't bring food or chairs. What are we going to do?" Manny asks.

I grin at him. "Let's climb."

He gazes at the towering bluffs. "Here? Now?"

"Why the hell not? Remember when we were kids? You could never beat me to the top."

"I don't have the bod for climbing anymore." He strikes a pose that makes me laugh. It's true; he's a lot bigger than when he was a kid, but fitter too. His pudginess has turned to thick muscle, and he can lift more weight than any other guy at the gym. No one fucks with Manny, but I want to climb, and I think he can still do it. Manny scratches his head. "You okay? It's not like you to ditch school two days in a row."

My stomach clenches. "What are you getting at?"

"Nothing. It's just—everyone thinks you did something to Tegan. You should probably act normal." He smiles, and I see he's not accusing me. He's just worried.

But I don't want to talk about it. "You're afraid I'll beat you to the top, aren't you?"

He gives a shake of his curly hair and rips off his shirt. "It's on, brother."

I pull off my shirt too, and we wrap them around our heads. I prefer to climb barefoot, but because of the gash in my foot, I leave my shoes on. We each find our favorite spots.

Wind, sand, and rain have changed the hillside, but it's like going back in time for me. Back to when I was little, and my dad was alive, and climbing the bluff was all that mattered. Above us is Falcon's Peak, the place where I was supposed to meet Shawna last night and where the local kids come to drink and screw and watch the sunset on the weekends. "Ready?" I ask.

"No," Manny says, laughing.

The sun glints off his black hair, and his smile makes me smile. "Race you to the top!"

We scramble forward, assessing the rugged terrain. The bluffs lift from the beach, almost straight up, a mix of soil, rocks, and short, thick plants that are heavily rooted into the hillside. With the sun still rising over the hill, I search for hand- and footholds to pull myself up. In moments, I'm ten feet off the ground, then fifteen.

Manny is to my right, a little lower and breathing hard. "Shit, this was a lot easier when I was lighter." His shoulder muscles ripple, tightening and loosening as he climbs, as he gains on me.

I face the hillside and focus, my fingers searching, my feet testing. Step by step, hand over hand, I rise higher off the beach. I whoop when the wind whips harder, pushing me sideways and roaring in my ears. I grab tight to a bush and freeze, waiting for the gusts to die down.

I glance at Manny, see he's still climbing. I pull myself into a new position. There are no good handholds ahead, so I edge sideways. Peering down, I calculate how far I've come, and my stomach lightens. I'm thirty feet up, maybe more. Seagulls glide below, riding the drafts, their wings shaping the wind. The waves appear smaller from here, but the ocean spans as far as I can see. The little cave where I first kissed Jess is a dark smear at the base of the sheer rock cliffs farther south. Beneath the water, I glimpse a large shape, maybe a seal.

The wind bites as I continue climbing, straining and sweating. I've done nothing but cry since Sunday morning. Now I feel strong, in control. I climb higher.

Placing my left hand on a rock, I squint upward and see I'm almost at the top of the bluff. Just as I grip the rock's edge and pull, I hear the sound of breaking glass in my head, and Tegan's voice. *Let me go. That hurts.* The shale comes loose, and I backslide toward the beach.

"Jake!" Manny cries out.

Gritting my teeth, I clutch desperately at whatever I can; my heart hammers, my blood squalls. I slide faster and faster down. My foot strikes a big rock and twists, sending sharp pain up my leg. At the same time, my hand finds a root and I grab it. My slide ends with a sudden jolt, and I'm left hanging about fifteen feet over the sand. My breath quickens, louder than the wind.

"I'm coming," Manny calls.

"No, I got it!" I find another thick root, grab it with my free hand, and settle my feet against the hillside, my left ankle throbbing. I set my jaw and keep climbing because it's easier to go up than down. Manny is to the right of me, shouting encouragement as we finish our climb.

When I reach the top, I crumble, exhausted, and examine my ankle. It's cut and bruised, but not broken.

"I thought you were a goner," says Manny.

"So did I." My body shakes but not from the effort, from Tegan's pleading voice in my head. If I attacked her, it wouldn't be the first time I assaulted a person, but it would be the first time I assaulted a woman.

I spread my fingers and study my hands. They make good strong fists, but I like them best on soft skin, touching, stroking, and holding. Tremors run down my spine as I contemplate whether my hands betrayed me, betrayed Tegan.

Manny shoves me gently. "Can't catch your breath, old man?"

I blink and take in the ocean that undulates toward the horizon. I imagine dropping my problems into it and watching them disappear.

"I wonder if Tegan's in there," he says, nodding toward the sea.

My mouth goes dry. "Why would you say that?"

"She could have gone for a night swim after, you know . . . you two got together. She did it at her bonfire party this summer."

"Yeah, I heard about that. Jess went in too. Fucking stupid. But someone would have seen Tegan and told the police about it."

He shrugs. "Unless she went alone."

I shake my head. "She'd never do that." I toss a rock over the ledge and watch it fall forty feet and land with a dull *plunk*. I wipe my palms on my jeans, feeling twitchy and hot. "You have any water in your car?"

While Manny walks down to the parking lot, I unwrap my T-shirt from my head and wipe down my sweating chest. He returns with a Yeti that's half-full of filtered water, and we share it on the bluff with our legs dangling. "The police started organizing search parties for Tegan," Manny says. "Can you believe it?"

I nod. The police haven't made too much information public yet, and Grady hasn't been at school, but yeah, I believe it.

Manny swallows another gulp of water. "Her parties have gotten pretty wild these days, with the drugs. Smokin' bud is one thing, dude, but that rave shit's no good. I'm done with that crowd."

I shove him with one hand. "Fucking liar."

A smile twitches across his face. "The music is all right, but seriously, it could be more chill, you know."

"Says the metalhead."

"Fuck you." Manny hands me the water bottle. "Ready to go?"

"Dude, I was born ready."

As we climb into his Charger, it strikes me again how serious this is. All these hours that I've been crying and missing Jess and hiding out—Tegan's family has been searching for her, hoping she's not dead.

I try to remember what I did after I thought *I have to hide this*. The time period during which Tegan went missing is mostly blank.

And I was the last one with her.

My heart thuds harder. If that video was a prank, it's gone too far. Tegan needs to come home or someone needs to fess up with the truth before I end up in prison. I might be "too young" to consent to sex, but I know for a fact I'm not too young to be tried for murder.

22

Tegan, July

The day before my Fourth of July bonfire, Shawna came over early to help me gather driftwood. She flung open my front door, spotted Grady and me watching TV and eating cereal, and shouted, "What up, bitches!" Her voice ricocheted through the house, making our goldendoodle bark, which he never does.

"Quiet, Boomer," said Grady, grabbing the dog's collar.

Shawna slammed the door shut and plopped onto our designer sofa with her shoes on. "Tomorrow night's going to be epic." She plucked at her clothes and fidgeted, her gaze shifting around the room. "Your parents home?"

I finished my last bite of cereal. "Dad's in Dubai. Mom's at a meeting for her new 'foundation.'" I put *foundation* in air quotes because so far it was just Mom and her friends, drinking wine and planning outrageous fundraising parties. They hadn't even chosen a cause yet—water pollution and illiterate adults were the current options.

I grabbed my cereal bowl and carried it into the kitchen. The glass doors that lead to our balcony were open, and the brine-scented breeze ruffled my hair as I passed.

"Are you hungry, Shawna?" Grady asked, ever the gentleman.

"No, nope, never. Hurry up, Teg. We have a lot to do." She stood up rapidly and Boomer growled at her.

"Hey, knock it off," Grady scolded, and then he caught my eye and nodded toward Shawna, his face a question mark. Besides her frantic behavior, Shawna's dilated pupils filled her eyes like black saucers against a pale blue sky.

I raised my eyebrows and shrugged. Yes, she was high, but what could I do about it? Marcus had gotten her hooked on whatever crap she was taking. "Just a sec," I called to her. I rinsed my bowl and left it in the sink for the housekeeper.

"You're coming to the bonfire, aren't you?" Shawna asked Grady, sliding closer to him and messing his golden hair.

He laughed. "Wouldn't miss it."

"Bringing a special girl?" She poked his stomach until his cheeks turned pink.

I padded back into the living room, barefoot. "Leave him alone. He's just a baby."

"A big baby," she said, lifting my brother's long, lanky arms and throwing them over her shoulders like a shawl. "He's gonna be a lady killer as soon as he gets his driver's license."

I snapped a photo of them. "He's already a lady killer. Too bad he only has eyes for Chloe."

Grady wiggled free of Shawna and stood up, stretching. "I'm not into Chloe."

Shawna laughed. "Liar, liar, pants on fire."

"Chloe doesn't date when she's competing, anyway," he added.

"That's stupid!" Shawna cried. "It's not like she's going to the Olympics, not after that beam disaster. We'll hook you up with a full-size girl. What do you like, redheads?" She flipped her spiraled curls into Grady's face, making him blush harder.

"I'm taking Boomer to the beach," he said. "Hasta la vista, chiquitas."

Shawna rolled her eyes as he left the room. "Let me guess. Tenth-grade Spanish?" she said to me.

"Yep, with Maestro Velasquez." My mood flopped. "That's the class where I met Jake."

"I remember! He still had braces and I didn't know what you saw in him—until, bam, he *glowed up*."

"He sure did." I closed my eyes, and the scent of the ocean mixed with my memories of Jake—his salty skin, his hands on my body, his deep voice in my ear. It hadn't been the same with anyone else, but it wasn't just the sex. Jake didn't care about being seen or driving the right car or making a sports team or getting into the best college. When we'd been together, he'd wanted the media off, the friends gone, the expectations erased—just him and me and nothing between us.

But I'd been the opposite. I'd photographed and posted every moment, kept a frantic social calendar, complained about his old truck, bought him better clothes, and threatened to leave him if he didn't try harder at school. When he dumped me, he said I was just like my mother. No one's ever loved me better or hurt me worse.

And now I wanted a second chance.

"Forget about Jake," Shawna said, drawing me back and flipping me around to face the ocean that filled my eyes like a dream. "There are millions of fish in the sea. Billions. Let's pick our outfits for tomorrow. You need a hookup as badly as your brother does."

I'd promised Shawna first pick out of my closet if she helped me gather driftwood for tomorrow's party, so I let her pull me upstairs to my room. Maybe it would be nice to try again with a new guy. Jake wasn't coming to the bonfire anyway. He'd replied to my group chat, *Have fun. I'm out*. I'd forgotten that each summer he and his family drove to Fort Bragg to visit his mom's cousin, usually around the Fourth of July.

What burned me was that Jake's girlfriend was coming. Grady had invited Chloe, and she'd invited her bestie—Jessica—who'd been *my* bestie until Chloe had come along. I didn't like the memories—those two racing like horses at recess and wasting our Saturdays at Chloe's boring gymnastics competitions. Jessica begged me to include Chloe in *everything* because Chloe didn't have any other friends.

It would sting less if Jessica had grown up or moved on by now, but no. She still hung out with Chloe and hadn't changed her look since the fifth grade. Long straight hair, no highlights or layers, same boring outfits—jeans and white T-shirts and cheap shoes. Jessica's body had filled out, but that was it. She was like a female duck, plain and practical, but somehow she'd scooped up the one boy I couldn't have. If she was the duck, Jake was the drake—gorgeous, proud, and frustratingly loyal, from his pea brain down to his big feet.

I hated them together. Maybe it was because they'd both dumped me, or maybe it was because they liked each other more than they liked me. Whatever it was, they didn't deserve to ride off into the sunset.

Shawna and I reached my bedroom, and she sprawled on my satin coverlet and rolled all over it. "I love your bed!"

"What are you, a dog? Get up." I glimpsed myself in my dresser mirror. The beach workouts prescribed by my personal trainer had done wonders for my stomach. It wasn't just flat; it was bronzed, cut with muscle, and narrower than ever. I wasn't sure why my ass and thighs continued to grow, but the contrast was kind of cool.

I decided to go all out tomorrow tonight—not for the boys but for Jessica. I would show that ugly duckling she wasn't a swan.

23

Jessica

Tegan's phone pulses beneath my mattress like the tell-tale heart. *Thump-thump, thump-thump, thump-thump.* I wake up more tired than when I fell asleep. It's as if Jake transferred his guilt to me with that phone.

He gave it to me Tuesday night, and now it's Thursday morning. Tegan hasn't come home or been found yet, and the tension in Crystal Cove is thickening. Grady's back at school, but he's not allowed to talk about his sister. The police questioned Alyssa and Chloe, who confirmed everything I told Detective Green. Neither friend mentioned Sunday morning's accident with the deer because we don't want to get Alyssa in trouble for taking her dad's BMW.

The coast is clear for my friends and me, but I can't hand this damaged phone over to the police without an explanation, any easier than Jake can. I'd have to lie about where I got it, and nothing sounds plausible. *I found it lying in the street? It showed up in my locker? It was in the bleachers at school?* It's insanity! But if I leave it out for a stranger to find, it could get thrown away—the phone looks like garbage—and then vital evidence would be lost. No, I need to figure out something else.

Besides all this, I'm curious. There might be answers in Tegan's phone, and I have questions, a lot of questions.

I tromp downstairs and pause in the kitchen doorway, watching my parents busy themselves with breakfast. Yellow sunlight stripes through the windows, turning the airborne dust to dancing glitter. The meteorologist said it's going to hit eighty-five degrees today, compliments of the sultry wind currents from Mexico. There was a story about Tegan on TV, but the police have remained vague about what happened to her, making noncommittal statements about "concern for her well-being," "doing everything we can to bring her home," and replying "no comment" to most questions. They're holding their cards close.

The day feels innocent and harmless, like any other day, but if my parents knew what I had squirreled beneath my mattress, it would shift into a nightmare. The kitchen walls would warp and weep, darkness would descend, and bitter cold would ice over the kitchen. The color would seep from our house and the sky. We'd become walking corpses.

"Morning, sweetie," Mom chirps, and just like that, the kitchen is warm and sunny again.

I yawn. "Morning." Mom's going into the office early to prepare for a new client, and she looks nice. Her hair is curled and she smells like hair spray. When she sees my face, she gasps. "What happened?"

"What?"

"You look like you got beaten up."

I peer at my reflection on my phone screen. The bruising from my injured nose, which was a pink splotch yesterday, has seeped upward toward my eyeballs and turned light purple. Dad's expression sharpens. "What happened?"

"Nothing. It was a few days ago."

"That's not nothing. Does it hurt? Can you see?" Dad examines the skin below my eyes and runs his fingers over the bones.

"My eyes are fine. I bumped my nose."

"How?"

I hesitate too long, and Dad's chest swells. He glances toward Jake's house.

"It wasn't him. I smacked it getting into Chloe's car." Why am I lying and dragging Chloe into this? Keeping my eyes lowered, I pour myself a cup of coffee and then offer them my brightest smile. "I'm fine."

"Should we take her to the doctor?" Mom asks Dad.

"If you want. I need to go to work."

"So do I. Are you sure you're fine, Jessica?"

"Other than looking like a raccoon, yes." I laugh, and my voice rings hollow in my ears. Jake tackled me in the woods and smashed my face into a tree, but it was an accident. I believe that.

As I busy myself making toast, my mind dives deeper. This happened *after* he drank too much, *after* he cheated on me, *after* he tried to sneak into my house, and *before* he gave me a missing girl's phone that he'd been hiding in his bedroom. None of this is normal, none of this is right, and none of this is *accidental*.

"Have a good day at school," Mom says, kissing my head on her way out.

After breakfast, I race back upstairs and apply makeup, a lot of makeup, and then walk to my car with a steaming coffee. Fifteen minutes later, I park my Honda in the student lot and walk to class, wearing shorts and a white crop top. Crystal Cove will pay for this balmy, glorious weather from the south later. The tropical winds will bring heat first, lightning and rain later—but for now I'm determined to enjoy it.

◆ ◆ ◆

Jake skipped school again on Wednesday, but today he's here, following me around, and I don't feel like talking. I try to avoid him but he's determined, and when he corners me by the student bathrooms, I whirl to confront him. "Why are you following me? We're not together."

He recoils, stung.

I lower my voice to a whisper. "You put me in a bad position with that phone, you know. Then you skip class? Everyone keeps asking me where you are. It's annoying."

Jake shuffles from foot to foot. "I couldn't deal with the people here. I'm sorry."

"You're always sorry."

"I know." He lowers his long black lashes and chews on his lip, wetting it. He's sexy and sad, and I feel a strong urge to punch him.

Instead I plow on. "Did Shawna tell you anything at Falcon's Peak the other night?"

"She didn't show up."

"Classic Shawna." I sweep back my hair.

"Hey, are those bruises?" He touches my cheek and sends tingles across my skin. When I don't respond, his body starts to shake. "Did I do that to you in the woods?"

The bell rings and I turn to leave, but Jake grabs my arm and spins me around. I misstep, and my ankle twists. "Jesus, back off."

His dark eyes brim. "I'm not trying to hurt you. I just want to see if you're okay."

I wiggle free. "You don't have to maul me. You could just ask. And no, you didn't hurt me. You can't anymore."

I walk away and leave Jake standing there, alone. I was stupid, stupid, stupid to take that phone from him.

Chloe finds me at lunch time and taps my shoulder, making me flinch. "You're jumpy." Her eyes widen. "What happened to your face?"

My hands flutter to my cheeks. Yesterday no one noticed, but like a rotting apple, the bruising has gotten worse. "Is it that obvious?"

"The makeup helps, but I'm a gymnast, Jess. I can spot a bruise a mile away." She sits next to me and smiles, showing her straight white teeth, and I hate knowing why they're so perfect. It's because they're fake. Chloe knocked out most of her front teeth in the balance beam accident years ago that cost her the all-around medal and a place on the Junior Olympic team. Tegan was there too; it was the last meet the three of us attended together. Chloe nudges me. "What happened?"

I shake my protein drink and explain about talking to Jake in the woods.

"You told me he borrowed your bike to meet Shawna. How did that lead to injury?"

"We—I didn't recognize him at first and I ran. We collided." I smile at her, adding quickly, "It was an accident. I promise."

She sucks in her lower lip, and her smile vanishes. "Collided? Is that a euphemism for something else?"

"No." I lift a shoulder—she doesn't know the worst of it—and my thoughts skip over the phone stashed beneath my mattress. It's been giving me bad dreams. I had another nightmare about hitting that deer and the blood dripping down the front of the BMW. I shudder and try to focus on Chloe, who doesn't look like she slept any better than I did. "Jake feels bad. He came over to say he's sorry."

Chloe's highly toned muscles ripple across her body, the way they do when she's about to perform a stunt. Her full lips tighten. "You're not going to take him back, are you?"

"No. No way. I mean, I don't think so."

"Jessica," she growls. "He cheated on you. Everyone is saying you lost him to a *bet*."

My anguish about this rises up, and I don't want to cry in the middle of the quad, so I stand and glance toward the library. "I need to get a book."

Chloe's eyes bulge. "Don't give in to him, Jess. You were going to take Tegan back too, remember. Aren't you glad you didn't?"

After our falling-out in fifth grade, Tegan tried to win me back—she courted me with notes in my desk, invitations, and smiles that made me forget she could ever be mean. I wanted to give in, I missed her so much, but having Chloe to lean on helped me resist. Over time I saw that Tegan hadn't changed; she'd just turned on the charm. Jake's tactics are worse—tears and apologies—harder for me to resist, but I'm older now, stronger. "This is different," I answer.

Chloe snatches up her backpack as the bell rings. "If you're sure. I never thought Jake was the type to—"

"Neither did I, Clo." We hug goodbye. I duck into the library. To further torture myself, I pull up a photo of Jake on my phone. It's him giving me a piggyback ride at the beach earlier this summer, back when we were happy. He adores this picture because of how trusting I look with my chin on his shoulder. He's smiling, his face open, his eyes brimming with love. On that day, I would have bet a million dollars he'd stay true to me.

"Oh, Jake," I breathe, my heart pulling toward him. "Why did you do this to us?"

24

Jessica

After school, I drive to Layers for the four to six o'clock shift, and the sandwich shop is packed when I arrive. The customer line weaves between our plastic chairs and out the door to the side-walk. Almost every table is full, including the window seats. My coworker, a junior named Amara, doesn't look up from the sand-wich she's making. There's a news crew out front, interviewing people. This morning the *Crystal Cove Gazette* headline read:

SENATOR'S DAUGHTER STILL MISSING

The article mentioned that police have identified a "person of interest" in Tegan's case. I hoped that person wasn't Jake. Turning in Tegan's phone might provide answers, but I haven't figured out how to do it yet.

"What's going on?" I whisper to Amara as I don my apron and hat to help.

"Search party volunteers," she whispers back. "They were looking for Tegan up at Cow Mountain, and the family gave them vouchers for free sandwiches after the search."

"Why Cow Mountain? That's pretty far away."

"I don't know." Amara's hands tremble. One of our schoolmates is missing, and I get it, she's scared.

I grab a serrated bread knife and take my place beside her. "What can I get for you?" I ask the next customer in line. He orders a foot-long tri-tip sandwich with almost every topping we have. As I slice the French bread and layer the ingredients, I manage another question to Amara. "Did they find her?"

Her agile fingers halt suddenly above the peperoncini. "No." She glances at me, frozen in place while customers impatiently fidget. I imagine they're hungry after tromping through the forested hills of Cow Mountain in the heat, prodding the bushes for a teen girl's body. Amara's dark eyes glisten. "Do you think there's dirt in her mouth? I keep imagining dirt in Tegan's mouth."

"Jesus, Amara, are you all right? Maybe you should sit down?"

She blinks and grabs a handful of peppers. "No, I want to stay busy." She gets back to work without noticing, or at least commenting, on my purple bruises hidden beneath my makeup.

I finish up the tri-tip and move on to a turkey with Swiss. Now Amara's got *me* imagining dirt in Tegan's mouth, and the sweet smell of processed meat makes my stomach churn. Snippets of conversation reach me over the scraping of my knife as I apply mayonnaise to the bread.

A bearded customer wipes his forehead. "It was hot as blazes out there today."

The woman beside him frowns. "Heat speeds up the decomposition process. I don't think that poor girl is at Cow Mountain. The smell would have attracted vultures by now."

"If she's buried deep enough, there won't be a smell," says a guy I recognize. He bags groceries at Crystal Cove's Safeway.

Saliva erupts between my teeth, and I close my eyes for a moment, flashing back to the party and the blood dripping on the BMW and the terrified eyeball in the darkness. Is the deer I hit rotting on the side of Blood Alley? If I drive there tonight, will I see vultures circling?

I wipe my lips and take a long slow breath because they're not talking about an animal. They're talking about Tegan—Tegan with her big smile, glossy sheets of hair, and muscular curves—a girl who would rather die than decompose in the foothills of Northern California. An airy giggle escapes my lips. *Rather die*—she is dead. No, no. We don't know that.

I move on to the next sandwich.

◆ ◆ ◆

When the rush ends, Amara and I wipe down the counters, cover the meats and cheeses, and start counting the tips in the jar. The volunteers were generous, either because they didn't have to pay for their sandwiches or because Amara and I are the same age as the missing girl and their tips were like a monetary compensation for our lost peer. We split the money now that my shift is over, and Amara finally notices my bruises. I give her the same dumb story I gave my parents.

As I sling my purse over one shoulder, Amara taps her long

fake nails on the countertop. "I don't believe what everyone at school is saying," she offers.

"Hmm?" I'm reordering my cash so that all the presidents' heads are facing the same direction.

"I don't believe Jake killed Tegan."

My head snaps up. "Is that what *everyone* is saying?"

"Most people," she concedes, tugging on a long curl. "But the way I see it, Jake got . . . what he wanted from her, so why would he kill her after that?"

My jaw clenches. "Yep, he got what he wanted, all right." I can't stop the flow of tears that follow.

"Shit, Jess." Amara jumps off her chair. "I was trying to make you feel better."

The sobs make a sharp U-turn into hysteria. "If this is you trying to make me feel better, don't become a therapist."

"I'm sorry. I figured you were worried about Jake."

My feelings explode. "Why does everyone think I'm worried about Jake? Why would I even care? He's not my boyfriend! He's not my problem. Why isn't anyone worried about *me*? I'm the other girl he hurt."

"Other girl?" Amara's eyes grow wider.

"No." I try not to think about the scratched phone Jake gave me. "I didn't mean it like that."

She slides one arm around my shoulders. "Oh, Jess, I'm sorry. I'm such a shit. Forgive me?"

"I'm not mad at you. I'm just mad. I gotta go."

"Are you okay?"

"Yeah, totally." I slip out the door, making the bell jingle. Usually I'd bring Jake a roast beef sandwich, but tonight I leave empty-handed.

Alone in my car, I wipe my cheeks and blow my nose, reach for my phone and then set it down. I want to call Jake, tell him I had a horrible day. He would listen and he'd promise me that tomorrow would be better, and then he'd bring me flowers or wash my car or take me somewhere special. He doesn't like me to feel bad, even for a moment.

Turning the key to my engine, I wonder at Amara's question. Why *would* Jake harm Tegan after getting what he wanted? Motive—what's his motive? I hadn't thought about this before because I was sure Tegan was hiding, but now I'm not sure. Why do people murder? Out of passion or insanity, to make the victim disappear, or to cover the tracks of some other crime, or all of the above?

If Jake didn't look at his phone until he woke up Sunday morning, he wouldn't have known before then that anyone saw him cheat with her, or that *I* saw it. Maybe in his drunken logic, he believed he could erase his mistake by getting rid of her?

If that theory is true, then Tegan's body should be close to her house, not at Cow Mountain. The Sheffield home sits on a high cliff, overlooking the Pacific. There's only a thin metal guardrail protecting people from falling over the edge. What if Jake tossed Tegan into the ocean? Or what if she simply fell?

My brain feels hot and clunky in my head, like an old computer. I'm done thinking about this. I slide on my sunglasses and drive home.

After showering and eating pizza with my parents, I start my homework. Not an hour later, Chloe texts: *They found a body. A teenage girl.*

My stomach tightens; my hairs lift. *At Cow Mountain?*

No. Blind Beach.

OMG! On shore or where?

Blue dots, and then Chloe responds: *In the water. It's on TV.*

Blind Beach isn't far from Tegan's home. It's a natural place to end up if she was flung off her balcony. It's as if the universe read my thoughts and made them come true. I rush to my bedroom window and shut the blinds so Jake can't see me across the side yard. Did he do this terrible thing for *me, for us?* How far will he go to keep us together?

Then full comprehension dawns—the police found a body. *A body.*

Tegan Sheffield is dead.

PART TWO

The Body

25

Jake

Since Mom won't let me drive my truck, Manny is on his way to pick me up for the gym.

Glancing out the front window, I see that Jess's car is gone. She's either at work or at Chloe's, and before I cheated on her, I would have known exactly where she was. I left a peace offering on her doorstep yesterday—homemade muffins with a note. I hope her dad doesn't throw them away.

A strange car is parked at the end of my road again, and there's someone inside it, waiting. I think the cops are watching me in the hopes I'll lead them to Tegan, or maybe the Sheffields hired a private investigator. Whoever it is, they switch vehicles and try to blend in, but this town is too small for a lurking sedan to go unnoticed. I decide to ignore them because I don't know where Tegan is anyway.

Manny turns the corner in his Charger and parks along the

curb. When Cole and Otis hear the familiar rumble of his engine, they rush full speed out of the house. "Manny!" Cole pounces onto my friend as Manny exits the car and tries to wrestle him to the ground. Otis whines and leaps, his paws scraping Manny's stomach.

"Otis, down!" I say, coming outside. My dog flips onto his back, and I swear he wasn't this needy before Dad died. During Dad's last weeks, Otis kept watch over his rented hospital bed, and Otis was the first to notice when Dad stopped breathing. He howled, which alerted the rest of us. The memory grabs me in its jaws and shakes me so hard, I feel dizzy. Losing the pack leader did some messed-up shit to Otis's little brain. It did some messed-up shit to all of us.

"Cole! You're getting strong." Manny squeezes my brother's biceps and turns him upside down, making my brother squeal with laughter. "But not as strong as me."

Cole grabs his glasses so they don't fall off his face. "Can I work out with you?" he asks Manny.

"When you can lift that rock, you can work out with me." Manny sets him down and points to a huge landscaping rock that came with our house.

"Yes!" Cole runs to the rock and tries to lift it, grunting and straining, but he can't.

"That's not fair," I say to Manny.

"It is fair. By the time he's big enough to lift it, he'll be old enough for a gym membership."

"I can't do it!" Cole screams.

"Keep trying, and eat your dinner every night," Manny says. "One day, you will. See ya, little man."

Cole lets go of the rock just long enough to wave goodbye, and then we slip into Manny's car. As he pulls smoothly away from the curb, Manny clears his throat and shifts nervously in his seat.

"What is it?" I ask.

His eyes sweep toward me, then back to the road. "There was a search party at Cow Mountain today. The police think she's dead, man."

I stare down at my hands that are scarred from punching walls—which I did a lot after Dad died—and from punching faces. Twice my skin has been sliced open by a guy's teeth. I remember these hands on Tegan's hips, squeezing. Her voice—*Let me go. That hurts.* Her beat-up phone in my glove box. Fuck, she'd better not be dead.

Manny offers a sad smile, showing his uneven teeth as he continues. "My mom was on that search party, and people were saying that Shawna's boyfriend is the 'person of interest' the police are after. I guess they went shooting at Cow Mountain this summer and Marcus told Tegan to watch her back. The police can't find him."

"What do you mean they can't find him? They're the police."

"He ditched his apartment; no sign of him or his car. He's hiding out, man, and did you notice Shawna hasn't been in school? They're probably together. Bonnie and Clyde."

"Did they find anything at Cow Mountain?"

"Nah, but I think Marcus is the one, man. It never made sense Tegan would go missing over a stupid video."

Heat glides to my cheeks, and my heart rate kicks up a notch. "It's more than a stupid video."

"It'll be forgotten by homecoming. Don't worry about it."

I slam my fist into his dashboard. "You don't get it! You weren't *in it.*" Tears fill my eyes. What the fuck is wrong with me?

"Okay, calm down. I guess it's a big deal from her point of view. I mean, her mom was a senator and she's a chick."

Manny nods as if that's all there is to it, and suddenly he seems a million miles away. No one gets that I'm not okay with people ogling my dick just because I'm a guy. I change the subject. "Want to work on our science paper after the gym?"

Manny chuckles. "Dude, I know you're lonely, but I'm not doing homework with you."

I laugh and don't know why I even asked, except that's what Jess and I would be doing tonight if we were together. We'd be sprawled on her living room floor, me squeezing her legs and making her laugh while she reads aloud from our textbooks. Her mom would sneak past every hour or so to offer food, but really to make sure we weren't getting pregnant.

My stomach heaves as I remember the STD testing. I have an appointment to get that done tomorrow. Tegan and I were idiots. Fucking idiots.

As Manny and I enter the gym, the smell of sweat and the sound of human grunts fill the air. "Oh shit," says Manny. The varsity baseball team is here, using the free-weight room, and they eyeball me warily. Grady Sheffield is with them—their star pitcher—and since people think I did something to his sister, the whole team hates me.

"Hey, fuckboy," says Chase Waters, one of Grady's best friends even though he's two years older. "What makes you think you can just show up here?" He strolls toward me, flexing his arms. Grady and the team shadow him, arcing around Manny and me.

"I'm just working out, man." Shit, Chase and I clunked beers last weekend at the party.

"Not here, you're not. Get the fuck out." Chase's jaw muscles quiver as he snatches my arms and tries to shove me toward the door.

Manny drops his big hand onto Chase's shoulder. "It's *Jake*, dude. Back off."

"Can't fight your own battles, fuckboy?" Chase shouts at me. "Or are you more comfortable beating up girls? Saw Jessica at school today. You give her those shiners she's trying to hide?"

I lunge at him, and Manny yanks me back, his voice rumbling in my ear, "Not worth it, man."

"You're a pussy, you know that?" Chase growls. "Tegan's too fucking good for you."

The manager of the gym turns down the music and starts walking toward us. Manny holds me tight so I don't start swinging.

Then Grady steps up, and the team parts for him. He's only fifteen, but he's taller and bigger than I am. His jaw muscles flutter; his lips quiver. "Where's my sister? What did you do to her?"

My gut loosens; I don't know what to say. Even the manager freezes in place. Everyone knows who Grady is.

Tegan's brother tilts his head, considering me, and I notice his resemblance to his sister—same full lips, sharp blue eyes, and gold-tinged hair. He rubs his face. "You were there," he rasps. "If you're not the one who hurt her, then why didn't you protect her?"

He might as well have slugged me. "I—I don't know. I'm sorry."

His eyes glitter and his hands ball into fists. "You're *sorry*?" Grady's not going to leave this gym until he hits me; I feel it. I toss a glance at Manny, and his grim smile tells me he feels it too. I give a small shake of my head. *Don't help me.* Manny's eyes widen, and I know he's thinking, *Fuck that!*

But it's Chase who strikes me first. He charges, muscles rippling, and slugs me in the jaw, and then we're both swinging. My fist snaps his head back. His return blow connects with my eye socket. "You total fucking loser!" he cries as I fly off my feet and land on my back. For a second, I can't breathe.

Manny grabs Chase in a choke hold.

"No," I wheeze, getting up. "I'm not fighting these assholes." I glance at Grady because I don't mean him, but he stares at me, uncomprehending, and I realize he's in total shock about his sister. "Let's go," I say to Manny.

But Chase breaks free and shoves me again. "Why won't you fight? Is it 'cause we're not girls?"

Manny punches him in the mouth, and Chase falls onto an onlooker, who gets pissed and shoves Chase into someone else, and then the gym erupts into a full-on brawl—fists flying, voices grunting, flesh bruising, blood dripping. Members flood out the gym doors; others pull up their phones to record the fight.

A fist strikes my jaw. I land a punch on someone's back. Fingers claw at me, but I'm quick to spin away.

That's when Grady comes for me. The baseball team notices, and there's a collective cease-fire as they open a pocket of space. This is Grady's fight, after all, but his wide eyes tell me he's never fought before, and his pursed lips assure me he'd rather not. I motion for him to come and get me, and he does. He lands the first punch, and the second, and the third. I curl over and let him pummel me.

"Jake, what are you doing?" Manny cries.

But the steam leaves the others when they notice I'm not fighting back. Their arms relax and their breathing slows. I let Grady release his rage about his sister onto my body, grateful he's a lousy puncher.

Manny halts Grady's final swing with an outstretched hand. "That's enough, yeah?"

Grady glances around, breathless. Then he smooths his hair, straightens his tank top, and reaches down to help me up, a Southerner to his bones. "Are you all right?"

"Yeah," I lie. Lousy puncher or not, he got me pretty good. I'm going to feel this tomorrow. Shit, I feel it now—head ringing, flesh on fire. I take Grady's hand, let him pull me to my feet, and the bystanders disperse. I can tell that Grady doesn't know what to say. Does he apologize, or leave me with a final verbal jab?

I don't think this is the time to bring up his sister, but I do it anyway, turning my eyes to his. "If I knew what happened to Tegan, I'd tell. I promise."

Grady's tight expression melts, and his eyes squeeze shut. He seems to retreat into himself. "Do you mean that?" he asks.

"Yeah. I'm not hiding. I'm not running. I just don't remember."

Grady nods. "Maybe my sister will, when they find her."

"I hope so, man. I do."

"Look," shouts a gym member. He points at one of the televisions mounted to the wall. "They found a body. Turn it up!"

Coverage from Blind Beach plays on the television, showing footage of divers pulling a female body out of the sea. Grady collapses to his knees as his teammates surround him.

My breathing stills as I watch three divers carry a clothed female body out of the ocean, her face blurred by the TV station. "No," Grady cries. His labored breathing fills the gym as detectives and cops comb the shoreline on TV. The camera operators are careful to shield the body from us, but we don't miss the sudden glimpse of long sea-tangled hair.

"It's not her," Chase murmurs to Grady. "That's not Tegan."

My insides float as if I'm falling. The ends of the girl's wet hair dried quickly in the wind, revealing unmistakable copper-red ringlets.

Manny wipes his face. "That looks like Shawna Moore."

The camera pans out, showing Falcon's Peak, where they believe the girl fell.

"Isn't that where you were supposed to meet her?" Manny hisses under his breath. Suspicion crosses his face like a bank of clouds, blurring his features, riling a storm.

Panic claws my stomach. "She wasn't there. I swear it." Is this why Shawna didn't show, because someone killed her after she texted me?

Manny's eyes twitch, and his lips flatten. But then he reshapes his expression, absorbing his thoughts so I can't see them. "Dude, it might be time to call a lawyer."

My scattered thoughts crumple into one: *If the dead body belongs to Shawna, then Tegan is still missing.*

26

—

Jessica

The headline in Friday's *Crystal Cove Gazette* reads:

BODY DISCOVERED AT POPULAR
BEACH IS NOT MISSING TEEN

I'm at school with Chloe and Alyssa and Manny, huddled together before class starts. Unexpected fog drifted in early this morning and blotted out the sun, leaving the campus damp and chilly. Students who were fooled into believing they could wear cute outfits—like Alyssa and Chloe—now regret it.

"That's harsh," says Alyssa about the headline. "Shawna's not 'the missing teen,' but she's still *someone*. Do you think she jumped or fell?"

"Let me see that." I snatch the paper out of Alyssa's hands and scan the article. My stomach drops. The story confirms that

Shawna fell from Falcon's Peak into the sea, where she became trapped between two boulders. "Time of death has not been determined," I say, summarizing the article. "Her mom didn't report her missing because Shawna spends the night elsewhere quite often. They mention the possibility of foul play."

Chloe rips at her fingernails with her teeth. "At least the sharks didn't get her."

Manny grunts, and I cover my mouth. "God, her mom . . ." If there is a worst nightmare for a parent, this is it. Shawna's mother identified the body last night, so it's confirmed. Shawna Moore is dead. Even the word is awful—*dead*—heavy, final, and short. "The school should let us go home," I say.

"Right?" Alyssa snaps her gum. "No one's getting any work done. Everyone's freaked out. Like, is there a murderer loose in Crystal Cove, or did Shawna kill herself?"

I read more of the article. "It says here that Shawna agreed on Tuesday to cooperate with the police in exchange for immunity in Tegan's case, which means she was involved in something illegal. No one saw her after that." *But she texted Jake on Tuesday night*, I think.

Alyssa jumps in, poking Manny in the ribs for emphasis. "She was going to cooperate, and now she's dead. Does that sound like an accident to you?"

"Maybe a coincidence?" Manny says, poking her back.

"Are you all right?" I ask Chloe. "You don't look good."

She wipes away a tear. "I'm just freaked out. When is all this craziness going to stop?"

"It might be over soon," Alyssa says. "Read the rest of the article. It says Shawna's boyfriend is a person of interest in her death and Tegan's disappearance. He isn't a college student, and Marcus isn't his first name. He's Daniel Marcus Lancaster, and he broke probation by leaving Nevada, where he assaulted an underage girl last year. He's been lying to Shawna. And look"—she points at the paper in my hand—"the police can't find him. He ditched his apartment in a hurry, left behind handgun ammunition and a pile of drugs. They have an all-points bulletin out on him. They'll catch him."

"Maybe he killed them both," I say.

Alyssa picks up her backpack, just as the first bell rings. "That's the million-dollar question."

As she and Manny walk away, holding hands, Chloe locks eyes with me and lowers her voice. "Didn't you say Jake had a meeting with Shawna at Falcon's Peak? Did he do this?" She rattles the newspaper in my hand.

I burst into tears, shocking myself. "I—no, of course not. Murder? That's crazy."

Her eyes glide over my face. "It could have happened by accident?"

"No, Jake's harmless."

"Your bruises might disagree."

"Chloe, seriously, let that go."

We glare at each other a moment, and then she smiles, a wide, perfect grin, and holds out her pinkie. "I'm sorry. Peace?"

I wrap my pinkie around hers. "Peace." Wiping my eyes, I hug her. "I miss you, Clo. You're always at the gym. We haven't hung out at all."

She hugs me back. "As soon as this college showcase is over, that will change. I promise." We part ways for class.

◆ ◆ ◆

As I walk to first period, I pass people gathered in the quad, crying. Reporters line the school property, and there are two police cruisers in the parking lot. I spot Hailey and Chiara, sobbing as a reporter interviews them. Brendon Reed is at their side. He nods at me as if we're friends, and my mouth falls open. The balls on that guy! I turn the corner and slam straight into Jake.

"Jessica." He drags me into an alcove and leans against me, pressing my back into the brick wall. "I've been looking for you. I'm scared." His chest quakes as he buries his head into the crook of my neck.

I'm frozen at first, overwhelmed. His clean scent fills my nostrils, and his hard chest feels achingly familiar beneath my fingertips. But he's heavy. "You're crushing me," I rasp.

He wraps his big hands around my skull, his face inches from mine. His skin is raw and bruised. His lips quiver and his eyes bounce across my features. His thumbs gently sweep my cheeks. "I love you so fucking much, and I—I don't know what to do. I can't believe Shawna's dead. I'm going to get blamed for this too." His body shudders.

He's so close that I feel his breath on my cheeks, and I force a whisper past my slamming heart. "You told me she didn't show up."

His long lashes flutter. "She didn't, I swear." A quiet groan escapes his chest. "Jess, someone is setting me up. Please believe me. I *know* I didn't kill Shawna."

"But you don't know if you killed Tegan?" My eyes dart to the breezeway, where students are walking to class, just a few feet away.

"No, no, it's not like that." He nuzzles me again, his stubble rough on my cheek. "I need you more than ever, Jess. My life is ruined."

His desperation leaves me feeling shaky, off balance. I push him back a step. "What happened to your face?" I ask.

"I got the shit kicked out of me by a fifteen-year-old." He inhales my scent, and I see that it calms him. *Grady must be the fifteen-year-old,* I think.

We stand there, unmoving, and every hair on my body angles toward him as if he's the sun. How does he have this effect on me, even when I'm upset? "I got the muffins you made," I manage. Jake left them on my doorstep Wednesday with a note: *Roses are red. Violets are blue. I made these muffins, just for you.* Then, in typical Jake style, he wrote, *P.S. Don't eat them. The box was expired. Sorry.*

Our eyes meet, and his are opaque, surrounded by his thick forest of tangled lashes. They remind me of Jake in other lighting, in other places—beneath the covers, where his dark pupils expand like universes; in the back seat, where his ruddy cheeks blaze like irons; and in my shower, where his chapped lips taste like raindrops.

His gaze grows hotter, and his breathing quickens. "Things are crazy, aren't they?" he murmurs. "Like everything is turned upside down."

I clear my throat. "Yeah, like we're living in a nightmare and can't wake up."

"That's for sure." He licks his lips. "Jess—where's Tegan's phone? Did you turn it in yet?"

My body tightens as if a puppeteer has just picked up my strings, getting ready to make me dance. I shake my head, and he releases his breath in a steamy gasp. "Okay, good. Will you do me a favor?"

I blink at him, horrified at what he'll want from me next.

"Wipe it clean, real clean. Get rid of my fingerprints." Tears wash his eyes. "I know how that sounds, okay, but I didn't think of it before. I didn't believe Tegan was really missing, but now . . . after what happened to Shawna . . . something's not right."

I have to wipe the phone down anyway, to remove *my* prints, so I nod silently.

He relaxes. "Thank you. I think I'm in serious trouble, Jess."

Goose bumps erupt across my arms. "Why? Have you remembered something?"

"I wish . . ." He trails off. "Can we—" The bell rings, interrupting him. "Can we talk later?"

I should say no, but now I have the damn phone. He's roped me into his . . . his *crime?* Our fates are intertwined, for better or for worse. "Maybe after school?" I offer.

"I work until six. After that?"

I sigh. "I work from six to nine. I'll call you later." I wonder if he wants to talk about Tegan or Shawna or something else. Either way, I'm not sure I want to hear it.

+ + +

All day, it's impossible to concentrate, and the teachers understand this. A test is postponed in English, and our government teacher decides to play a movie. Everyone's whispering about Shawna and wondering if Tegan will come out of hiding now that her best friend is dead, *if* she's hiding. I hear Jake's name spoken often, whispered like a curse. The idea that he murdered both girls is taking root.

My last class is world history with Jake. We sit five rows apart, and the teacher plays a documentary. The lights are off and the blinds shut. I'm chewing the gum that Alyssa gave me at lunchtime and doodling in my notebook because the movie is boring.

Halfway through, the classroom door slams open and instant sunshine blinds us. Our teacher startles and knocks his hot cup of tea into his lap. He dances behind his desk, yelping, but also trying to assess what's happening in his classroom.

Two police officers enter, their radios hissing, and they don't look happy. "Jacob Healy?" says the female, her eyes scanning the room.

Jake flies out of his desk and scrambles to the far corner of the classroom.

A few students scatter and gather around the teacher, their notebooks clutched to their chests like shields.

"Everyone, remain calm," says the female cop, whom I recognize. She was a student here a few years ago, Ivy Lee, an ex-cheerleader. Her focus lands on Jake, and she and her partner slowly approach him, their hands outstretched, closing in on him like they would a cornered animal. Officer Lee speaks. "Jake, we need you to come with us. We'll explain at the station."

His body trembles; his breathing grows ragged. His battered face looks horrified, and I will him to be still and not to run. The cops' guns are holstered, dark and shiny at their hips.

"Will you walk with us, Jake, or do we need to restrain you?" asks the male officer.

Jake's gaze flits toward the door, and his legs flex.

The male officer advances. "Don't do it, Jake."

"He's just scared," I blurt, and everyone in the classroom turns to me, including Jake. When this happens, the cops rush forward and zip-tie his wrists behind his back.

"What did I do?" Jake asks, terror in his eyes.

The male cop holds him steady while Lee speaks quietly. "You have the right to remain silent. Anything you say can and will be used against you in a court of law. You have the right to an attorney.

If you cannot afford an attorney, one will be appointed for you. Do you understand your rights as I've stated them?"

"Am I under arrest?" he asks.

"We're detaining you for questioning with our detective. Do you understand your rights?"

Jake nods, and his legs go weak beneath him. "Yes. I—I want my mom." He's so quiet, I barely hear him. I rise halfway out of my chair, and my heart knocks in my chest. He looks so scared, and I realize how much I still care about Jake. I can't just turn that off. I want to help him and a tear slides down my cheek. I wipe it off before anyone notices.

The officers guide him out of the classroom with his head down. I wonder if they discovered new evidence in Tegan's case, or if this is about Shawna. And how does Marcus fit in? He was at Tegan's party too.

The image of Tegan's phone flashes through my mind. I've been paralyzed about what to do with it, but I can't wait any longer. Maybe it'll exonerate Jake, or implicate Marcus, or someone else. Either way, it could reveal the truth.

But I need to see what's on it first. There might be a few damning texts from *me*. The reason I don't judge Jake as harshly as I should is because I've been hiding something too. Something that happened this summer.

The trick will be turning the phone on without the police tracing the signal. If I don't play this right, I could be the next person they arrest.

27

—

Jake

The back of the squad car stinks of dried vomit, worse than the Uber that Jess and I took in downtown San Francisco last month. A cage of steel separates me from the officers in the front seat. They have handguns, a rifle, batons, a computer, and a busy radio—everything one needs to haul a stupid teenager to jail.

All because of Tegan Sheffield.

"Will you call my mom?" I ask Officer Lee.

"We already did. She's meeting us at the police station."

My legs bounce and my pulse speeds. "Is this about Shawna?"

Officer Lee turns around and faces me. "Why, do you have information about her?"

I shake my head and decide to shut up.

When we arrive at Crystal Cove's tiny police station, the officers sit me in a chair while an interrogation room is prepared. A few moments later, Mom's harried voice rings in the lobby. "My son is here, Jacob Healy."

An officer leads her to where I'm sitting, and Mom bursts into tears when she sees my hands behind my back and my swollen face from the gym fight. I hid out in my bedroom so she wouldn't fuss over me last night.

"Oh, Jake, did you get into a fight?"

"Yeah, yesterday, but I don't think that's why I'm here."

She crumples into the chair next to mine and wraps her arms around my chest. I lean into her like I did when I was younger.

Officer Lee rounds the corner, offers an unreadable smile. "We're ready for you, Jake. This must be your mother?" They talked on the phone but not in person, so Lee introduces herself and then removes the zip ties around my wrists. "Sorry about the cuffs, Ms. Healy. Jake looked like he might run."

"I'm sure you scared him," Mom says through clenched teeth. She juggles her purse and keys and sunglasses as we follow Officer Lee into a stale white room. There's a small wooden table, several plastic chairs, a camera mounted to the wall, and a box of tissues. The floor is carpeted and the other walls are bare except for a PROTECT AND SERVE poster.

"Have a seat," says Lee. Then another woman enters the room with eyes like darts. "This is Detective Underwood," says Lee.

Underwood is an older woman with a trim athletic body, thick shoulders, and long fingers. She doesn't offer a smile or a handshake, just waves at the chairs, indicating that we sit down. *Is this good cop, bad cop?* I wonder.

"Get us some water," Underwood orders Lee. The younger woman departs and returns with plastic water bottles for each of us.

Detective Underwood begins, hard and fast. No foreplay. "Well, well, Jacob Healy. We have a lot to discuss."

"I don't understand why Jake is here. Is my son under arrest?" Mom asks. "Should we call a lawyer?"

Underwood waves her hand. "Jake's not under arrest. I've detained him for questioning, to go over some facts. If he chooses not to cooperate, I may escalate this to an arrest, but I would prefer not to file the paperwork." Her smile is broad but somehow unfriendly.

"Okay." Mom peers nervously at me, and I wipe my palms on my jeans.

Underwood turns to me. "I'm going to record this because I don't want to put words in your mouth later, if that makes sense. All you have to do is tell the truth. Let's begin." Underwood nods to Officer Lee, who presses record on the camera. "Time is two-thirty p.m. at the Crystal Cove Police Department located at 220 Spinnaker Street in Crystal Cove, California. Present in the room are Jacob Healy, Mona Healy, Officer Ivy Lee, and myself, Detective Samantha Underwood. Please state your names for the record and to establish your voices."

We each state our name, and Mom squeezes my leg. I hate that she has to see this, but I'm also glad she's here. Mom withdraws a tissue from her purse and starts shredding it in her lap.

"All right, Jake. I have some follow-up questions about the party you attended Saturday night that ended early Sunday morning. We have a missing student, Tegan Sheffield, a sexually explicit video recording, and now a deceased student who also attended the party. Shawna Moore was about to give evidence regarding the video before she died."

Mom's breath hisses, and my heart gives a painful beat.

Underwood consults a manila folder. "First I'd like to ease both your minds about the video recording. The special agents who flew in earlier this week took it down and did a deep scrub on all the posts from that night and subsequent days. The bureau has methods for tracking the shares and removing the layers as the content moves toward the dark web. It's not a perfect science, but they've done their best."

"Dark web?" Mom whispers.

"That's right."

The school cheeseburger I ate for lunch churns heavily in my belly.

Underwood studies our faces, rubs her chin. "We've opened a separate investigation into Tegan's alleged production of the video. Regarding that case, you are the victim, Jake."

I squirm in my chair, repelled by the word *victim*.

Officer Lee interjects, her eyes scanning mine. "We can't emphasize enough the seriousness of this crime, Jake. It's a felony to film sexual acts with a minor and share the footage. All persons responsible will be prosecuted."

Mom sets her jaw and fiddles with her purse handles. "That's good."

I wish they'd stop calling me a minor; they might as well call me a child. I'm not a fucking child.

Underwood resumes command. "That is assuming we can gather the evidence we need for an arrest, for instance the camera that was used. Do you know what happened to it, Jake?"

"No idea," I answer, still trying to wrap my brain around the word *felony*. Tegan really threw herself under the bus with this video stunt.

Officer Lee grows more earnest. "This wasn't your average hookup, Jake. From our perspective, it appears that it was planned. Who else might have been involved besides Tegan?"

I remember Shawna's words. *You were only supposed to kiss.* And her fears. *The FBI is here, and everyone is lying. No one wants to get arrested.* And the bet—who made the bet? My head pounds harder and I stare at my shoelaces, but I'm too scared to even mention Shawna's name in front of this detective. "I don't know."

"All right, let's move on," says Underwood. "As stated, we discovered the body of one of your classmates yesterday, a close friend of Tegan's. Our investigation into her death has just begun, but it escalates our concern for Tegan's well-being."

Mom grabs another tissue to shred, and I release a deep breath. I don't think they know I planned to meet Shawna at Falcon's Peak before she died—not yet anyway—and that's good. I told Manny and Jess about it, but no one else. If the police don't have Shawna's phone, they may never find out. Below the tabletop, I slide my cell out of my pocket and quickly delete my text thread with Shawna, just in case.

Underwood continues. "We've questioned many of the students who attended the party. They report that you were the last one seen with Tegan before she disappeared. The family's home security cameras were disabled remotely at two forty-two a.m., which makes you our only witness, Jake."

I sit taller. *Witness?* Maybe they don't suspect me.

Underwood continues, "We need your help to piece this together, and this isn't the time to protect your friends. I'm going to ask one more time, for the record, do you know where Tegan is or what happened to her?"

I shake my head. "Nope."

"Are you saying you don't know, or you don't remember?"

"Both," I answer. "Wherever she is, it's got nothing to do with me." My pulse quickens because I'm not sure if I'm telling the truth.

Officer Lee's sharp eyes roll across my face, curious. "But if you don't remember, how can you be sure?"

"Look, I had a few beers, okay?" I feel utterly miserable, dehydrated, and tired. I just want to go home.

"What's the last thing you are sure about? Walk us through it," says Underwood.

I slide my palms down my thighs, close my eyes, and teleport back to the party. "I argued with my girlfriend by the pool and then went looking for her later, but I started dancing with Tegan. Or she started dancing with me. I don't know. It gets blurry after the dancing." After the tequila, actually, but my mom doesn't need to hear about that.

"Jake?" prods Officer Lee. "Try to remember. It's important."

I squint, thinking harder. "I followed Tegan upstairs. We started kissing, and then I woke up in my bedroom at home." For a moment, I relive the touch of her silky skin and that blistering electric moment when I entered her. I don't mention the burst of shame afterward or my horrible first thought: *I have to hide this.* I don't mention Tegan's angry voice, the sound of shattering glass, or the sharp pain in my foot. It's all noises and impressions, but I can't see it. It's like my eyes were closed. "I guess I blacked out," I finish.

Detective Underwood grunts. "You definitely had more than a few drinks. Did you drive yourself home?"

I believe they want to charge me with *something,* and the last thing I need is a DUI, so I simply shrug. Mom stays silent too, not mentioning that I parked my truck on our lawn.

"We've checked CCTV in the surrounding area, from two-thirty a.m. to midmorning on Sunday. We know that a vehicle matching the make and model of your truck left Tegan's neighborhood at five-fifty-five a.m. and traveled straight to your house."

Underwood glances at my mom and then amends her statement. "Though *straight* is not an accurate representation of what we saw. The drive home was erratic, but it was dark and we didn't get a good look at the driver. Was it you, Jake?"

I shrug. "I think so."

Underwood grimaces, and then to Officer Lee she says, "Re-examine the existing footage from the Sheffields' home security cameras, before they were disabled. I want eyes on Jake and how much he drank that night."

"Got it," says Lee with a quick nod, and I feel a DUI charge barreling toward me.

Underwood inhales and then slowly lets out her breath, switching gears. "Jake, I've kept these details from the media, but I'd like to show you a few pictures." Underwood slides the first one over, and Mom gasps. I scoot away from it and almost fall out of my chair. Underwood leans closer, her breath crisp with mint. "Do you recognize this bedroom?"

I nod, my heart banging.

"Whose blood is that Jake?"

In the photos, large droplets of blood are splattered across Tegan's white satin comforter. Her dresser is dislodged from where it stood against the wall. The large dresser mirror is shattered, the wood frame smashed. Shards of mirror litter the floor, along with more blood droplets. It appears as if someone went on a rampage in her bedroom. Nausea washes through me.

Underwood's lips tighten. "We've had an undercover cop watching you since Sunday, Jake. We believed you were our best chance at finding Tegan and finding her quickly. We hoped you'd lead us to her location or confess to a friend what you did, but we found this instead." She shows me a bag that contains the shards of glass from my foot and my clothing from the party. "The under-cover officer collected these items from your garbage can early Wednesday morning."

Mom emits a surprised shriek. "You went through our trash?"

Underwood nods. "Once you put the cans on the city curb, we don't need a warrant." She turns to me. "There's blood on the T-shirt you wore to the party, Jake. You might as well tell us now. Will the blood belong to Tegan Sheffield?"

"Stop," Mom whispers, her fingers trembling against her face. "No more."

"He doesn't need to answer the question, Ms. Healy. We'll have lab results soon enough." Underwood's hazel eyes impale mine. "Or he could just answer."

Blood—on my shirt? I didn't notice any blood, it must have been a small amount. I rub my head, guessing that I'm totally fucked. But the thing is, if I believed I'd hurt Tegan or made her disappear, I'd have turned myself in. Shit, I got nothing to lose. I already lost Jess, I'm barely on track to graduate on time, and I'm not good at anything useful—can't fix cars, can't build shit out of wood, can't do math. The only things I'm good at are surfing, kissing, and screwing things up.

But until I'm positive about what happened at that party, I don't know how to defend myself. My lips remain sealed.

Underwood stares into my eyes as if she can pull the truth straight out of my brain. "The sooner you cooperate with us, the better it will go for you, Jake. What do you say?"

I gaze helplessly at my mother and then back at Detective Underwood. "I want a lawyer."

28

Jake

"Wait a minute." Mom shoves Underwood's evidence away from us. "You said my son's not a suspect."

Underwood smirks. "I said he's not under arrest."

Mom reaches for her purse. "Jake and I are leaving."

Underwood shakes her head. "Not yet, Ms. Healy. Jake doesn't have to answer our questions, but he can't leave until these search warrants regarding Tegan's missing-persons case are executed."

She retrieves several official forms and hands them to my shocked mother, her smile turning grim. "We would have served these last Sunday but Judge Singh was reluctant to sign them then. Mainly because Jake is Tegan's victim in another case and because we didn't have enough physical evidence for probable cause. Judge Singh didn't like the 'optics.'" She puts *optics* in air quotes.

"But after learning that Jake disposed of broken mirror shards and bloody clothing in the garbage, the judge agreed that we have probable cause to search, and he signed these this morning." She taps the papers. "These warrants give us permission to collect your son's DNA, impound his truck, search your home, and inspect his person."

Mom's fingers clench around the papers, and her eyes blaze. "But you just said he's not under arrest. I don't understand."

"I'm not arresting him, at least not yet. Your son is a witness, a victim, and a person of interest in Tegan's case. Look at this." She holds up the photo of Tegan's bedroom. "A struggle occurred and a former senator's daughter is missing. Your son was the last one with her. We're not messing around, Ms. Healy."

Mom recoils. "Can we decline the searches until we talk to someone?"

Underwood grunts. "A lawyer can't stop this. It's happening now."

I glance at the papers and read the confident scrawl of Judge Singh across each one. My stomach slides out of me.

The detective taps the warrants that have whisked away my privacy. "We can do the physical exam here. We're looking for cuts, bruises, offensive wounds, that kind of thing."

Mom rights herself, her hands shaking, and I know exactly how she feels because my heart is racing too. We're both thinking about the mirror shards she pulled out of my foot Sunday morning. The wound is still visible, still healing.

Underwood lifts her hands in a peaceful gesture that feels false. "You may remain with your son, Ms. Healy."

Mom's long eyelashes flutter as if she's going to pass out.

"The warrant includes seizure of your cell phone, Jake, so hand it over, please." Underwood wiggles her fingers at me and continues speaking. "You will need to buy a new phone. You're not getting this one back."

Everything inside me clenches and retracts. "But I need my phone."

Underwood narrows her eyes. "You understand that a girl is missing, don't you, a girl you know intimately?"

I slam my cell onto the table and meet Underwood's sharp hazel eyes. "She can stay missing, for all I care."

"Jake!" Mom cries. Lee snaps her head toward me, her eyebrows knitting together.

"It's all right," says Detective Underwood, placating Mom while palming my iPhone. "I understand why your son might feel reluctant to help us after what happened to him at Tegan's party. I'd be upset too if someone put me on display to win a fifty-dollar bet."

"A bet?" Mom asks.

Underwood nods. "At her beach bonfire this summer, Tegan entered into a wager that she could kiss your son. We believe the video recording was her way, or someone's way, of proving that she won."

I sink deeper into my chair as it hits me. My troubles didn't begin last week; they began with that fucking bonfire. That's when the gauntlet was thrown down—*Kiss Jake or pay up*. I know Tegan doesn't care about fifty bucks; she bleeds cash. No, she cares about winning. Whoever made that bet is to blame for *all of this*.

"Who would do that?" Mom asks.

"Her friends aren't saying," Underwood admits. Her eyes flick toward me.

Mom rises and stands over Underwood, glowering down at her. "Tegan and Jake used to date. Did you know that? She's never gotten over him. She filmed him and now she regrets it. He's the victim; you said so yourself." Mom slaps her hand on the table. "Why don't you do your job and find her?"

Officer Lee intercedes before Mom and Underwood start to brawl. "Ms. Healy, we appreciate your son answering our questions. We'll want to speak to him again, and I suggest you listen to your son and retain counsel immediately." She hands Mom and me two business cards, looking apologetic. "Please call if you're harassed by the media. Once these new details get out, it's going to be a feeding frenzy. Reporters already smell a story—former senator's daughter and all—but please don't speak to them. It can only hurt the investigation."

Mom gives a curt nod, and Underwood takes charge again. "Jake, follow me for the exam. Ms. Healy, come along. There's no sense in rushing home. A CSI team has been deployed to your house and they're searching it now."

"Already?"

"When we move, we move fast, Ms. Healy. Come along." Underwood escorts us down a bare hallway, and I hate this detective with every breath I take.

Two male cops join us, and they usher Mom and me into a windowless room while Detective Underwood waits outside. One of the men opens a sealed container and pulls out what looks like a long Q-tip. "Open your mouth." He swabs me and places the stick into a tube and labels it.

Then he asks me to remove my clothing. The room is fluorescent and cold, and Mom looks away as I strip down and stand naked in front of the officers.

Wearing gloves, they measure me, photograph my body, scrape beneath my fingernails, which aren't clean, I notice, and inspect every inch of me, including the bottom of my feet. "What happened here?" They remove my bandage and note the fresh gash in my skin. An officer measures and clicks half a dozen photos of the wound.

"I don't remember." It's mostly true.

Mom chews on her knuckles, and then finally the exam is over, my foot is re-bandaged, and we're released into the parking lot. An arrest is imminent, and we both know it.

"Can we get the court-appointed lawyer?" I ask Mom as we climb into her car.

"Let me worry about that." Her hands shake so badly, she drops her keys twice, and then she turns over the engine and drives to the next street, where she pulls over to take deep breaths. We sit in silence for a moment as her eyes fill with tears. "Is there anything you want to tell me, Jake?"

I shake my head, feeling numb. I can't tell her anything.

Her eyelashes clump into thick black spikes. "How did we get here?" she asks.

How did we get *where?* I wonder. In a family with a dead father? In a beach town that's rarely sunny? In a police interview room with an ex-cheerleader and a mean detective? I have no fucking idea. "I don't know, Mom. I'm sorry."

"It's not your fault," she says automatically. She pulls back onto the street and drives toward home.

"Dad would be so mad at me," I say. He was ex-army and worked in machinery repair. He was strict, expected me to make my bed every morning, never miss a day of school, and work with 110 percent effort. He would not be proud of me right now.

Mom wipes her eyes. "Dad would *help* you, honey, and so will I. I know you didn't hurt that girl." She pats my leg, but her eyes say more than that. They say *I love you no matter what, I forgive you, I'm not mad at you, and I don't judge you.* I love her too, and I probably don't tell her that enough.

When we get to our house, we pause down the street and watch with our mouths open. There's a police van parked in the driveway, and a tow truck is wheeling away my pickup. Some neighbors stand on their front stoops, and there are three news vans parked on our curb, filming the action. Somebody leaked my name, probably someone from school. I rub my hands across my shaved head. "I can't deal with this."

"Neither can I," Mom says. "Let's grab Cole early, go see a movie, and buy you a new phone."

"Really?"

She smiles bravely. "Yes, you pick the show." She steps on the gas and flips a U-turn, and my fists unclench as the sight of gloved detectives going in and out of my house vanishes in the sideview mirror. At least Tegan's phone is with Jess and I know they won't find anything else in my bedroom.

I face forward, wondering for the first time since she went missing if I'll ever see Tegan again.

29

Tegan, July

The morning of my Fourth of July bonfire, I lay in bed, stalking Jake on my phone. Ever since he'd plucked me out of the ocean the week before, I'd been thinking about him harder than ever. His feed was boring, though. He'd driven to Fort Bragg with his family, and he'd only posted one picture—a shot of Cole at the beach holding up a starfish.

I kept scrolling and stopped at the one photo of *us* he'd never deleted from his account. It was from Spanish class, a few weeks before we started dating—Jake and me with our "authentic" dishes from Mexico, a class assignment. I'd made churros and he'd brought chips and salsa, not exactly a "dish," but he got an A anyway.

The teacher had made us conversation partners a few weeks earlier, so we sat at my desk and shared our food. Jake made such a seductive show of eating my churro that Shawna got up and took a photo and then AirDropped it to everyone in the classroom, making all of us laugh. Jake turned ten shades of red. He hadn't realized anyone else had been watching.

After Shawna went back to her desk, my gaze dropped to his lips, which were dusted in sugar, and then up to his eyes. Jake didn't look *at* me like the other boys did; he looked straight *into* me. The classroom vanished and a wave of heat roared through me. That was the moment I noticed the impossible length of his eyelashes and the dark hair curling at his neckline. We *linked*, and I had never unlinked.

Now this photo of him, sucking on my churro with me laughing in the background, was like mockery. He hadn't captioned it—he never captioned anything—but he also hadn't deleted it. I'd been analyzing what that meant since the tenth grade. Did he want me back? Was he keeping the door open? But it was Jake. He probably just hadn't scrolled down far enough when he'd deleted our other photos.

I tossed my phone onto my pillow. Sometimes I wished he'd block me.

◆ ◆ ◆

Shawna and I never got around to gathering the driftwood yesterday, so she came over at three to help, and she was so tired, she could barely drag herself down the cliff trail to the beach. "Are you high?" I asked.

"I wish," she said longingly.

"You need to stop. You know that, right?"

She rubbed her forehead and squinted at the sun. "Why's it so bright?" And then she started crying.

I glanced at the beach, at the driftwood scattered far and wide.

We needed to collect it and then dress for tonight. We didn't have time for a meltdown. I strode toward a piece of gnarled wood. "Tell me what's wrong," I said without looking at her.

"I think Marcus is seeing someone else."

Did a dog chase cats? Of course he was seeing someone else. I kept walking, and she trailed after me. I studied her wilted shadow, galled by her weakness. "Break up with him, then."

She sobbed harder. "I can't. I love him."

I whirled on her. "Why? He's an ass. He uses you."

Her fiery ringlets whisked across her face. Veins bulged in her eyes. "You don't know what he's like when we're alone. He's sweet. He tells me his problems. His dad used to lock him out of the house, you know, and once he had to eat dinner out of the garbage. He's struggling, Teg."

I picked up the big driftwood log. "Those are his problems, not yours. Are you going to help me, or am I on my own?"

She grabbed the other end of the log. "He bought me a ring."

This news halted me in my tracks. "An engagement ring?"

"A promise ring. He says maybe someday we'll get married."

I dropped the driftwood and took her hand in mine while the surf lapped at our toes. Sure enough, she wore a new etched silver ring on her finger. I forced a deep breath. "Do you really want to marry Marcus? The guy you're in tears over for cheating on you?" The ring glowed in the sunlight, a pretty manacle binding her to him.

"I don't know for sure he's cheating," she said.

"But you suspect." I crossed my arms. "Women are usually murdered by their husbands, you know."

She ripped her hand from mine. "Why would you say that?"

"No idea. Maybe because he hits you?"

Her freckled face turned pink; her pale eyes swam in tears. "He's right; you're a bitch. No wonder no one wants you." She stomped away from me and up the trail toward my house.

"No one wants me?" I shouted after her. "Are you fucking crazy?"

She kept walking.

I kicked the log, jammed my toe, and wanted to scream. There were seven guys chatting my ear off on Snap, and two full-grown men had asked me out in the previous week. People wanted me. It was the one thing that remained constant even as my grades slipped and my volleyball serves veered out of bounds—I was *hot*. A glance at the sand confirmed it; even my shadow was hot. Who on God's green earth did Shawna think she was talking to?

I sucked for air as if I'd run a mile, or been punched in the stomach. "People want me," I said out loud. I had texts and likes and offers to prove it.

But a contrary voice whispered on the breeze. *Then why are you alone?*

30

Jessica

The sight of Jake in handcuffs at school crushed me in a million different ways. How could he look so guilty and so helpless at the same time? I don't know if the cops apprehended him for hurting Tegan or for killing Shawna—or both—but I have to turn off my phone because everyone is asking me. It feels as if Jake and I are still attached, but like an amputated limb, there's nothing there.

I race from my last class to meet up with Chloe and Alyssa in the school parking lot. We signed up to join a search party on the coast after school. The urgency to find Tegan has grown exponentially since Shawna was found in the ocean yesterday. I spot Alyssa first, standing beside Chloe's Tahoe. "Holy shit, are you okay, Jess?" she asks. "Did Jake really run from the cops in world history?"

"He didn't run," I whisper. "They handcuffed him and—" My voice cracks as tears burn behind my eyes. Seeing Jake like that scared me worse than I thought.

Chloe wraps her arms around my waist and leans into me. "He brought it on himself, Jess. Don't feel bad."

Alyssa nods. "You know how much I adore Crystal Cove's cutest couple, but I'm with Clo; he brought this on himself, like he always does. You guys remember ninth grade when he tossed his chair at the wall in English because the teacher made him read out loud?"

I let out a breath. "That's not fair, Alyssa. You heard Jake read—he was embarrassed, not angry."

"You make a lot of excuses for him, Jess."

My throat tightens against a fresh onslaught of tears. Am I making excuses or giving viable explanations? The difference between the two has grown fuzzy since the party. "I have to work tonight. Let's get this over with."

We pile into Chloe's Tahoe, and the mood in the car deflates as we ride the rest of the way in silence. As Chloe's Tahoe approaches the coast, we drive straight into thick fog. It envelops the SUV and forms a ceiling above the grassy pastures that line each side of the highway. Cow and alpaca herds dot the greenery, and a salty scent reaches through the damp, beckoning as the sea does.

Chloe's headlights beam on as she follows the gently curving road through the foothills and then crosses over the Russian River into Jenner.

"Almost there," she says as the coastline appears ahead, a thin vein of yellow sand separating the endless ocean from the tall, sheer cliffs that contain it. The Sheffield home is just a mile south, at the top of one of these outcroppings. It sits smug on its perch, a modern geometric masterpiece, a blazing prism of glass against the fog-filled sky, a stubborn stand against Mother Nature, who will one day blow the house down.

I inhale the chilly air and release a long slow breath. Here, my problems feel small.

◆ ◆ ◆

When we arrive, the parking lot is full of volunteers who want to find Tegan. Chloe pulls into a parking spot and then hesitates before getting out of the car. "There's Grady," she whispers. Tegan's brother is standing with Hailey from school, talking.

"You don't look happy to see him," Alyssa comments.

"No, I am." Chloe bites her lip. "I told you, it's been weird since his sister went missing. I don't . . . I don't know what to say to him."

"Say you're sorry," Alyssa offers.

"For what? We don't know if Tegan's dead or alive."

Alyssa shrugs and points toward the boulders in the sea beneath Falcon's Peak. "Shawna's body was found out there."

That sobers us, and we spill out of the car and walk to the back of the volunteer line. Officials stand beneath a temporary canopy that is threatening to fly away in the blasting wind. It's twenty degrees cooler here than it was in town, and I shiver in my hoodie.

"Thanks for coming," Grady says, leaving Hailey and approaching us warily.

"What can we do to help?" Chloe asks. She avoids his sad gaze, and I feel sorry for Grady. Everyone probably acts weird around him; I know I'm not comfortable.

He ushers us to the front of the line, since he's a member of the family. The volunteer in charge guides us through the steps of registering, and Tegan's situation feels direr by the minute. "Write your names and school or driver's license ID numbers here," says the volunteer, consulting her clipboard.

"Our IDs?" Chloe asks.

The volunteer nods distractedly. "The police are keeping track of everyone who shows up."

I spot the detective I talked to Monday after the party, the one who was searching the woods around Tegan's house. I lied and told him that I'd just hit an animal on the road, and remembering that makes my bladder shiver. Detective Green frowns at first, as if he can't place me, and then recognition dawns and he nods.

The volunteer official interrupts the moment. "You'll be in area seven, over there. See the tall gentleman in the red baseball cap?"

Grady nods.

"That's Arjun. He'll tell you what to do. Here, have a water bottle." She hands each of us a plastic water bottle, and we make our way through the damp sand toward Arjun.

He's in his late twenties and sporting a broad grin, and he gets even more excited when he sees us. "More helpers, yes, good. We're just about to set out. Quick recap, folks: We're looking for anything unusual, anything that might not normally be on a beach. You're looking for thingamajigs, yes, just like the Little Mermaid—jewelry, utensils, cigarette butts, beer cans, bottles, coins—anything a human would use!"

Alyssa squints at me. "Little Mermaid?" she mouths.

Grady gazes at Arjun, nodding as if this volunteer is going to single-handedly find his sister. God, this kid is killing me. He's fifteen, the same age Jake was when he lost his dad, but Grady's a young fifteen—so trusting, the kind of person who believes that adults tell the truth, that the nice guys always win, that bad things don't happen to good people. Our heartless ocean has taught him nothing.

Passing by the smashing waves, we hike south to a staked

flag stuck in the sand, the marker for area seven. "If you find something, *do not touch it,*" Arjun warns us. "Find me and I'll radio it in to the authorities on hand. Spread out and don't go past that marker." He points at a flag farther away and then releases us.

We separate, but Grady's not moving. He glances at the volunteers scattered around the beach, his eyes watering. Every one of us is shorter than he is, but he looks so small and lost with the Pacific Ocean raging behind him. I grab his arm. "Don't turn your back on the ocean."

"What?" he yells over the surf.

"Never turn your back on the ocean, Grady. This beach is dangerous. Why don't you head toward the cliffs, and I'll search by the water?"

He nods, and then our eyes lock and I see the boy I used to play with at Tegan's—except now he's almost grown.

"Do you know why your boyfriend made that video with my sister?" he asks.

I gasp, stung. "Why is this Jake's fault? It was her bedroom, her TV downstairs!" I get that Grady wants to avenge his sister's honor, a true Southern boy, but I can't help him.

He shakes his head like he used to when he was little, quick, like a shiver. "Y'all think you know my sister, but you don't," he says quietly. "She's changed since her group hooked up with Marcus, but I know she wouldn't broadcast herself doing . . . that."

Now is not the time to tell Grady what I know about Tegan—she's a mean girl who wraps her insults in charm and honey. *Stunning jacket, Jess. Only you could wear that color. You're dating Jake? What a catch for you! I wish I had your figure; my boobs stretch out all my tops.* And straight from the mean girl's handbook, she has a posse of minions that do her bidding and flatter her—like Shawna, Brendon, Chiara, and Hailey.

Grady lifts his chin. "You're jealous." His words slice straight through me because they're true.

"Just stay away from the water, okay?" I bend my head and start walking. The dark wet sand is strewn with tangy-smelling seaweed, broken crab and abalone shells, driftwood, and lots of thingamajigs. The cave where Jake and I first kissed is a dark smudge against the cliffs and the tide is high at this moment, making it inaccessible.

I spend most of the two hours marking things as small as bottle caps—a piece of food wrapping, colored string, a girl's hair clip—and then wait for the forensic squad to send over an intern. Everyone got pretty excited about the hair clip, but it's plastic with a little heart at the end, nothing Tegan would wear. They bagged it up anyway.

Grady wanders around, mostly in circles. He shouldn't be here.

By the end of our shift, we're tired, wind-chapped, and defeated. I believe we've witnessed the most organized beach cleanup in Crystal Cove's history, but I doubt a single recovered thingamajig will help us find Tegan.

Grady slumps by Chloe's car, his shoulders quivering. "The police are bringing search dogs, but if Tegan's in the water . . . how will they find her?"

"Oh, Grady, don't think about that." Chloe rubs his back.

"If Jake didn't do this, that bastard Marcus did. He threatened my sister. He beat up Shawna. The police told my mom they found human skin and blood beneath Shawna's nails. They believe she fought with someone before she died."

"Holy shit," says Alyssa.

"Y'all best not repeat that," he adds. Grady faces the sea, his cobalt eyes scanning the waves. "One of the dogs is a cadaver dog." His jaw muscles clench.

Do you think there's dirt in her mouth? Amara asked me at Layers. Suddenly I feel light-headed.

Chloe stares up at Grady, who's a whopping seventeen inches taller than she is. "I'm sorry," she whispers, touching his hand.

His shoulders quake, and we're all silent a moment as he gains control of himself. "If we just had her phone, I—I think we'd know everything," he says, and my heart starts a slow gallop in my chest.

"Look, there's Brendon." Alyssa points out the Cameraman, who's arrived to help search. Brendon spots us too and starts to walk over, looking like he wants to talk.

"Such a jerk," I whisper. "I can't believe the police cleared him." After his interview, Brendon posted a picture of himself outside the police station, smiling and giving a thumbs-up with the comment: *Nothing to see here, folks. #IAmInnocent*

"An alibi is an alibi," Chloe says, guiding me into her SUV. "Let's go before he tries to talk to us."

The drive back to Crystal Cove is subdued, and my guilt explodes. *If we just had her phone, I—I think we'd know everything,* Grady said. The fact that his sister's phone has been beneath my mattress the last three nights is beyond unacceptable. I vow that tonight I'll power it on and see what's there, and then I'll figure out a way to turn it in without incriminating Jake or me.

On the way back to town, Alyssa brings up graduation and then quickly drops it. With each day that passes, it's starting to look more and more like Tegan won't finish high school. Ever.

31

Jessica

After the beach search, I work the late shift at Layers, but I'm anxious to get home and get to Tegan's phone. It's slow after the dinner hour, and normally I'd do homework, but I can't focus. I'm also freaked out about what I did today—searched the beach for Tegan's body. I'm cold and can't get warm, so I keep busy, sweeping, mopping twice, scrubbing, and doing all the prep for the morning crew.

Alyssa texts me right before closing: *There was a press conference after the search. Here's a link.*

I click on the video that was filmed in front of the police station at six. Tegan's parents, the police chief, a female detective, and Grady stand at the podium. Tegan's mom is immaculate, as usual, but looks tired. The police chief, who has slicked-back hair and a sharp widow's peak, speaks first.

"I'm Chief Waylon with the Crystal Cove Police Department. Yesterday we discovered the remains of Shawna Moore, a twelfth-grade student at Crystal Cove High School. Her body was submerged off the coast of Blind Beach in twelve feet of water. We do not have information on cause or time of death at this time, but it appears the student fell from Falcon's Peak into the sea, where she became trapped between two boulders."

Waylon draws a breath, looking shaken, and then a photo of Shawna's boyfriend fills the screen. "A person of interest in this case is Moore's boyfriend, Daniel Marcus Lancaster, age twenty-two. We've issued an all-points bulletin for his arrest. If you have any information regarding his whereabouts, please contact the Crystal Cove Police Department, but do not approach him. I repeat, do not approach this man. He's wanted for a prior assault on a young girl and we believe he could be armed and dangerous."

A shiver rolls through my body as Waylon continues. "It's possible that Shawna Moore's death is linked to the disappearance of her classmate Tegan Sheffield. As reported earlier, eighteen-year-old Tegan Sheffield disappeared without a trace from her family home during a party early Sunday morning. Our investigation began immediately and will continue until Tegan is found. We're exploring every angle of this young woman's sudden disappearance."

He adjusts his belt and continues as reporters click photos of him and the Sheffields. "I can tell you this: Security cameras in the home were disabled remotely at two forty-two a.m. by someone with knowledge of or access to the family's passcode. The girl's younger brother discovered Tegan missing at nine-thirty a.m. when he returned home from a friend's house. This window of time has become the focal point of our investigation."

My heart patters as I set down my cleaning rag.

"We're continuing to conduct interviews with the students

who attended Tegan's party, reviewing CCTV, and processing fingerprints and DNA collected from the scene to match to possible suspects. In the meantime, we'd like the public's help in locating Tegan Sheffield."

Tegan's portrait appears on the screen. "If you have knowledge of her whereabouts, or if you noticed any suspicious activity between two-forty-two a.m. and nine-thirty a.m. Sunday morning, please contact us immediately. Several community searches are in progress, with more scheduled. Call this hotline for information on how you can help." He pauses for questions.

A tall reporter yells out, "Tegan has been missing for six days, Chief Waylon. Did you suspect foul play immediately?"

Waylon averts his eyes from Senator Sheffield standing beside him. "The condition of the young woman's bedroom indicated that a struggle occurred there, and a county CSI team immediately processed the scene and searched the area. So yes, we suspected immediately, but we have standing arrest warrants out on Tegan Sheffield for lewd conduct with a minor and statutory rape, among other possible charges in a separate case. We had to consider the possibility that she panicked and fled after the illicit video she allegedly recorded went viral." In reaction to this comment, Tegan's mom flinches as if she's been struck.

I lean against the sandwich counter and turn up the volume on my phone as another reporter speaks. "How is this case related to the recent death of Shawna Moore? Were the girls friends?"

"They were, and yes, there's a strong probability the cases are connected."

"Was Shawna involved with the video Tegan allegedly recorded with a younger student? Do you believe Shawna was murdered?"

Waylon's eyes narrow. "I cannot comment further on the video. As for Shawna's death, it's suspicious and still under investigation."

"Will Tegan be arrested once she's found?"

"Yes." Waylon nods, and Tegan's mom leans hard on her husband, her fingers digging into his arms.

"Chief, you mentioned Tegan might be hiding to avoid criminal charges, but how likely is that, given the amount of days that have passed and her apparent lack of access to funds or a vehicle?"

Waylon shakes his head. "I won't give odds on that, sir. In conjunction with the family, we're organizing search parties and bringing in dogs to aid in Tegan's recovery. Blood droplets discovered in her bedroom have been matched to her DNA. If she fled on foot and she's injured, she might be in need of medical care."

Fled on foot? I remember the eyeball and the squeal of tires in the rain. My fear that I hit Tegan resurfaces. Right then, I hear a noise outside and glance up, but it's just the wind blowing.

A young female reporter speaks. "Chief Waylon, have you identified any real suspects? Could it be the male classmate Tegan allegedly molested?"

He purses his lips. "No comment. Senator Sheffield would like to make a brief statement and she will not be taking questions. Thank you."

He steps back, and Tegan's mom shoots him a nasty glance as she takes her place at the microphone. Then she looks directly into the camera. Her family stands three steps behind her.

She clears her throat and speaks in a slow, gentle drawl. "My husband and I are offering a fifty-thousand-dollar reward for any information that brings our daughter home to us. The idea that she is *hiding* is preposterous. Please, if you have Tegan or know where she is, call the hotline. If you do not wish to leave your name, you may remain anonymous. We—we love our daughter very much, and we just want her back." Her tightly threaded expression unravels, and her husband leads her away from the podium.

The reporters attempt to ask questions as the family walks away. I slide my cell back into my pocket, hands trembling. Chloe's at the gym, so I call Alyssa. As soon as she answers, I blurt out my fear. "What if I killed Tegan?"

"What the fuck are you talking about?"

"She went missing sometime after two forty-two a.m., and I hit the deer a little after three."

"So?" Alyssa hisses.

"The timing is right. What if she ran like they said on TV, and I hit her with your dad's car?"

"I was there. You did not hit Tegan." She takes a deep breath. "What's really bugging you, Jessica?"

I close my eyes and come face to face with the truth—I feel guilty about *everything*. A tear skids down my cheek. "I . . . god, this is awful. Part of me is glad Tegan's in trouble and glad she's gone. Just once, I don't want her to win."

Alyssa snorts. "Tegan's not *winning*. She vanished into thin air and her best friend is dead."

My cheeks burn. "I know that."

Alyssa turns down her TV. "She wanted payback, that's all. Tegan lost you in the fifth grade and she lost Jake in tenth. You both hurt her."

Her words stun me. "We hurt *her*? You're serious?"

"As a heart attack, but that doesn't mean you should feel bad or guilty. Feuds don't end well; case in point."

I swallow and wipe my tears. She's right, and I feel better but also blown away. I never considered this from Tegan's point of view, that Jake and I each dumped her. "The fight with her seems stupid now."

Alyssa laughs. "It was always stupid, Jess."

◆ ◆ ◆

After my talk with Alyssa, I finish locking up the sandwich shop. It's dark outside. Clouds mask the moon and the stars as I drive home wondering if there is a murderer loose in Crystal Cove or if it's my ex-boyfriend Jake. When I arrive, his pickup is gone and I wonder if his mom gave him his keys back, but when I glance up at his window, his blinds shift as if he's home. Is he watching me? I loved being neighbors when we were together, but now—it feels claustrophobic.

I think I'm in serious trouble, he said at school today. So vague! On Tuesday night he was not so vague. He promised that Tegan and her friends would *pay for what they did.* Then he went looking for Shawna, and now she's dead. Today he asked me to wipe his fingerprints off Tegan's phone. He has lied and could still be lying—to himself, to me, to the police.

I enter my house quietly, but a door creaks upstairs and Mom steps out of her bedroom, wrapped in a robe. She leans over the banister. "There's lasagna in the fridge if you're hungry."

"Okay, thanks."

She pads downstairs, smelling of night cream and toothpaste, and hugs me, releasing a long slow breath, the kind you make after a good cry. "How are you doing, sweetie? I know you and Shawna haven't talked in a while, but you used to be close when you played soccer."

An unexpected whimper escapes me, but this is not the time to break down.

"You have so much to deal with," Mom says quietly. "I'm so sorry. Do you want to talk to anyone? Can I help?" I consider this from her point of view—a dead body and a sex video. It's not far from what she expected with raising a teen. Mom is like a prepper at the end of the world, thinking, *I'm ready for this!*

"I'm fine, Mom," I say, sniffing back tears. "It's just a lot, you know?"

"I know." She strokes my hair and hugs me.

We say good night, and since I can't leave until she falls asleep, I heat up a plate of homemade lasagna, trudge to my room, and text Jake. He said at school that he wanted to talk tonight, but I don't have the energy for his tears. I text him: *I'm tired. Can we talk tomorrow?*

After a long pause, he texts back: *I need you jess. The police took my phone, my dna, my truck.*

My heart thrums. *How are you texting me then?*

Jake: *mom got me a new phone today. same number. can I come over pls*

Not now, I write.

Jake: *r u mad at me*

I stare at my screen in disbelief. Am I mad at him? He slept with my worst enemy and *enjoyed* it. He saddled me with her missing phone. He destroyed *us*, and I miss him with all my heart, but I'm also glad Tegan's gone, and that makes me sick. My feelings give me whiplash, and I can't respond to his question. I turn off my phone and confront my bed.

Sleep hasn't come easily since the party, and it's been worse since I hid Tegan's cell beneath my mattress. It bothers me all night like a rock in my shoe.

I slide it out, this cold and dented phone, this *evidence*. It's like holding Tegan's brain in my hands—her thoughts, memories, plans, and secrets. I wonder if she told anyone what happened between us at her Fourth of July bonfire. I wonder if she saved our texts. I have six attempts to guess the password before her phone locks me out.

Six attempts to guess a combination of six numbers or letters.

But to do that I have to power the phone on, and the second that happens, her cell will ping the nearest tower, the police will be alerted, and they will come, sirens blaring. They'll arrest Jake and me for hiding evidence. I need to do this somewhere else, somewhere safe, and I know the perfect place.

I leave my house at midnight, dressed in black.

32

Jake

"Come on, come on," I say to my phone, willing Jess to text me back. I watched her come home and stare up at my window, but then she scurried into her house as if she's afraid of me. My truck is gone, my house has been searched, and reporters were on our curb all day, and she missed the whole thing. I need her, but she's not answering my question, *r u mad at me.*

As the minutes tick by and my screen doesn't light up, my chest tightens, my eyelids twitch. I need her to *believe* me, or believe *in* me. I would never hurt anyone without a good reason. How do I know Tegan didn't attack *me?* Maybe I defended myself? No one can be certain.

I close my eyes and remember how good Jess smelled at school today when we talked in the alcove. It took everything I had not to kiss her until she forgot her first name—but then she took off, as if being around me scares her. Losing Jess to college would be less painful than this, seeing her every day and being rejected.

I text Manny: *can u come over*

He texts back right away: *On a date with Alyssa*

I scroll through people's stories, and it seems like everyone is out—at the movies, at restaurants, on dates, or throwing parties in honor of Shawna. Life goes on for everyone except me—and Shawna, I guess.

I turn off my brand-new phone and glide down the steps to the kitchen. The vodka bottle Mom keeps on the top shelf sings my name: *Jake, drink me.*

Fuck it.

My life can't get any worse.

The first drink is a memorial toast to Shawna.

The second is in honor of the Crystal Cove Police Department that I expect will arrest me at any moment. I don't know how blood got onto my T-shirt, but if it's Tegan's blood, I'm fucked. And if the police have Shawna's phone or pull her last texts out of the cloud, they'll see we were supposed to meet at Falcon's Peak, where she died. I will be even more fucked.

The third drink is for the hell of it, and now I'm just drinking. "Cheers, asshole!" I say to my reflection as I pour another screwdriver and swallow it in two greedy gulps. I don't think Jess is coming back to me, and the feeling is all too familiar, like when Dad died, like falling into a bottomless pit. She's gone and it's my fault, all because I followed my dick into a bedroom.

And now Shawna—fuck! Her body was lodged between the rocks while Manny and I were racing to the top of the bluff, feeling so alive. Was that seal I glimpsed beneath the surface *her?* It feels too close to home, too coincidental—no one will believe I wasn't involved.

And Tegan is still missing.

Or is she?

I grip my glass and peer out the kitchen window into the dark woods. "Tegan, are you out there? Are you behind *all* of this?" If Jess is right and the live feed was set up as a joke on Tegan, then maybe Tegan *isn't* missing. Maybe she's getting revenge on her friends for double-crossing her and she's setting me up to take the fall. If so, then who is next on Tegan's list? And where is she hiding? She must be close.

I lean over the kitchen sink and drink water directly from the faucet.

In my mind's eye, I imagine Shawna's body falling off that cliff, briefly flying, and then crashing into the waves, striking unseen boulders, becoming trapped underwater, and then her bright blood reddening the sea. *Jesus.* I pour another shot and swallow the liquor, reveling in its hot and numbing sting, then toss the glass into the sink and stumble into the family room.

People speculate online, saying that I've snapped and gone on a vengeful rampage—that I murdered Tegan and Shawna to prove my devotion to Jessica—but if I've lost my mind, how would I know?

Thinking of Jess reminds me of Brendon Reed, the Cameraman, and how he posted her reaction on YouTube. That reminds me of my promise to beat the shit out of him. I grab my laptop, pull up his channel, and watch the last seven of his stupid-ass videos. The FBI took down the one starring Jessica, but the Cameraman has over fifty thousand new subscribers since Sunday morning. The more I think about Brendon, the angrier I get.

People loved watching my girlfriend fall apart on his channel. He even zoomed in on her face, cutting between her horror and my tongue in Tegan's mouth. I don't care if he has an alibi or not; he must know something. I should *not* go to his house. I know that, but fuck it, I think it's time I paid the Cameraman a visit.

If I'm going to jail, I might as well get answers first.

33

Jessica

The wind has blown the ocean clouds inland, and the sky is clear on the coast, the stars glittering, the nighttime noises amplified. I park at Blind Beach and slip out of my car, shivering. The surf hisses in and out like dragons' breath, and the waves lick the shore like thirsty tongues. I pause, surveying the beach for driftwood bonfires or any other sign of life, but no one's here. My ankle boots echo across the pavement, and my keys rattle loudly in my hand as I walk toward the beach, with Tegan's phone an unwelcome passenger in my pocket.

When I reach the sand, my boots sink into its softness and my body takes on a lurching gait. I focus on the dark maw in the distance, the cave where I first kissed Jake. It's low tide—I checked the tide chart before I left—and the cave is accessible now. On the way, I pass a ring of flowers, photos, notes, and toys near the bluff below Falcon's Peak. It's a makeshift memorial to Shawna that someone set up after the beach search.

Keeping my eyes averted, I pass the wilting flowers and continue walking.

The sand near the cave is wet, and I have about an hour before the tide rolls in and traps me inside. The deepest recesses remain dry year-round because the cave slants up in the back, but the entrance gets blocked every high tide. However, I'm here for one of the cave's lesser-known features—it completely blocks cell phone signals.

With the ocean behind me, I flip on my cell's flashlight and sweep the cave's entrance. "Hello?" I whisper, not wanting to startle any lovers or a seal, both of which have happened before. My voice echoes back to me, and no one answers or moves. No seal lunges out of the darkness.

I walk several feet inside, just enough to scramble a cell signal, and sit on a rock that's been polished smooth by endless strokes of seawater. As I slide Tegan's phone out of my pocket, my heart rate speeds a notch. The scratched plastic cover is cold but still glittering, like Tegan herself. "Here goes nothing."

I power it on.

The cracked screen remains blank for what seems an eternity. Then it turns white and a black apple appears—the fruit of all knowledge. My breath hitches when the password screen materializes. I have six tries before the cell locks me out.

When Tegan and I were friends, her password was her parakeet's name along with the number one. I don't know if she still has the bird, but it's worth a try. I type *DOLLY1*. The phone shakes and orders me to *Try Again*.

I have five more attempts and decide to stick with the pet motif. The Sheffields' goldendoodle is named Boomer; I know this because whenever Grady is away for sports or vacations, Chloe takes care of the dog. I type *BOOMER.*

Try Again.

I glance out the cave entrance to the sea. One of the most common passwords on earth is 111111, and Tegan's arrogant enough to use it. I type it in, get the same response. *Try Again.*

Three more tries.

My thoughts flit to the past. Tegan and I were close once—true best friends. Everything that was mine was hers, and everything that was hers was mine. We traded clothes, toys, and secrets. We rode all over town on our bikes, buying ice creams and lip glosses, and attending library programs.

Everyone wanted to play with Tegan, but she was content with me. We had countless sleepovers where we made popcorn from scratch and watched movies in her basement. We teased Grady and made him run errands for us. We were happy—just the two of us, and her beloved Irish setter, Maggie.

Maggie died last year, and Tegan posted that she was "the best dog ever." The name *Maggie* has six letters.

I peer toward the lapping waves, feeling alone and hidden inside this cave, but not safe. I need to hurry. Holding my breath, I type *MAGGIE* into the phone.

It unlocks.

I did it! A slew of pent-up texts vibrate Tegan's phone and my heart thrums, expecting sirens or the whir of helicopter blades as the police descend upon me, but the night remains silent except for the pulse of the sea. I move deeper into the cave and switch the phone to airplane mode.

Swiping to Tegan's photos first, my hungry eyes swallow them.

Tegan on vacation; Tegan with her friends; Tegan posed in a hundred different outfits; Tegan with multiple cute boys, her pink tongue sticking out. She looks so happy, so *confident*. It's hard to believe she's missing and not the one pulling the strings.

I check her stored albums and find one titled *The One That Got Away*. It includes a single photo—a selfie of Tegan and Jake, taken when they were dating. They're cuddling in her canopy bed. He's shirtless with a mouth full of braces, and she's wearing his T-shirt, her hair tangled. They're each smiling at the camera, and I recognize the dreamy look in his half-lidded eyes. He's just had sex. She added a virtual heart-shaped sticker to the photo that reads *First Time!*

Gross! I almost hurl the phone across the cave.

This is too much, too intimate. I can't. I just can't. But I have to.

Breathing the cold sea air, in the very cave where I first kissed Jake, I skip to her text messages. My fingers tremble as I carefully swipe the damaged screen, and my eyes scan the cave entrance, hoping no one shows up to get high or make out.

I read all of Tegan's messages, from the beach bonfire up to her end-of-summer party. Most are innocent, just talk about what music to play and what time her parents would be back from Santa Cruz on Sunday. The texts between Shawna and Tegan are chilly. I heard at school they'd been fighting.

Then I read the newest texts from her friends, the ones that had been building up since she went missing on Sunday: *Where are you? Are you okay?* Or: *Stay away, the FBI is going to arrest you.* There's a cryptic one from Shawna on the night she died that reads *beetlejuice, falcon's peak.* I have no idea what that means.

The waves grow more aggressive, sending sea spray into the cave. I need to get out of here before high tide. I scroll faster through the messages, noticing Tegan didn't respond to any of the recent texts, but then, how could she? Jake had her phone, and now I do. I open her contacts and find Jake's number, but there's only one undeleted message between them, and it's from Jake on Sunday morning after the party: *Why did you film us?*

Us? Jesus.

I grip the phone so hard, a piece of plastic shatters off and cuts my hand, drawing blood. I suck the wound, my heart thudding. Even though the signal is blocked and the cell is in airplane mode, I feel like I'm holding a ticking time bomb. I need to finish and get out of here, but there's nothing on this phone that incriminates Jake *or* lets him off the hook. It doesn't explain what happened to Tegan or where she is now.

I find the texts I sent her after the disastrous Fourth of July bonfire. I read our exchange over and over until tears blur my vision. These messages are private. They have nothing to do with where Tegan is now, and I have the power to get rid of them. A crab scuttles out of the rocks, startling me into action. I swallow and then do it—I delete the messages.

But I know that deleting our text exchange isn't enough; a forensics lab could recover them. A full factory reset would be better. I open the settings, scroll to the reset button, and hover my finger over it. Swiping the button will destroy my texts and her responses forever, but it will also erase Tegan's entire history—all her photos, videos, texts, and upcoming plans. It will be like erasing *her*.

My heart knocks against my ribs. No, I can't do it.

I'll leave the phone here, in the back of the cave where it's dry. The whole town knows that Shawna's body was found near these waters. A battered pink phone in a cave will warrant their attention. Someone will find it and they'll turn it in.

I grab the sanitizer wipes I brought, and begin to wipe the phone clean of my fingerprints and Jake's as I walk deeper into the cave. On the way, my boots get tangled up in something, maybe seaweed, and I trip forward. My head smashes against a jagged rock on the ground, and hot blood dribbles down my forehead.

I pull my cell from my pocket and shine its flashlight. "Oh!" I tripped over a dark blue sleeping bag. Next to it is a small pile of food wrappers and fresh bottles of drinking water.

Someone is living here! Oh my god, what if it's Tegan? What if I found her hiding spot?

"Okay, okay," I mutter to myself, heart banging. I need to go. Now! Crap, I dropped Tegan's phone! I crawl around the cave floor, reaching and feeling into the nooks and crannies of the rocks. Empty abalone and crab shells clatter beneath my fingertips.

"What the fuck are you doing?" says a man's voice.

I leap to my feet, my breath steaming around me. The man stands at the mouth of the cave, carrying a bag of takeout. He's filthy; I can smell his body odor from here. He's wearing a baseball hat, but I recognize him.

It's Shawna's missing boyfriend, Marcus.

34

—

Tegan, July

"How is tonight so perfect?" I twirled barefoot in the sand, my phone clutched between my fingers. The boys watched me—Marcus, Brendon, and Chiara's new boyfriend, Dylan. My brother glowered from a beach chair, watching them watch me, ever my protector. It was July Fourth, Independence Day, and the bonfire was stacked and ready to light. Using my cash, Marcus had come through with two kegs of beer, six cases of hard seltzer, fireworks, and what he called "a little something for later"—blotters of ecstasy.

"Drugs?" I snapped at Shawna when I got her away from Marcus. We'd never included them at our parties before.

She gave me a dark look, still pissed about earlier in the day when I'd mentioned that it wasn't unusual for husbands to murder their wives. "Don't be a child," she said, and Hailey's eyes darted nervously between the two of us.

I rose to my full height, feeling like an overweight Barbie doll next to Shawna, who was stick thin and as white as milk. She looked exotic and chic in my old black micro dress and large black sunglasses. Her red hair blew around her chiseled face like curling flames. "Child?" I repeated. "Unlike you, Shawna, I'm eighteen. I'm old enough to go to prison."

She lifted her glasses and slanted her eyes at me. "You act like this is illegal."

"Did you seriously just say that? Drugs *are* illegal."

"Not in small amounts." Her eyes shot toward Marcus, and he ignored her.

I threw up my arms, thinking of what my mother would do to me if she found out about this. Mom encouraged parties—it was how *she* networked, after all—but a drug bust would quickly change that. I quelled my anger, forced calm breaths and what I hoped was a cold, reptilian gaze. "I guess I'm not up on current drug laws."

"It's no big deal." Shawna swiped her hand as if erasing me, and went to cuddle with her boyfriend. Rage swarmed through me as I imagined spiking her head like a volleyball and smashing it onto the court. If she hadn't been high already, this would have been the end for us.

I glanced at Brendon, and he approached me as if summoned. "Want a sunset photo?" he asked.

I wasn't really in the mood, but like Shawna, I'd pulled out all the stops on my outfit—ice-white ripped jeans with an American flag scarf threaded through the belt loops; a loose-fitting, furry half sweater, also white; and fresh three-hundred-dollar platinum highlights. The stylist had flat-ironed and then curled my hair into flowing golden-cream waves, and had added eyelashes that reached the moon, and silver glitter that made my blue eyes pop like planets. Hammered platinum hoops decorated my ears, and the low-cut top offered flashes of a star-spangled red bikini. I'd exfoliated and oiled my skin until it glowed like bronze. I'd be stupid not to pose for a picture.

"Sure," I said. "With the girls." I beckoned to Hailey and Chiara. They'd worked hard decorating all afternoon, and the beach was festive with a dozen tiki torches staked around the bonfire; circles of Adirondack chairs around smaller fire pits for roasting marshmallows; coolers full of water; and wooden bowls filled with fruit, energy bars, and candy laid out for our friends. The girls deserved recognition. "Sunset photo!" I called out to them.

They dropped their conversations and skipped to my side, and we headed to the waves. On the way, my gaze tangled with Shawna's. She lifted her chin and looked so much like her childhood self that I instantly forgave her and smiled.

She grinned back and tried to join us for the photo, but Marcus yanked her back onto his lap, his fingers clutching her flesh like talons. She dropped her eyes, and my anger resurfaced. He was stealing Shawna just like Chloe had stolen Jessica. He'd even given Shawna a promise ring. I shot him a nasty look that made him laugh.

As Brendon took the photos, the orange sun sank into the Pacific. Afterward he turned up the wireless speakers he'd connected to his phone, and my mood lifted. The few adults hanging out on the beach did exactly what I expected them to do—they left. Our first guests arrived, dressed in red, white, and blue.

I cracked open a White Claw and stood next to Brendon, whispering rumors into his ear about each person who showed up, while he giggled. "Photograph everything," I commanded him before I turned him loose. He nodded and left, lifting his camera to his eye. "Hailey," I said, "get Brendon a beer."

"Okay!" She bounced across the sand and retrieved a beer for him. Next to the massive pile of driftwood, Marcus watched everything.

That's when Chloe arrived with Jessica Sanchez in tow. The sight of her felt like razor blades in my stomach. Perfect, plain Jessica—wrapped in plaid. Jake's "girl next door." Her lack of effort mocked me. At least he was out of town and I didn't have to watch him follow her around all night. Jake was obsessed with Jessica, and it drove me crazy. What did she have that I didn't?

"Penny for your thoughts." My brother sidled up and threw an arm over my shoulder.

"Chloe brought Jessica. I told you she would. This is *my* party, Grady." My voice trembled with resentment. It was bad enough that Chloe came to my house and walked her dog with my brother, but to bring Jessica was a slap in the face, and everyone here knew it.

Grady sighed. "It's been years, Pea, and you never gave Chloe a chance when we were little. She's a good person. She works hard." He tightened his arm around me. "Jessica's all right too. Why do you hate her so much?"

The answer came, unbidden. "She thinks she's too good for me."

He lifted a dark blond eyebrow and quirked his lips. "You sure you don't have that backward?"

I shoved him. "Go fall in love with someone. Not Chloe. And don't drink."

"I don't love Chloe."

"Just go," I said, and he sauntered away, so handsome, so *young*. Grady still played with his magic set and obsessed on his dog like a little boy, taking Boomer exploring and teaching him tricks. My brother could pitch a ball at eighty miles an hour, and at six foot four he towered over most adults, but he was a baby, and his crush on Chloe was left over from his childhood fixation with her, but he didn't understand her like I did. Chloe's obsessive energy was not for him. It wasn't for any boy. It was for athletic glory. But Grady watched her as one watched a wild bird, hoping that one day it would land on his finger.

I sipped my drink, galled, as Jessica and Chloe help themselves to my food.

Over by the huge stack of driftwood, Marcus grabbed a container of lighter fluid, held it to his crotch, and then squirted it all over the stacked wood as if he were peeing on it.

"Don't!" I started, but it was too late. He lit a match and tossed it, and the bonfire roared toward the sky like a monster. Everyone screamed and cheered.

I'd planned to make a speech about freedom and then light the fire myself while Brendon played "The Star-Spangled Banner" through the speakers, but Marcus had ruined it. My stomach burned and sparked like the fire.

Confused, Brendon played the national anthem anyway, and our friends sang at the top of their lungs. Someone lit off an early firework, and it arced over the sea like a missile. I clenched my jaw. The fireworks weren't supposed to go off until midnight. Nothing about tonight was going the way I'd planned, and I felt like I was losing control.

If this was a preview of senior year, I already knew I was going to hate it.

35

Jake

"Shhh," I hiss to Otis as he follows me to the back door. "Be very, very quiet." He cocks his head, and I laugh and bump into the wall. "Where'd you come from?" I ask the wall. I have to bite my hand to keep from giggling. Otis whines as I shut the door on his face.

Outside, I toss the empty vodka bottle into the garbage. "Steal that," I mutter, addressing the cop, who has either stopped following me or has gotten better at hiding it.

The fresh air flows through my nostrils and chills my good humor. Jess never answered my text: *r u mad at me.* It's pretty damn obvious we're done. I'm probably wanted for murder. The police have my truck. And I might have an STD. I'm royally fucked.

I fix Brendon Reed's image in my head. All that matters is wiping his stupid smile off his face. Where the fuck is Jess's bike? I kick around the weeds until I find it where I left it Tuesday night. One tire got knocked loose when I went looking for Shawna, and now it wobbles as I board the seat and pedal out of my neighborhood.

After a mile of fresh air and pumping blood, my head starts to clear, but the ankle I injured while climbing the bluffs on Wednesday throbs, and I have a huge shiner around my left eye, compliments of Chase Waters at the gym. My life is falling apart, but I'm just drunk enough not to care. It's been almost a week since Tegan went missing—and Crystal Cove is asleep. It's the perfect time to have a little chat with the Cameraman.

Brendon lives in the Cherish Heights neighborhood off Blood Alley, the same dangerous road where Tegan lives. I haven't biked it since I got my driver's license, and never in the dark and never after drinking screwdrivers. The edges of my vision fuzz, my muscles are loose, and I'm pedaling in flip-flops, but I'm sober enough to ride in a mostly straight line.

The pavement unfurls beneath my tires, black and shiny with a bright yellow stripe down its center, like a poisonous snake. This unlighted road kills people with its blind curves and deep, nearly invisible ditches, and I keep looking back to make sure no car is coming. My legs burn with a buildup of lactic acid, my throat is parched, and my tires hum on the road like engines.

When I arrive at Brendon's house, I'm damp with sweat and out of breath. After laying down Jess's bike, I wait for my breathing to settle, then walk straight up to Brendon's double front doors and ring the bell.

It's after midnight and there's no porch light on, so when his mom finally answers, she looks confused. "Did you forget your keys— Oh, you're not Brendon." Mrs. Reed has known me since kindergarten, but she doesn't recognize me, maybe because I shaved my head, or maybe because she's never paid much attention to anyone besides her precious son.

"Is Brendon home?"

Her forehead wrinkles. "Are you his friend?"

A lopsided smile curves my lips. *The fact that you don't know if I'm your son's friend, lady, probably means I'm not his fucking friend.* But I can kiss ass as well as any other teen, so I smile wider. "Not really. Is he home?"

She gives a rusty laugh, as if I'm joking. "Brendon's working the late shift at the theater. Why don't you come back tomorrow?"

I sway slightly on my feet. Beyond Mrs. Reed, the pungent tang of fried fish wafts from the kitchen. "Sure, okay." It's a lie; I'm not leaving.

The sound of Mr. Reed's nasally voice drifts from between the house's cracked siding. "Who's here? Is it the police again?" His wife murmurs something as she closes the sun-damaged front door.

The police *again?*

There's a worn spot outside their home where Brendon parks his car. I wander over to it and lean against the trunk of a cypress. There are no streetlights here and there's not much noise, just the calming breath of the ocean. I'm warm in my sweatshirt, so I close my eyes, thinking about Tegan and her friends and the video.

Brendon not only filmed Jessica's reaction. He edited, titled, and posted the video on YouTube to try to get more popular. I've been distracted, and this won't bring Jessica back to me, but it's time for a reckoning.

Sometime later, Brendon's car appears and drives up the long gravel driveway, plunking over potholes. I don't bother getting up, just watch him park, check himself out in the rearview mirror, and then get out of his car. He stretches, slides his keys into his pocket.

"Hey," I call.

He leaps like a startled cat. "Who's there?"

I push myself up, stretch my shoulders. The sight of him kicks my adrenaline into high gear and flushes out the last of the alcohol. "It's Jake."

Brendon's eyes flit to his house. "What're you doing here?"

I circle him, blocking his path to the front door. The sky is bright with stars, and the moon is a sharp band of silver, illuminating the Cameraman—his sweaty spikes of hair, his bleary eyes. The scent of movie theater popcorn permeates his designer clothes. "I'm here because of what you did to my girlfriend."

His mouth twitches. "I made her famous."

"Fuck you." I snatch Brendon by the throat and drag him into the dark shadow of the cypress. He's taller, but I pin him against the scraggy trunk. He owes me answers. "Where's Tegan?"

He tries to slug me and I knee him in the groin. "Where is she?"

"I don't know," he wheezes. "She took off, I guess. Why can't anyone take a joke?"

"Because it wasn't funny."

He laughs. "But it was!"

"Shawna's *dead*, Brendon." I punch him in the mouth, and his smile vanishes. He breaks free and knocks me sideways. I twist, crack him in the jaw. "You know what's going on. You have to tell me!"

"Get the fuck off me!" he screeches. His knuckles slam into my injured left eye socket, and hot tingles splay across my skin. My fist smashes into his chest, then his face again. There's a snap when his nose breaks. Blood gushes, soaking his sweatshirt. My knuckles graze his teeth. Saliva spray floats in the air.

"Stop!" he screams.

I shove against him, my face an inch from his. "Tell me the truth—where's Tegan? What happened in her bedroom? I can't remember anything."

Brendon reels back and laughs, blood dripping from his lips. "You're so fucking stupid. You still have no idea, do you?"

I shake him. "No idea about what? Tell me!"

He taunts me, laughing. "Jake and Tegan sitting in a tree, K-I-S-S-I-N-G."

My skin turns cold; these are almost the exact words Tegan said to me at the party. The sudden roar of the ocean drowns him out—but no, that's my voice, screaming obscenities and questions at Brendon with each punch and kick to his body. "Where's Tegan? What don't I know? Stop laughing!"

But he's not laughing anymore; he's covering his head and crying, "Go away!"

I cock my fist. "Tell me or I'll fucking kill you. Did I do something to Tegan? What do you know?"

His tears shift to hysteria. Blood leaks onto the soil as he starts singing, "First comes love, then comes marriage—"

My fist launches, catching him again across the jaw.

His mom and dad fly out of the house, and Mr. Reed knocks me to the cold ground. I flail, still screaming and cursing.

Brendon sinks to his knees, dazed.

"Stop it!" Mr. Reed snarls as he pins me to the gravel driveway. His breath stinks. "Leave my son alone!"

Precious, perfect Brendon. Fuck. I watch the stars wink overhead, impassive, aloof. I can't believe my life has come to this. I don't like beating people up; I like to have fun. But I guess fun can lead to trouble.

"I'm calling the police. You—" Mrs. Reed points at me, crying, her mouth a red slash. "You said you were his *friend*."

I don't bother to correct her. I want to give up, give in.

Mrs. Reed snatches Brendon's phone from his back pocket and presses three buttons. She's using speaker, and I hear a voice on the other end of the line say, "Nine-one-one. What is your emergency?"

My heart wallops and before I know it, I shove Mr. Reed away and I'm off, running.

"Get back here!" screams Mr. Reed.

I stumble down the gravel lane and into the redwood forest. Why the fuck did I ride here in flip-flops? Rocks and tree needles stab my feet, and the gash I got in Tegan's bedroom threatens to re-open, but I keep running. These woods go on for miles and miles, meet up with a state park, and continue for miles more. There are bears, mountain lions, and illegal-marijuana growers, but none of that scares me more than the cops.

I don't want to run from them, but I don't want to face them either. Not tonight, not ever. If I get killed out here, maybe it won't be the worst thing.

I sprint faster.

36

Jessica

"I said, what are you doing here?" Marcus repeats.

My body starts to tremble. No one hides in a cave unless they did something very, very bad. He glares at me, and I drop my eyes. He's only seen me twice before, once at Tegan's bonfire and once at her end-of-summer party, and I don't believe he recognizes me. I focus on his shoes. "I—I . . ." How do I explain why I'm here, after midnight, dressed entirely in black?

"That's my shit," Marcus says, pointing at the sleeping bag and the water bottles.

I retreat from the nest he's made for himself. The police said he could be armed. They said he's dangerous. I raise my hands to show him I'm harmless. "I wasn't taking it."

He jerks his head north, toward the parking lot a half mile up shore, and strides toward me. "You should get out of here."

I nod, but where is Tegan's phone? It flew from my hands and could have landed in a crevice or slid beneath an outcropping.

Panic flutters in my chest. I was going to leave it here—but with Marcus? The thought niggles at me because it's not a bad idea.

"Is that blood?" he asks.

I touch my forehead and feel a hot slick substance where I smacked it. "Um, yeah, I think so." I hug the edge of the cave as I make my way to the mouth. If he murdered Shawna, and maybe Tegan too, then he has nothing to lose by killing me. I need to get out of here before he realizes I recognize *him*.

As I approach the mouth, Marcus steps aside. It appears he's not looking for any more trouble, and my insides shudder with relief. I duck past him, exit the cave, and splash into the surf. Crap! The tide has come in and the waves are shoving against the cliff. I'm ankle-deep in seawater.

Marcus walks deeper into the cave, where the floor shifts up and the water cannot reach. Soon he'll be trapped in there until low tide, unless he swims out. I see why he chose the cave; it's an excellent place to hide since it can only be accessed a few hours per day. Some locals believe it's never truly safe. A large sleeper wave could fill the cave and drag its occupants out and into the open ocean, where they would surely die.

Not my problem.

I slap through the surf to the main expanse of beach and then break into a flat-out sprint. Marcus isn't the college student he claimed to be—he's a liar and maybe a killer.

In the parking lot, I jump into my Honda and lock the door. My engine turns over with a violent shake, and I speed out of the lot, thinking, *Come on, little Civic. Get me out of here!* I feel as if someone is watching me, and my skin tingles.

All the way home, I peer at my rearview mirror, believing every lone car I see is Marcus, following me, if he has a car. Most of the vehicles turn onto side streets, but one car does not. It follows me at a distance, taking every turn I take. My heart ratchets up a notch.

I flip on the music and push my preset buttons until I find a happy song. I'm being paranoid. Marcus isn't following me. He didn't recognize me. When I reach my neighborhood, the car behind me keeps going, and I let out my breath. It was nothing. No one.

Safe in my driveway, I pull up my friends' accounts and study the party photos again. There's Marcus, glaring at Tegan, but is that anger on his face, or is it lust—or both? Hard to tell, but everyone says he abused Shawna. He could have killed both girls. It makes a hell of a lot more sense than Jake killing them.

Excitement rumbles in my chest. The fact that Marcus abandoned his apartment for a sea cave feels like proof of his guilt. And if I turn him in, the police will search every inch of the cave and find Tegan's missing phone. They'll believe he's had it all along, and I won't get in any trouble.

The police listed an anonymous tip line during the press conference. Trembling and chilled, I find it on the police website, dial, and reveal Marcus's location.

"Are you sure you don't want to leave your name?" the operator asks. "If this leads to Tegan's return, you'd be entitled to the fifty-thousand-dollar reward."

"I'm sure," I say, and end the call. It's done, and the police should already be on their way. I let out a long hopeful breath.

My windows have steamed up, and as I wipe away the condensation, I gaze at Jake's darkened window next door and imagine him in bed, frightened and alone, and my bitterness about his cheating cracks, just a little. I want to talk to him, tell him that I believe he's innocent. Innocent of murder, anyway.

With a deep breath, I exit my car, then creep around to Jake's back door, which his family never locks. Staying quiet, I tiptoe up his stairs and into his bedroom.

His scent assails me when I open the door, and my heart swells with memories. "Jake," I whisper, reaching for the large body on the bed. "Jake?"

A wet tongue swipes all over my face. Otis! I turn on Jake's lamp and ward off the attentions of his needy Lab. "Otis, shhh!"

Once the dog is calm, I glance around, see that Jake's favorite shoes and the wallet he keeps on his desk are both gone.

It's Friday night, and a sweep of jealousy brushes through me. Where is he?

I pull up Snap, and when I locate Jake on the map, my heart stutters. He's in Cherish Heights—in Tegan's neighborhood. I call, and his cell goes straight to voicemail. What is he up to now?

37

Jessica

Back in my car, I refresh the Snap map and see that Jake's avatar is no longer in Cherish Heights. He's deep in the woods. I call him again, and this time he answers, his breath panting. "Jessica?"

"Where are you? What are you doing?"

His footsteps are quick and noisy, the wind whistles on his end of the call. "Some shit went down at Brendon's," he says. "His mom called the police and I took off."

"You're running from the police? Seriously, Jake, that's—"

"They're going to put me in jail, Jess!" Jake's footsteps slow until he comes to a halt. He's winded and takes a moment to catch his breath. "You think I'm stupid, don't you?"

"I didn't say that."

Emotion throttles his voice. "But it's true. I'm running through the woods in fucking flip-flops and I don't know where to go. I keep getting in trouble, and I really, really don't want to go to jail." He starts to cry. "If I hurt Tegan, I'll turn myself in, I swear, but

I—I don't believe I did. I just want someone to tell me the fucking truth about that party." His voice cracks.

I start my car. "Don't move. I'm coming to get you."

Jake sucks in his breath. "Stay home, Jess. I don't want you getting in trouble too."

"Already on my way." I drive out of my neighborhood and accelerate, switching Jake to speaker. "You're close to the river, so meet me at the old rope swing, okay?"

"Jess—"

"Just be there." I end the call.

◆ ◆ ◆

Fifteen minutes later, I pull off the main road and park beneath a massive oak, hoping the tree will shield my car's presence in case the police drive by. Stumbling over rocks in my ankle boots, I find the hidden trail that leads to the rope swing, our summer hangout from middle school.

The trail curves through the redwoods toward the river. Here the air is thick and heavy and warm, unusual for the coast. Fresh rain clouds roil overhead, and the crescent moon shines between them, creating silver streams. As I descend toward Jake and the rope swing, my broken heart beats a little faster, a little stronger.

Discovering that Marcus is hiding out, not dead or on vacation or anything, has changed everything. What if Jake has been innocent all along—of everything except the cheating, of course?

It was easy to suspect him at first. He had Tegan's phone, and he said Tegan and her friends would pay for what they did. But Jake can't bake muffins without screwing them up. If there was a category for "Most Likely to Get Framed for Murder" or "Most

Gullible" in the yearbook, Jake would win. Maybe someone is setting him up, and that someone is probably Marcus.

The idea that I've misread Jake makes me question everything else about him, and about us. By the time I reach the rope swing, tears threaten to cascade down my cheeks, because the truth is, I haven't been totally honest with him.

"Jessica!" he calls.

I don't see Jake at first, but there he is, standing by the water's edge, hunched like a fugitive. Filthy mulch, webs, and stringy redwood tree bark cling to his clothing. His cheeks are flushed, and his half-lidded gaze burns into mine. The only time his body is still is when he's looking at me.

I grow anxious the closer I get to him. Jake's knuckles are raw and crusted with blood, and his face is swollen and bruised, but I'm not afraid. I'm worried. If he's innocent, then he's been fighting and skipping school and running from the cops because he's *scared*, not guilty. If he's innocent, then he's been putting up with false accusations and public humiliation without support from anyone, including me. If he's innocent, it explains why he's been so terrified, erratic, and desperate. How is this suddenly so clear?

He watches my face, his eyes glowing hotter. Right then the clouds darken and thunder booms. Warm rain spits from the sky, splattering our shoulders, and as the water drips down Jake's face and darkens his shirt, he strides across the shoreline until we're inches apart. I touch his rough, bruised face with my fingertips, and my throat closes. "Are you okay?"

He licks his lips. "I am now."

"My parents would kill me if they knew I was here."

He steps closer, and I feel the heat radiating from his wet skin. "I think they'd kill me, not you." His forehead crinkles when he smiles, but his eyes remain focused, piercing me, scattering my thoughts.

The world shrinks as it fills with the sound of our breathing. The way his wet shirt clings to his muscles makes my heart beat faster. I slide my fingertips across his flat stomach and then slip them beneath his T-shirt, where his skin is hot and damp.

"Jess," he whispers, his voice shuddering.

I miss him, I want him, and while I don't totally forgive him, the last of my reserve crumbles. "Come here," I whisper.

He blinks, and then swoops me into his arms. My stomach twirls and I block out all we've been through as he wraps my legs around his waist.

Our lips meet, and we kiss as if it's the first time, eyes closed, lips eager, tongues exploring. Goose bumps spread across my skin as Jake holds me tight. Our bodies fit together like they always have, and when I squeeze him back, he smiles against my cheek. I didn't expect us to fit together as if we've never been apart, but we do, and now I don't want to stop. "Let's go to the shed," I say, surprised at the huskiness in my voice.

The shed is a small abandoned building that middle schoolers have fixed into a hangout. It's stocked with camping chairs, a card table, curtains and pillows, coolers, graffiti on the old wood walls, and a large window seat that fits two. There's usually only one reason for a couple to hang out in the shed, but Jake appears confused.

"Let's go to the shed *together*," I clarify.

He laughs, and a happy smile erupts across his face. "I'll go anywhere with you, Mrs. Healy." I startle at the nickname, but let it go for now.

Taking his hand, I lead him farther down the path. When we

arrive at the shed, he kicks open the door and carries me inside like a bride. After setting me down, he pulls off his dirty sweatshirt, turns it inside out, and lays the clean side on the window seat like a blanket.

"Give me your jacket." I remove my coat, and he spreads that out too, making a clean bed. He turns on his phone flashlight and sets it on the table, gently lighting the room, and then he turns to me. "Are you sure you want to do this, Jess? What's changed?"

I kiss him. "Don't talk." After trailing my fingers down his stomach, I tug on his belt loop, pulling him closer and smiling at the combination of joy and concern on his face.

"I don't have a rubber," he says.

"We can do other stuff." I kiss him harder.

A soft moan rumbles through his chest, and my body starts to hum. I pull his shirt over his head and balk at what I see, more bruises across his ribs and stomach. "Jake?"

"Shhh, I'm fine." He covers my lips in kisses and starts to remove my top, but I stop him and do it myself. He watches, his pulse thrumming as my sweater hits the floor. I'm not wearing a bra, and our eyes meet over our naked chests.

His hands sweep down my back as he squeezes me against him. I open my eyes, see that his are closed. He's lost in me, lost *with* me. This—I've missed *this*! Kissing Jake is still like riding a rocket—body floating, heart thudding, breath gone.

The rest of our clothing slides off like water, and we're skin to skin, his cheeks blazing, my body humming. Our feelings swirl like fairy dust, rising, rising. As the rain showers the earth outside, the rest of the world disappears.

◆ ◆ ◆

Afterward we cuddle together and listen to the rain pelt the thin roof. Jake traces patterns over my bare skin until I get cold and pull on my warm fuzzy sweater. "Tell me what happened at Brendon's?"

"We had a chat," he says vaguely, rubbing his chewed-up knuckles. "But he didn't tell me anything new. I'm so tired, Jess. Nothing's made sense since the party."

I tell him the news I've been holding in—that I found Marcus. "He's been hiding in a cave, Jake, *our* cave."

His head snaps up. "Whoa, whoa, how did this happen?"

I tell him the whole story, except the part about deleting my texts with Tegan. No one needs to know about that. "Marcus didn't recognize me, but I called the hotline and turned him in. The police said at the press conference he's a person of interest. Once they have him, they can question him. He did something wrong, Jake, or he wouldn't be hiding."

"I guess. Are you sure he didn't recognize you?"

"Yeah, don't worry about that. Listen. Shawna told you everyone is lying, right? Well, would she have said that to you if you were one of the liars? I think it was a warning; she was trying to help you. I don't think you did anything to Tegan."

"Really?" A grin breaks out across his face, followed by a frown. "Why did I have her phone, then? The simplest explanation is that I did it."

"The law of parsimony?"

"The law of what?" He rubs his tired, swollen eyes, and I reach for his hand but then think better of it. I don't want Jake to confuse sex with getting back together, especially after the *Mrs. Healy* comment. Instead I touch him with words. "The simplest explanation is that you can't remember because you didn't do it. I believe in you, Jake."

He exhales as if dropping a huge weight, and then leans back, arms behind his head. "That's all I needed to hear, Jess. I can survive anything. I can survive the zombie apocalypse, as long as I have you."

I smile and look away, my body still cooling from our encounter. He *does* think we're back together, and I get how he misread this, but how do I fix it without crushing him? I'm not ready for more. I want to forgive him for cheating on me, but I haven't yet. I owe him the truth, though; I owe him more than that, actually. "Jake, I have something to tell you."

He grins. "Yes, beautiful?"

A strange voice shouts from the woods, interrupting us, "This is the Crystal Cove Police Department. Identify yourselves and come out with your hands on your heads!"

38

Jake

Heart knocking, I roll off our makeshift bed and tug on my jeans. Jessica does the same. Our eyes lock, round and panicked as we dress. "How did they find us?" I hiss.

She lifts one shoulder. "Your phone?"

"Shit, I forgot to turn it off." Truth is, once I saw Jess teetering down the path in ankle boots, tight black jeans, and a high ponytail to save me, I forgot *everything*. Now we're caught and trapped like rabbits. "I'm sorry," I say to her.

She offers a worried smile. "Don't run this time, please."

"I won't." As we lift our hands to our heads, the sight of my swollen knuckles reminds me that I beat Brendon pretty good. "I think I'm going to jail, Jess."

She rushes to my side, and we hold each other one last time as footsteps stomp around the shed and the glow of a flashlight pierces the black windows.

"You have one minute to exit the building," shouts the cop.

Our hearts collide against our chests, and Jess quivers in my arms. "It's going to be okay," I promise as I nuzzle her neck, absorbing her, memorizing her as if I'll never see her again.

"Ask for a lawyer," she says.

I groan because my mom can't afford a private lawyer. A trial will be expensive, and my mistakes are going to ruin my family, fucking ruin them. I should never have dragged Jessica into this either. "I'm sorry. I'm so fucking sorry," I whisper into her ear.

"Shh," she says. "We'd better go."

I nod and call toward the door, "We're coming out." The cop asks us to identify ourselves, so we give our names, state that there's no one else in the shed, and then exit, hands on our heads.

Seconds later, I'm on the ground with my arms wrenched behind my back, my wrists zip-tied. An officer I don't recognize leans over me, his slick hair hanging over his forehead. "You're in serious trouble, Healy." He yanks me to my feet.

Officer Lee is here too and she questions Jessica, asking what time she arrived at the river and if she knows anything about my assault on Brendon. My girlfriend stammers over her answers.

The other officer warns me of my rights, his voice echoing in the silent forest. "You're under arrest for the assault and battery of Brendon Reed. You have the right to remain silent . . ."

When he's finished, Officer Lee speaks. "I have some news for you, Jake. We found Tegan Sheffield earlier this evening."

"Oh my god," Jessica cries.

I sag toward the ground as relief washes through me. Holy fuck, they found her. "Good, that's good."

The male cop recoils. "It's not good, Jake." He guides me into the squad car. Officer Lee releases Jessica after she promises to drive herself straight home, and then I'm carted away. The ride is quiet, and even my tears are silent as I realize what Officer Lee didn't say.

She told me they'd found Tegan, but not if they'd found her dead or alive.

39

—

Jake

Posing for my mug shot reminds me of school pictures. Do I smile, or is that creepy? Do they want a side view? Turns out they don't care as long as I hold still.

I'm at the Juvenile Justice Center ten miles from Crystal Cove. Processing me takes forever because they're short-staffed and have to wait for the day shift. Around seven in the morning, officers finally fingerprint me, search my body, photograph my bruised face and knuckles, make me shower, and issue me a cheap set of clothing and bedding.

"You need to call your parents but you can eat something first," says the guard, who heard my stomach rumbling during the fingerprinting. He leads me to the boys' dormitory, shows me my cell, and then walks me to the cafeteria.

The inmates grow excited when they see a new person entering their domain. There's posturing and curious looks, but after a few lewd jokes and sizing me up, they seem to accept me. A couple of the older guys make room for me to sit with them for breakfast, blasting me with questions about what I did to end up here that I evade. I fully expected to have the shit kicked out of me as soon as I walked through the door, so this isn't bad.

Soon after I finish eating, a guard collects me to call my mother. As I dial, my stomach tenses. She's going to be upset.

As expected, Mom jumps all over me as soon as I say hello. "You didn't come home last night. I was so scared, Jake! The police said you fought with Brendon. Is this about Tegan? Are you okay?"

"Mom, I'm fine. It was just a fight."

Instantly she's crying. I assure her I'm not hurt, not badly anyway. She collects herself. "I know you're angry, Jake, and you must feel helpless, but every decision you make is hurting you. I don't understand this rage." A fresh sob ripples through the phone line. "What am I supposed to *do*? I want to help but I don't know how."

I clear my throat, unsure how to respond. "I'm just a fuckup. I'm sorry."

"You are not!" She's silent a moment. "Don't speak to anyone without a lawyer, okay? You'll only make things worse. I'll find you a good one."

"I'll use the court-appointed lawyer. Don't waste your money."

There's another long pause from Mom, and then she says, "I'm not sure we'll qualify for the free one."

"Why not? We're broke, aren't we?" Mom makes one dollar over minimum wage.

"Will you stop arguing and let me be the parent? They charged you with"—it sounds like she's rattling a piece of paper—"lying in wait, assault and battery, and causing great bodily harm. An ambulance took Brendon to the *hospital*, Jake. A good lawyer could mean the difference between coming home or . . . not coming home for months."

I hear our refrigerator door open and close, and wish I were there with her and Cole and Otis. Mom's footsteps click across the floor as she talks. "Dad's insurance money paid off the house, so I can borrow off that. Just don't talk to the police. You need professional advice. Promise?"

My jaw clenches. No way am I going to let Mom borrow money off the house. Dad insisted she pay it off with his life insurance money so we'd have a cheap, safe place to live. The leftover cash went into the bank, but then Mom's car died, and she had to buy a new one. Also, Cole's sports and summer day care is expensive, so she dips into savings each month for that. She can't afford to pay back a loan. The guard signals me. "Hey, Mom, my time is up."

"Jake—"

"I love you." I hang up on her. I know she's going to hire a lawyer anyway, so to prevent that, I tell the guard I want to speak to Detective Underwood now. Right now.

◆ ◆ ◆

Forty-five minutes later, I'm in an interrogation room at the juvenile center. "Handcuffs off," Underwood orders, and the guard unlocks my hands.

Officer Lee is still on duty, and she joins us, not unfriendly but not smiling either.

Underwood wears her usual battle-hardened expression. "Good morning, Jake. I hear you've decided to talk?"

I nod slowly, wondering if she's expecting a confession about Tegan, because I only plan to talk about Brendon.

Underwood repeats the process from the other day, explaining that the interview will be recorded. She confirms for the record that I have voluntarily declined my right to have an attorney or parent present and that at seventeen years old, it is within my power to do so. I give verbal consent, feeling queasy.

"Jake, you were arrested for assaulting Brendon Reed, and we'll get to that—"

"There's nothing to get to. I did it. Can we fast-track this?"

"Are you *sure* you don't want a lawyer?" Officer Lee asks, her dark eyes blinking rapidly. "It's your right to have one present."

"We've established that, and he declined," Underwood growls. She ticks something off in her notes. "We'll take your written statement about Brendon in a few moments, but first let's talk about the Sheffield case. Officer Lee informed you that we found Tegan?"

My heart skitters, but I'm curious. "Yes. Where was she?"

She leans back in her chair. "A team of search dogs arrived last night and found her body." Underwood studies me. "What do you think about that?"

My stomach plummets. My fragile world collapses around me. Body? Tegan's dead? "I think it's terrible," I murmur.

"That we found her?"

Her words make me flinch. "No. It's terrible that she . . . that she died."

"That's the thing, Jake. Tegan's not dead. She's alive."

I glance from Underwood to Lee, confused. "But you said you found a body?"

"Semantics," Underwood says, smirking. "It surprises you, doesn't it, that she's alive?" There is a long awkward pause where none of us says a word.

They're trying to trip me up, make me confess. After squirming a minute, I fill the silence. "I guess so; she's been gone almost a week."

"Your hiding spot was clever," says Underwood. "We searched the Sheffields' grounds and the swimming pool area the day Tegan went missing, and then focused on the woods surrounding her house and the beach. But Tegan was crammed inside her family's poolside storage bench this entire time. She was so lifeless beneath those chaise lounge cushions, the officer who looked inside didn't detect her presence. For a person to survive"—she glances at her notes—"six days without food or water, I imagine you're very surprised to learn she didn't die."

I glance helplessly at Officer Lee. "I—I didn't put her there."

Lee sighs. "Tegan's at the hospital in a coma, Jake. We're waiting on an official report, but it appears she's been unconscious since Sunday morning. Her body expended so little energy that she was able to endure without food or water."

I nod along with her words, but I can't fully process what I'm hearing. This should be good news, but it feels very, very bad. "Is she okay?"

"No, Jake, she's not okay." Underwood peers at me with undisguised distaste. "Tegan has visible abrasions and contusions that indicate a struggle. The doctors suspect severe head injury, and possibly a broken arm. We're still waiting on DNA results for the blood on your clothing, but we suspect it will be hers."

My head drops, and sweat breaks out across my shaved scalp.

Officer Lee takes pity on me. "Tegan's not off the hook for

having sex with a minor or for creating the explicit content with you, Jake. We will file charges, and while she's in the hospital, we'll be testing her for STDs and pregnancy. As her victim, you'll be notified of those results."

I gape at her, my pulse speeding. Did she just say *pregnancy*? Tears bite the backs of my eyes, and I blink to keep them from falling.

Underwood raps the table with her knuckles, bringing my attention back to her. "Last night, while you were assaulting Brendon Reed, we found this, thanks to an anonymous tip." She retrieves a bagged cell phone from her satchel and places it in front of me—Tegan's phone. I recoil from it, and my throat clamps shut.

"I see you recognize it, Jake. We found it at Blind Beach, in a cave allegedly inhabited by Daniel Marcus Lancaster, another person of interest in Tegan's case."

Underwood collects a sheet of paper from her file. "We lifted two sets of fingerprints off the phone and ran them this morning, and guess what? Neither belongs to Marcus or Tegan. One belongs to *you*, Jake, and the other is not in our database. Who do you think the second print belongs to?"

I swallow and shake my head, feel my panic rising.

She flares her shoulders. "We don't know either, but we have a new theory regarding your girlfriend, Jessica Sanchez. We believe the second print will match to her. Are you two working together?"

Working together? Jesus. I close my eyes, feel my stomach crinkle into a ball. Yes, this is very bad. Why didn't Jessica wipe the phone clean like I asked?

Underwood stands and hovers, her tall body shading mine. Her voice drills into my brain. "If you want to *fast-track* things, why not start by cutting the bullshit."

She throws a glance at Lee, who takes over. *Good cop*, I think. Officer Lee touches my arm, real sympathy lurking deep within her eyes. "It's time to tell us the truth, Jake. We can help you and Jessica if you cooperate. If you don't, our hands are tied."

I sit up and draw a deep breath. No fucking way am I going to throw Jessica under the bus. She's the only good thing in my life right now, and she's trying to help me even though I cheated on her. But I feel like I have to give the detective something. Maybe it'll make her leave me alone. "The only thing I didn't tell you before is that I had more than a few beers, okay? I drank tequila too, and that's why I blacked out."

Lee pats me. "This is a good start."

But Underwood loses what patience she had left. "That's it? Come on. Walk us through this, Jake. What compelled you to cram a five-foot-nine-inch varsity athlete into a five-foot-long box? Did Jessica make you do it?"

"No," I roar. "Leave her out of it."

"Look at these texts we pulled off your phone." Underwood shoves a transcript of messages in front of me—random, unanswered texts that I've sent to Jessica since Sunday morning.

please call me

tell me what to do and i'll do it.

im yours jess. i dont want to live without you

i told you the truth im not into Tegan. im glad shes gone.

jess please all I want is to make you happy. i'll do anything. i'll make sure they never hurt you again

My scalp tightens across my skull as I read the texts. I should ask for a lawyer; it's not too late. But having one won't change my story.

Underwood wiggles the paper and imitates my voice. "*I'll make sure they never hurt you again*. This is the problem, Jake. You're caught in a feud between two girls that, according to your classmates, dates back to the fifth grade. They're using you to hurt each other, but you're the one who's going to end up in prison. Is this you?" She throws down another photo, a grainy nighttime image of a male riding a bike near Falcon's Peak, taken from a traffic camera.

My lips tighten.

"We know from Shawna's cell phone records that you had plans to meet her, the same night the coroner says she went over the bluff. You told Jessica you'd do *anything* for her. Does that include murder?"

Terror shreds what's left of my nerves. "What about Shawna's boyfriend? He's the one living in a cave!"

Underwood pounces. "He's running from a warrant in another state, and his fingerprints aren't on Tegan's phone. Tell us, Jake, is Jessica using you to get revenge?"

"No, fuck no!" I think about last night, remember the slick feel of her skin against mine, the heat between us, the taste of her lips. Loving Jess is the opposite of flying or floating or any of that bullshit people think is romantic. Being with her is like landing—it's the only time I feel grounded and strong and safe. I *would* do anything for her, that's the truth, but she hasn't asked me to hurt anyone.

There's a long silence as the officers watch me, waiting. My adrenaline subsides and I fold into myself. "If you think I killed Shawna or put Tegan in that bench then arrest me, but leave Jessica out of it."

Underwood and Lee exchange a glance that seems to say *He's hopeless*, and then Underwood gulps her coffee, which must be cold by now, and switches gears. "Let's talk about Brendon Reed. Why did you hide outside his house and ambush him?"

"Ambush?" I scrape at the seam of my jeans. "I wasn't hiding. I was just waiting."

"But you planned the attack?" Lee probes.

Something shifts inside me, and my anger resurfaces. "Look, they started this—those three. Tegan, Shawna, and Brendon. They hurt Jessica on purpose and filmed me, and they're the fucking criminals. Why aren't they in jail?"

Lee writes furiously on her paper, and Underwood circles me, a triumphant gleam in her eye. "They aren't in jail because one of them is dead and the other two are in the hospital, and the common denominator for each crime is *you*."

"But you're going to charge them, right?" I wipe at the fresh sweat dripping down my forehead, because no matter what I say or don't say, I'm probably incriminating myself. It's time to stop talking, probably past time.

"You're very concerned about their punishment, aren't you, Jake?" Underwood grimaces. "Let me ask you this. Do you see yourself as a knight in shining armor, vanquishing your girlfriend's enemies? Because from what Officer Lee witnessed last night at the shed, it's working. You got your girl back."

I drop my head into my hands, feeling cold and scared, and ready to give up. "Please leave Jess alone. She didn't do anything wrong."

"Of course she didn't. She has you for that."

Underwood shoves a new photo in front of me, and when I look, the buzzing in my head abruptly ceases. It's a crime scene photo of the Sheffields' dirty pool house storage bench with the lid open. Tegan's body is inside, her legs bent, her head tilted to fit. Her eyes are closed, and she's so pale, she looks blue. Her hair curls around her shoulders, still glittering from her hair spray. One set of false eyelashes is stuck on her cheek, black and spidery. She looks like a crumpled corpse smashed inside a coffin, and bile flows up my throat. "I didn't do that to her," I whisper.

Underwood paces in front of me, turning on her heel with each point she makes. "This is how we see it, Jake. You had *motive* to get rid of Tegan; you wanted to punish her for the live video. You had *opportunity*; you were the last person with her. And you had *means*, the physical ability to subdue and carry your victim."

She strides closer, her eyes flaming. "By your own admission, you don't know if you kissed the queen of England that morning. The *truth* is that you have no alibi and no memory, but we don't need your confession. The evidence tells the story, and Chief Waylon wants an arrest in Tegan's case *yesterday*. If you have any hope of receiving a reduced sentence, you need to cooperate."

I imagine my mother, visiting me in prison for the next twenty years, and shudder. Maybe I should admit I did it, get this over with. Maybe I'll get ten years instead of twenty. I'll be twenty-seven when I get out. And it's possible I'd get paroled sooner than that. I could have a life. . . .

Underwood rises to her full height and pounds the table, causing both Lee and me to flinch. "The truth is that on Sunday morning, *you* fought with Tegan in the bedroom, cracked her mirror, and broke her arm. *You* used her phone to disable the Sheffield security cameras at two forty-two a.m. And then *you* carried her—under cover of darkness—to the storage bench. There you stuffed her inside and *left her to die!*"

Something roars up within me, some truth that I know about

myself. I like girls, but I don't like *hurting* girls. The person who did this horrible thing is fucking *not me*! I kick back my chair and face her, my muscles quivering. "I didn't do that! I would *never* do that."

Lee jumps out of the way, knocking over her water bottle, and I glare at them both. "You have the wrong guy, and I think you fucking know it. That's why you haven't arrested me." My breathing ratchets up higher, louder. "You don't want the truth. You want what's easy."

"The truth?" Underwood sits back down and appraises me. "You're the one in the dark, Jake. Remember the fifty-dollar bet?"

I sit also and resume picking at my pants seam, trying to look unconcerned.

Underwood crosses her arms. "If you care so much about the truth, you should ask your girlfriend about the bonfire party."

My breath whooshes out of me, and a sick feeling invades my body. Something tells me I should walk out of this room and not look back, but I can't, I fucking can't. I lift my head. "Why would I do that?"

Underwood slides over a transcript of text messages between Jessica and Tegan from July, then drops the hammer. "Because your girlfriend is the one who made the bet."

40

Jessica

"Jessica!" Mom calls from downstairs.

"What?" I mumble from beneath my covers. It's Saturday morning, and my head is swirling with everything that happened last night—unlocking Tegan's phone, running into Marcus, making out with Jake, getting ambushed by the police, and learning that Tegan's been found. I had nightmares about Blood Alley too, the screeching tires and that flash of eyeball. Did they find Tegan near the road? Is she dead? Did I kill her?

When I wasn't having nightmares, I was plagued by visions of a cave filling with blood instead of seawater. And when I cleared my mind of that, I remembered Jake's blissful expression when we kissed, and then the horror on his face when the police took him away. I want to help him but not for the reason he thinks. I was so shocked he cheated with Tegan that I suppressed my part in it, but now my guilt has roared to life.

I text Chloe: *Did you hear they found Tegan?*

She responds in seconds: *What do you mean found her? Where!!!!*

Me: *That's all I know.*

Chloe: *Is she alive? omg*

Me: *I don't know*

"JESSICA!" Mom shouts.

"WHAT?" The crackle of the television and the sound of Dad noisily clearing his throat drifts toward me from downstairs. Did I forget to unload the dishwasher or something?

"Come here!" Mom calls.

Whatever she wants, it's not good. I pull on a pair of sweats and a clean University of Colorado Buffaloes T-shirt and skip downstairs. "Why are you yelling at me?"

"Sit down," she says. Dad is dressed for golf, and Mom's robe hangs listlessly off her shoulders, but they're like two frightened horses, jumpy and wide-eyed. Dad points to the television. "They're going to repeat the story in a minute."

My pulse flutters. This has to be about Jake and Brendon's fight or about the police finding Marcus and Tegan's phone. I face the screen, my fingernails tapping my hips.

A male newscaster stationed outside the police station speaks. "More information is coming from Crystal Cove's police department this morning about the dramatic hunt for Jacob Healy that led to his arrest. It began around one o'clock this morning when officers responded to a nine-one-one call in the elite Cherish Heights neighborhood about an assault in progress on a local teen.

"The police released the alleged attacker's identity this morning because he's now the lead suspect in Tegan Sheffield's missing-person case. His name is Jacob Healy, and he's a local Crystal Cove twelfth grader. Healy fled on foot into the woods. The police apprehended him at an abandoned shed near the Russian River where he'd met up with another teen from Crystal Cove."

I grunt, grateful they didn't mention my name.

As the man reports, photos of our high school, Brendon's neighborhood, the river, and Jake's handsome eleventh-grade photo flash across the screen.

"As reported earlier, Tegan Sheffield vanished during a party at her home last Sunday morning after allegedly recording a sexually explicit video with Healy that went viral online. Evidence discovered in the girl's bedroom indicates a violent struggle occurred."

The reporter takes a breath, briefly consults his notes. "The Sheffield case heated up last night when search-and-rescue dogs led detectives to Tegan's location—a five-foot-long poolside storage bench on her family's property. The popular eighteen-year-old student was discovered inside beneath a pile of seat cushions, comatose but breathing. The officer who initially searched the bench has been put on administrative leave. The missing teen has been transported to Saint Joseph's intensive care unit, where she remains in a coma. Should she regain consciousness, Tegan faces possible criminal charges regarding the illicit video."

The reporter's words slowly sink into my brain. "Tegan's been home this entire time?" I ask Mom. "How could she survive a week without food or water?"

"The coma protected her," Mom answers.

Drone images of the Sheffield home and swimming pool fill the screen, and there is the dirty old storage bench, tucked near a supply shed. It's as if whoever hid her there wanted her to be found, or didn't have time to hide her somewhere better. But she was *too* close, it seems. The searches have been focused on the beach and the woods, and on her friends' homes and properties—not her own backyard, not since the first day.

The pool footage is followed by charming images of Tegan herself, posing with her volleyball, riding a horse in Lake Tahoe, and hugging Grady on her balcony.

I sink onto the sofa, and my parents sit next to me as the news continues.

"Local authorities have been tight-lipped about this investigation until today, but embattled teen Jacob Healy has been a suspect from the beginning. Multiple search warrants were served on the teen yesterday after officers collected evidence from Healy's garbage can that revealed blood on his clothing and broken fragments of a dresser mirror, believed to be from Tegan's bedroom.

"The Crystal Cove Police Department continues to investigate the suspicious death of Tegan's best friend, Shawna Moore, but an arrest in either case won't be forthcoming until all the evidence is reviewed and processed. Back to you, Teresa."

My breath leaves my body. "I don't believe it," I say.

Mom grips my hand. "I know, honey, it's terrible. I'm sorry."

"No—someone set Jake up. Shawna told him everyone at the party is lying."

Dad curses, and Mom's expression goes blank with surprise. Then her eyes shift to Dad. They believe I'm blind to Jake's faults, but they don't know what I saw last night. "It's the only thing that makes sense," I explain, wondering why the newscaster didn't mention Marcus. Didn't the police find him after I reported his location? And what about Tegan's cell?

"What makes sense is the evidence," Dad grouses.

The anchorwoman asks the reporter a follow-up question.

"Have the police indicated a motive for these horrible attacks, Alan?"

The reporter grimaces after a short video delay. "No, they haven't, Teresa, but it appears the attacks are related to the illegal recording we reported on earlier in the week. The FBI has since removed the footage from the internet, but Healy's alleged assault victims—Tegan Sheffield, Brendon Reed, and possibly Shawna Moore—have each been implicated or questioned in the video's production. Apparently, it was a prank against Healy that some students say got out of hand. He'll be arraigned in juvenile court on Monday."

The news anchor nods. "This type of behavior is not uncommon—drinking, pranks, and sexting—but this case really highlights the criminality of it when a student is underage, turning what might have begun as a fun evening into jail time."

"It sure does, Teresa. It's a caution to teens across America."

"Thank you, Alan." The anchor turns to the people at home, and the split screen vanishes. "We'll keep you updated as further details develop in this shocking case that, for many high school students, hits too close to home."

Dad gets up to turn off the TV. "Do you see Jake for who he is now?" An angry tear slips from his eye that he quickly wipes away. "I'm changing the locks on our doors and getting an alarm system." The skin beneath his jaw quivers as he lays down the law. "You are to drive *straight* home from school and work, and no more runs to Blind Beach alone. You hear me?"

I rise from the sofa and back away. "Why are you punishing me?"

"It's not—that's not what I'm doing. If Jake posts bail, he'll be out while the authorities investigate."

"But—"

Dad inhales, and his body grows larger. "Do you think he's

attacking these kids for *you*, Jessica? Because it's not romantic; it's dangerous."

I cross my arms. I don't know what to think. Jake beat up Brendon. That's all I know for sure, and I can't say I feel bad about it. And why didn't the news mention Marcus? Didn't the police find him?

Dad pushes harder. "A girl is dead, and Tegan is close to it. Brendon is in the hospital with a broken face. Jake did that!" He grips my shoulders. "Snap out of it."

"He would never hurt me, Dad."

"Just because he hasn't bitten you yet doesn't mean he won't."

"You're comparing him to an *animal?* That's low. I'm going back to bed." But I don't feel as calm as I sound. My entire body trembles as my brain slowly begins to comprehend that Tegan is in a coma.

Upstairs, I check my phone. I have an unread message from Chloe: *call me*

A second later she answers and I start talking. "Can you believe someone put Tegan inside a bench? How is that even possible?"

Chloe is silent a long moment. Then she asks: "By *someone*, don't you mean Jake?"

My spine contracts. "No, it was Shawna's boyfriend. Look at the party photos people posted; check out the way Marcus was glaring at Tegan. He doesn't like her. Didn't Grady say he threatened her—that's why they searched for Tegan at Cow Mountain? I think he attacked her and planted her phone in Jake's truck—"

"Wait, what? Jake has her phone? The police didn't mention that."

I stumble over my words. "It—it doesn't matter. The point is, Marcus set him up."

"How involved in this are you, Jessica?" When I don't answer right away, Chloe gets angry. "Jake is dragging you down, Jess. He doesn't want you to go to college, he suffocates you, he attacked you in the woods. . . ."

"You're exaggerating."

"He threw you into a tree, Jess!"

"Why are you mad at me?"

"Because you're letting him do this to you. You're better than he is. Can't you see it? Even if he didn't hurt Tegan, Jake's going nowhere. You need to stay focused, like me, if you want to get anywhere in life."

My mouth falls open. Tears sting my eyes. "Why are you telling me this?"

"Because I care about you," she says, softening. "I'm on your side, not his. I'm sorry if that upsets you."

"You sound like my dad."

She laughs softly. "Absolutely *not* my intention, but it's probably because he loves you too."

Tears skid down my cheeks. "I'm so confused."

"I know. It's okay. I'm sorry I've been wrapped up in the college showcase, but I'm here if you need me."

"Thanks, Clo. What are you doing later?"

"Beam, then bars. What else would I be doing on a gorgeous Saturday afternoon?"

We talk a few more minutes before hanging up. All that's certain is that Tegan's alive, which means Jake didn't kill her. And neither did I. Whatever I hit on Blood Alley, it wasn't her. Maybe now the nightmares will stop.

✦ ✦ ✦

During dinner the following evening, Dad notices the Band-Aid on my forehead from my cave injury. "You're getting clumsy," he says, forcing a smile.

"I'm fine." I offer no explanation, and Dad lets it go. He's trying to keep the peace since our last fight about Jake. Besides, he thinks I'm safe, with the new security cameras he installed and Jake still incarcerated at the Justice Center. It's Sunday evening, Jake's arraignment is tomorrow.

Mom sips her wine, one sharp eye on me. The school sent home a letter telling parents to watch their children for signs of mental distress. The letter is taped to our refrigerator door with the mental health hotline highlighted in pink.

Doctors are keeping Tegan in a medical coma so her body can heal without the accompanying mental stress of what happened to her—attempted murder, it appears—and what she did—recorded herself having sex with a minor. It's a lot to wake up to. Also, they had to rebreak her arm for it to heal properly, and they're monitoring her brain activity because of her concussion. It'll be at least a few more days before they let her wake up, and she might have brain damage.

All this is tumbling through my mind when colored lights swirl through the front window and across our walls in shades of red and blue, jolting me to the present. "Oh no." I drop my fork and rush to the window. My parents stand behind me as a police cruiser pulls up to the curb. Two officers step out, clean and polished, badges gleaming.

"What's he done now?" Dad mutters, glancing at Jake's house even though he's not home.

But the officers ignore Jake's walkway and walk up ours. My

spine tightens. The grilled chicken rolls over in my stomach. There's a knock at our front door.

"What in blazes?" Mom says.

Dad opens the door, and a blast of wind ruffles my hair. The officers lean back on their heels. "We're looking for Jessica Sanchez," says one.

Dad's mouth falls open and I step forward, trembling. "I'm Jessica."

"You've been identified as a person of interest in the Tegan Sheffield case. We need you to come with us for formal questioning. You have the right to remain silent and to refuse to answer these questions. Anything you say can and will be used against you in a court of law. You have the right to have an attorney present during questioning, and if you cannot afford an attorney, one will be provided. Do you understand?"

Chills sweep my skin. "Yes, I think so."

"Mr. and Mrs. Sanchez, you can follow in your own vehicle."

The officers take hold of my upper arms, and I scamper to keep up with them as they walk me toward the squad car, my thoughts pulsing. I need a jacket, my purse. I have nothing with me but my phone. A few neighbors are watching, so I stare at my feet as the officers march me toward their car, usher me into the back seat, and drive away from the curb.

I let out a shaky breath. This must be about Tegan's phone and the texts I deleted—maybe the police recovered the messages.

Maybe they know what I did at the bonfire.

PART THREE

The Truth

41

—

Tegan, July

The bonfire popped and crackled on the beach, swirling embers into the breeze. Brendon's music roared through my body, propelling me as I danced.

Shoes—gone.

Sweater—off.

Brendon put on my top and pranced around as if he were me, making everyone laugh. I twirled in my jeans and star-spangled bikini top, arms high, feet stomping and twisting in the sand, girls and guys all over me, grinding and kissing. Silken skin. Warm fingers. Hot tongues. Fun.

Grady watched, his eyes as big as an owl's, worried. I waved at him, the ogre.

Then he strode over and tried to get me to stop, to go home. "You're high," he screamed over the music. "Let's go."

I peered up at our glass-prism house on the cliff, a nest for eagles. "I can fly," I said.

Grady wiped his face. "You can't fly, Pea. Let's go home." He grabbed my arm, and I fought him like a marlin at the end of a fishing line.

"Let her go." It was Marcus, shorter than Grady but bigger.

"What did she take?" my brother shouted.

"Love, man. Just love." Marcus's shirt was off, and I ran a hand down his chest, curious. He looked rugged in the firelight, like a cowboy, with his storm-cloud eyes and bearded jaw, his low-slung hat. Why did I hate him so much? I couldn't remember.

He drew me in and we danced, gliding away from Grady. My brother, watched us go. A lost boy. I wiggled my fingers at him and then forgot him as Marcus and I spun closer to the flames. He licked my neck, and my head fell back. I laughed. His hand slipped inside my bikini top and his fingers knew right where to touch, like Jake's. My Jake.

Jessica watched us from the shadows, her face scrunched like a pig's.

Marcus leaned toward my ear. "I got something to show you." His arm snaked around my waist, and we began to walk away, toward the cave where couples had been disappearing all night.

But the dark opening in the cliff gaped like a monster's mouth. "No," I managed, my tongue thick, my jaw clenched. The cave was full of teeth and blood. I didn't want to go there.

His arm locked around my waist like a roller-coaster restraint, no getting off until the ride was over.

"You fucking bitch!" Shawna flew up from her Adirondack chair and ripped Marcus away from me, but I'd already forgotten where we were going, what we were doing.

"What did you call me?" I asked her, light-headed.

She pushed me, and I fell onto the sand, and my bikini top

barely held me in. Our friends laughed, and phones appeared in their hands, like evil eyes, recording, recording. Shawna stood over me, spit flying from her mouth. "You think you can have anyone you want, don't you?"

I forced myself to my feet, my head clearing just enough to fight back. "I *can* have anyone I want." I adjusted my bikini top and leaned toward Marcus, ignoring the rot I felt in my stomach.

Jeers arose around us, and I blinked, confused about the battle I was fighting.

Shawna inhaled so deeply, I thought she might pop. "That's a lie. You can't have Jake Healy. You begged him to come back after he dumped you."

My breath hissed from my lips. "He didn't dump me."

Then the bonfire popped again, shooting embers into the night sky, and Jessica appeared, shrouded in smoke, Chloe by her side—my former friends. Jessica's gaze impaled me like a challenge, and Chloe crossed her arms, the ever-vigilant sidekick.

I stepped back, reeling, slipping. Behind me, the dark water was smooth, a rare miracle for the Pacific. "I can have anybody," I repeated, throwing a violent glance toward the boys. "If I wanted Jake, he'd come back to me."

Jessica's expression melted and reformed into metallic rage. An answering ripple shot through Chloe. I felt naked in front of them.

"You always want what you can't have," Jessica growled.

My eyelashes fluttered and the party felt ruined, but I could save this moment. I would not go down at my own bonfire. I straightened and dug into my ammunition for my greatest weapon, my smile, the big one, the one that said, *I'm prettier than you, richer than you, smarter than you, and better than you.* I beamed it out and blinded everyone with it. The phones dropped, the mood shifted.

I lifted one shoulder, casual, effortless. "I'll tell y'all what I want," I said, voice sultry. "I want to go night swimming. Anyone brave enough to join me?"

Without waiting, I shed my jeans and walked into the water in my swimsuit, followed by Brendon and Chiara, several boys, and one very angry girl—Jessica Sanchez.

42

Jessica

It turns out criminal defense attorneys are available twenty-four hours a day. My parents found one online, and she's sitting across from me, Ms. Jackson, wearing a pantsuit and looking alert, as if it's not eight-thirty on a Sunday night.

She consults privately with us first. "We're going to let Detective Underwood do the talking and show us what she has on you, Jessica. She didn't arrest you, which means either she's building a case or she believes you have information that could incriminate yourself or someone else. Without knowing her angle, we're here primarily to listen. If I allow you to answer a question, say yes or no only. Don't embellish or try to explain. If you're confused or worried, tell the detective you'd like to consult with me. Understand?"

I wipe my hands on my leggings and nod.

My parents cling to each other as Ms. Jackson opens the interrogation room door and allows the detective inside. Her name is Detective Underwood, and the way her wiry muscles ripple beneath her suit jacket gives me the impression she plays some kind of sport and that she's competitive, very competitive. A camera records the interview.

"Jessica, Jessica." Underwood glances at a pile of notes stacked in front of her. "Your name has come up one too many times in our case against Jacob Healy. It's always interesting when a suspect's girlfriend gets so involved."

"Ex-girlfriend," I whisper, wondering what she's talking about.

Ms. Jackson squeezes my arm and shakes her head, a reminder not to speak.

"Right," says Underwood. "Ex-girlfriend. That's even more interesting. You've worked harder than we have to solve this case."

"I was trying to help Jake," I say, then bite my lip. Do they know I called the tip line? It was supposed to be anonymous.

"Jessica," Ms. Jackson hisses. Then to Underwood, "It's late. Tell us why we're here, Detective."

Underwood purses her lips. "Let's begin with the lie your client told Detective Green."

My breath catches, and I'm glad my parents are sitting behind me so I can't see their faces.

"On Monday afternoon at four-ten, you gave a statement to a Sonoma County detective in the woods behind Tegan's home. You claimed you had just hit a deer on Blood Alley and were looking for the body."

The word *body* floats in the room, almost visible, like a word from *Sesame Street*, and I wonder why she's bringing this up.

"He didn't believe you, Jessica. On a hunch, we questioned Alyssa Jung again about your drive home from the party. After informing her about the penalties for giving false information to the police, she changed her story. Alyssa stated you struck an unidentified creature with her dad's BMW at approximately three-fifteen a.m. on *Sunday*, during the time frame when Tegan went missing. Then you cleaned the blood off the car. Did you have two accidents on that road, Jessica?"

My mind reels, and I feel terrible that Alyssa got dragged into this.

"Don't answer that," Jackson says to me. Then to Underwood, "I'd like a copy of that statement."

Underwood nods. "Everything we discuss tonight will be made available to you. I'm not hiding anything." She gives me a pointed look. "Alyssa's father gave us permission to tow his BMW to a forensic lab, where it will be examined. I have a team at his house right now, picking it up."

My shoulders go rigid. "Alyssa wasn't allowed to drive it. That's why I didn't—"

"Jessica, stop," warns Ms. Jackson, and then she turns to Underwood. "Are you alleging that Jessica struck Tegan on Blood Alley and left her there? Because the victim was not found on the road but in a storage bench at her home, right under your nose."

Underwood rolls her shoulders. "I'm not alleging anything. I'm asking your client why she lied and why she scrubbed the blood off the front grille with bleach, potentially or willfully destroying the evidence."

"Evidence of what? Roadkill?" Ms. Jackson snorts and shuffles her notes. "You are wasting our time, Detective."

Underwood flares her nostrils and glances at her notes. "After Jessica struck the creature on the road, she dropped Chloe at her house and then drove Alyssa home at approximately three-fifty-three a.m. There, she scrubbed the car, and then jogged home. Tegan was discovered missing at nine-thirty a.m. Sunday, which means Jessica had *five and a half hours* to return to Blood Alley, retrieve Tegan's injured body, and stuff it into that bench."

"After she got home, she went straight to bed!" Mom blurts, and Ms. Jackson shushes her.

"Can you prove that?" Underwood asks. "Did you watch your daughter sleep?"

Jackson jumps in. "Jessica's parents have not been cautioned, and they are not the subjects of this interview. Strike Mrs. Sanchez's words from the recording."

Underwood talks over my lawyer. "Jessica, did you put Tegan in the bench?"

"No!" I sputter.

Ms. Jackson raises her voice. "Stop trying to get a rise out of my client, Detective. Jessica's seventeen years old and this isn't a courtroom; let's cut the theatrics."

"Theatrics," huffs Underwood. "From all accounts, Tegan has bullied and harassed Jessica online since she started dating Jake. Then Tegan slept with him in front of all their friends. That is *theatrics*. It's enough to push a downtrodden girl toward revenge. It's a compelling motive to make Tegan disappear."

"No, no, no," Mom whispers.

Ms. Jackson clicks her pen. "Your theory doesn't explain the destruction in Tegan's bedroom."

Underwood smiles. "Why would a popular girl abandon her party and race down a dark road at night? Here's a theory—she was terrified. In a moment of regret, Jake assaulted Tegan in that bedroom, but she escaped and fled, and your client struck her with the car. Jake and Jessica paired up after the accident to get rid of what they believed was a dead body." Underwood considers me, one eyebrow lifted. "Am I warm?"

"That's a wild story," says Jackson. "I can think of a number of counter scenarios."

The women square off, and I want to speak so badly that I have to clamp my mouth shut. Underwood recalibrates. "Alyssa Jung indicated you swerved *toward* the creature on the road, Jessica. Did you hit it on purpose?"

"Don't answer that," says Jackson.

"Were you drinking?" Underwood prods.

"Don't answer that either."

My blood seeps from my brain, and suddenly I have to pee.

Underwood appears satisfied with herself and places her hand on her laptop. "Last night, our tip line received this call at one-oh-two a.m. about a person of interest named Daniel Marcus Lancaster. The caller discovered him hiding in a sea cave." Underwood plays the recording of my phone call. "Is that your voice, Jessica?"

Shock steals my breath. "They told me it was anonymous!"

Underwood's face splits into a grin. "It is, well, it was. Thank you for confirming your identity as the caller."

My father groans, and I feel my face flush.

"I need a word with my client," says Jackson. She ushers me out of the room and leans over me, her perfume swirling around us. "Jessica, I'm going to hold your hand and I'm going to squeeze it every time you to start to open your mouth, to remind you to stay quiet. All right? You're not helping."

"I'm sorry."

Back in the interrogation room, Underwood steeples her fingers. "It fascinates me that you were exploring caves after midnight by yourself, Jessica. One look at your parents' faces right now indicates this is not normal behavior. Did someone tell you Marcus was hiding there?"

"No comment," says Jackson.

"Okay, then what was your client doing in an ocean cave in the middle of the night?" Jackson squeezes my hand, and Underwood keeps pressing. "I'd like to suggest that she was destroying more evidence. I'll go a step further and suggest that you're the one pulling the strings, Jessica. You're controlling Jake and seeking revenge against a girl you had a falling-out with in elementary school."

I suck in my breath, and Jackson squeezes my hand so hard, it hurts. I shake my head.

Underwood consults a sheet of paper. "The texts to you that we pulled from Jake's phone read like a bad soap opera: 'Please call me. Tell me what to do, and I'll do it. I'm yours, Jess. I don't want to live without you. I told you the truth. I'm not into Tegan. I'm glad she's gone. Jess, please, all I want is to make you happy. I'll do anything. I'll make sure they never hurt you again.' What did you ask him to do for you, Jessica? Hide Tegan in the bench, beat up Brendon Reed, murder Shawna Moore?"

I'm frozen to my chair. I can't think or breathe.

"That's enough," says Ms. Jackson. "You're reaching and you know it. Do you have anything substantial, Detective? If not, we're leaving."

"I'm just getting warmed up." Underwood removes her suit jacket, revealing a burgundy blouse and a gold chain with a shamrock on it. Two small sweat stains darken the armpits of her silk blouse. "Inside the cave, we found this." She pulls from her briefcase a pink phone wrapped in a clear evidence bag, and I recoil from it as if it might explode.

"Marcus was gone when my officers arrived," Underwood continues, "but the fingerprints found on discarded water bottles match his fingerprints on file. What doesn't make sense is why he left behind Tegan's phone when he fled, which links him to her disappearance. Feels sloppy."

Jackson waves her hand. "Living in a cave is sloppy."

Underwood concedes and turns to me. "We lifted two sets of fingerprints off the phone, but neither matches to Marcus. One belongs to Jake, and there's an unidentified second print that I believe will match to you, Jessica."

"If Marcus isn't involved, then why is he hiding?" Jackson asks.

"He violated his probation in Nevada, he was dating Shawna Moore, an underage girl, selling drugs to minors at Tegan's parties, and in the possession of firearms. He is involved," counters Underwood, "but not in the way you think."

"There's enough speculation in this room already, Detective. Do not presume to know what I think."

Underwood absorbs the scolding and hands my lawyer a signed document. "I have a warrant here to collect your client's phone and fingerprints."

Cold sweat rolls down my sides, and I glance at my parents, who are ashen and stiff, as if they died in their chairs.

"Based on what probable cause?" asks Ms. Jackson.

"Based on the suspicious timing of Jessica's car accident and this," says Underwood. She slides over a transcript. "We pulled these text messages between Jessica and Tegan from the cloud. They were exchanged this summer, and they speak to Jessica's state of mind. They were deleted from Tegan's device at twelve-forty-eight Saturday morning, just fourteen minutes before Jessica called the tip line, which implies Jessica was in the cave with the phone when these incriminating texts were deleted."

"Bloody hell," my dad mutters.

My stomach clenches. My pulse speeds.

"I want a copy of that recording, the fingerprint reports, and this text transcript," says Jackson.

"You will have it all." Underwood smiles at me. "Read the texts aloud for the camera, please, Jessica. They were exchanged between you and Tegan this summer on July fifth."

"I'll read them," offers Jackson. "But you cannot prove Jessica sent these." She clears her throat and reads them out loud:

Jessica: *Are we still on?*

Tegan: *What are you talking about?*

Jessica: *The bet.*

Tegan: *We shook on it didn't we? you want me to kiss jake. I'll kiss jake. Done deal*

Jessica: *He has to kiss you back or it doesn't count. It has to be real.*

Tegan: *just get your $$$ ready loser* 😘

Jessica: *you're the one who's going to lose* 😘

When Ms. Jackson is finished, the room throbs from the sudden silence. I drop my head and fight back tears.

"Oh, Jessica," says Mom.

Now they know the truth—that I made the bet with Tegan, that I'm responsible for everything that happened next.

Underwood releases me, indicating that she'll be in touch after examining my cell and running my fingerprints against the unidentified print on Tegan's phone, but they will match. I already know that.

I leave the station with my head down, my façade smashed. I can't hide a moment longer from what I did.

I started this; I'm the one who must end it.

43

Jake

It's Monday, and after chewing me out for talking to the police by myself, Mom hires an attorney named Mr. Cline. He's a tall, thin guy with a goatee and some dandruff on his shoulders, and he meets me at the courthouse for my arraignment hearing. Regarding my fight with Brendon, the police charged me with felony battery and causing great bodily harm with malice aforethought. Mr. Cline says I'll plead *not guilty*.

"Why?" I ask in the chilly conference room. "His parents saw me do it."

"It's so I can form a defense," he answers. "Your classmates put you through grievous personal trauma and then amplified it on social media. When you attacked Brendon, you were drunk and upset, but you surrendered peacefully to the officers at the shed. We're lucky the damage to Brendon's nose is minor, a hairline fracture."

He pats my shoulder. "Look, Jake, no one wants to put a

confused and traumatized high school student in prison. I think I can get your charges reduced to one count of misdemeanor battery and get you into a diversion program and anger awareness counseling. Brendon seems willing to let bygones be bygones."

I nod, but really, I don't give a damn anymore. All my problems started with that fucking bet and it was my girlfriend's idea. I can't believe it. Jessica goaded Tegan into kissing me and then let me cry and grovel at her feet, all without admitting her part in it.

Yeah, I went too far, I get that, but Jessica gave Tegan *permission*. I would never ask a guy, let alone one of her ex-boyfriends, to kiss Jessica. I'd never put her in that position, but if I did and she fell for it, I'd blame my fucking self, not her.

When Shawna said *everyone is lying*, did that include my girlfriend? Am I the only asshole who didn't know what was going on?

My lawyer nudges me. "It's time, Jake." When we walk into my arraignment hearing, the first person I see is my mother, and she's wearing makeup, something she hasn't done since Dad's funeral. She forces a smile for me.

Then I notice the reporters, four of them sitting in the front row, scribbling notes. The judge reads my charges, my lawyer makes my plea, and I receive a date for my preliminary hearing, along with an admonishment from the judge—and then it's over. I'm released to my mother, and she is the proud owner of one juvenile delinquent and a shiny new credit card bill. "I'll pay you back," I tell her.

"Stop it, Jake. I'll pay *any* price to keep you safe. You boys are all I have."

I let it go and change subjects. "Where's Cole?"

"At school. Talk about upset, he wet the bed last night."

"Shit, no kidding?"

She rolls her eyes at me since we both know she'd never joke about that. "There were reporters at our house yesterday, Jake, and you were gone for three nights. He's worried."

Her words crush me because Cole doesn't deserve this—reporters at the house, his brother in juvie. It can't feel good. "I'll talk to him, take him out for ice cream or something."

Mom drives us home, and when we pull onto our street, she curses quietly. Two news vans are parked at our curb. "Duck down. I'm going straight into the garage."

I do as she says, and soon the car cabin darkens as the garage door shuts behind us. Mom turns off the engine and we sit a minute. I laugh bitterly. "I'm so confused. I loved Jessica. Why did she do this to me?"

"Oh, honey." She hugs me awkwardly between our seats. "You got caught in the middle of teenage bullying. That's what this is."

I pull away from her and stare at our messy garage, which is full of Dad's tools, bins of old ski clothes from long-ago vacations, and bikes that have flat tires. "I wish Dad were here."

Mom's eyes fill with tears. "He is here, honey."

Mom claims to sense Dad's presence, but I don't. I feel the place he used to be, which is cold and empty and fading fast. Sometimes I forget the color of his eyes. "I'm sorry you had to leave work again," I mumble, and dart into the house for a shower.

◆ ◆ ◆

Now it's Thursday. I've been home "sick" all week, and I had to promise Mom I'd go to trauma counseling for her to excuse so many school absences. The police questioned and released Jessica on Sunday night, and she's been calling me ever since and leaving messages, but I haven't called her back. It's one-thirty p.m. and Jessica should be at school, but I notice her car in the driveway.

The investigation against each of us has stalled due to delays at the forensic lab, and the police haven't held a press conference in days. The Sheffields are livid that their daughter wasn't discovered immediately and the headlines in the *Crystal Cove Gazette* are belligerent:

POLICE STYMIED BY MISSTEPS
IN SHEFFIELD CASE

HIGH SCHOOL SEX PRANK BAFFLES POLICE

SENATOR'S DAUGHTER BRAIN-DEAD?
BEST FRIEND MURDERED? SUSPECTS LOOSE?
WHO'S IN CHARGE IN CRYSTAL COVE?

I haven't been charged with anything other than my fight with Brendon. If the police truly suspect me, or Jessica, or Marcus, they're holding their cards close. Tegan is still in a coma, and the tension in Crystal Cove is as thick as the storm clouds developing over the ocean. Another arrest feels imminent, but of whom? Waiting is surreal, like being in the eye of a storm, like that calm moment before the world is torn to shreds.

Rumors are spreading that Jessica and I assaulted Tegan together and tried to hide her body. People post memes online about us that imply what the cops suspect—that Jess is in charge and I'm the idiot doing her bidding. Everything is hashtagged #CrystalCovesKillerCouple. I deleted all my accounts.

I pad into the kitchen for orange juice, pour a glass, and drink it while staring across the side yard to Jessica's house. Then, like an apparition, she appears in the window. I try to duck, but it's too late. She spots me and motions for me to come over.

"No," I mouth.

"Please," she mouths back. Her amber eyes are swollen and red-rimmed from crying, her bottom lip is quivering in a way that would have driven me mad a few days ago, and her hair is tousled and tangled. She looks destroyed.

Fuck it. I have to face her eventually. I nod and pour the rest of my juice down the drain.

44

Jessica

After five minutes of trying to figure out the new alarm system my parents bought to keep Jake out, I disarm it and let him in.

He stands in the foyer, chest heaving. "How could you?" he croaks.

My hand flutters to my mouth. "Jake, I'm—"

"You're sorry?" He brushes past me into the house. "Why? Because you offered my ex fifty bucks to kiss me?"

"It wasn't like th—"

"I said don't." His voice rings through the house. "No more lies." He paces the hallway and then enters the living room and collapses onto the sofa, his head in his hands. "Why didn't you tell me that you made the bet?"

I try to sit beside him, but Jake thrusts out his hand. "Not so close."

A lump forms in my throat. I perch on the recliner across from him and start to cry.

Jake watches me, waiting. He hasn't shaved, and his eyelashes are spiked with dried tears. His long fingers tap his thighs, but his pupils are huge, as if his eyes are melting in their sockets. I sense the fury that underlies his hurt like a shark coasting beneath the waves. "You sold me out for fifty bucks and you didn't have the nerve to tell me," he says, voice raw. "Fifty fucking dollars. Is that all I'm worth to you?"

My breath scrapes across my throat in a gasp. Jake's right, there's no point in saying sorry, because there's no excuse for what I did. I made a bet that broke us up, turned his private life into national TV coverage, and ended with him in juvenile hall. And then I was too cowardly to tell him the truth. I knew he'd be upset, and I was right.

He lifts his head, and our eyes meet. "Did you even care if your gamble broke us up?" he asks.

My first answer dies on my lips, because of course I care, but ... there's more to it. "I—I don't know."

Jake sits taller, squares his shoulders. "What's that supposed to mean?"

I squirm as feelings I haven't addressed bubble to the surface. "Maybe I was testing you."

Jake thinks about that and then shakes his head. "No, nope. Do not throw that shit on me, Jessica. I gave you no reason to test me." He taps the arm of the sofa. "I told you how much I loved you *every single day*. We were happy; I was, anyway. I think you did it to push me away, to break us up. You wanted your freedom for college."

There is truth in his words, even though that's not why I did it, and he reads it in my expression.

"It would have been kinder to break up with me," he says, trembling.

I slide off the recliner and crawl closer. "It's not that I wanted my freedom, but if you want to bring that up . . . You were a lot, Jake. You watched me, followed me, kept track of me. You didn't trust me."

"Bullshit," he cries. "You act like I'm a stalker or something. I thought you liked being together all the time. It doesn't help that we're neighbors."

I blink, and tears spill from my eyes. "You didn't want me to go to Colorado for college."

He rips off his windbreaker and tosses it. "Of course I didn't! It makes me sad and I'm going to miss you. Fuck, what am I supposed to say, that I want you to leave?"

His words slice me like knives, and it hits me how much we've avoided talking about this. We've been dancing in a burning building, not wanting to acknowledge that it's falling down around us.

"If I clung to you, it was only because I knew you were leaving." Jake rubs his forehead as if it hurts. "I wanted to spend every last second with you and give us the best senior year ever."

I shake my head, confused by his perspective, because from mine, it felt like he would never let me go.

He meets my gaze, his eyes liquid. "I was proud of you, Jessica. I was glad you were getting out of here, and I was jealous. I'm the one staying behind, and I didn't want to think about that."

Jake's words slay me. "I didn't know."

"You didn't ask," he growls. "You always think you know everything." He leans back and wipes his palm on his jeans. "If you weren't trying to break up with me, then why make the bet? Did you think that winning would end your war with Tegan?"

My mouth drops open, and he stands up to leave.

"Maybe this was never about me. Maybe it was always about *her*. But you know what? I don't care. We both fucked up."

"Jake, stop!"

"Why?" He pauses with his shoulders sloped, his jaw loose, the fight in him gone.

I've never hurt Jake before, never seen him sad because of me, and my heart shatters. There are no magic words to repair the damage I've done. He doesn't trust me but he deserves the truth. I exhale a long, slow breath. "You're right, I did it because of her. At the bonfire party, Tegan made a comment about getting you back, and I wanted to prove she couldn't. I wanted to beat her at something. I wanted to win. I should have told you. I'm sorry that it went so far."

Jake hooks a thumb into his pocket and nods as if he understands, but then his sad eyes harden. "The only way to beat Tegan Sheffield is not to play."

He strides out my front door without bothering to close it.

45

___

Tegan, July

The Pacific Ocean wrapped around my body like fluid ice. "Lord, it's cold," I cried. But the chill sharpened my senses, sobered me, and reminded me why I didn't like night swimming.

Brendon splashed me as he swam past, and I splashed him back. Chiara, her new boyfriend, and his friends bobbed around us, the ocean swelling and dipping as if it were a monster, breathing. Moonlight left a pale seam across the dark water, and the bonfire crackled onshore. Our other friends danced around the flames like living shadows.

Brendon dived beneath the surface and began tugging on our legs, trying to scare us. I floated on my back, buoyed by salt water, and watched the stars hold court overhead, the same stars that watched over the whole wide world. Brendon bumped me, and I felt the thrill of something big and dangerous beneath the water before he moved on. There was no undertow tonight, no danger of sleeper waves. For the first time since I'd moved here, I felt safe in the water.

Then a slick head popped up next to mine and blinked in my face, and I floundered away. My first thought was, *Seal*, but it wasn't a seal. It was Jessica Sanchez. "You scared me," I said.

She swam closer, her wet hair like silk, her eyelashes clumped in long spikes, her skin dripping like a storm. She glided smoothly, a vengeful mermaid, eyes pointed at me, her limbs pale in the inky water. "You'll never get Jake back, and I'm sick of you talking about him. You need to leave us alone."

"Have you been drinking?" I asked, then paddled away, glancing toward the shore. This wasn't a version of Jessica I'd met before.

She cut me off. "Did you hear what I said?"

"I'm not doing anything to you and Jake." The frigid water had frozen my skin, and my body quivered.

Brendon eyed Jessica and me with curiosity. "We're going back. Too cold," he said.

"Coming," I called, but Jessica swam the angle, blocking me again. Her eyes blazed beneath the icy moon, searing me and forcing me to look at her, really look at her.

She was raw and sublimely pretty with only her head and shoulders above the water, a goddess raised from the deep. But beneath those silken cheeks and velvet eyes, I glimpsed the face of my ex–best friend, the little girl I had loved with all my heart, the girl who'd torn out my feelings and shredded them when we were eleven years old. My heart whirled. The memory was monstrous. "Get out of my way," I snarled, stroking past her.

She snatched my arm and twirled me around. "Not until you promise to stop."

"Stop what?"

"Obsessing over Jake. Let him go."

I laughed in her face. "Let *him* go? Are you aware he watches me when he thinks I can't see? Just the other day we sat on his surfboard together. Maybe you should be having this conversation with him." We rose and dipped with the waves, and I felt dizzy. My lips were stiff and numb, and I was growing tired of paddling.

Emotions raced across Jessica's face. "Jake's not interested in you."

"His dick is." A crude blow, but I needed to end things before we drowned out here.

Jessica surged forward, her lips curled back. "You're wrong. He wouldn't want you if you were the last girl on earth. You're mean. You're selfish."

Jessica's words caved my chest in, turned my legs to jelly. I was not mean or selfish. I was generous and honest and loyal. I glared at her. "I gave you *everything*, Jessica. I never said no to you, not once. No one will ever have your back like I did."

"You said no to Chloe. You treated her like crap."

"I didn't like Chloe."

Jessica's eyes widen. "But *I* did! You never let me make my own choices. And now I have Jake and you don't. Stop harassing us."

I gaped at her, saw she believed this—this myth about me. I swam straight at her. "What Jake wants is Jake's choice, and he wants me. All the guys do."

"Prove it," she cried, paddling out of my way. "I bet you fifty bucks you can't even kiss Jake."

I laughed. "You're on."

"What?"

I extended my hand toward her. "I said you're on. I'll take that bet."

The blood that had darkened Jessica's cheeks drained away, but she took my hand and shook it. Right then the hour struck midnight and Marcus lit a firework. It soared over the ocean and exploded, lighting our faces in all-American shades of red, white, and blue. "You're going to regret this," I said, and then swam back to my party, leaving Jessica bobbing like a cork.

✦ ✦ ✦

The following day, Jessica texted me: *Are we still on?*

I swiped my hair off my face and texted her back: *What are you talking about?*

Jessica: *The bet.*

The bet? Lord, I'd forgotten about it. She'd bet me I couldn't kiss Jake, but I didn't believe she was serious. My pulse thrummed faster. Jessica wanted me to lose, to fail. As if I'd let that happen. My fingers flew across my screen: *We shook on it, didn't we? you want me to kiss jake. I'll kiss jake. Done deal.*

Jessica: *He has to kiss you back or it doesn't count. It has to be real.*

Has she lost her mind? I thought, and texted: *just get your $$$ ready loser* 😘

Gray dots and then: *you're the one who's going to lose* 😘

I slammed my phone onto my desk. She was right, there was no way Jake would kiss me while they were still dating—I knew that like I knew my middle name—so how was I going to win this bet?

46

Jessica

The transcript of the texts between Tegan and me are released to the media on Friday.

Now everyone in the *world* knows that my wager led to all that happened next—the sex, the video, Tegan's coma, and possibly Shawna's murder. Overnight, I become the villain, the girl who set her boyfriend up to fail, and sympathy for Jake skyrockets.

News headlines reach the *Daily Mail* in the UK:

AMERICAN TEEN SNOGS
CLASSMATE FOR FIFTY DOLLARS

It's worse in the US:

TEEN GIRL BETS ON LOVE AND LOSES

TWELFTH GRADERS WAGE WAR
OVER EX-BOYFRIEND

AN INDECENT PROPOSAL IN CRYSTAL COVE

Even Chloe is livid when she hears the news and FaceTimes me. "This whole time I've been defending you, and you freaking *asked* for this?" She stomps around her bedroom and slams her door. "How could you hide this from Jake, from me? I felt terrible for you, Jessica. I can't believe you made the bet and didn't tell me!"

"How do you think I felt?" I whisper. "I didn't want Jake to find out."

"I wouldn't have told Jake. I—I—can't deal with this right now. I'm leaving for Arizona soon. Don't talk to me until after the showcase." She ends the video call, and I fall onto my bed, sobbing.

Then my lawyer calls to tell me my fingerprints matched perfectly to the unknown print on Tegan's phone. "Are you surprised by this?" Ms. Jackson asks on the speakerphone with my parents.

"No," I whisper, which upsets my dad a lot.

But Jackson absorbs my response like a pro and continues, "Detective Underwood sent a new warrant to Judge Singh for your DNA, Jessica, and he'll sign it. The detective is building a case against you for interfering with a police investigation at minimum, and for aiding and abetting your boyfriend in Tegan's attempted murder at maximum. The BMW came back clean; there are no traces of blood, tissue, or hair—human or otherwise. The lack of physical evidence is good news for you, Jessica."

It might be good news, but it makes me feel queasy. After the call, Mom retreats to her bedroom for the rest of the day.

Tegan promised I'd regret our bet, and she was right, but I won't let things end this way with Jake. She may never wake up and tell us what happened to her, but maybe I can redeem myself and help him out of the legal mess he's in—that we're both in. I have an idea that involves breaking and entering, and it might be the stupidest thing I've ever done.

Okay, maybe the second-stupidest if you count the bet.

◆ ◆ ◆

Shawna Moore's house is nestled in Dune Hills, a neighborhood of 1950s bungalows that were once small beach cabins for wealthy families. Behind the neighborhood are the sand dunes, and just to the north is Falcon's Peak, the bluff where Shawna fell to her death.

It's Friday night, almost two weeks since the party, and I'm outside Shawna's bedroom window, once again dressed in black, except this time I'm wearing thin gloves and my hair is pulled into a tight hair-sprayed bun. I'm not leaving any of myself behind, no fingerprints, no DNA.

I had to sneak out and jog through the woods to get past the smattering of reporters that watch Jake's house and mine. It's a three-and-a-half-mile trek to Shawna's, and I made it in twenty-eight minutes flat. *Not bad for a noncompetitive run,* I think as I catch my breath.

Shawna was going to tell the police everything she knew before she died—but she never got a chance. I think Marcus killed her and attacked Tegan too. It's too late for Shawna to talk now, but maybe not too late for her to reveal *something*. The police still haven't found the camera that was used to film Jake and Tegan—

a camera that might have also recorded the violence that occurred afterward—and it's possible Shawna took it and hid it. This is why I'm at her house, to look for the camera and for clues. I need to get Jake and myself out of this mess.

There's a candlelight memorial and vigil for Shawna and Tegan at Blind Beach tonight, which is how I know her mom isn't home. My feet sink into the loamy soil as I push on Shawna's window. Only outsiders lock up their homes in Crystal Cove and the glass gives way and slides open. Seconds later, I'm in Shawna's bedroom.

The overhead lights are off, but the moonlight illuminates the room. Her bed is made up with a quilt and a throw blanket. Her clothing is put away, but there's a laundry basket standing in the corner, as if she'll return and use it.

After turning on my flashlight, I flip through the loose pictures that cover her desk—photos of Tegan, Brendon, Marcus, and others. Her old sporting equipment—soccer ball, cleats, track shoes, and a softball glove—is displayed neatly outside her closet. Fairy lights decorate her headboard, and the walls are studded with flags from other countries, places Shawna hoped to visit, I imagine. The room is pungent with essential oils and incense.

"Here goes nothing." With a gulp, I drop to my hands and knees. Then I roll onto my back and squeeze beneath Shawna's bed. Years ago, when we were kids on the same soccer team, I caught her stuffing her diary into a hole in her box spring during a team sleepover. It's a place that authorities, or her mother, might not have searched, and it's possible she still hides things there—diaries, notes, the camera, or anything that might shed light on what happened to her.

It's a tight fit, and I can't lift my head without banging it on the slats. My nostrils fill with disturbed dust, and I sweep the flashlight, checking for spiders that might be hiding in the bed frame. The hardwood floor is littered with insect husks and dust bunnies, and when my hair gets wrapped up with a crispy-looking dead fly, my stomach heaves. "Gross," I mutter, tasting the dust on my tongue.

Squirming farther beneath the bed, wiggling like a snake on my back, I study the box spring above me. The fabric is ripped in several places, revealing the framework. I don't remember which side of the bed her secret spot was on, or which end. I'll have to explore each little hole.

Swallowing, I reach my hand into one of the dark openings and feel around for any thingamajig that doesn't belong. My fingers encounter a layer of dust, more dried-up insect bodies, and sticky webs. I reach deeper, my lips twitching in disgust. Nothing.

I try another dark, filthy opening. Then another.

Finally my fingers close around a small notebook and I slide it loose, inhaling more dust through my nostrils and sneezing. A critter crawls across my fingers, and I yank back my hand. A brown house spider clutches my pinkie for dear life.

I squeal and slam my head into the box spring as I slide out from under the bed. I fling the spider off, and it lands in a patch of moonlight and then scurries across the floor, its eight legs a rapid blur.

I didn't find the camera, but at least I found something. Opening the notebook, I flip through the lined white paper, growing excited. It's a diary and the dates are recent.

I scan half a dozen entries about Marcus. Shawna describes going to parties with him, taking drugs, and having sex in his apartment. There's one about Tegan's Fourth of July party that includes two sentences about the bet. *Jessica bet Tegan fifty bucks she can't kiss Jake. This is going to be hysterical.*

The ugly, bitter side of me thinks, *Look who's laughing now,* and I instantly hate myself for it.

I flip forward and read more about Marcus. Shawna believes she loves him, but it seems more like obsession to me. There are several entries where she's upset because Marcus doesn't call or text her, or he shows up with hickies from other girls. He flirts heavily with Tegan, and Shawna's afraid he likes Tegan better than her. She also berates herself for being "just a high school girl." One of the last entries is dated on Tuesday, two days before a kayaker found her body in the sea. My pulse jumps as I read.

Just talked to the police—I am so fucked! Prison! I should turn him in. I don't want to go to prison! If I tell the police what he did, they'll go easier on me, but he'll be so mad. Shit! Everyone is lying and Jake is clueless. If Jake knew the truth . . . he would kill us all. Stupid! Stupid! Why did we ever think this would be funny????????

My hands shake as I finish reading. "What did you do to Jake?" I wonder out loud. When Shawna wrote this on Tuesday, Jake already knew about the video and the broadcast, so Shawna must be talking about something else. Something he *doesn't* know about.

Brendon said something similar, that Jake's stupid and has no idea what's going on. Maybe they're talking about planting Tegan's phone in Jake's glove box. Shawna wrote: *I should turn him in.* But who is "he"? Does she mean Marcus or Jake?

I think back to the night of the party and everything weird that happened after—hitting a creature on Blood Alley, lying to the detective in the woods, Shawna's death, and Tegan getting stuffed into a storage bench like a discarded toy, and then Jake beating up Brendon and getting arrested. This all started because Jake and

Tegan did more than kiss. That's what turned the live feed into something criminal.

I inhale and shove that memory aside. It seems obvious that Tegan's friends played a joke on her that backfired with that illegal broadcast—and one of them is picking off the others so they don't confess. And I think they're setting up Jake to take the blame. He doesn't know if it was really Shawna texting him to meet her at Falcon's Peak. It could have been her killer, trying to make *him* look guilty.

I bet whoever has the missing camera is the one responsible, and it's not here. Brendon the Cameraman is the obvious choice, except the police questioned him and let him go. The word at school is that after he left the party, Brendon stayed up all night watching movies with his insomniac father.

No, everything circles back to Marcus. If he snuck into Tegan's room and assaulted her like he did that girl in Nevada, maybe he kept the camera recording as a souvenir, or a trophy. That footage could be my best hope to clear Jake's name, and I have an idea how to get it.

I search Shawna's diary for a clue about Marcus—his address, his social media handles, anything—and as I flip through the pages, I travel back through Shawna's life. When I reach a page from seven months earlier, the day Shawna and Marcus first met, I find something promising—phone numbers, two of them. Shawna drew a heart around them and wrote Marcus's name. One number is starred and the other is labeled *extra*.

Using the new phone my parents bought me, I snap a photo of the numbers and then one of Shawna's final diary entry. Her mother deserves to have this notebook, so I leave it on Shawna's bed, where it will be found tonight or tomorrow—her daughter's private thoughts.

They are hard to read but they are honest, and some of them are sweet: *I got an A on my essay! Mom is so proud of me.* And: *Watched a movie with Mom last night. We both cried. I should hang out with her more.*

Gazing down at Shawna's bed, my life feels surreal, bizarre. Senior year was supposed to be exciting—not morbid.

After jogging back home, this time in thirty-one minutes, I shower and remember one of Jake's silly notes from last year: *Roses are red. Violets are blue. I might be failing math, but at least I have you. P.S. I'm not actually failing. I have a D.*

Having a D is failing when it comes to college admissions, but Jake's never been one to pay attention to details. He doesn't keep scores or hold grudges—he's *nothing* like Tegan or me—but because of our bet, he's caught in a web he doesn't understand.

It's time to end this. I pull up the photo of Marcus's two phone numbers. I know he deals drugs, so I believe the "extra" number is a burner phone, and hopefully it's still active. I compose a text to the extra number, swallow a breath, and hit send.

I've set the bait; now to see if he bites. If this works, I could soon be face to face with a killer.

47

Jake

"You died, Jake," says Cole.

I glance at the TV screen and there's my video game character, lying flat on his face. "Shit, sorry."

My little brother squints at me, his disappointment in my gaming skills splayed brilliantly across his face. "I thought you wanted to play. You're not even trying."

I drop the controller and take a swig from my Yeti, which is full of orange juice and vodka. There's a soft glow over the world, a bloom of heat in my belly, and numbness in my brain. I can almost forget that Jessica Sanchez ever existed. I pick up the controller, get a new life, and try again.

Our house feels hot despite the drafty windows letting in the night air. I pull off my shirt and wipe the sweat off my shaved head. The bruises from my fight with Brendon have spread like rotten spots across my face, as if I'm spoiling from the inside out. I also have a nagging pain in my shoulder socket, but none of that compares to how battered I feel on the inside. I close my eyes, resisting the blackness that rises up when I imagine life without the girl I loved with all my heart.

Someone egged our house last night and spray-painted *Crystal Cove Killer* on our garage door. Today I painted it white to cover the words.

I did receive a piece of good news. My STD results and Tegan's pregnancy test came back negative. It's good, but I'm not as elated as I thought I'd be. I feel more like someone who narrowly avoided walking off a cliff—relieved and grateful—but also stupid and sad. The truth that someone brutally attacked Tegan hits me full force. Someone broke her arm and stuffed her in that bench, someone who hates her, I imagine, and she may never be able to tell us who. I fixed a drink to absorb all that, and now I can't stop. I want to scream—I want to go outside and scream at the sky.

I lean against Otis, using him as a backrest, and his loose hair makes me sneeze.

Cole scoots away from me. "Are you sick?"

I snatch him up and breathe all over his face. "If I am, then so are you."

He rolls and kicks me hard, right in the center of my chest. "That's not funny!" His cheeks redden as he tries to scrub my germs off his face with his T-shirt. Otis circles us, whining, and then a defeated noise from the video game we're playing makes Cole groan. "You died again, Jake."

"I think we need snacks, you know, to keep up our strength." Cole and Otis follow me into the kitchen, where I try to open the refrigerator door, miss the handle completely, and stagger into the counter. Laughing, I try again.

Cole stomps on my bare toes. "You're drunk!"

Collapsing, I grab my foot as the kitchen floor spins and the dog tries to lick my face. Shit, I wasn't feeling those vodkas until I stood up, and my poor little brother has me to thank for knowing what *drunk* means. It's probably a good thing his friend Sawyer isn't allowed over anymore.

I glance up at Cole with his naturally pointy ears sticking out of his hair, and swirl my finger at him. "You look like an elf."

He swats my hand away. "You'd better not let Mom see you like this."

"Like what?" Our mother's clipped tone fills the room as she returns from running errands all day. Otis greets her with soft whimpers, upset because Cole and I are fighting. As soon as my mother's eyes meet mine, hers harden with suspicion. "Jacob Monroe Healy!" After clacking across the tile, she drops the grocery bags onto the counter and then yells at my brother, "Cole, go to your room."

"What did *I* do?"

Otis darts behind my brother, shaking because he hates yelling.

Mom rubs her head. "Nothing. Let me talk to Jake, alone. You're not in trouble."

My brother glares at me. "You ruin everything! I just wanted to play with you." He grabs Otis's collar and drags him out of the kitchen.

I watch them leave, floating in the glorious glow of oblivion. Mom squats next to me. "How much have you had?"

She scrunches her face, and I laugh. "You look like a squirrel."

Mom groans and then grabs all the liquor out of the high cupboard and starts pouring it down the drain while throwing words over her shoulder. "You need help, Jake. Your uncle is an alcoholic; you know that. This drinking is out of control. You drove home drunk, you—you made that video—"

I heave myself to my feet and roar at her, "I didn't make any fucking video!"

Her weary eyes search my face. "If you hadn't been drunk—"

"No!" I slam my fist on the countertop. "No! The camera was hidden. Tegan and Jessica tricked me!" I snatch a dirty glass from the sink and hurl it against our tile floor, and feel a huge sense of satisfaction when it shatters. I reach for another.

"Stop it! Just stop. You're right. I'm sorry." Tears fill her eyes. "I don't know why I said that. I'm just—so angry about that bet."

"*I'm* angry," I growl, smacking my chest. "I'm the one—I'm the one that . . ." Sobs fill my throat, choking me. "I'm the one everyone's laughing at."

She crosses the floor, avoiding the broken glass, and presses her forehead against mine. "No one's laughing at you."

I push her away. "You have no idea what it's like. My teachers, the principal, all the other moms, and the fucking middle schoolers—they *saw* me. And now everyone knows my girlfriend bet on me and lost. The looks I get, Mom. Everyone in Crystal Cove has seen . . ." Shaking my head, I can't finish my sentence.

She nods. "You're right, I don't know what it's like, but I know drinking won't help."

"It doesn't hurt! It makes me forget. It makes me feel fucking good."

She grabs the broom from the pantry, sweeps the ragged glass shards into a safe pile, and throws them away. Then she returns to me and tilts her head, lowers her voice. "Why are you so angry?"

My arms flail. "Because I'm stupid. I'm mad at myself."

She shakes her head, and her dark hair shimmers. "I don't think so. What are you really mad about?"

I lean against the wall to steady myself. "I just told you," I rasp.

Her lower lip trembles. "I think this goes deeper than the party. Do you remember when you first started drinking like this?"

"No." I reach for my Yeti, and she yanks it out of my grasp.

"Do you remember the night I found you in the bathtub with a bottle of tequila, Jake? The water was cold. You were shivering and crying, and you wouldn't speak to me."

I hiccup, and that draws a bitter, sadistic laugh from my gut. "Didn't you ground me for, like, a month?"

She offers a tight smile. "I did. Will you talk about it now?"

I shake my head. "Fuck, Mom, I don't know what you want."

She inches closer, tears sparkling in her dark eyes. "I want us to talk about what happened that day, before you ended up in the bathtub."

The floor dips beneath me. "There's no reason to."

"This drinking is a reason. It's when you started using alcohol to forget."

I cover my head. "You know what happened. You were there."

"Yes, but I don't have anyone to talk to about it either, just you. Why won't you discuss it?"

My heart bursts and I slide to the floor. "Because it was the worst day of my life. Because we buried Dad and everyone said he was in a better place, but he's not!" I close my eyes, try to hide. "This is the better place—here with us! Are you happy now?"

She releases a breath, nods, and sits next to me.

I twist away as memories of Dad blast through me—Dad lifting me to the sky; Dad praising me as I climbed the bluffs; Dad teaching me how to surf; Dad hugging Mom, keeping her grounded, keeping me grounded. Then he died and we blew away. My shoulders tremble with the weight of his absence.

Mom keeps pushing. "We talk about everything, Jake. Why not this?"

"I don't want to." Fury at the unfairness of it unfolds its wings, and I rise to pace the floor, breathless.

"It's okay to feel angry that your father died."

I inhale a ragged breath and fresh tears drip from my eyes, my nose. The truth squirms inside me, ugly and oily. I open my mouth and it spews out, all over the kitchen, all over Mom and me. "It's because he didn't fight. He quit! He gave up."

Mom catches me in her arms and wraps them around me. "He did fight, honey."

I shake my head as ugly sobs pour from my chest. "No, I heard him. He told you to stop the treatment, but Dad was strong. He could have beat it."

Mom's fingers dig into my shoulders. "What are you talking about, Jake?"

I wipe my eyes, my throat raw. "I heard you guys talking, like a week before he died. He told you to stop the drugs. I heard him. He quit, and the cancer won." My body shakes as an avalanche of grief shreds my insides. I never told anyone about this—how my dad gave up on us. I know it's selfish to think that—I fucking know it and hate myself for it—but maybe, with more of the cancer treatments, he would have lived.

"Oh no," Mom says, covering her mouth. "Oh, Jake, that's not what happened."

I stare at her, my breath coming faster.

"Dad asked me to stop the *morphine*, not the medicine. He hated how it knocked him out. He didn't want to lose a minute with us, with you. He never gave up on us. The doctors are the ones who ended the treatment when it started causing more harm than good."

"But—" Her words shatter me, and I can't finish the sentence.

She pulls me into her arms. "Dad never wanted to leave you," she murmurs, crying.

A soft, warm body joins us. It's Cole, followed by a wet nose—Otis. My brother burrows between Mom and me and looks up, his glasses steaming. The kid likes to eavesdrop; he probably overheard everything. "I thought I killed Dad," he whispers.

"What?" Mom rasps, and we both stare at him.

Cole is calm, not crying, but his body is taut like a spring. "I forgot to wash my hands. Dad was talking and I couldn't hear him, so I got into his bed. He wanted to tell me something and I touched his face. Then I went to get you," he says to Mom, "and you yelled at me for digging in the yard and getting dirt on Dad."

She nods. "I remember."

I swallow hard and finish Cole's story because I was there too, sitting in the corner of the room, keeping watch. "And then Otis started howling." Silence falls between us as we look at Otis. His tail sweeps the kitchen floor, and he whines, as if he's remembering it too—the moment Dad died.

"I thought I gave him germs," Cole finishes.

"Oh no," Mom says, cradling and kissing us both. "It wasn't your fault, Cole, and Dad never gave up on us, Jake. He loved you boys with all his heart. He loved you so much that he held on longer than any doctor believed he would."

We hug her back for a long time, and then I ask Cole, "What did Dad say to you? Do you remember?"

My brother slips off his glasses and wipes them on his pajamas. "He told me I smell good."

Mom smiles. "It's true. You do."

Cole shrugs. "That's all I remember."

We remain in the kitchen for a long time, talking about Dad and crying. After a while, our memories make us smile. I guzzle water, and the effects of the alcohol slowly leave my body.

The kitchen is warm, and Mom turns on some music, sways to the beat while she puts the groceries away. Cole makes hot cocoa, just like Dad would have, and Otis barks for attention.

Dad didn't quit. It's like a rock off my chest. I let out my breath, and Mom whispers to me behind Cole's back. "Will you stop drinking?"

I gaze at her and shrug. "I don't know how."

"We'll figure it out, get you some help. You're not alone." I nod, and she pats my arm and then joins Cole in the family room for a movie.

I glance out the kitchen window toward Jess's house. I felt nothing but alone after my dad died—until I met her—and now she's gone too. My gaze shifts to my mom and brother, cuddling on the sofa, and then to the photo of my dad on the fridge. His eyes stare back, happy, fearless, and *green*. His eyes are green.

I'm not alone. Mom and Cole lost Dad too, but we have each other. I decide to be a better son and brother. I lean into the family room. "Hey, Cole, I'll kick your ass at that video game tomorrow, okay?"

"Jake!" Mom scolds.

But my brother laughs and jumps on the couch. "Promise?"

I draw an X on my chest, and my voice thickens as I say, "Cross my heart and hope to die."

48

Jessica

"I'm going to work," I shout to my parents. It's Sunday afternoon, and they're sitting on the back porch, eating shrimp cocktails. They want me to lie low until we hear back from the detective about what's going to happen to me, but I have a shift at Layers. Besides, Marcus took the bait. Tonight is the night.

"Come straight home after," says Mom. She attended her monthly book club luncheon today, and she's rosy-cheeked from the wine.

"Don't forget to reset the alarms after you get inside," Dad adds. "Love you."

Before Tegan went missing, we were like everyone else, we never locked our doors. "I will! Love you too."

I drive straight to Layers with a queasy stomach. If Marcus doesn't chicken out, I'll see him tonight, alone. God, *this* is the stupidest thing I've ever done, but I owe it to Jake to try to get that missing camera.

When I reach the sandwich shop fifteen minutes late, I rush through the door. Amara is off today, so I'm working with Simon. "Sorry I'm late. Has it been busy?"

"Does it look busy?" He's painting his fingernails black.

"You're not supposed to do that in here."

"It's low-odor polish." He blows on his nails to dry them. "Besides, it's been dead since I got here. No one wants a sandwich today." The western horizon is dark, and another dreaded lightning storm from Mexico is supposed to make landfall next week. Thick fog crossed the bluffs this afternoon, and when it's gloomy outside, either we get a mad rush or everyone stays home. Looks like they stayed home today. After a beat, Simon adds, "We're low on Swiss cheese."

"I'll cut some." In the back room, I start slicing and then restock the Swiss and American cheeses, cut more turkey, and put away the avocados for tomorrow. Simon serves a customer who takes their food to go, and I do homework in between cleaning the countertops and sweeping the floor.

"Another light just burned out in the parking lot," Simon says, peering through the large front window that overlooks our little Crystal Cove strip mall. "Maintenance needs to fix that shit. It's not safe when it's dark."

A half hour later, he glances at the clock. "Time to go." In October, Layers switches to winter hours, but until then, two people are on shift until seven, and then I'm alone until nine.

"Don't forget to sign out," I remind him.

"Have fun doing your homework," he sings as he shoves open the door, letting in a blast of cold air, and then he vanishes into the fog.

I hate the last two hours of my shift. Even on a good day,

customers rarely want sandwiches between seven and nine, so it's lonely and boring, and I'm the one stuck with the cleanup. The best part about the last two hours is getting paid to do homework.

But tonight I can't concentrate. I pace, sweep the tiles, and keep one eye on the door. My text to Marcus went like this: *I found your number in Shawna's diary. She wrote about the party. I know what you did.* I included the photo of Shawna's journal that I took at her house.

Marcus: *whos this*

Me: *Jake's girlfriend Jessica. I want to make a trade*

I explained what I wanted, and he agreed to meet me. Marcus made me swear not to involve the police, and I made him swear not to hurt me. I believe we both lied.

After staring at the glass front door for an hour, I turn to put the mop away, and that's when the bell jingles. Marcus hunches through the doorway wearing a gray baseball cap, a stained plaid flannel over a gray T-shirt, and faded jeans with dirty cuffs. His head is down and the cap shields most of his face, exposing only his lips and cleft chin. His fingers twitch against his jeans, and without looking at me, he asks, "Are the security cameras off?"

"They don't record," I answer, my heart thudding.

"Show me."

I expected this, so I lead him to the back office and show him the camera screen. The record light is off. Through lowered lashes, I inspect his clothing for gun- or knife-shaped bulges. He appears unarmed.

Marcus grunts and we return to the sandwich counter. Lifting the bill of his cap, he meets my stare head-on. His eyes are the same light gray as his T-shirt, and he flicks them nervously across my body. "I remember you from the party. Big ass, pretty face, no sense of humor." He waits for a reaction, gets none, and goes on. "So why do you want a camera that shows your man banging another chick?"

My stomach gurgles, but I keep my expression flat. It hits me that he doesn't look tired; he looks *haunted*. In that second, I believe he murdered Shawna. I reel backward as he talks.

"You say my girl confessed everything?"

"Yes." My bladder shudders as it does when I lie.

He peers at me harder, and his eyebrows shoot up. "Fuck me! You're the chick from the cave; you turned me in." He reaches for me.

I fly backward and flatten myself against the wall. "No. Yes," I sputter. Oh god, he looks like he wants to murder me. "I'm sorry. I got scared, but then I thought we could help each other." Lies, lies, lies!

He beckons with his hands, eyes bouncing all over the shop. "Fuck you. Just give me the diary. I need to see it."

"Show me the camera first." His jaw muscles flutter, and then he pulls a miniature camera out of his front flannel pocket and holds it up, out of my reach.

"You didn't answer me before," he says, his sour breath blowing across my face. "Why do you want this?"

I sidle against the wall toward the back office because I'm going to need a head start when the time comes to act. "The FBI erased the online footage, but Jake and I know it still exists in that camera. I want it for him, so he can destroy it. He's not proud of it."

"He fucking should be."

Anger flushes out my nerves. I want to ask him if he put Tegan in the poolside bench, if he pushed Shawna off Falcon's Peak, and if he set up the live broadcast at the party, but I can't because then he'd know that I *don't* have the diary and that Shawna didn't confess anything. Not in enough detail to get him arrested, anyway. *Stay focused, Jessica! Don't react.*

"I like that you're loyal to your boyfriend," he says, snatching a piece of my hair and smelling it. "I wish Shawna'd been more like you. She was going to spill everything. I'm not going down for what that bitch Tegan did to your boyfriend. I was just the middleman."

I tug my hair out of his hands. "Middleman for what?"

Marcus lowers his voice to a growl. "Just get the fucking diary. Now."

My heart bangs in my chest, I'm breathless. "It's in the back office. I'll get it, and you can read it while I check the footage on the camera."

He snatches my arm with his free hand and squeezes hard. "Do you think I'm stupid? I'm going with you."

Panic crawls through my belly, and I rip my arm out of his grasp. "I'm not supposed to let anyone back there and I already broke the rule once. Just wait. I'll be quick."

Our eyes clash and I'm trembling, but I can't chicken out. I need to help Jake, to redeem myself. I lower my fingers toward a button hidden below the cash register.

Marcus grows skittish. "What are you up to?"

Before he can stop me, I smash the emergency button. There's a loud click as the front door locks shut.

"What the fuck?" He rushes to the door and rattles the handle. Security bolts have slid into the metal framing, locking him inside the store.

"Jessica?" he snarls.

The owners installed the system six years ago after a gunman attacked a nearby strip mall. It allows employees to lock themselves inside the shop without having to approach the floor-to-ceiling glass storefront and risk getting shot or seen. It's meant to keep the bad element *out*, but in this case, I want to keep him in.

Marcus charges me.

I sprint toward the back office.

"You fucking bitch!"

As I pass the sandwich counter, I slide across the damp tiles that I mopped twenty minutes ago and slam into one of our refrigerators. It wrenches my shoulder, and I slip onto my rear with a yelp.

"Come here!" Marcus skids around the counter that separates us, eyes locked on mine, lips drawn back.

Oh no! I try to stand, slip again, and scurry toward the office on all fours.

When his sneakers hit the wet tile, he falls harder than I did. The camera slides across the floor toward me and I snatch it. "Fuck!" he cries.

The tile is layered in grease, and when it's damp, it's like walking on ice. Marcus crawls toward me and reaches for my leg.

I kick at his hand and he misses. As I yank my body through the doorway into the office, he reaches again and his fingers curl around my ankle. He jerks hard, dragging me toward him.

"No!" I toss the camera into the office and clutch the door trim with my fingers. As he tugs my body, my grip begins to slip. I kick at his head and neck with my free leg, making him curse, then heave the rest of my body into the room and slam the door on his arm, crushing his wrist.

Marcus shrieks with pain.

I slam the door two more times—*Bam! Bam!*—whacking his wrist bone until he lets go of my ankle.

"I'm going to kill you!" he screams.

The door bangs shut, and I lock it. My breathing fills the small office. My heart hammers; my stomach loosens and floats. There's a small metal desk in here and a tiny industrial window that doesn't open. I grab the landline and dial 911.

Outside, Marcus pounds on the door, cursing and threatening me.

"The police are coming!" I shout, just as they answer the phone.

He retreats while I explain what happened to the operator. Next I hear Marcus attacking the front windows. It sounds like he's battering them with our plastic chairs. Over and over, I hear the shock of his swings, but the tempered glass doesn't break.

I pick the camera up and sit with my back against the wall, trembling hard. I did it. I not only got the camera, I caught Marcus too. My ankle and shoulder throb, and I can still feel his fingers gripping my skin. A few tears slide down my cheeks from the shock of it all.

Then I hear police sirens outside and exhale in relief.

It's over.

49

Jake

Monday morning, the sound of Mom's phone ringing wakes me. Stretching in a patch of sunlight, I feel calm inside, as if I've landed on my feet and can't spin away. Dad didn't abandon us; he didn't give up. He just didn't win his last fight. I guess none of us do.

Mom knocks on my door.

"Yeah." I sit up, rubbing my eyes with one hand and reaching for a T-shirt to throw on with the other.

She enters my room, pale and shaking. "That was Detective Underwood. She needs to speak to us right away."

"Why?"

"I don't know. Something's happened and we have an appointment at ten. Mr. Cline will meet us there. Oh, Jake . . . what if—"

"Hey," I say, hugging her. "It's going to be okay."

I'm not talking about the appointment, and I think she knows that. No matter what happens, I think I'm going to be okay.

At ten o' clock, a cop escorts Mom and me to the same cold interrogation room as before. I gave Cole a huge hug before school today because I don't know if I'm coming home or getting arrested.

My lawyer, Mr. Cline, is pacing when we enter the room, and I calculate how much this is costing my mom, at three hundred bucks an hour. He spots us and he's excited. "Jake! Mona!"

I smile. Was he expecting some other mother-and-son duo?

We sit, and Mr. Cline inhales a deep breath and closes his eyes, seeming to gather his thoughts.

I can't stand the waiting. "What's going on? Did Tegan wake up?"

The lawyer answers. "No, she didn't. I don't know where to begin." He places his hands delicately on the table between us. "First, the police captured Shawna's boyfriend last night. I don't have all the details, but Marcus is cutting a deal. He's confessing to some things that could be very good for you, Jake."

"Like putting Tegan in that bench or killing Shawna?"

Mr. Cline frowns. "No, not that."

I curl my hands around my head. "Then how is this good for me?"

"Detective Underwood will explain everything. You have Jessica to thank for this break in the case." Mr. Cline meets my confused gaze. "After abandoning his cave at Blind Beach, Marcus holed up on an illegal cannabis farm in Mendocino County. But last night, Jessica lured him to the sandwich shop where she works, trapped him inside, and called the police."

"*What?*"

"She's safe now, don't worry, but I'll be honest with you. They were each injured in the altercation. They were treated and released, but his injuries are worse. Jessica broke his wrist."

Fury and terror roar up from my gut and mix sickeningly in my chest. I imagine Jess battling Marcus, a man bigger than her, stronger than her, meaner than her—and I know she did it for me. "I need to see her."

"She's home safe. Ah, here's Detective Underwood."

When Detective Underwood and Officer Lee enter, Underwood offers each of us a cup of coffee, and her tone has completely changed since the last time I saw her. She's humble, like my dog Otis after a scolding. Officer Lee winks at me, a friendly, almost conspiratorial gesture that I can't interpret.

"Is the room too hot or too cold?" Underwood asks. She's never cared about my comfort before, and I shake my head.

"Let's begin, then." She doesn't read me my rights or record the interview, and that also sets me at ease. "Jake, you probably heard that Jessica Sanchez's actions led to the arrest of Daniel Marcus Lancaster, who goes by his middle name, 'Marcus,'" Underwood says with an undertone of grudging respect.

"He broke probation for a prior conviction in Nevada, which is why he's been hiding from us, but now he's cooperating as much as his lawyer will allow. Between Marcus's statements, the discovery of some new evidence, and some creative detective work"— she points at Lee—"we've come to view Tegan's party in a new light. What happened there is layers deep, Jake. Layers deep." She pinches the skin between her eyes as if weary of the whole thing. "We've informed Mr. Cline as to the basics, and Officer Lee will take over from here."

Crystal Cove's ex-cheerleader sits taller in her chair and smiles warmly. "Thanks for coming in today," she says, showing more confidence in front of Underwood than she has in the past. "I want to show you something." She turns a laptop around so my mom, Mr. Cline, and I can see the screen. "I'd like you to watch these clips I've singled out."

Lee touches the play button, and then Mom and I are transported back in time to Tegan's party.

"Big house," Mom comments as her eyes scan the screen.

The first clip shows me by the keg in the kitchen with Jess where I fill my cup with beer, and subsequent clips show us separating, then Manny and me playing pool. Lee taps on her pad of paper. "It took you thirty-two minutes to finish your first drink."

I blow out a breath and glance at my lawyer. "Is this an intervention or something?"

Officer Lee answers. "Nothing like that. Bear with me, okay?"

I nod and shift my gaze back to the laptop and the next clip, which is of me drinking a second beer and playing another round of pool. Then the time stamp jumps to over an hour later. I'm by the swimming pool, arguing with Jess. I gulp my third beer and slam it down. She leaves, angry. "I told Jess she wasn't any fun," I explain to Mom.

She frowns at me.

The following clip shows Tegan approaching me with two shot glasses, and I start to squirm. "Do we have to watch this? I was there. I remember this part."

"I'd like you to watch, Jake. It's important." Lee's eyes plead with me to give her a chance.

I cross my arms behind my head. Fuck it, I can face what I did, but I don't know why my mom and lawyer need to see this. Tegan's swimming pool glitters on the tiny laptop screen, taking me back to that night. The Jake on camera is oblivious to how badly he's about to fuck up his life. I watch myself toss back the small shot glass that reads *Drink Me*.

"This is where things get interesting," says Lee. "After that shot, you dance for forty-three minutes, but watch how your demeanor changes."

I study the screen. Before the shot of alcohol, I was standoffish—my arms crossed, my eyes scanning around for Jess. Twenty minutes after the shot, I'm wide open, letting girls get close, stroking their skin, grinding against their bodies, including Tegan's—especially Tegan's.

Sitting beside my mother at the police station, my cheeks flush with heat because this—this isn't me. I don't flirt when I have a girlfriend, not even when I'm drunk. "What the fuck?" I whisper.

Lee forwards to the last clip. "This is when you follow Tegan into her bedroom."

My eyes dart to my mother's face, which is twitching but expressionless.

On-screen, Tegan and I check upstairs for Jessica and then arrive at Tegan's door. She hovers behind me, her lips smiling. Then we disappear into her bedroom. Watching it makes me sick. I wave my hand. "Can we stop? I already admitted I got wasted."

"Please let her finish," says Mr. Cline.

"That's the thing, Jake—you didn't get wasted," says Lee, her gaze triumphant. "The family's home security system covers almost every inch of their house. Until we lost coverage at two forty-two a.m., we could see everything. I've watched the footage half a dozen times, and you're never out of sight until you and Tegan enter her bedroom."

She consults her notes. "You drank a total of three beers and one shot of tequila over a two-and-a-half-hour period. Given your height and weight, our medical expert doesn't believe you consumed nearly enough alcohol to black out and still be sick and hungover the next morning. What I found interesting is that you grew more intoxicated *after* you ceased drinking, and the evidence shows you didn't accept any drugs offered at the party."

Lee watches my reaction and continues. "I began to develop a theory about what happened to you, Jake. And now—thanks to the quick thinking of your girlfriend—we've apprehended Marcus. After confronting him with my theory last night and doing some more digging, I've confirmed it. The truth is, Tegan Sheffield drugged you."

Mom's hands begin to shake. "You're saying my son was *roofied?*"

"This changes everything," says Mr. Cline.

Lee nods. "Marcus sold Tegan what he referred to as a 'love potion' for Jake's drink. But then someone drugged her too, and that was *not* part of the plan."

My stomach drops. "Why would she do that to me?"

Underwood grimaces. "To win the bet. According to Marcus, Tegan told Shawna she was very worried you would refuse the kiss, so she bought the potion from him to spike your drink."

"Holy mother of God," Mom says, crossing herself.

My lawyer smiles encouragingly at me as Underwood continues. "When Officer Lee visited the evidence locker last week, she located all the shot glasses labeled *Drink Me* and had them tested. *Two* glasses, not one, contained trace elements of illegal substances. The fingerprints and saliva on those glasses matched your and Tegan's profiles.

"The reason you don't remember anything, Jake, is because Tegan laced your drink with GHB and liquid ecstasy. Everything you experienced afterward is consistent with the effects of these powerful drugs. GHB causes memory loss and compliance, and the stimulant in ecstasy enhances libido and sex drive, ensuring your ability to . . . perform."

Lee clears her throat. "What we don't know yet is who drugged Tegan and whether or not she set up the camera and synced it to the TV. There's no evidence that Tegan planned to record herself or authorized any of her friends to do so. We believe that whoever drugged her thought it would be funny to watch her lose control. Overall, this appears to be a double cross against Tegan that went horribly wrong."

Mom pales. "A double cross?"

"I'm sorry," Officer Lee says. "I know this is hard."

Underwood produces a notebook from her packet of papers and shows us the opened page. "Ms. Moore found Shawna's diary after Friday's vigil. We believe this line—'If Jake knew the truth . . . he would kill us all'—refers to the spiked drink. And this line—'I should turn him in'—refers to her drug-dealer boyfriend who sold the chemicals."

"But who drugged Tegan?" I ask.

"We're still looking into that and into Shawna's death." Lee glances at me, saddened and curious, and I can't believe any of this.

Underwood releases a loud sigh and nods at Lee. "Our wunderkind officer didn't solve every mystery, and that includes who put Tegan in the storage bench. It wasn't Marcus. He left the party at one-forty a.m. and showed up on casino CCTV footage at two-thirty a.m. He stayed until about five Sunday morning, playing blackjack, and then drove home. Also, the missing camera is still at large. Marcus told Jessica he had it, but he lied. The one he brought to the sandwich shop was a fake. Tegan's attacker is still at large."

I start to fidget. "How do you know it's not me?"

"We don't," says Underwood, folding her big hands in her lap. "My theory remains that you and your girlfriend colluded to seek revenge for the video."

I laugh at that, and Mom shakes her dark hair, her body vibrating with emotions. "My son would not hurt *any* girl."

Mr. Cline nods vehemently. "If this goes to court, it will be a very tough case for a prosecutor to win." He stabs the table with his finger. "My medical expert will argue that Jake can't be held responsible for his actions while drugged, and I will prove that Tegan Sheffield is a predator. She stalked and harassed my client online, dosed him with mind-altering chemicals that lowered his inhibitions and induced amnesia, and then seduced him. While her assault may have backfired against her, Tegan planned a dangerous attack against Jake that could have ended in his death. If my client had to fight his way out of that bedroom, it was self-defense." Mr. Cline trembles with fervor. "Tell Jake about the blood."

Underwood deflates. "The blood on your T-shirt doesn't belong to Tegan. It's yours, Jake. You must have wiped your injured foot with it. And we swept the storage bench for fingerprints. None of them are yours."

"Tell him about Shawna," says Mr. Cline.

"The DNA beneath her nails did not match yours, Jake."

"Unbelievable." Mom rocks in her chair, shaking her head. "So you don't have *any* evidence against him?"

Underwood bristles. "What we have are two students, Jake and

Jessica, who lied to the police and hid Tegan's cell phone from us, Ms. Healy."

Mom stands up. "No, what you have are two kids who got scared and can't see around corners. You have put my son through hell, you know that?"

The taller woman flushes. "That was not my intention."

Lee pours each of us a cup of water and clears her throat. "I want to assure you both that if we have enough evidence for a conviction, the DA will prosecute Tegan for what she did to Jake."

My guts twist. "But after she drugged me, someone drugged *her*. How can she be held responsible if I can't?"

Lee nods. "That's a good question, but Tegan was of sound mind when she purchased the drugs from Marcus, plotted to seduce you, and possibly set up the camera. We don't believe she intended anything more than the kiss, but that doesn't reduce the criminality of her actions."

Next Officer Lee slides a pamphlet across the table titled *Drug-Assisted Sexual Assault*. I stare at it, stunned, and then it hits me—all of it.

I was drugged and raped.

Suddenly I can't breathe. The veins in my arms bulge as I clench and unclench my hands. "No!" I shove the pamphlet off the table. "No, no, no." The room spins. My chest tightens. I reel out of my chair.

Everyone stands up; the fluorescent bulbs hum. "Jake, you're okay. Put your head down and take deep, slow breaths," Lee says.

I prop myself against the wall, warn them to stay away with my hands. I'm not going to let these people baby me, and I'm not going to pass out. I count to one hundred and get myself under control. The room is so quiet, I hear the wall clock ticking.

Officer Lee's voice fills the silence. "What happened isn't your fault."

Tears blur my vision and I point to the laptop. "But—I—she didn't force me. I saw the video."

My mom reaches for the tissues, crying silently.

Lee leans closer. "Jake, please hear me, truly hear me. She overcame your defenses with chemicals. It was an attack as real as a physical attack. Your mom tells me you've been very emotional since the party. You're not going to heal from this until you accept the truth."

The truth. I squeeze shut my eyes as my heart thumps in my chest. Then fresh understanding floods me. I *didn't* betray Jessica. The horrible thing that happened—that's been plaguing me—it wasn't something *I* did. It was something horrible that was done to *me*. Deep tremors roll through my body.

Mom guides me back to my chair, her hands gentle on my shoulders.

My brain continues to whirl. I didn't cheat, but to accept that, I must face the disgusting truth that I was drugged and manipulated for the sick pleasure of someone else. I must face the fact that I was used—completely and helplessly against my will while my classmates watched—that I am a *victim*.

My soul darkens and my anger rises like smoke. I manage to speak without yelling. "So, I couldn't have done anything to stop it?"

"No, Jake, you couldn't," says Officer Lee.

Fury chomps at me like the waves of the Pacific, heartless and cold and relentless, taunting me, threatening me, but leaving me only half drowned, and I groan from the weight of it. I want to run or hide or explode, but I can't do anything. It happened.

Victim. I reject the word even as it sets me free.

"What now?" Mom asks. "What about the missing camera with the footage of Jake?"

Underwood closes her yellow folder. "It's a mystery. We'll continue doing our jobs, processing evidence, and unraveling the lies from that night until we understand everything. As soon as she wakes up and her doctors and lawyers allow it, we'll interview Tegan."

Officer Lee turns to me. "The offer for counseling stands, Jake. Please let us know if we can be of assistance."

I shake my head at them, feeling whiplashed by the meeting. They called Tegan a predator, called me a victim. They'd still like to arrest me, but they also want to offer me counseling. I turn to my mom. "Let's go."

We walk out of the police station and into the sunshine. Mom grabs me and hugs me so tight that we both start to cry. "I love you," she whispers.

"I love you too." A coiled and ugly burden unfolds and lifts from my chest. I *didn't* betray my girlfriend. After inhaling deeply, I release a breath that flows toward the sea, fresh and free, like the wind. As Mom and I walk to the minivan, I feel lighter. I feel redeemed.

I am the man I thought I was.

50

Jessica

Two incredible headlines blare on the front page of the *Crystal Cove Gazette* on Wednesday morning. The first makes me physically ill:

FORMER SENATOR'S DAUGHTER
DRUGGED MINOR FOR SEX

The related article drops a bombshell. Tegan drugged Jake to win our bet, and then in a double cross, someone drugged her—the prank of all pranks. The revelations ooze like oil through Crystal Cove, dirtying and smearing our once idyllic beach town in suspicion and shock.

I'm pinned to my mattress, unable to leave my bedroom, my house. Every angry thing I said to Jake after the party comes back to me in violent breaths. I unleashed Tegan on him with that bet and then believed the worst about *him*. I never considered that she'd cheat to win. My boyfriend was drugged because of *me*.

I called Jake as soon as I heard. "I'm sorry! Oh my god, I was so awful to you," I cried. "I didn't know."

After a long silence, he said, "But you know *me*." And he hung up.

Mom says it's not my fault. "You shouldn't have made the bet, sweetie, but Tegan went too far. Her decision is not your responsibility."

Maybe that's true, but I goaded her, and Jake paid the price. At least he seems better, now that he knows the truth. He got his truck back from the police, and he pulled out of his driveway this morning with the windows down, his music thumping.

The online news media heats up again with the idea that Jake and I worked together for revenge against Tegan:

BULLIED COUPLE FIGHTS BACK

WHEN PARTY PRANK BACKFIRES, VICTIMS SEEK DEADLY REVENGE

IS CRYSTAL COVE'S CUTEST COUPLE ON A RAMPAGE?

But the second headline in the *Crystal Cove Gazette* is good news:

SLEEPING BEAUTY AWAKES!

Tegan is out of her coma and able to speak. The entire town, including me, is holding their breath, wondering what she'll say, who she'll accuse. I hope we get answers, because none of my efforts to crack this case have explained what happened to her, or Shawna either. The waiting is like watching a hammer before it falls, wondering whom it will strike.

I think back to the beginning, to what Shawna told Jake: *Everyone is lying.* Who is everyone? Not Jake, because she was speaking to him, and not Shawna, since she planned to tell the police the truth. Who does that leave? I make a list of Tegan's closest associates.

+ Brendon
+ Marcus
+ Chiara
+ Hailey
+ Grady

And what was everyone lying about? Probably drugging Jake. To be fair, blackout drinking is nothing new for Jake, which is why it never occurred to me that he'd been drugged. But who spiked Tegan's drink and put her in the bench, and who killed Shawna?

The latest press conference indicated that Marcus has an alibi for Tegan's assault *and* Shawna's death. Brendon has an alibi too. That leaves Chiara and Hailey, but they're too afraid of Tegan to hurt her. My gut tells me that whoever crammed her into that bench is *passionate* about her—and not in a good way—as weird as that sounds.

Since Chloe's at the gym, I call Alyssa on our landline. She's a voice of reason, and she answers on the first ring. "Jess! The internet is on fire about you and Jake! Are you okay?"

"Yes. I mean no. I need to talk something out." I take a breath, knowing that what I'm about to say sounds crazy. "I can't stop thinking about the car accident. What if I hit Tegan and broke her arm? What if someone found her and put her in the bench, or she got confused and crawled in herself?"

Alyssa chokes on something. "Jesus, Jess! You hit a deer. Chloe saw it."

"But I can't get the accident out of my head. I've had nightmares since it happened. I—I saw an eyeball; it looked human. Maybe Chloe is wrong. It was pretty dark."

Alyssa doesn't respond for a moment, then says, "Okay, going with that train of thought and assuming that you hit someone, why does it have to be Tegan?"

My spine stiffens, and tingles splay across my stomach. "Who else could it be?"

Alyssa bites on something crunchy. "I don't know, but they kept running after you hit them, right? There had to have been a reason, and we both know Tegan would have stopped. No way could you run her over, break her arm, and not get an earful."

I laugh softly. "True."

"Maybe the person kept running because they didn't want to be identified. See? What if you hit Tegan's *attacker?*"

"Seriously, Alyssa! Do you think that's possible?"

She chews loudly. "No, I think you hit a fucking deer, but it's plausible, I guess. Too bad you cleaned my dad's car. The blood's gone. We'll never know."

We talk a bit longer and then hang up. I strip off my running clothes and throw them onto the floor. I'm pissed about the BMW. That blood on the grille was the only evidence I had that might explain what I hit on the road. As I pull on fresh clothes, my heart stalls.

My jeans!

I wiped some blood on my jeans that night! I rip through a pile of unwashed clothes, and find the pants I wore to the party. Lifting them out, I close my eyes and send up a silent prayer. Then I lay them flat on my floor.

There it is—the crusty bloodstain. "Gotcha," I whisper.

✦ ✦ ✦

I call Officer Lee, and an hour later, she's at my front door to collect the jeans. "So maybe you didn't hit a deer," she says wryly.

"How long will it take to find out whose blood it is?"

She purses her lips. "We can't match it unless the person's DNA is already in our database. We've been swabbing every party guest who will allow it, and we're still processing those samples. It could take another week to finish, but the lab will expedite this test. At least we can find out if the blood is animal or human." Lee smiles and encases the jeans in a plastic evidence bag.

"Hey," I say as she turns to go. "I heard you're the one who figured out Jake was drugged. I—I never even considered it."

Lee lowers the volume on her police radio and leans against the front door. "Something similar happened when I was in college. My best friend drank at a party and woke up the next morning in the guest room with the door locked. The student who threw the party told her she'd gotten very drunk and he'd put her there to keep her safe."

Lee's eyes go vague, as if she's looking at something far away. "My friend was grateful, even bought him a gift card. A year later, he got busted for drugging and kidnapping a freshman girl at college. During the investigation, police found naked photos of my friend, and several other students, on his computer. She was devastated."

"That's awful."

Officer Lee nods and sighs. "Since then, I pay attention. This is more common than people think, and the perp is often someone the victim knows well, even trusts."

The air around us goes still as I contemplate this, and then gratitude washes over me for Jake's sake. "Thanks again," I tell her.

"It's my job, Jessica. I'll have these jeans sent to the lab and we'll be in touch."

As she's driving away, I glance up at Jake's window. His light is on, but for the first time in a long time, he's not watching me.

51

—

Jessica

The police have gone silent as Crystal Cove waits for more answers. Tegan is awake, but her lawyers won't allow her to talk until she's had a few more cognitive tests, and Jake still isn't speaking to me. This weekend he went surfing with Manny and Alyssa. No one invited me, and I can't blame them. Chloe is at the college gymnastics showcase in Arizona, and Shawna's mother held a Celebration of Life yesterday. I wasn't invited to that either.

Sunday evening my new phone rings. It's Chloe, calling from the showcase in Arizona. She's breathless. "I made it, Jessica! I committed to UCLA, and as long as nothing goes wrong, I'll sign in November!" Her words bubble across the phone line, effervescent, without a trace of her prior anger.

"Chloe! I'm so proud of you. I knew you could do it."

She leaps into a retelling of her competition, all the highs and lows and slight bobbles and perfect landings. "I nailed my beam routine, finally! Didn't even chip a tooth." She laughs about the beam injury that almost ruined her career, which is so unlike Chloe. She's high from her success. She won her prize. "It was all worth it," she whispers.

I imagine the hours in the gym, the missed parties and date nights, the injuries, the pain, the surgeries. "Of course it was," I tell her.

Her breath catches, and she's quiet a moment. "Jess, I'm sorry I got angry about the bet thing. I understand why you didn't want to tell anyone. We're flying home tonight and my parents are having a dinner for me tomorrow. Will you come?"

"Yes!" A feeling of hope washes through me. Chloe and I are okay, and she accomplished her dream. Maybe Jake will forgive me too. Maybe everything will be okay.

◆ ◆ ◆

The following evening, I drive to Chloe's. The second lightning storm from Mexico is expected to arrive soon, bringing rain and high winds, another gift of global warming. Our meteorologist dubbed the storm "rainopalypse." It's gray and miserable and windy outside.

Chloe lives near the mouth of the Russian River on the north side of Blind Beach. Her house is small, just two bedrooms with a wraparound porch. I brought flowers for her, and Grady is here too with his dog, Boomer. He gives Chloe a solid gold necklace with a cursive pendant that reads *Champion*.

"It's not a gold medal, but it's gold metal," he says, blushing.

"That's cute." I snap a photo of them with my phone.

Her parents serve a six-course salmon dinner that is delicious. No one speaks about Tegan, or about Shawna's unsolved death, even though we have a clear view of Falcon's Peak from the windows.

After dinner, Chloe, Grady, and I decide to walk their dogs on the beach before the storm makes landfall.

"I'll be right behind you," I say, nodding toward the restroom.

Chloe and Grady gather the goldendoodles and run, laughing, to the beach. I hit the restroom and then stop in Chloe's bedroom to snap a picture of her new trophy. Her shelves are lined with them and dripping with medals and photos, a lifetime of dedication and talent.

The photos progress with her age. She was so cute as a toddler, already at the gym, tumbling. Fifteen years later, she's not much bigger, but her body is banded in muscle. She's stiff but graceful, light but powerful, with eyes like portals that see the future. You don't work as hard as Chloe if you can't see the finish line.

I trace my finger along her older trophies, and stop at the one she earned the day she busted out her front teeth. It was the last event we attended with Tegan, before the friendship fell apart. Chloe won the trophy for her bar performance, but balance beam was next and that routine was difficult. She'd struggled with it for weeks before the competition. Still, everyone expected her to win the all-around and qualify for the National Junior Olympics.

But that day, she was not herself. She didn't work the beam; it worked her. When she flipped backward, she under-rotated and landed on her face, almost snapped her corded neck. The gym erupted, officials running, her parents crying, her blood spurting. Chloe crumpled like a baby bird fallen out of its nest. Tegan and I watched, horrified.

Winning the cup for bars meant nothing to her that day, and here it is, crooked on her shelf, like a twisted tooth. I realign the trophy so it's as perfect as the others, and hear a rattling noise. Reaching inside the metal cup, I pull out an object that makes my heart tumble into erratic thudding. No, no, no! This is not what I think it is. It can't be!

I rewind it, hit the play button, and my world, my childhood, and my friendships—they implode.

52

Jessica

"It was you!" I storm the beach, shouting over the wind. The coast is socked in by fog, and the froth-tipped waves of the Pacific Ocean churn up the sediment, making the water look brown.

I catch Grady and Chloe in the middle of a kiss—their first? They break apart when they hear me shouting. Their dogs splash and play at the river's mouth, oblivious.

"Explain this, Chloe." I hold up the tiny camera, the missing evidence that contains the video of Jake and Tegan having sex, but also more—much, much more.

Grady draws his eyebrows together, and Chloe backs away from both of us.

"What did you do? What did you do!" I cry, clutching the camera in my fist, terrified of dropping it into the water.

Her mouth pops open; her eyes fill with tears. "No—nothing." Her body breaks into deep shivers.

"I watched the recording."

Chloe blanches.

"It was *you* in Tegan's bedroom. You fought with her and smashed the mirror."

Grady staggers. "What are you saying, Jessica?"

But my eyes remain fixed on Chloe.

"Tegan attacked *me*," Chloe rasps, walking backward.

I shake my head, my voice rising with the wind. "No, you're lying. You went into her room and fought with *her*. Tegan saw the posts on her phone and accused you of syncing the camera to the TV. You admitted it, Chloe. I heard you!" I wave the camera at her, and she lunges for it.

"Give it back!" she cries.

"No." I toss it to Grady, hoping he can catch as well as he can pitch. He's startled, but his long arm snakes out and the camera lands safely in his palm.

Chloe starts to cry, and I snarl at her, "When Tegan tried to get the camera back, you attacked her. It's all there, and Jake slept through it. You *knew* he was innocent this whole time. You let everyone believe—" I choke back tears and press on. "The camera kept recording by the pool house. I heard everything. I know what you did."

Grady can't breathe. He stares at Chloe in horror. "You put my sister in the bench? You—you tried to kill her?"

"No." Chloe's arms lift up to block her face. The tumbling surf swipes at her legs, licking her hungrily, but Chloe seems suddenly more dangerous than the sea. Her fake teeth chatter. "I—I was trying to climb the f-fence behind the pool house but she . . . she gr-grabbed me. She fell."

"Tegan didn't fall," I sputter. "You kicked her to the concrete with those." I point at Chloe's legs, the thick pistons that power her into the air, fling her into triple flips, and then catch her landings like solid bolts of steel. "You knocked her out, broke her arm, crammed her in that bench, and then let the world believe Jake did it." My voice warbles.

"Why?" Grady asks, looking destroyed.

Chloe's voice pitches so high, the dogs bound over to lick her hands. Her head swivels from me to Grady. "You don't see how your sister treats me. Sh-she hates me." Her face twists. "Tegan tried to k-keep me away from both of you. She—she tried to ruin me. Do you know wh-what she said right before I took the b-beam that day?"

Chloe glances at me, and I know exactly what day she's talking about—the day she busted out nine of her front teeth and lost her chance at the National Junior Olympic team. The day that ended her international gymnastics career.

Chloe's voice turns cold, slick. "After my perfect uneven-bar score, I went to the restroom, and Tegan was there, waiting for me. She said, 'Beam is next, right? I'm filming it for Grady. Don't fall like you did in practice.'"

Grady flinches.

"Tegan knew I had a crush on you," Chloe growls. "She said that to get into my head, and then she sat in the front row, waving her camera at me, and it worked. I couldn't focus. It almost killed me."

Tegan's brother pounds his chest. "She was a *kid*," he snarls. "It was years ago. My sister could have *died*, Chloe! Why did you leave her in there so long? Why didn't you tell anyone?"

"I thought she *was* dead."

"Oh god." A wave of nausea rolls over me. "You thought you were hiding a body."

Chloe sniffles. "I needed to focus on the college showcase. There was no point in getting help if she ... was gone."

Grady charges her, his arm cocked back, his huge hand balled into a fist.

"Grady, no!" I shout, but he stops himself, inches from Chloe's face.

"I hate you," he rasps. "I hate you, I hate you!" His words batter her worse than any punches could.

"Stop it!" she screams, covering her ears.

"Did you drug her too?" he asks. "Did you want everyone to see her and Jake together?"

Sobbing, Chloe shakes her head. "No. I didn't know about that, just the bet, and I didn't believe Jake would go for Tegan. I wanted him to *reject* her. I wanted her friends to watch her lose, like I lost. All I meant to do was film it. I—I had no idea she'd drug him."

I flash back to Chloe's contortionist show at the party. "Did you do those tricks on the dining room table so that everyone would be near the TV?"

Her stricken face confirms what I've said. She glances at the dark sky. "But when Tegan and Jake kept going, I—I couldn't believe it. That wasn't supposed to happen. When everyone started posting, I knew there'd be an investigation, because it happened to that girl on my team. My fingerprints were on the camera, and I just wanted to grab it. I didn't plan to fight with Tegan. I'm sorry, Grady."

Chloe is hunched now, shivering harder and soaked with sea spray. She glares at me. "None of this would have happened if you hadn't made that bet, Jessica."

"What you did to Tegan isn't my fault," I cry.

Grady swipes back his hair, still stuck on the details. "You turned off our security cameras, didn't you?" he asks. Chloe looks away, tearful, and he drops his head into his hands. "Jesus, I gave you the password when we got the puppies, so you could walk Boomer. The police asked if anyone had access, but I totally forgot. Damnit! You—you . . .". He can't finish. He stares at the camera in his hand, which holds the truth about what happened to his sister.

Chloe takes another step back, deeper into the water. "I'm sorry. Please, I'm sorry."

Her face shifts, so raw, like I've never seen it. I cross my arms, sickened. "Did you put Tegan's phone in Jake's truck?"

Chloe cries louder.

I glance at Grady. "We should call the police."

"No," she pleads. "I just committed to UCLA. I worked for this my entire life." Her eyes dart to Grady. "Don't do this to me."

His eyebrows lift and his cheeks flame. He exhales, almost involuntarily. "Tegan always said you were no good for me. She saw you for the monster you are."

I think back to Tegan's hatred when we were kids, calling Chloe a parasite and a clown, taunting Chloe at her meets. I remember Tegan slapping me in fifth grade and then Chloe shoving her into a table. Were each of my friends capable of violence? Then there was me, daring Tegan to kiss Jake and then blaming him for it. I'm no better.

Chloe shakes her head, her wet hair slapping her skin. "Tegan's the monster."

"Maybe we all are," I whisper. We each took things too far, but no one further than Chloe. "I'm calling the police." I slide my phone out of my pocket. Shawna's voice whispers across the water, *Everyone is lying*, and my throat constricts with a new, more terrible realization. "Did Shawna find out you synced the camera? Did you kill her and set up Jake for that too?"

Chloe's expression hardens and her shoulders lift. "He shouldn't have cheated on you."

"He was drugged!"

"I didn't know that." Chloe's eyes morph into those opaque portals from her photos. She sees the future and it scares her; I can tell by the tremble in her chin. It's the beam routine all over again, and Chloe's afraid of what's next. "They don't have gymnastics in prison," she murmurs.

Grady and I cock our heads, noticing she didn't deny killing Shawna.

The waves swell behind Chloe as the heat and wind from Mexico tangle with our fog and icy water, creating a pile of sodden, heavy, gray clouds that sparkle and rumble overhead. As the first droplets of rain splatter us, Chloe dashes into the sea.

"Chloe, stop," I shout, and then turn my back on the ocean to dial the police.

Mistake number one.

A sleeper wave swamps Chloe and then me, knocking us off our feet. Ice-cold salt water floods my mouth, sand scrapes my skin, and tumbling waves drag me out and roll me into the deep. Murky, swirling sediment confuses my senses. Grady's muffled shouts pierce the surface like bullets.

Then suddenly I'm sliding through the water, as if something strong, something angry is pulling me. A ghost. Shawna.

No, it's Chloe.

Her fingers wrap around my arm, and her eyes bulge, terrified, and then a new wave breaks us apart. I kick harder as my muscles catch fire. My lungs seem to swell and shrink at the same time. I scream into the current.

The riptide sweeps us into the open ocean. To the sharks. To the watery graves of fish.

Mistake number two.

Chloe is not more dangerous than the sea.

53

Chloe, End-of-Summer Party

9:15 p.m. My eyes tracked Tegan as she glided through her end-of-summer party like a queen. She was her best self when she was in charge, the center of attention, calling every shot. I understood because I felt the same when I competed.

I was standing beside the nachos, salivating even though I ate three thousand calories a day, and my eyes drilled into Tegan's back. Winners had a glow that regular people lacked, but they made mistakes. Then they lost.

Tegan was going to lose tonight, and I couldn't wait.

I grabbed a handful of the cheesy tortilla chips and fed myself. Chew and swallow. Chew and swallow. If I didn't enjoy the food, it felt okay to eat junk. Chew and swallow. The processed cheese and salt flooded my system, calmed my nerves.

I first heard about Tegan's bet the day after her Fourth of July party. Grady called and begged me to help him clean up the beach.

Tegan and Shawna were hungover and he needed help. I brought my dog, Celeste, and we spent the morning tossing empty cans, bottles, plastic trays of half-eaten food, and expended fireworks into garbage bags.

Afterward, Grady cooked me breakfast and asked if I'd run upstairs to grab his laptop. There, through the door of their shared bathroom, I overhead Tegan on her phone.

"I'm going to kiss Jake," she was saying. "No, I don't want him back. Well, maybe . . ."

I craned my neck as her voice dipped lower.

"I'm not kidding, Shawna, I got fifty bucks riding on this kiss." Tegan laughed. "I think I'm going to do it at my end-of-summer party."

My stomach flipped over. What the hell?

"No, it's not crazy. But look, I have to win this bet. Like, if I lose, you know, I'll look really stupid."

I slid my phone out of my pocket and switched it to silent, terrified a notification would go off and Tegan would catch me eavesdropping. I couldn't believe she was talking about kissing Jake—my best friend's boyfriend!

"No shit," Tegan whispered into her phone. "Of course Jake won't *want* to kiss me, but I have an idea. If it doesn't work, though, no one can ever know about this. You got it? . . . Good. Come over later, okay?"

They went on talking about other things, and I grabbed Grady's laptop and slunk back downstairs. I wondered who'd made the bet with Tegan, but it didn't really matter. What mattered was that she planned to kiss Jake.

That's when I came up with an idea of my own, because if I knew one thing about Jake Healy, it was that he was head over heels in love with Jessica Sanchez. Tegan was going to lose this bet, like I lost my shot at the Junior Olympics that day on the beam. A smile crept across my face. The only thing a winner hates more than losing is losing in front of a crowd.

* * *

9:35 p.m. After chatting with Jessica and Alyssa by the snack table, I hunted down Brendon Reed, found him in the basement, and pulled him inside an empty bathroom. "Is everything set with the TV in the family room? Are you sure it will sync to the camera?"

He blinked at me, looking drunk. "Yeah, it's set."

What Tegan didn't know about Brendon was that he hated her. I knew this because Brendon and I had taken photography together the previous year. We'd partnered on a project, and one day he'd unloaded on me about how Tegan used him, teased him, and bossed him around. He put up with it for the social status—not how he verbalized it, but I got the drift. Brendon had sold his soul to be popular.

So when I suggested we live-broadcast her attempt to kiss Jake—a feat destined to fail, and fail big—the Cameraman was all over it. He showed me the motion-activated camera the day before Tegan's party and went over how it worked. I went to Grady's and slipped into Tegan's room through their Jack and Jill bathroom—where there were no security cameras to catch me. I set the camera on her bookshelf between two of her old stuffed animals. It was so small, she'd never notice it.

Brendon had an app that connected to the motion-sensor camera. When Tegan and Jake entered her room, the camera would start recording. Brendon would get an alert on his phone and then switch the input on the big TV downstairs to the live camera feed. "You're one hundred percent sure it will work?" I asked again.

"Yeah, it'll work. I've got the remote." He slid a thin black TV remote from his pocket and dangled it in front of my eyes. "You're pure evil for coming up with this, you know that?" He leaned forward and tried to kiss me.

Our heads bumped, and when I pushed him away, he looked sad. Then he hiccuped, and I laughed because I was generous enough to pretend none of that weirdness had just happened. No one liked rejection, especially not assholes.

"This is going to be epic," Brendon added. "You have no idea."

"No idea about what?"

He laughed again, wiped his lips, and left the bathroom. "You'll see."

◆ ◆ ◆

2:35 *a.m.* Brendon was right, it was epic! Tegan didn't just kiss Jake and win the bet; she went *all the way*. And Jake was into it. I wouldn't have believed it if I hadn't watched it on a ninety-inch screen.

I got Jessica out of that family room as fast as I could. What the hell was Jake thinking? What an asshole!

While Jess sobbed beside me, I shifted into full panic mode. I doubt anyone could tell by looking at me—I'd learned to control my face and body—but my mind was in turmoil. I almost couldn't breathe because of the terror.

Tegan and Jake had had *sex*, and everyone had posted it online. I knew there'd be an investigation. Jake was underage and Tegan was a former senator's daughter; those posts would spread like wildfire.

Brendon and I were screwed. We had texts between us talking about the live feed and both our fingerprints were on the camera. If either of us were caught, detectives would take our phones and figure out we'd planned this. We could be arrested, sued, fined! I'd be kicked off the team. I'd miss the college showcase.

Everything I'd worked for since I was two years old was on the line because Tegan and Jake couldn't control themselves. My only consolation was that I'd succeeded in humiliating her—just not in the way I'd hoped.

But that didn't matter now. What mattered was getting the camera back.

"I'll grab us some food while we're waiting," I mumbled to Jess and Alyssa, and then slipped out of the guest bedroom.

I crept through Tegan's house toward the utility staircase. The Sheffields' security cameras blinked at me from all over the house, watching silently. Three years before, Grady had given me access to the system so I could take care of Boomer whenever his family was out of town. I opened his security app on my phone and disabled the Sheffields' cameras at two-forty-two a.m. I didn't want a record of what I was about to do.

I bumped into Brendon at the bottom of the staircase. He had just snuck in through the back door. "I thought you went home?" I asked. Right after the video had played on the TV, I'd seen him pull out his car keys and leave through the front door.

"I did, but this shit is blowing up online. I came back for the camera. If Tegan finds it, she'll know it's mine and fucking kill me." A shadowed smile creased his face. "Told you it would be epic."

My scalp tightened. "Did you know she planned to screw Jake, because I still can't believe it?"

He shrugged. "Maybe, maybe not."

Anger flared in my stomach. "Jessica is destroyed," I added, crossing my arms. "And do you know how much trouble we're in if anyone finds out?"

"Trouble with Tegan?"

"With the police," I hissed. "Our fingerprints are on that camera. We need to get it and delete our texts too."

"The police?" Brendon scoffed. "I doubt it, but I'm here to grab it anyway."

I considered our options. Even with the security cameras disabled, there was the risk of a person seeing us enter Tegan's bedroom. I wasn't her friend, but Brendon was. "All right, you get it," I agreed, and he tromped up the stairs.

On the way back to the guest room, I grabbed a few snacks for Alyssa and Jess.

◆ ◆ ◆

3:16 *a.m.* Holy fuck! Jessica just crashed into Brendon with the BMW. Could tonight get any worse? Why was he bolting across the street like a fucking deer, anyway? It was dark and raining hard, and he didn't stop. After the car hit him, he just kept going.

The lie slipped easily from my lips. "It was a deer, Jess."

Later, at home, I texted Brendon: *I saw you on the road, are you okay? Did you get the camera?*

After a long pause, he answered: *sorta okay and no i didn't*

Me: *WHAT???*

Brendon: *Tegan was awake and super sick, like scary sick. i got the fuck outta there. Ill get the camera later*

Later? The sun was about to rise, and once the town was fully awake, and the school, or Tegan's parents, became aware of the posts, the shit show would begin. I lived on the other side of Blind Beach from Tegan's house. I slipped on my hoodie and jogged back to the party. If you wanted something done right, you had to do it yourself.

+ + +

4:50 a.m. When I opened Tegan's bedroom door, neither of them noticed at first. She and Jake were still here, on her bed. A sliver of light from her bathroom created a yellow stripe down Jake's naked body. He was facedown, breathing deeply, passed out cold. Tegan sat beside him, her yellow hair clumped and knotted around her face as she angrily swiped her phone screen. I smelled vomit, saw it splattered across her bathroom and down her top—bright red, the same color as Shawna's Jell-O shots.

Rage filled me, unbidden and unexpected. This wasn't Brendon's fault or mine or Jake's—it was *hers*. Tegan had wanted Jessica's boyfriend, and now she had him. She hadn't changed a bit since fifth grade. I stepped out of the shadows. "Looks like you just won fifty bucks."

She fell back, clutching her nightshirt.

I nodded toward Jake's body sprawled languidly across her sex-stained comforter. "Congratulations."

Her jaw worked in circles. Her spine tightened and her cheeks flushed. "Fuck you, Chloe. How long have you been in here?"

"Did you see all the stories? You're famous."

She started to pant. "Did you do this?"

"It was all you. Bravo!" I began a long, slow clap.

Tegan jumped on me, but I was stronger and she was clumsy from alcohol, even after throwing most of it up. We spun around the room and knocked into her desk, sliding it across the hardwood. Her hand clutched for purchase and landed on her floor-to-ceiling white curtain, and tore it down.

We smashed into her dresser, shattering the mirror. The glass cut Tegan's arm, and blood splattered across her satin bedding. Jake moaned in his sleep, and Tegan gasped. "Look what you did!"

I gripped her arms, my fingers clawing into her pampered flesh.

"Let me go. That hurts," she cried, her blue eyes tearful but furious.

The past bubbled up in my chest. I hated Tegan. I wanted to slap her, but instead I let her go. She clamped her hand over her wounded arm. "What do you want?" she rasped.

"This." I snatched the hidden camera.

Her eyelids sprang wide. Her voice rose. "Did you—are you the one who filmed us?"

I smiled. I couldn't help it.

Tegan shook Jake's body. "Wake up!" He flipped over but didn't wake up. She snarled and stumbled after me.

I raced toward the staircase. Tegan's footsteps followed as we roared down the stairs and out of the house. It was still raining buckets outside, and I couldn't see well in the dark. Tegan chased me past her swimming pool and toward the pool house. Eight-foot-tall iron security fencing edged the manicured portion of her property. I sprinted along the fence line like a trapped dog, looking for a way out.

"Stop!" Tegan shouted.

I glanced back at her dark house. Her parents were still out of town, and Grady had left with Chase Waters. Tegan's friends were gone. We were alone.

I stopped behind the pool house and whirled, startling her. Tegan swept her wet hair out of her eyes. The muscles in her face twitched. "Why are you running? Just give me the camera, Chloe."

The lens peeked from my pocket, cold and powerful, still recording. It could destroy me. I would never let her have it. "Over my dead body."

"You're kidding!" she screeched. "What are you, ten years old?" Obviously nothing had changed between us in all these years. Her eyes narrowed. "You still blame me for that beam accident, don't you?"

I shifted my jaw.

She laughed at the wet sky. "Lord almighty, you could never take a joke, Chloe."

"Looks like you can't take a joke either."

She stomped toward me, eyes brimming with rage and tears. "This is different. You hid a camera in my *bedroom*. My mother will put you in jail for that. Your gymnastics career, if you can actually call it that, is over. Now give me the fucking camera." She dropped her phone and closed the space between us in one giant step.

My gut loosened as her eyes bored into mine. Tegan had always terrified me. I leaped onto the eight-foot security fence and climbed it.

⋅ ⋅ ⋅

5:12 a.m. As the rain streaked from the sky, Tegan reached up and grabbed my leg, her face screwed tight, her mascara sending black rivers down her cheeks. "I think I will take that camera over your dead body," she growled. Her anger sobered her and gave her strength.

But I was stronger.

I cocked my foot back and kicked her arm with it. She clawed at my jeans, trying to drag me off the fence. I twisted and climbed higher, swift and effortless.

"Get down here, you clown." She paced below me like a tiger.

"Come and get me," I taunted.

"I swear to the stars and back, I'm gonna kill you, Chloe Hart." Tegan leaped into the air, rocketing toward me with all the jumping power of a varsity volleyball player. Her hand wrapped around my calf.

"Let go!" I kicked her, over and over, battering her arm with my free foot. She cried out but didn't let go. I coiled and kicked again, and we heard her bone snap. Tegan let go and fell to the ground. She landed on her feet, reeled back, and then looked up at me in shock.

Her beautiful face, twisted with pain, kindled something rotten within me.

Still hanging from the iron fence, I lowered myself, swung my legs, and then kicked her like a horse would—a double-barrel shot to the chest that sent Tegan flying into the side of the pool house. Her head smacked the wood siding and then bounced forward. Her eyes spun around like a cartoon character's. She slid to the cold wet concrete, as limp as a doll.

360

"Chloe," she rasped. "Chloe . . ." And then her eyes closed.

I dropped off the fence and watched her, my legs trembling. Whatever had ignited inside me, now splintered through my body like buckshot. Oh fuck, what had I done? I dropped beside Tegan and listened to her chest, heard nothing. Nothing! Falling back, I covered my mouth to hold back a scream. I'd killed her.

The sun was rising quickly, and the panic I'd been struggling to subdue since the video had gone live spread its wings in my chest. Every somersault, every flip, every bruise and broken bone, every missed party, every missed kiss, every skipped dessert, and every golden trophy flashed before my eyes. At my feet, Tegan's mouth had gone slack, and her skin had turned waxy and pale. I put my ear to her wet lips, felt nothing, heard nothing.

Tegan was gone, holy shit, but I wasn't.

I lifted her long lifeless body. *Should I drop her into the sea?* I wondered. The ocean waves rolled and crashed below the cliff, but my stomach gurgled at the thought.

Right then Shawna stumbled out of the basement, jingling her keys, heading home. I thought she'd left too and I ducked. If she turned her head, she'd see me. I swallowed my breath and carried Tegan into the shadows beside the pool house. There was a dirty storage bench there, shoved up against the wall, almost big enough to fit Tegan.

I plopped her down, opened it, and pulled out a few abandoned chaise lounge cushions, thinking hard. No one knew I was here. The security cameras were off, and I'd been dropped off at home earlier. Not even Brendon knew I'd come back. I could put Tegan inside this bench and she'd be safe from the rain and sun until her family found her body. No one would ever suspect I'd killed her.

Decision made, I folded Tegan into the bench, bending her legs and arms as if she were a Barbie doll. Then I gazed at her. Even with a torn shirt, her arm bent at an odd angle, and her wet hair plastered to her skin, she looked pretty.

I covered her with the cushions, wiped my fingerprints, and closed the lid. I found her cell phone where she'd dropped it, noticed it had cracked, and then stashed it in Jake's glove box since his truck was still in the driveway—that's what he got for cheating on Jess. Meanwhile, the rain poured from the sky, erasing our footprints, our scent, erasing everything.

On my way home, I didn't hurry, I didn't cry, but deep within my chest, my heart pounded, and deep within my mind, a thought screamed, *Don't walk away!* But I had learned to control my body and my mind, and I shoved those feelings aside and didn't look back. What would be gained by getting help? Nothing. But everything could be lost.

By the time I got home, I was sure of only one thing—this was Tegan's fault, not mine.

54

Jake

As soon as they let me see Jessica, I rush to the hospital, but her dad stops me in the lobby.

"Jake," he starts.

"I just want to see Jessica. Please."

"It's okay," he says. "You can see her. I wanted to tell you I'm— I'm sorry for being so hard on you." He shakes my hand and Mrs. Sanchez offers me a quick hug, and then they tell me her room number.

Up on the third floor, Jessica looks like she's been to hell and back. Her rescue, and the revelation about Chloe assaulting Tegan, played on TV two days ago, and I watched it from home. The rescue footage claws at me each time I close my eyes, because Jessica could have died. The current swept her and Chloe into the Red Triangle into water so deep that rescuers would have needed a submersible to collect her, had she drowned.

It was Grady's quick call to 911 that made the rescue happen, before hypothermia or something worse killed her.

"Hey," I say, sitting on a chair by her bed, "next time you go swimming, stay in the shallow end."

She smiles, but it fades quickly. "I can't believe it was Chloe, Jake. I'm so confused."

"Yeah, me too." Jess looks hollow and pale in the bed, and I resist the urge to touch her.

"Am I blind, Jake? Did I miss something with Chloe? Tegan never liked her; maybe she sensed something I didn't. I wonder if I'd listened . . . if I'd chosen Tegan over Chloe . . ."

I shake my head. "They both have their issues, Jessica."

"Have they found Chloe yet?"

I rub the skin between my eyes as she blinks back tears. "The Coast Guard is still looking."

"God, the sharks . . ."

"Don't think about it."

The camera Jessica found had recorded Chloe's attack on Tegan and her admission to setting up the camera. The police searched her house and phone records, and they found evidence that she killed Shawna. DNA collected from Chloe's toothbrush matched to the skin collected from beneath Shawna's fingernails. Also, Chloe's phone GPS shows that she traveled to Falcon's Peak and back during the window the coroner set for the time of death, which included the hours before I got there.

It's anyone's guess what happened, but there's no doubt the two girls fought at the top of the cliff before Shawna fell. Then, using Shawna's cell, Chloe texted me, saying to meet at Falcon's Peak. She knew that when Shawna's body was found, I'd be blamed.

The way I see it, if the death was an accident, why set me up? But I also wouldn't describe any of Chloe's recent behavior as rational or understandable.

The camera also recorded Chloe putting Tegan's cell in my glove box. *That's* how angry Chloe was that I'd cheated on Jess. The police plan to charge her for murder and attempted murder, if they find her alive.

"Chloe was scared," Jess says from her hospital bed. "I don't believe she meant to hurt anyone."

"She covered her tracks and set me up to take the fall," I retort. "Don't kid yourself about Chloe, Jess. All she cares about is herself."

Let me go. That hurts. Tegan must have said that to Chloe while I slept through the whole damn thing. Not my finest moment.

I wipe my palms on my jeans, feeling antsy. Talking with Jess feels too familiar, too comfortable, and I'm not here to go backward. "I'm just glad you're okay," I tell her.

She reaches for my hand. "I'm so sorry about the bet and what Tegan did to win. I—I don't know what I was thinking."

I pull away from her before my anger can sprout to the surface. "It's fine; it's over." Her amber eyes meet mine, and I hold her gaze because I need to make sure she understands my next words. "We're over too."

"I know." A tear slides down her cheek, and it's like I can hear her heart splitting in half, because that's how I felt when she first broke up with me. It sucks, but I can't help her, not anymore. "I gotta go, Jess. I have an AA meeting in thirty minutes."

She sniffles, wipes her eyes. "That's good."

I study her and she looks different, still beautiful, but different.

Maybe it's because I'm no longer hers and she's no longer mine. Our connection was like a filter that washed out every flaw. Now she could be anyone's girl, or no one's.

I offer a smile. "Guess who DM'd me? Tegan Sheffield. She's doing okay, except for all the legal trouble she's in. Says she's sorry. Can you believe it, a DM apology for what she did to me?" I laugh, but Jess looks appalled. "It's all right. It's more than I expected."

She bolts upright as I start to leave. "Jake, will you apply to college too? Please. For me?"

"Already did," I tell her. The school counselor convinced me I could squeak into a state college if I brought up my math grade. I didn't apply for Jessica, though, or for me; I did it for my dad. "Bye, Ms. Sanchez."

She hiccups silent tears. "Bye, Mr. Healy." Like lovers returning gifts, we give each other our names back.

I leave feeling better than I thought I would. At home, Cole is waiting for me. We're going to play soccer and go for ice cream and then watch a movie with Mom tonight. In between all that, I'm hitting the gym with Manny. The fiasco with Tegan and me is over, but I'm still on the hook for beating up Brendon. The charges were reduced and my record will be expunged. Being a minor isn't always a bad thing.

There's one question still unanswered: Which of Tegan's friends spiked her drink? Who double-crossed her? Maybe we'll never know.

55

Jessica

As Jake strides out of my hospital room, he leaves a chill in his wake. I cry for a long time—for him, for Chloe, for Shawna, for me. Officer Lee charged me with interfering with a police investigation because I lied to Detective Green and because I didn't immediately turn in Tegan's phone.

But it's not over. The lab finished processing the DNA swabs from the party guests against the bloodstain on my jeans, and there's been a match! It's good, but it means I hit a human being, not a deer.

Officer Lee told me the person has been questioned and is in custody. She isn't charging me with a hit-and-run offense since I stopped and checked the scene, and there wasn't a victim on the road. A police press conference is scheduled for two o'clock today. My hospital television is turned on and ready.

My door creaks open and I glance up, expecting my nurse, but it's Tegan Sheffield. Our rooms are on the same floor, but I didn't expect a visit. She stands on the threshold, her broken arm in a cast, and she's wearing a fluffy blue robe with a pair of Uggs. She passed all her cognitive tests and is recovering quicker than doctors expected, but she looks tired. Her hair is pulled back and she's not wearing makeup. Her nose is slightly red from crying, or maybe she's just cold. "Hi, Jessica."

My stomach clenches and my throat constricts. The last time I saw her, she was tonguing my boyfriend in a blue lace bra. "What do you want?"

"Can I come in?"

I lift a shoulder, and she takes the chair Jake vacated. "I'm glad you're okay," she says, echoing Jake.

My heat rises; my thoughts crumple. "I'm not okay."

She scoots closer. "Jessica, look at me."

I force myself to meet her gaze. Her big blue eyes water, and her chin quivers. "I'm not okay either. I did terrible things. My lawyers are cutting a deal with the prosecutor, but I'm not getting away with this, Jessica. I may have to serve time in *prison*." She whispers the last word.

I can't imagine her serving any time, not with her mother's connections, but she should. You can't drug people to get your way.

When Tegan doesn't get sympathy from me, she waves her good hand. "I'll be fine. Lord knows I deserve it."

Our eyes clash, and the past rises like a shark from the deep— the battles over Chloe, the obsession with Jake, the video. Tegan shivers in her thick robe, and without her veil of makeup and attitude, I can finally look at her without feeling singed.

"Can I ask you something?" Tegan asks. "Something I've wondered about for a long time?" I nod, and her gaze becomes fixed. "Did you date Jake to hurt me, or did you really love him?"

The air leaves my chest, and my thoughts speed back in time—to Jake crying outside his house the day I befriended him. His dad had died but he'd also just broken up with Tegan. I knew from her red-rimmed eyes at school that she was devastated. Did I date him to get back at her, to score a point in our war? A loose cog clunks into place in my brain. *Maybe this was never about me. Maybe it was always about* her, Jake said at my house. Oh no.

Tegan sees the truth in my eyes. "I thought so."

I shake my head. "I did love him, though."

"Everyone loves Jake." She sighs. "I don't want to rehash the past, but we shouldn't have made that bet."

"You're right," I say, sniffling.

She folds her good arm across her chest. "I didn't understand how awful my plan was until I woke up. I hurt Jake so bad, and then someone did the same thing to me."

"Was it Marcus?" I ask.

"I don't think so. He sold me the drugs for Jake, but he likes his girls awake." She pulls a face. "I think it was one of my friends. How about that?"

"That sucks," I murmur.

Her face scrunches and she dissolves into tears. "But Shawna didn't deserve what happened to her. My best friend is dead, Jessica. Her last text to me said, 'Beetlejuice, Falcon's Peak.' It was our code for 'I need help. Come now.' Shawna was in real trouble and I didn't go. She must have thought I abandoned her after the party."

"You couldn't have gone; you were in a coma."

She nods. "Yeah, that was crazy. I knew Chloe was bad, but not *that* bad. I threw up most of the drugs, so I kind of remember wrestling her for the camera and then chasing her. I couldn't get a grip on her. She's tiny, but she's really strong. And fast."

"She panicked," I say. "She knew she'd get in trouble for the live feed once it got shared online, and she was right."

"All because Jake is seventeen," Tegan says, wiping her eyes.

"All because we went too far," I counter. "With everything."

Tegan holds up her cast, offering a wry grin. "At least I won't have to play volleyball this season."

"I thought you liked volleyball?"

She shrugs. "It stopped being fun years ago."

Right then an image of our school appears on the TV. "Look," I say, turning up the volume. We watch the news report side by side.

"A recent break in the Crystal Cove High School video scandal has revealed new information. Alan Chavez is on location with more. Alan."

The camera cuts to a reporter standing on the narrow shoulder of Blood Alley. After a short delay, he speaks. "During the early morning hours of Tegan Sheffield's end-of-summer party, a fellow student struck a creature on this stretch of road while driving home. Blood evidence from the accident, recently turned in by the driver, has been matched to a classmate named Brendon Reed. Brendon originally told police he was home when Tegan went missing, and his father corroborated his story, but this new evidence proves the student lied about his whereabouts."

Alan takes a breath, and Tegan's body goes stiff.

"With his alibi destroyed, police were able to obtain Brendon's phone, DNA, and fingerprints, and this new evidence has led to a profound discovery. The police charged Brendon today with dosing his classmate, the former Alabama senator's daughter, Tegan Sheffield, with a combination of GHB and ecstasy. Brendon confessed that he entered Tegan's bedroom just after three a.m. to check on her and found her vomiting what appeared to be blood into her toilet. Afraid he'd be implicated, he panicked and fled, and was then struck by the car right here, on Blood Alley."

The anchor frowns. "What was the motive for this drugging, Alan?"

He grimaces and refers to his notes. "Brendon said, and I'm quoting now from the police report, 'When I heard Tegan planned to roofie Jake, I thought it would be funny to roofie her too. It was a joke—something for my YouTube channel. It was Chloe's idea to set up the broadcast downstairs, but that's because she didn't know about the drugs. The whole thing backfired, though. I couldn't have put what Tegan and Jake did on YouTube anyway.'"

Tegan rips off her sheepskin boot and hurls it at the TV. "That asshole!" she screams.

"Shhh," I say. The reporter goes on to explain that Brendon and Chloe kept each other's secrets after the party and that Chloe convinced "the driver"—me—that I hit a deer to keep Brendon's alibi intact. In return, he didn't tell anyone she'd set up the live feed. But Brendon didn't know the whole story, that Chloe had gone back to the house later and fought with Tegan or that Chloe had stuffed her inside the storage bench.

I turn off the TV and cover my head. "I knew it wasn't a deer."

Tegan lurches around my hospital room in one good boot, wheezing as if she's been plunged into ice water. "I can't believe *Brendon* drugged me. I knew it was a friend!"

She stares at me as if I have answers. "I wouldn't call him a friend," I say.

Tegan snorts. "The doctors told me that if I hadn't thrown up in my bathroom that night, I could have *died*." Her eyes roll back, and then suddenly she's clutching her head and crying huge tears. "All I wanted was a kiss. This is crazy; I'm going crazy."

She collapses back into the chair and peers at me. "Were you the driver? My lawyers mentioned something about you and a BMW on Blood Alley."

I nod. "It was me." I think back to the day I confronted Brendon in his backyard, and the blood seeping from his thigh. I thought he'd hurt himself on his wrought-iron chair, but I think the chair reopened his wound from the car accident.

I recall Shawna's words to Jake at school: *Everyone is lying*. No wonder she was afraid to tell the truth. All her friends were involved—Brendon had drugged Tegan, Tegan had drugged Jake, and Shawna's boyfriend had provided the chemicals. Even Brendon's father lied.

After a long moment, Tegan's lips quiver into a fluttering smile, like a baby butterfly trying to fly. "You hit Brendon with a BMW?"

"A classic," I say, smiling back.

"That's fitting." She plays with her long glossy hair. "This is a lot to sort out."

"Yes," I say in a soft breath.

Tegan watches me with her large, sad eyes, bluer than any sky—the same eyes that first saw me in second grade when I tried to carry my lunch, my jacket, and my art project onto the bus. She didn't ask if I wanted help, she just helped, and when the bus stopped, she got off at my house. We played the rest of the day and every day after. "Do you think we could be friends again?" she asks.

A gasp bursts from my lips.

"I'm sorry. I shouldn't have asked that." She retrieves her boot and puts it on. "Remember when my mom wouldn't buy me that scarlet dress I wanted in *Vogue*?" I nod, vaguely remembering Tegan threatening to run away to New York to steal it. "And when I didn't get it, I ripped up the magazine and said the dress was ugly?"

"Yes, and then we burned the pages."

"Yes, we destroyed it and I swore I hated the dress."

"I remember." I feel my stomach sink because I think I know what's coming next, and it's going to break my heart all over again.

Tegan collects herself. "You're that dress, Jessica." Then she exits my room and shuts the door.

I lie back on my pillow. Senior year spans ahead of me like a yellow brick road—homecoming, senior pictures, winter ball, spring break, prom—but it won't be the same, not without Jake and Chloe.

And I won't be the same. Not after this.

If I could go back in time, further back than the party, all the way back to fifth grade when Tegan and I battled over Chloe, and Chloe and Tegan battled over me, I would whisper into my ear, *Whatever happens next, stay away. You don't need friends like these.*

Or maybe I would shout it.

ACKNOWLEDGMENTS

Thank you for reading *Friends Like These*! Huge thanks to the early readers who helped me shape the novel—my mother, Sheila Nelson; one of my dear friends and favorite librarians, Tiffany Bronzan; and my fellow writers and thriller fans: Shells Legoullon and Nikki Garcia.

Much love to my agent, Elizabeth Bewley, for her early insights and encouragement. At one point, overwhelmed by the pandemic, I scrapped the novel and decided not to write it. In a phone conversation with Elizabeth, she assured me this was my "next book." I decided to believe her and pushed on.

However, the manuscript needed more work, and I received invaluable input from my primary editor, Wendy Loggia at Delacorte Press, with additional feedback from Hannah Hill and Lydia Gregovic. Utilizing their insights, I dug deeper into the relationships between the friends and added Tegan's flashback chapters. I am forever grateful to this talented trio for their notes and vision—and to editors in general. I would never want to write a book without one.

Virtual hugs to my readers! First and foremost, my goal is to entertain you, and I hope you enjoyed the story.

Spoiler ahead. If you haven't read the book, please stop here until you finish.

At the heart of this tale is an issue that's important to me—the very real experience of drug-assisted sexual assault, processed through the unexpected lens of a seventeen-year-old boy. Through Jake, we experience the rage, denial, confusion, and shame that come with being victimized, but also the onset of healing. As a survivor, I enjoyed giving Jake the voice and the justice that so many victims never receive.

Drug-assisted sexual assault is incredibly nefarious because the victim is often robbed of their memory, or told a story about what happened that isn't true, but it is never the victim's fault. It doesn't matter how they got into an altered state, whether they chose it or someone drugged them—it is just as illegal to harm an unaware person as it is to harm an aware person. Incapacitation is not permission.

Waking up confused or in an unexpected location is a warning sign of drug-assisted sexual assault. The perpetrator might be someone the victim trusts or would never suspect. The perpetrator might even be the person who took care of the victim during their period of confusion or unconsciousness. I hope, dear reader, you have never experienced this.

If you suspect it has happened to you, there is help. Call the **Rape Crisis National Helpline** on 0808 802 9999 or for help and advice, visit their website: **www.rapecrisis.org.uk**

Thank you again for reading, and if you enjoyed the story, please share it with a friend.

ABOUT THE AUTHOR

Jennifer Lynn Alvarez is the author of ten published novels, including the YA thriller *Lies Like Wildfire* and two middle-grade fantasy series, but this is not where she started. After earning her BA in English Literature from the University of California, Berkeley, Jennifer went into finance, of all things. It was many years and several rejected manuscripts later before she accomplished her childhood dream of becoming an author. Jennifer no longer works in finance and spends her days dreaming up stories. She also teaches creative writing classes through her local library, encouraging others to write their own stories. Jennifer spends her time between Northern California and Middle Tennessee with her husband, kids, and more than her fair share of pets.

jenniferlynnalvarez.com

Where there's smoke, there's a liar . . .